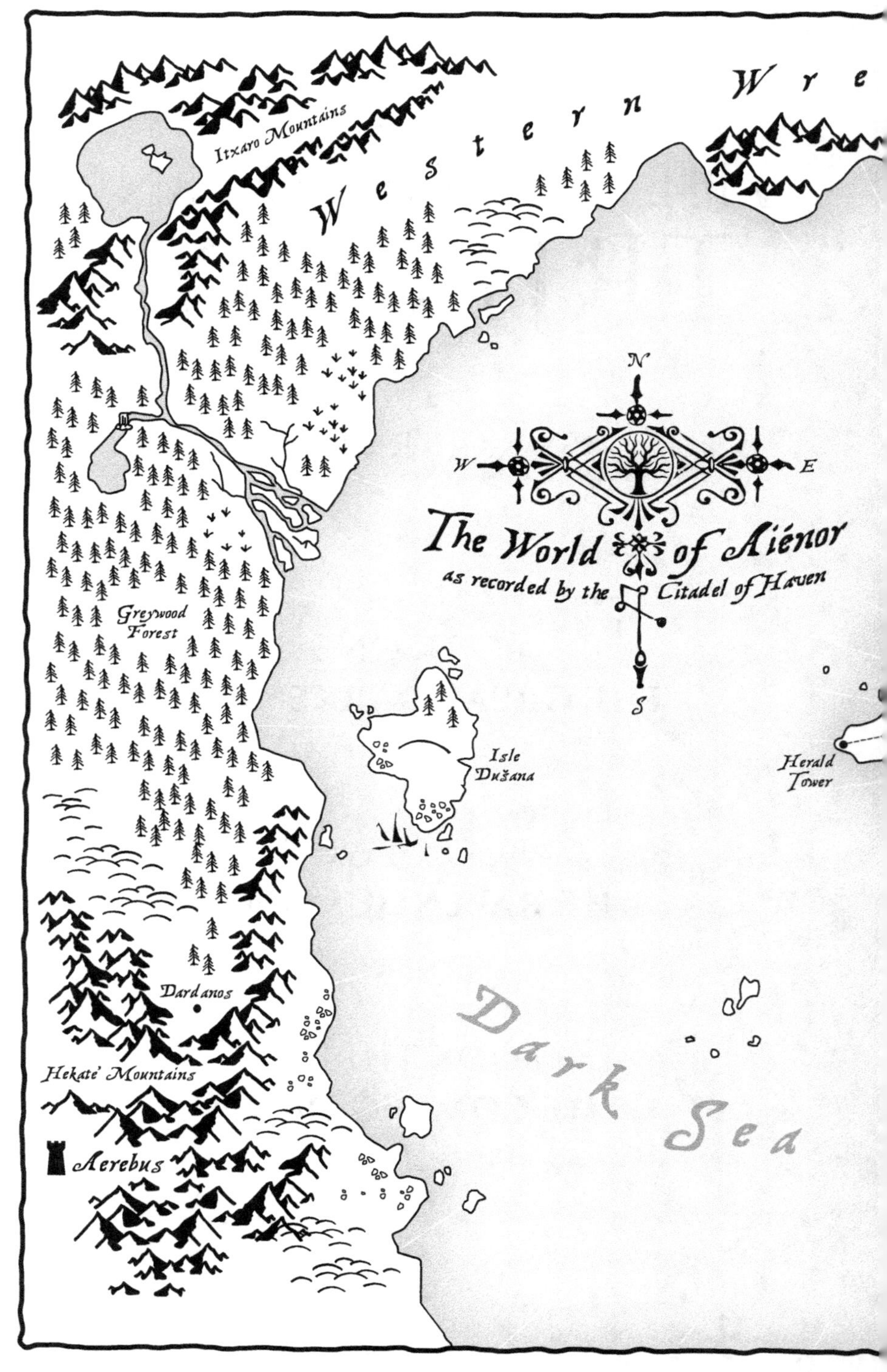

Itxaro Mountains
Western Wre
Greywood Forest
Dardanos
Hekate' Mountains
Aerebus
N
W
E
S
The World of Aiénor
as recorded by the Citadel of Haven
Isle Dušana
Herald Tower
Dark Sea

th
Terriah
Hilgari Mountains
Northern Altar
of the Priest
The Retreating Forest
tyros
Pool of Eilwned
River Aborris
Piney
Creek
The
Capitol
Haven
Mt. Aureole
Black Mountains
of Cair
Halward
Meinir
River Ithelum
Westriver
Outlying Lands
Abondale
Lake Riene
The Talffyn Pass
Bright Harbor
Maris
Bay of Eurwen

THE COMING DAWN

By R.G. Triplett

EDITED BY MELODY FARRELL

PRONOUNCIATION GUIDE

CHARACTERS

Abaddon (A-bah-dohn)

Ádhamh (AH-dahm)

Æðelric (AY-oh-ehl-rihk)

Æsc (Aysk)

Aius (AHY-uhs)

Alon (AH-lahn)

Amaian (ah-MAHY-ahn)

Anahiera (A-nah-HEER-ah)

Angrah (ANG-grah)

Ardghal (AHRD-gahl)

Armas (AR-mahs)

Arthfael (ARTH-fay-ehl)

Asier (Ah-SEER)

Asierians (Ah-SEER-ee-ahns)

Astyræ (A-stir-ay)

Aysa (AY-sah)

AŽDAHĀ (Az-dah-HAY)

Azrael (AZ-ray-ehl)

Bakaren (BACK-ah-rehn)

Barkas (BAR-kahs)

Basajuan (BASS-ah-wahn)

Blodeuwedd (BLOW-day-wehd)

Brádách (BRA-dak)

Branwen (BRAN-wehn)

Caedmon (CAYD-mohn)

Calarmindon (cal-ahr-MIN-duhn)

Celrod (KEHL-rahd)

Clivesis (CLAHYV-zees)

Črotmir: (CROHT-meer)

Deryn (DAYR-ehn)
Durai (Doo-RAH-ee)
Ealhstan (EEL-stahn)
Edur (ee-DOOR)
Éimhear (ahy-MEER)
Elior (Ehl-ee-OHR)
Eógan (YOU-gahn)
Ermendrud (EHRM-ehn-drood)
Faolan (FAY-ow-lan)
Faramund (FAR-ah-muhnd)
Farran (FAIR-ahn)
Fryon (FRI-ohn)
Garaile (Gah-RAEEL)
Gelinda (Gehl-EEN-dah)
Goran (GOR-an)
Gormlaith (GORM-layth)
Gvidus (GVEE-duhs)
Haizea (Hi-ZAY-ah)
Harmier (Hahr-mee-AYR)
Hildræd (Hihl-DRAYD)
Hlíf (Hihlf)
Iker (AEE-kehr)
Illium (IH-lee-uhm)
Iolanthe (ee-oh-LAHN-thay)
Isme (EES-may)
Johnrey (JOHN-ree)
Julen (JU-lehn)
Kahri (KAH-ree)
Keily (KAHY-lee)
Kemen (KEE-mehn)
King Cascarie (KAS-kah-ree)
King Kaestor (KAY-stohr)
Klieo (KLEE-oh)

Linnaea (LIHN-ee-ah)
Llinos (LEE-nos)
Mågąn (May-gahn)
Mahlah (MAH-lah)
Mal'akhim (MAH-lah-keem)
Meledae (MEL-eh-day)
Mezulari (Meh-zoo-LAR-ee)
Moa (MOH-ah)
Navid (nah-VEED)
Niniané (nih-nee-AH-nay)
Nogcwren (NOHK-ren)
Oier (oh-ee-AIR)
Oren (OH-rehn)
Oskar (OH-scar)
Oweles (OOLS)
Payam (PAHY-yam)
Portus (POR-tuhs)
Pyrrhus (PAHY-ruhs)
Ragnarr (RAG-nar)
Remiel (reh-mee-EHL)
Roshan (RO-shuhn)
Ruarc (ROO-ahrk)
Šárka (SAR-kah)
Seig (SEEG)
Sendoa (Sen-DO-ah)
Shameus (SHEY-mus)
Sigrid (SEE-grihd)
Soma (SO-mah)
Soren (SOAR-ehn)
Tahd (TAWD)
Tarrthála (TART-hah-lah)
Tersk (Tersk)
Timorets (TIH-moor-ehts)

Uriel (YOO-ree-ahl)
Völker (VOHL-kehr)
Walha (WAHL-hah)
Wielund (WAHY-lund)
Yasen (YEAH-sehn)
Zigor (ZEE-gor)
Zuriñe (zur-EEN)
Zuzen (Zoo-ZEHN)

PLACES/LANDMARKS/THINGS

Abonris (AB-ohn-rihs)
Aerebus (AIR-eh-buhs)
Ágoni gi (Ah-GO-neh-gee)
Aiénor (ahy-NOR)
Argiñe (ahr-GEEN)
Arianrhod (AY-ree-an-rud)
Asier (ah-SEER)
Bay of Eurwen (YOOR-wihn)
Clarus (CLAY-ruhs)
Dardanos (DAR-dah-nohs)
Enguerrand (EHN-ger-uhnd)
Falls of Sarangrael (Ser-ahn-grey-EL)
Fionnuala (fee-oh-NOO-lah)
Gwarwyn (GWAHR-wihn)
Halvard (HAHL-vard)
Harel Lior (Hah-REHL LEE-or)
Hekate' (Heh-KAH-tay)
Hilgari (hihl-GAR-ee) Mountains
Ikehr (Ahee-KEER)
Isle Dušana (doo-SAH-nah)
Islwyn (IH-sehl-wihn)

Ithelum (IH-theh-luhm)
Itsaso (it-SAH-soh)
Itxaro (Ihx-TAH-ro)
Kalein (kah-LEEN)
Maris (MAH-rihs)
Mathgham (Mahth-guhm)
Meinir (Mah-ee-NEER)
Melania (meh-leh-NEE-ah)
Mount Aureole (AH-rohl)
Oroitz Guardia (Or-oh-ihtz Guard-EE-ah)
Petros (PEH-trohs)
Shaimira (Shahy-MEER-ah)
Sleth Aodh (slehth ay-OHD)
Terriah (TAIR-ah)
Tristura Eremua (Trih-STOO-rah Air-OO-mah)
Viðarr (vee-OHR)
Ziohnia (Zi-oh-NEE-ah)
Zuhaitz Dolu (Zoo-Hah-EEtz DOH-loo)

Preface

Stories are told, day in and day out, in this maddened world of ours. Most stories cost very little to tell, and thus are hardly even remembered by the teller, let alone those who paused briefly enough to listen to them.

But good stories, deep stories, are never just fanciful flights of a distracted imagination, or whims of fiction caught in the hot afternoon sun. No, good stories are fought for, tooth and nail, and paid for with blood and bowel, wrestled with and labored over until the tale that is being told is one that is indeed worth listening to.

Good stories grab our attention by way of adventure and avarice, comedy and consequence, romance and ruin; but for how long, and why? It is when our attention is turned from a sense of mere listening to one of enraptured yearning that we have crossed the threshold from goodness into greatness. No longer are we content to just notice the tale in our peripheries for a moment in time; rather, we become consumed with a desire to never forget it.

May the wars that we have fought to tell the story true bring forth the kind of tale that is worth remembering.

Oh story, you have found me.
Found me wanting,
Found me desperate,
Found me unsure how to tell you.
So I will write and try,
And live and die,
To fashion words to fit the muse.

Oh story, you have caught me.
Caught me toiling,
Caught me guilty,
Caught me worried that I've wronged you.
For I wrote and wrought,
And bled and fought,
To tell the story true.

Oh story, you have left me.
Left me wondering,
Left me maddened,
Left me searching everywhere for you.
Did I force and fit,
And bridle and bit,
The wild from out of you?

Oh story, I have found you.
Found you waiting,
Found you hopeful,
Found you finding me again,
As I fought to follow you.

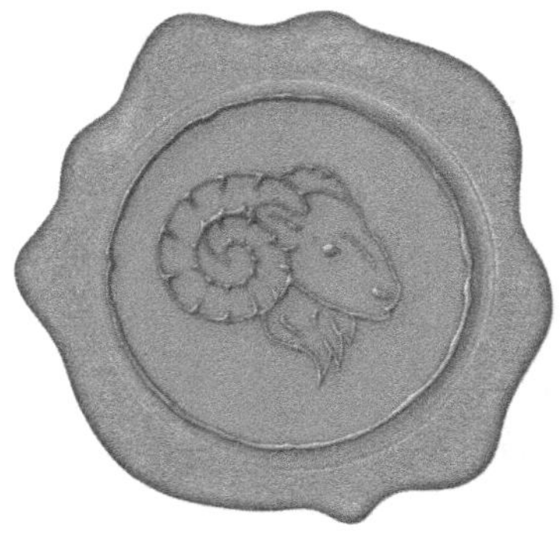

Prologue

The sound of running water was ever before them, drowning the anxious thoughts of anxious minds.

The long caravan of desperate travelers followed the hunter to a place that seemed unreachable. The darkened, treacherous journey had exacted a toll as the days went onward, and already the complaints and grumbling of the road weary Asierians began to drown out the faint roar of the water that compelled their guide forward.

"What have we done?" an older councilman asked, without heed for discretion. "We left the walls of our city, we left the safety of our defenses and the provision of our holds … for what? To wander forever in the darkened bowels of this … whatever *this* is?"

"How short your memory becomes, Oier," Zuriñe chastised from the front of the line. "Do you not remember, it was but a score of days ago that Isme came, with the winds of the Raveness at his command? Do you not remember the burning of our Palladium? Do you not still smell the fear and the fired flesh of our citizens?" The aged councilman shook his head. "How dare you forget!"

"We were unprepared, taken by surprise!" Oier argued. "We could have resisted, we could have…" His voice trailed off as he searched for the right argument. "It would have been better to die defending our home than to wander helplessly in this folly of a cave!"

"Yes. We could have resisted. We could have made a stand, we could have called upon Soren and all of his warriors, demanded spears to be brandished and lives to be given in service of our city!" Zuriñe conceded. "But for how long?"

Oier breathed angrily through his clenched mouth, and Zuriñe answered the question for him before he could make his rebuttal.

"How long before our strength ran out, or before there was no city left to defend? How long before we had no choice but to bend the knee and pledge our banners?" the councilman said sadly. "She is not just another invader, Oier. She is … unnatural."

"You don't know that!" Oier bit back. "You don't know what that future would have held … but this?!" He pointed to the endless leagues of dank, dripping, cavernous stones that they had traversed without relief. "This is insufferable. We should have stood our ground and made a defense!"

Tension began to fill the air like the building sound of boiling water, and the frustrations of both committed and unconvinced threatened to burn them all.

"Perhaps that is what we are doing, right here, right now," Bakaren said. "I, for one, did not wish to leave. I wept, and I weep even still. But perhaps Zuriñe is right; this might be the best way to defend our people."

Just then, a blast of a horn cut through the sound of debate. Tired footsteps halted as every weary eye looked up to see what the alarm had signaled.

"Is that a good sound?" a young boy nervously asked his father.

"What is it? Are we alright?" a pregnant widow asked her own mother as she tried to soothe away her fear by rubbing her swollen belly.

Husbands held their wives and children clung to their parents' legs, while Soren's watchers held tight to the hilts of their blades, all waiting. Some feared the worst while some hoped for news from the vanguard. The grumblings of the exiled people ceased for the moment as the heavy silence held the attention of each and every eye.

"People of Asier!" came the booming voice of Lord Julen. "The hunter has found the hiding place for us! Come! Come now, my friends, and soon behold for yourselves our new home."

"The boy did it!" Zuriñe said proudly. "Well done, Kemen!"

"I know these days have been long, and dark. I know your bones are weary and your feet have traveled far. I know that all of you … all of us … have left and lost everything we have called home." Julen's tired yet hopeful voice echoed off the walls of the tunnel. "But at the end of what we have known, we will begin anew. Asier is gone, she has been broken under the weight of a ravenous evil. But here, hidden under the protection of this holy rock, at the end of all things … we will make a new home!"

The people released their collectively held breath, as relief and hope washed over the thousands that had made the journey north along the banks of the river Argiñe, through the foothills of the Itxaro Mountains, past the water gate and into this hidden passage beneath the soil of Aiénor.

"The Giver of Light has brought us to *this* end, but not to *our* end. From this day forward, no longer shall we call ourselves by the name of our fouled, red city, no longer shall we be known as Asierians. *Amaian* shall be our name, for we have come to the end … to begin again."

A wave of murmurs began to run through the crowd.

"What is this place?" the elder councilwoman, Bakaren, asked. "What shall we call our new home?"

Lord Julen looked to the young hunter, whom he had dared to follow into these hidden depths. "Perhaps it is only right for Kemen to be the one to name our new home for us." He slapped a proud hand upon the strong hunter's shoulder. "Tell us, Kemen, where have you led the Amaians?"

The young man thought for a moment, remembering the hard journey through the rock and through the water. He remembered his day of hunting the beast so white, like nothing he had ever seen in his thirty years upon this world. Though he tracked and followed its strange markings, it had remained ever just beyond the shot of his bow, somehow leading him deep into this unknown place.

He remembered when he first broke through the darkened passage and out into the hidden expanse. He remembered the wonder that coursed through him as he beheld the massive, rocky faces of the Itxaro and the mists and fog that veiled their existence. Their embrace seemed nearly impenetrable as it climbed high above and around this secret source of fertile land and clear springs.

He thought about the words of Julen, his lord, and about the deathly horde who had brought war and fire upon his home. He thought about his grey-haired uncle and about the failing light of the tree across the mighty Itsaso. And, above all of these thoughts and all of these memories, he thought about how safe he felt at this moment; hidden ... protected.

He knew what this place was, he knew that the Giver of Light had led him here. Although he never caught the white beast, he knew he had found something of even greater significance.

The long-haired hunter looked to his lord, and then again to the sea of eyes that flickered in the hazy torch light before him. "This place, this hidden and beautiful home ... is called ... *Shaimira.*"

Chapter One

The eyes of the horrified woodcutters beheld the wild, green fingers of lightning that erupted along the shores of their new home. A maddened tempest seemed driven upon the sea, threatening to extinguish their braziers with each malevolent gust of wind.

"What in the damnable dark is that, brother?" Goran whispered.

"Whatever it is, I am glad that it is not us who are there to welcome it," Alon agreed.

"Do you see that?" Gvidus asked as he pointed just above the sightline of the timber-walled stronghold. "It's blackness, it's the damned blackness!"

"The whole God-forsaken world is blackness!" Oren argued. "What are you talking about, brother?"

"Don't be a worm-eaten pine stump, Oren. *Look at it!* Do you see that ... where that green lightning is coming from? There! Do you see it? That's a completely different kind of dark right there, brother." Gvidus pointed again.

"It's just like the black we saw before those raven-fletched arrows riddled our cutter camp," Goran said, his throat going dry as he spoke.

"All the way over here?" Oren asked. "But how? That was half-a-world away."

"It hovers across land *and* sea?" Alon asked. "That's just not natural, if you ask me."

"No, brothers." Yasen spoke, interrupting the nervous speculation of his friends. "That fire, that darkness ... there is nothing natural about it at all."

"What would you have us do about it, North Wolf?" Gvidus asked his chieftain. "Should we not grab our blades and pursue it like we did that cold day in the north?"

Yasen stared ahead, looking out from the hills of the western timberline, just half a league from the gates of the colony's stronghold.

"If the situation were reversed ... do you think those colony guardsmen would have come up here to our aid in the midst of a terrible storm?" Alon said. "No ... you know that they wouldn't!" He spat. "You know damn well that they would have run as fast and as far away as they could. And besides, they were the ones that didn't want the likes of us anywhere near the stronghold anyways."

"Aye, but we know this isn't *just* a storm, brother," Oren answered.

"If it is the same black, the same arrows, the same devilish green light, then the men still there..." Goran paused, letting the weight of his next words roll heavy on his lips. "They are already lost."

The men stood in silence as the angry thunder crashed and rolled upon the eastern horizon. Other woodcutters from the line began to make their way to the gathered center, looking for direction from their chieftain. Grips began to tighten around well-worn axe handles, and worried whispers flew back and forth between these mighty northmen as they looked in horror at the greenlit display of power.

"My brothers," Yasen finally said. "It is no longer safe here for us ... of that much I am certain. I can feel it in my bones."

"Aye … that's plain enough to see," Rolf agreed.

"What will we do then, Yasen?" Goran asked. "Do we just leave this place? Do we let whatever hell that is claim the colony?"

"Not a single one of your lives are worth losing for the sake of those timber walls," Yasen told his men. "Besides, those were Seig's walls, not ours. And you all know the affections he had for us."

At that, a knowing laughter lifted the mood of the gathered woodcutters, if only for the briefest moment.

"We will need to get far away from here, my brothers, and we will need to be quick about it. You can be sure that whatever green-eyed devil that is out there will not be satisfied with a small victory," Yasen said as his gaze shifted to the north.

"But where will we go then?" Alon asked

"I know a cave. It should be safe enough for all of us; though its hospitality is rather disappointing," Goran suggested.

"And then what, brother?" Gvidus asked. "Just hide like wounded dogs in some darkened den out here in the middle of the wilderness?"

Yasen thought on it for a moment. "Cal mentioned a place… a refuge of sorts, hidden somewhere in the northern parts of this Wreath."

"What sort of place?" Oren asked. "Did he say where it was?"

"A hidden place," Yasen replied. "He didn't know where it was exactly." The North Wolf looked at his gathered brothers as a hopeful light lit his right eye. "But I know where we might begin to look."

The men gathered around eagerly as he told them Cal's tale of the abandoned prison tower in the heart of the Greywood forest, of the lady Astyræ, and of the strange markings that made him believe in a refuge that still stood in the wilds of this darkened world.

"Be warned though, my brothers. For although there may be a sanctuary somewhere in the North, there is also a sorceress, or so I have been told. Could be nothing more than folklore … but I do not think it so. There is something darker out here than just the lack of light. So be ever on your guard, and for the love of the THREE who is SEVEN, keep your axes at the ready and your blades sharp."

"Aye!" came the collective agreement of the woodcutters.

"Goran," Yasen said. "Take the men to the cave, and wait for me there. Stay out of sight for as long as you can manage. Whatever it is that is happening there at the stronghold, is doubtful to remain there."

"Aye" Goran said as he nodded his understanding.

"And what of this enemy?" Rolf asked. "I, for one, would like to know what it is that will be nipping at my heels in whatever is to come!"

"Very well then," Yasen agreed. "Go, and for the sake of your heels, be quick and quiet about it. Tell us what you can find about this ... this ... whatever it is."

"And you, North Wolf?" Gvidus asked. "Just what are you planning to do?"

Yasen thought on it a moment, turning his head to gaze into the darkened forestland behind him. "I must see this tower for myself. We need to know just what it was that made our groomsman brother believe there was something out here worth risking everything to seek."

"If there is some sorceress out there ... I mean ... if there is some kind of danger, I would be remiss to allow you to defeat it alone!" Soma, one of Yasen's riders exclaimed gleefully. "My axe hasn't tasted much more than dogwood and pine these last dark days. I'll go with you to the tower, brother."

"Alright then." Yasen agreed. "Gather your supplies. I don't think we have much time—"

His words were cut off by the sound of a violent crack, and the reverberations of a significant crash were felt upon the ground beneath their boots.

"What in the damnable dark?" Gvidus exclaimed.

"Let's go, brothers," Yasen ordered, his unpatched eye narrowing with a keen wariness of the danger all about them as he stared back towards the timber walls of the colony's stronghold.

The woodcutters began to grab their tools and mount their horses. Yasen and Soma wheeled their mounts westward, as Yasen called out to Rolf.

"Be safe, brother!" the chief of the woodcutters said to the spy. "And do not trust everything you see. Remember the isle and the witch … there is always more than meets the eye."

"Aye," Rolf agreed.

"At the cave, then," Yasen reminded him.

"The cave," Rolf acknowledged.

With that, the woodcutters split their company into three parts. The greatest number headed north along the forest line until they came upon the pebble-strewn bank of the very same brook where Cal had marked his passage. Yasen and Soma spurred their horses westward, deeper and deeper into the massive covering of the mighty trees, while Rolf turned toward the impending doom at the edge of the water.

Chapter Two

Rolf rode hard, trusting that the sounds of thunder and the unsettling reverberations of this storm would mask the sound of his horse's pounding hooves upon the ground. Though the distance was short enough, Rolf could not shake the unquieting sense that this was the most dangerous ride he had ever made.

As the watchfires of the twin guard towers drew closer and closer, it became all-too-certain that something indeed was not right here. "Where are the watchmen? Why are they not at their posts?" He said to his horse, Kader. "Careful now, girl."

The air about the timber walls grew instantly silent, save for the banners that whipped in the wind and cracks and pops from the watch fires. "Do you hear anything?" Rolf said to his horse as he threw his leg over her saddle.

Kader snorted her reply as the woodcutter tied her reins to a knot in the corner of the timber wall.

"Neither do I," Rolf admitted. "That is odd ... that is odd, indeed." Rolf tightened his grip upon his double-bladed axe, walking as silently as he could, careful to mind each step he took towards the suspiciously open timber gate.

His bearded face peered in through the ominous opening, and to his amazement he saw not a soul in the entirety of the stronghold. "This is madness," he said aloud. "Where are they? Why would they—"

His words were stolen as the sound of thunder rattled east of the now-emptied stronghold.

He looked about the square nervously, and then muttered, "Well, if you don't mind, Governor, my brothers and I could use some provisions for our journey."

Rolf ran towards the storeroom near the stronghold's kitchens, knowing full well that if he were ever caught for looting the supplies of the colony, he could be beaten or even hung for his trespasses. He grabbed a pair of leather saddle bags and began to fill them with wine skins, dried meats and fruits, and a few wheels of cheese. He knew that it wasn't much, and that he could not possibly carry enough to feed all of his brothers ... but he hoped that at the very least this would help.

When his bags were nearly bursting, he slung them over his shoulder and began to hurry towards his waiting horse. The air about him somehow seemed darker. Even though the braziers and watchfires burned with glowing flames, their light seemed to be nearly swallowed up by a heaviness that hung oppressively over this place.

Rolf walked back out through the timber gates, unnoticed by anyone but his horse. "This is so odd, girl. I have never been more unnerved by something that isn't even ... *here*." As he lay the bags across the back of the mare, he heard something on the wind that made his blood run cold.

"Did you hear that?" he said, straining his ears and turning his head. "That sounds like a woman." He looked up as he listened, eyes fixed upon the empty perch of the watchtower. "I'll be back, girl. I am going to see if I can get a better look."

Rolf left Kader, her back laden with supplies and her reins hanging limp upon the muddy ground below. He stole off toward the northern watchtower and climbed the wood-hewn ladder with such haste that he slipped and nearly lost his hold. "Come on, Rolf, don't be the damned fool that gets himself killed before the battle even begins!" he told himself through gritted teeth.

With only a few more rungs to climb, the tall woodcutter reached the perch of the watch tower. He scanned the horizon, surveying the perimeter of the stronghold until his eye caught the most unnerving scene he had ever beheld. "What in the damnable dark?"

There upon the shore, the mighty *Determination* lay beached and ruined. The same beautiful sails that brought them across the black waters of the Dark Sea were now tattered and desecrated by some crude, white marking, aglow with the sickly green blaze of the same torches that he and his chieftain had seen in the dying forests of the north.

He reached for the flint that hung around his neck as he watched a swirling storm of ravens circle in a hungry, brooding cloud over the heads of the governor and his guardsmen. At the center of the scene stood a woman whose eyes seemed to glow bright with a sickly yellow fire.

"God help us," he whispered as he kissed his flint.

At the sound of his lips upon the holy stone, the fierce gaze of the yellow-eyed woman broke away from the governor and turned to the woodman upon the wall.

Rolf's bowels began to churn as a cold sweat beaded along the nape of his neck; his mouth went dry with fear. He threw his axe to the dirt below and leapt down the timber ladder. His feet missed the last three rungs and he slipped, hitting the cold ground harder than he anticipated. The breath was knocked clear out of his already burning lungs, and he wheezed and coughed while trying to regain his footing.

The tall woodcutter began to run as fast as his fur-covered boots would let him. He reached the open timber gates in almost forty paces and as he did, the sky awoke in an angered display of power. Fingers of green lightning clawed at the black and cloudless sky above him.

"What kind of devilry?!" he exclaimed between labored breaths.

At the crack of the lightning, he heard Kader's scream. She reared up in a display of frightened madness and Rolf's heart sank as he watched. "No! Kader!" he whispered frantically. "Easy girl! Easy now!"

But Kader's loyalty was overrun with fear. The horse's front two hooves landed heavy upon the ground as she shook her blonde mane in protest. Before he could get to her, the horse shot off like an arrow towards the safety of the timberline. All that Rolf could do was watch her go.

The thunderous sound began to grow louder and deeper. The woodcutter spun around, his head whipping to the right and then again to the left as the brooding cloud descended upon the man of the North.

"Alright then!" Rolf shouted to the swirling tempest about him as he raised his axe. "Do not think that I won't stand my ground! I will cleave you like I have a thousand soldier pines before you!"

A raven broke away from the swirling mass and flew near enough to scratch his face. Rolf reached up to his cheek and felt the warm trickle of blood.

"Caw, caw!" The voices of the carrion fowl taunted him.

"Ravens?" He shouted to them as he swung his axe at the storm. "Is that all you are, ravens?" In that very moment, as if in response, they all opened their eyes in unison. A thousand little, green eyes stared him down.

"Oh, God!" he gulped.

The storm crashed down upon him. His blade caught their black bodies with a practiced strength, cleaving them clean in half, but only a score of them. Hundreds more began to claw at his flesh and his face with their talons, pecking and biting at his neck, his hands, and his eyes.

Rolf screamed in agony. He swung his axe despite his pain, but the onslaught was too much for any one man. As he yelled and shouted into the storm, the birds began to rip at his tongue and his face, and he choked and coughed against the taste of his own blood. He fell to his knees, bleeding eyes clinched tight, swinging desperately with what little strength was left in his bleeding arms. As he did, his grip failed him. The shaft of his axe was too slick with his own blood.

The moment his axe fell, the birds stopped their biting.

"What do you want?" He tried to say through his ripped and bloody mouth. The birds did not answer him. Instead they dug their sharpened talons into his fur cloak and into his raw skin. In a display of witchcraft he had not dared to imagine, the murder of carrion fowl lifted the large man into the air and flew him towards the wreckage upon the shoreline.

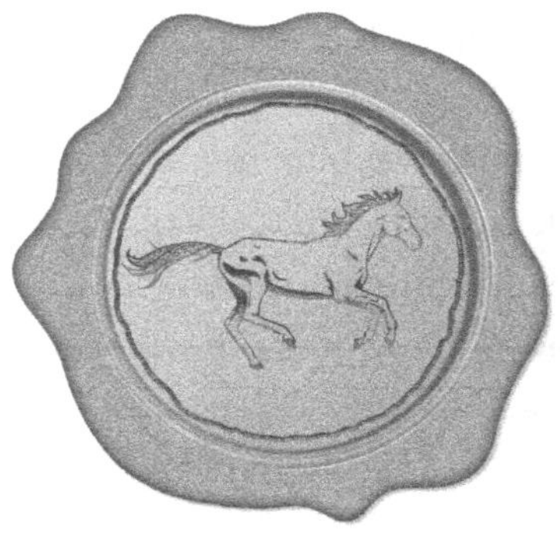

Chapter Three

"I am sorry, Cal!" she told him with great distress in her voice. "I didn't know ... we heard the Nocturnals, they were here, and Deryn and I fought against them ... I thought... I didn't mean to!" Her violet and yellow eyes welled with tears at the look of horror on his face.

Cal fell to his knees as if he too had been speared by the bolt of the fabled bow *Arianrhod*. His hand ran through the glowing, white fur of the wounded Stag. "What have you done?" Cal whispered. "What have you done, Astyræ?"

The magical beast exhaled his final, blood-gurgled breath without so much as a word of direction. The once-magnificent crown of triune antlers was now half buried in the moss and dirt, broken in the crash to the wilderness floor.

"No! You can't go! You can't be dead!" Cal shouted as he used all his strength to try and roll the Stag over, away from the deadly barb that had pierced its flesh. "You can't leave me ... you can't leave us!"

Frustrated sobs began to rumble in his shocked voice. "What will we do? How will we follow?"

"Cal?" Deryn called out to his charge, concern and uncertainty coloring his words.

"*How will we find the way?!*" Cal couldn't contain his grief. His whole body shook in the wake of this senseless death.

"Cal ... I didn't know!" Astyræ tried to explain herself.

"Cal," Deryn said, placing a steadying hand upon the shoulder of the lady Astyræ. "Think now. What did he tell you?"

Cal raised his hands to his face, the blood of the holy beast now crimson upon his own flesh. A storm of anger and fear, weariness and grief roiled about in the chamber of his thoughts and flashed in his eyes. "*You* did this!" he turned on the lady at his side. "All may very well be lost now... because of this... because of you!"

Astyræ stepped away from him, her breath catching in her throat as her remorseful tears poured from her frightened eyes.

"How could ..." he tried to ask, but the flood of emotions overtook his storm swept mind.

"We were defending you!" She blurted out. "Fighting to save you, while you were frozen in place!"

"But he was our guide!" Cal spat back. "How will we ever find Shaimira, let alone the new light?! This creature was the only one who *knew the way*!"

"I thought he was one of *hers*," she shouted back at him, her words sharp with the edge of innocence. "Another one of her Nocturnals bent on cutting us all down!"

"Cal!" Deryn flew to him now, his tiny hands holding the tear-streaked face of his friend. "Listen to me ... what did the cervidae tell you? What did he say?"

Cal stared at his hands, seeming to not have heard the words of his Sprite companion. Deryn grew worried in the silence, but held steady, willing their eyes to meet. When the shock of the moment released its strangling grip, Cal's eyes finally found his friend's. Deryn exhaled an anxious breath.

"What did he say, Cal?" he urged again.

The groomsman swallowed back his grief before he managed to answer. "He said that we were to retrace the ancient paths. He said that he would be our guide, that he would show me the way to find the light."

Cal's gaze broke again and he stared deeply into the forest before finally turning to his violet-eyed companion. "But how will he lead us … if he is dead?"

Astyræ hung her beautiful, golden-haired head in wounded shame. "I didn't mean to … I didn't know… I thought he was an enemy, Cal. I was trying to help you." Her tears began to fall again. Cal knelt in the dirt, watching her cry as he held his blood-stained hands out before him.

"This is why! This is why I should have never come with you, Cal!" she cried out. "I am *cursed*! If it wasn't for me, my father would have never taken that fruit of the tree, he would have never listened to that foul Sorceress of a woman. He would have never needed to surrender our home and our city… and I would have never been here to murder this poor beast!"

Deryn stared at Cal, wordlessly urging his compassion. The groomsman looked away, shifting uncomfortably on the ground, listening to the sobs of her shame.

"Astyræ." Deryn finally said kindly. "Come now."

"No! Stay away from me!" She argued. "I've ruined everything, can't you see that?"

"If it weren't for you and your bow, Lady Astyræ, we might all be weeping tears of an even greater sorrow," Deryn continued.

"I'm cursed, Deryn," she said.

"Enough of that, now," came the gruff and weary voice of the groomsman as he stood and walked towards her. Her shame seemed to somehow wake his heart. "I believe you. And though I don't know how, perhaps we might still find another way." He took another step towards her and raised his eyes to meet hers.

What she saw stole her breath. "Cal?" she whispered, concern coloring her words.

"You are not cursed," he said with a begrudged compassion as he wiped his own tears from his eyes with his bloody hands.

"Cal?" she asked again, and this time her slender hand reached out to touch his blood-smeared face.

"It's nonsense. You can't quite possibly hold yourself to blame for the choices of your father. Love is foolish, I know that-" He tried to explain, but her concern cut him off.

"Deryn?" she interjected.

"My lady?" Deryn asked worriedly, sensing the dread in her voice. "What is it?"

"I don't understand," Cal said, his brow furrowed in confusion.

"What is happening to him?" she wondered aloud. "What is happening to his eyes?"

"My eyes?" Cal asked, confused now at the turn of events. "What are you talking about, woman?"

Deryn flew to them in a hurry, and what he saw made a shiver run down his tiny, blue-winged body. "Cal," he said with both wonder and confusion.

"What in the damnable dark is the matter?!" Cal said in frustration. "What is going on with you two?"

Astyræ's fingers wiped at the blood of the Stag that had been smeared across the face of the groomsman. As she did, the dark brown color of his eyes was wholly replaced with a burning white glow. "Oh Cal!" she breathed. "Your eyes ... they are on fire!"

"What is it? What does that even mean?" he asked again, searching both of their faces for answers. "Deryn! What is she talking about? Tell me true, brother!"

"Look," Deryn said as he gestured to the reflective glass-like sand of the Ágoni gi. "See for yourself, my friend."

Astyræ took his hand without saying a word and led him to the hallowed gravesite of the long dead Jacaranda tree. The violet in her own eyes began to sparkle in hopeful wonderment, overcoming the yellow of self-loathing sorrow.

Cal searched her face for answers, but could not find what he was looking for.

"Look into the glass, my friend, and tell me what it is that you see." Deryn told him.

Cal turned his gaze from his friends and peered into the ancient mound. There, in the midst of the sacred glass, two white orbs stared back at him. As they came into focus, he saw his own reflection materialize around them. "What in the name..."

"Yes, my friend," Deryn agreed aloud. "What, indeed."

"My eyes?" Cal reached his hand up to cover one, and as he did the reflected light darkened. "What happened to me?"

"Perhaps the Stag was right," the Sprite told him. "It may be that he will show you the way after all ... only not in the way you might have first thought."

"But how?" Cal said, looking back at the lifeless body of the white cervidae on the forest floor. "How could he?"

"Perhaps he is also a fool," Astyræ said aloud, still mystified at all that had just happened. "Perhaps it was love that caused him to be so."

"Tell me," Deryn asked, "what do you see?"

"What do you mean, what do I see? I see you, Sprite, and I see the lady, and I see ... I see the dead Stag," Cal answered defeatedly.

"Keep looking," Deryn urged.

"I don't know what you mean, Deryn!" Cal blurted as he turned his head this way and that, scanning the land about them. "I see the clearing, and the trees, and I see-" His words caught in his breath. "*What?*"

"What is it, Cal?" Astyræ begged as she held onto his arm.

"What is that over there?" he mused aloud.

"Over where?" Deryn asked, looking in the same direction as his white-eyed friend.

"There! At the base of the large, soldier pine!" Cal called as he ran from their encampment towards the edge of the clearing. "Look! See? White markings!"

Cal bent down to examine them, his chest heaving with excitement. "They look like rubbings from a…"

"From a stag?" Astyræ finished his words for him.

"Yes, my lady," he said as his own heart softened at the smile on her beautiful face. "Like rubbings from a stag."

"Perhaps he will show us the ancient path after all," Deryn mused.

"Perhaps," Cal agreed.

"I am sorry, you know," she said once again, and her apology found his heart like the silver arrow of the fabled bow.

"I know," Cal told her.

"What should we do with him?" Astyræ asked. "It cannot be right to leave him here for the carrion and the beasts of the forest. It is my fault he is dead … the least I can do is honor him."

"Aye, my lady," Cal agreed with a tone of deep appreciation in his voice. "It is fitting for such a beast to be given a burial worth its majesty."

"May magic and beauty both rest eternal in their glass tomb," Deryn said, giving both his permission and blessing over the groomsman's thoughts.

"Thank you, my friend," Cal said as he nodded his head in understanding of the extravagant generosity of his Sprite companion.

The three of them dug their hands into the crystalline shards of the ancient tears, preparing a place to bury the White Stag who may very well have been sent by the THREE who is SEVEN Himself. When space had been made enough for the beast, they dragged the lifeless body and laid it to rest. Before they covered the holy cervidae, Astyræ reached down and removed the arrow of Arianrhod from his pierced body, seeing it right that the instrument of its demise not sully the tomb of its sacrifice.

"There," she said as she snapped the barbed bolt in two and threw it upon the clearing floor. "Never again will that shard of the *Silver Moon* draw blood from any beast of the ground, for it has flown recklessly this dark day."

Cal reached out and took her slender hand in his own as Deryn spoke words over the grave.

"*Bealtaine do íobairt chruthú ár baois an ciallmhar, agus is féidir leat maith dúinn ... ar feadh tréimhse nach raibh a fhios.*"

"What does it mean, Deryn?" Astyræ asked him, removing her hand from the groomsman's with a mournful look upon her face.

"May your sacrifice turn our folly wise, and may you forgive us ... for we did not know," he told her.

Astyræ's eyes slipped closed as a tear escaped down her cheek. "We did not know," she whispered.

Cal reached for her again, but Deryn's outstretched hand gave him pause. He stepped back, trusting in the wisdom of the Sprite and yet wrestling with the tension in his own spirit.

"May it be so." Cal agreed.

"Come now, my friends," Deryn spoke into the silence. "The path has been marked for us, and it is time that we follow it."

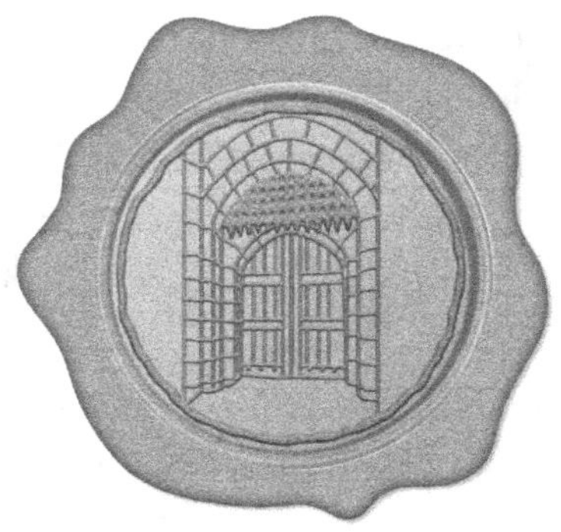

Chapter Four

"Where are we?" The crimson haired woman asked aloud. "Where does this pass let out?"

"North!" Portus, the tanner, replied. "I mean, that is where Engelmann told us it would lead us, right Margarid?"

"Yes," Celrod said. "But *where* north? North of the city could be a thousand different places."

"Not that I am complaining or anything!" Timorets, the brewer, said light-heartedly as he kissed his flint and looked nervously over his shoulder, trying to raise the spirits of the remnant of Haven. "As long as this place doesn't have dragons or soul-feasting butterflies, it will make do!"

The eleven weary travelers let out an exhausted laugh, both nervous for whatever lay next before them, and at the very same time grateful that they had indeed passed safely through the heart of the mighty Mt. Aureole.

"Where is that bird when you need him?" Harmier said, his eyes searching the darkened sky about them for the Owele that had led them to freedom.

"We are north of the city alright, but I can't see much more than that," Michael told his friends. "Except ... except that we are still in the mountains somewhere. I think we are still rather high up."

"Cair!" Celrod, the schoolmaster, exclaimed. "The Black Mountains of Cair. Leagues and leagues of inky-black rock, hard granite whose only relief is eastward."

"Eastward?" little Georgina exclaimed. "But what is eastward? My papa said that the only things east were outliers and witches, not to mention the shadow cats and ... and ... and giants!"

"My dear little girl," Harmier, the merchant, said with kindness in his placating words. "Outliers are the last of our worries. With any providence we might just find ourselves some friendly ones! And as far as witches and giants and the like ... no... no such things exist in this world."

"No such things?" Fryon said, amused at the merchant's dismissal of such evil. "Do you not remember what we just escaped? Oweles and *dragons*?"

"Of course I remember!" Harmier shot back. "That doesn't prove that a child's fairytales are true!"

"Aye, but it does change things a bit for me," Fryon argued. "I would have never told you that dragons are real either! But then ... we all know the truth of that matter now, don't we?"

"Fair enough then," Harmier relented. "Let's *hope*, shall we, that there is something more hospitable than whatever wild beasts your papa told you about, Georgina, and perhaps a little less wild than what we all might fear."

"So ... east, then?" Margarid said, her words coming out with trepidation. "That's not what Engelmann told us to do ... that's not where the arrows pointed."

"Aye," Michael agreed as he reached up to take her kindly by the shoulders. "But I don't think that Engelmann would have had us blindly walk off the face of these black mountains, in the pitch of this darkened world of ours, just to perish by following the direction of his arrows. Do you?"

"Mar, he is right," the tall tanner agreed.

"Besides," Michael said again. "I don't think we are done heading North. We just have to take a bit of a roundabout way."

"To the north, then!" Celrod said in an amused tone. "North ... by way of East."

"That might just be the smartest thing this old school master has said yet," Timorets said with a slap to Celrod's large, rounded shoulders.

"North by East," agreed Fryon.

"Aye," came the rumbling of agreement from the remnant.

"What do you say, Margarid?" Michael asked.

She nodded her understanding, squinting in the pale, violet glow about them. "North by East, then."

Michael kissed her dirt-smeared forehead. "Come on, my lady. We won't last long up here, not with that biting wind nipping at our backs. Grab what you can, and let's hope that Harmier is right; that there is something or someone out here that might have some hospitality to share with us."

With that, the eleven of them began the slow, winding, steep descent through the barren, black rocks of the Cair. Celrod held on to the brewer, steadying his wounded steps as best as he might, while Fryon, his brother, and Portus went ahead of the others to find a way down the mountain. Day after arduous day they travelled, and though they could see, dimly, by the light of their hope, there was not much more than black rock and black sand for them to notice.

"Do you think ... do you think it will always be like this?" Georgina asked Margarid as she held tightly to her hand.

"What do you mean, child?" Margarid asked sweetly as she helped steady her over a rather large step down.

"I mean ... is this how it is going to be? Running away from our home? Hiding from dragons? For always?"

Margarid thought on it for a while before she spoke. "I don't know; I suppose for a while at least. Though, no... I don't think this will be forever."

"What makes you say that?" Georgina asked. "Tell me, please."

Margarid looked to Michael for some kind of help as she did her best to answer the question that all of them were really asking. "Pain can't last forever, neither can sorrow ... I don't think it is in its nature to do so, try as it might."

"But what makes you so sure of that?" she asked her auburn-haired guardian.

"I have a friend ... well, more like a brother, really," Michael joined the conversation. "And he believed what the old Arborists did."

Margarid smiled her permission and nodded her affirmation at him as he spoke.

"That a new light would come, one that would chase away all sadness, one that would rid the world of all shadows and the evil that brooded in them. This new light would put the whole of Aiénor right again."

"My papa said those stories were just a fool's dream," the little girl replied.

"So, you would tell me that you believe his fairytales of witches and giants, but you can't possibly believe in something truly good, something long foretold?" Harmier said with unbelieving disgust. "Now tell me who is the fool here!"

She wrinkled her brow in slight offense at the merchant's harsh words, looking to Michael to defend her from the rudeness of it all.

"He is right, you know," Michael said with a knowing grin. "I would rather make this journey, this unbelievable journey that we have all found ourselves a part of, foolishly believing and foolishly hoping that this new light will come for all of us, than resign to a life without the possibility of a true home for us all."

"But how will we find it, Michael?" she asked him, tears stinging her eyes as she spoke. "Did your brother know?"

Michael thought of Cal, thought of how believing in this hope was always so natural for him. He thought about his Sprite friend and the great lengths by which he dared to trust his own life to this belief. He thought of how much he missed him, and how he wished and prayed that he was indeed safe right now.

"Michael?" Georgina asked again as she smeared away the tears from her eyes. "What did he tell you?"

"We will find it, girl; we will find this new light when we seek it," he replied, understanding coloring every utterance of every word he had heard Cal speak to him.

"But when? I want this light now ... I want those bad raven men to go away and I want to go home. Why haven't we found it yet?" she said as she started to cry all the more.

"I don't know when, I only know *how* ... and so seek it we shall," he answered her.

"One step at a time," Margarid added. "And together ... until we find it."

"Aye," Michael agreed.

The sound of anxious footsteps running towards them woke them from their rather heavy conversation, as Portus came running to them at the end of the line. "We've found something," he said in a whisper. "Not more than three, maybe four hundred paces down and to the east."

"What is it? What do you see?" Margarid blurted out.

"It looks like fires," Portus said, catching his breath.

"What color are they?" Michael asked nervously.

"They are not green, though they are not very big and they are not very bright," Portus replied.

"Well, that is a relief," Margarid said in an exhale.

"Maybe," Michael said warily. "What do you know? What could you see, Portus?"

"Not much ... but they seem muted, hidden behind rocks, or walls, or ... I don't know for sure," the tall tanner replied. "But they are below us, maybe at the bottom of these black rocks."

"Well, that is something good to know, at least!" Celrod exclaimed. "My leg is hurting something awful."

"Aye, and my back is beginning to strain under the weight of all of his hurting," Timorets chimed in.

"Alright then," Michael said to the remnant. "Perhaps Harmier was right, maybe we will find some unlooked for hospitality in these outlands."

"And what if we don't?" Portus asked.

"We have a few blades, don't we?" Michael said. "Let's just make sure we have them at the ready ... just in case. We need to stay together, though; I don't want anyone to be separated from the whole of the group. Tell Fryon and his brother to wait for us, we will meet them as one."

"Aye," Portus agreed and took off to tell the others.

"And if their blades number more than ours do?" Celrod asked.

Michael looked below them, unable to see the glowing fires Portus spoke of. "Then we will continue North, by way of East, as quickly as we can."

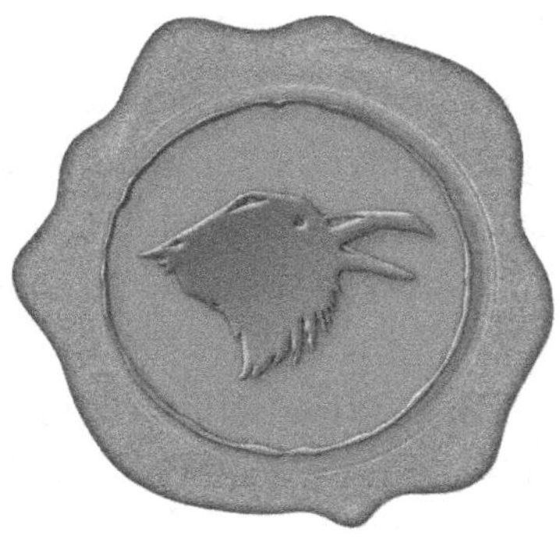

Chapter Five

"Who are you?" Seig shouted into the storm, both hands clasped on his upraised sword. "And what have you done with my captain? How did you come upon my ship?"

The man, the thing, the monster who commanded the storm of ravens stood at the bow of the ship, ashen arms outstretched in a display of grotesque strength. Seig watched in horror as he opened his mouth wide, letting out another blood-curdling screech.

A strange mass of soldiers appeared along the bridge deck; their eyes were the same sickly green as the ravens who drove the vessel.

"Men of the dead tree," came the sound of a woman's voice, spoken with a terrible calm. "It is *I* that should be asking *you* ... what it is that you are doing on my lands."

"*Your* lands?" Seig retorted. "I am the governor of this colony! This is my stronghold; these are my walls! And these," he said, gesturing to the gathered guardsmen, "are my blades. Choose your words carefully, lest I tell my men to shoot your damned birds right out of the sky!"

The guardsmen of the first colony watched, mesmerized by her terrible beauty, horrified by her unwavering, yellow gaze as she strode atop the deck of the ravaged ship.

"I remember the last lord who spoke with such arrogant ignorance," the woman said as she glided past the foremast and onto the bowsprit. "Don't you, Zviad?" she said playfully to a hulking beast of a man, whose face seemed sunken, and whose eyes bore the haunting glow of the sickly green.

"Yes, Raveness." The man spoke with little emotion. "But I have seen for myself a new light, and have repented of my folly."

"What in the damnable dark?" Pyrrhus said aloud, his skin crawling much the way it had on the godforsaken Isle Dušana.

"Who are you?" Seig demanded, impatient with her posturing.

"Who am *I*?" the Sorceress asked.

At the sound of her voice, the driver leapt from the bow of the ship and landed on the sandy shore. The Ravens at his command swirled about in a tempest as they began to take form, and with their bodies they hovered as an unholy set of stairs for the woman to descend upon.

"What kind of-" Seig began to ask.

"Soon all will be revealed, Governor," she said pointedly. "Soon there will be no need for questions." She stepped effortlessly atop the feathered staircase, descending on the backs of her feathered slaves.

The horses began to stamp and snort in protest, clearly unnerved. The guardsmen swallowed back their fear, counting their numbers against the green-eyed forces of this Raven Witch.

"Who am I, you ask? I am the savior of this darkened world," she said as her yellow eyes focused piercingly upon him. "I have ruled the west for many years, enlightening all who might wish to be free of the bondage of the dead tree, and ridding the world of all who refuse to see my *light*."

"Ruled the west?" Seig argued boldly. "Then how is it that we have never heard a single word about your reign?"

Six of her guards leapt from the deck of the beached vessel, then another six, and finally a third. As the contingent of her green-eyed soldiers landed upon the sand of the beach, they began to file in obedient rank to surround her.

"My lord?" Pyrrhus asked tentatively.

"What is this?" Seig said in bemused defiance. "Not even a score of untrained outliers? Do you expect this puny band of soldiers to defend themselves against the knights of Haven?" He spat. "You are sorely mistaken indeed. "

"But you forget yourself, dear Governor." Her words dripped with predatory cunning. "This is *my* land. It is not I, nor my men, that will need defending."

Seig continued with his show of strength, his haughty pride not allowing him to see the true danger gathering all about them. "We are here by right and by order of the Priest King Jhames himself! I have claimed these lands for him. I command these men *and* the armies of men that are yet to come."

"Ah, yes. Your Priest King." She paused, enjoying the sinister decadence of the moment before she demurely spoke again. "It would be fitting to inform you that I have also laid claim to your walled city, your citadel, your ship, and yes, even your Priest King, for myself. So I ask you … is this the full measure of *your* strength?"

"That's blasphemy!" Pyrrhus shouted out. "No one has ever taken our bright city, not while the light of Haven still-" His words fell short at his own realization.

"Dear brazen, flameless knight," she taunted. "Your precious light has failed you, just like its maker."

"Your lies will get you nowhere, woman," Seig scoffed.

Just then, the gaze of the Raven Queen shot up and to her left, for her eye had caught movement on the walls of the stronghold. "What do we have here?" she said slowly and deliberately. "It would seem that the full measure of your strength is not yet present after all," Nogcwren said hungrily.

The eyes of the Nocturnal soldiers scanned the beach about them, hands firmly gripping their feather-laden spear shafts.

"Bring him to me," she ordered her driver.

He acknowledged her order with a sinister grin, his lips spreading unnaturally wide and revealing a rotting row of yellowed teeth. He raised his arm like a great conductor, ready to unleash the fullness of his evil orchestration. The birds began to agitate, their voices cawing in unison, their black wings beating in rhythm to the wishes of the driver who commanded them.

"*Fly,*" he whispered in a tongue unfamiliar to the men of the colony. At his command, the hundreds of ravens shot through the dark sky, their little, black bodies tearing away the tiny thongs that had bound them to the arms of their master. His own blood began to trickle down his ashen arms as he let forth a soul-chilling laugh.

"What in the damnable dark?" Seig whispered to himself as he watched this twisted act of worship.

"That is what your *Priest King* said to me right before he kneeled to my display of power," she said coyly.

"Birds or no birds," Seig said, both afraid and offended, "I will not stand and hear you speak such lies!"

The wind about them began to blow, and the sounds of beating wings and cawing birds began to fill the tense darkness.

"This is a colony of Haven, and I am its Lord!" Seig shouted angrily now. "Neither our homeland nor this outpost will kneel to your witchcraft. I warn you now... leave these shores before my patience runs out!"

Seig threw his leg atop his mighty warhorse, and the rest of his men were happy to follow suit, for they did not wish to spend another moment in the presence of this witch.

"But Governor," she said as she smoothly strode over to his horse. "I am not quite finished."

At the last of her words, the angry Ravens barreled into view of the beach clearing, carrying a struggling, bleeding man in their tiny talons.

"What in the name of the THREE who is SEVEN!?" Seig said as he clasped his flint and kissed it without heed to the company he kept.

The birds held the man upright, hovering off the ground. Their sharpened talons dug mercilessly into his arms and shoulders, splaying his body there before them.

"Woodcutter?" the governor asked. The man turned his head toward the sound of Seig's voice. With great effort he opened his mouth to speak, but where words should have been, the spray of his own blood spewed upon the sandy shore.

"What do you want?" Seig turned to the Raven Queen with trembling rage.

"The same thing I have always wanted," she said. She approached the captive woodcutter and lifted her inked fingers to trace his bloody face.

"And what is that?" he spat. "Have it then, and be gone from here."

"Ha, ha, ha… ahhh! Tsh, tsh, tsh!" Her taunting laughter pricked the fear that had been quickly rising in the gathered colony. "So much pride, so much brawn, and yet, so… little… *awareness.*"

He breathed heavily through his nose, his offense buffeted by his uncertainty and fear.

"Aiénor," she said matter-of-factly. "I want Aiénor, all of it… and I will not rest, nor cease to raze every city and every stone until I have what I desire!"

"And just how do you intend to do that? It is going to take much more than a handful of blades and your little winged friends to conquer the world." Seig replied, contempt and arrogance dripping from his words.

"Oh, you are indeed right about that." An evil laugh erupted from the Sorceress as she threw her head back and raised her arms wide. The men of the first colony stared in shock and in horror as the very air about her began to choke and swell in a sickly, green mist of her conjuring. From within the fog, the image of two massive dragons slowly emerged, their eyes blazing with a hungry stare. Without warning, a soul-chilling roar screamed out as the image of a blast of fire erupted from within the sorcery.

A collective gasp rang out from the assembled company of guardsmen, and Seig looked back at his men, his bravado unnerved at such a display. His eyes searched their faces before he dared to look at the woodcutter, who still hung suspended by the murder of black birds.

"And..." He swallowed back the bile that threatened to choke his words from him.

"If my ravens are not enough to convince you, perhaps an army and a pair of dragons will." As she spoke, the fog grew thicker, larger, expanding above them and magnifying the size of the terrible beasts within. The horses grew nervous and the fight that had been nearly boiling over seemed to drain from every last soldier of Haven.

"Convince me of what?" Seig whispered.

"Governor!" Pyrrhus tried to interrupt, but neither Seig nor the witch seemed to pay him any mind.

"That you, like the rest of the *wise and powerful* lords of these lands, should aid me in my cause. That you should follow in the example of your Priest King and take for yourself and for your men the gift that I so freely offer," she said, gazing directly into Seig's terrified eyes.

"Gift?" he asked. "What is this *gift?*"

"The gift of *light,* dear Governor," she said. "Why toil and lay waste to the forests of this world for nothing but a fleeting and tepid glow? There is a light that requires no timber, that burns without a flame. I give the gift of sight in the darkness and freedom from the lesser illuminations."

"And then what?" he asked. "I seek both flame and glory, the glory of making my own light!"

"Dear Governor Seig!" she said, sweetly now. "If glory is what you still seek; I will not withhold it from you, for though my prize is ever close at hand... my labor is just beginning."

"Why not just take it all? Take the whole damned world for yourself if you want it bad enough," he said.

"I cannot force my gift upon anyone, well... not in the way you might think. Besides, what good is a world to rule with no one left to subjugate?" She laughed at her own words, her voice chilling the blood of all the men of the first colony. Nogcwren then returned her attention to the bloodied and bleeding woodcutter before her, studying him ravenously. "Now tell me, Governor. Where are the rest of your men? I would so like to meet them."

Chapter Six

Seig's gaze still fixated upon Rolf, suspended by ravens and spread before the Raven Queen.

"Where my men are is of no concern to you," he shot back to the Sorceress. "Besides, why would it matter to you anyway? You have your dragons, and I am sure a host of magic that could indeed divine whatever the hell it is that you would want to know." He spat as he spoke.

"Governor, that is not what I asked you," she said, rage beginning to bubble beneath her words.

"I know it's not," Seig replied. "But what does it matter? Dragons may have taken my homeland, but there are yet no dragons here to make me bend the knee. We are done here! Men of the first colony!" he shouted at the top of his lungs now. "You have seen conjurings and tricks, true or not ... I can't be certain. But what I do know is that no *conjuring* or smoke monsters will force my pledge of fealty to this witch, nor will I heed her orders."

The men of the first colony nervously grunted their agreement, while the eyes of the Raven Queen began to burn brighter and brighter with her fury.

"How dare you speak to me like this!" she growled.

But he didn't look to see her rage. Rather, he addressed his men from his mount, wheeling the black steed around to face his own men. "Move out!"

"If you refuse to share your findings, I am sure that *he* won't mind speaking on your behalf," she said as she gestured to the woodcutter. "Tell me, have you come across any that are native to this place?"

Rolf's eyes glanced back and forth, darting between his lord and this witch who held him by some dark magic. He coughed, choking on his own blood, trying to speak but unable to do so.

"What was that?" she asked him, toying with the bleeding man.

"Have you discovered any others here, living in this place?" she demanded again. "I wish to know if you have seen *them* trespassing upon my kingdom?"

"Let's go, then!" Seig shouted out his order.

"But what of the woodcutter?" came the voice of the young smithy. "My lord?"

Rolf began to cough now even more violently as he willed his mouth to speak. "Damn you!" he sputtered out his curse. "Damn you to whatever hell birthed you!"

"Oh, I have already been damned," she scolded him, her sickly, yellowed eyes burning with the wounded memory. "I remember the day my lover failed me, the day he would not raise his sword to defend me! I heard his wordless curses as he chose those ... those *things* over me! So, curse me all you like, woodcutter, for it was by his cursing, his choice, that I have found my destiny... and as *hell* would have it ... my destiny has now become your demise."

With a flick of her inked hand, the birds that held Rolf suspended there in front of the audience of guardsmen dropped him to the sandy beach. In a gruesome display of power, they ravaged and raked the flesh of the woodcutter as he screamed in pain. Seig and his men stared in horror at the nightmarish scene that whirled about and before them.

"This is my world, Governor, and all of Aiénor will bow before me; every man and every beast," Nogcwren raged. "The choice you and your men must make is whether to take my gift and serve me willingly, or choose to end up as another meal for my pets."

"I serve none save the Priest King himself!" Seig argued.

"Yes, yes!" she interrupted him. "And now your Priest King serves me, we have gone over this before."

Seig exhaled a tired breath, then kicked the flanks of his horse, moving to take his leave.

Nogcwren lifted her hand and the birds rose up like a black storm, flying over to the young smithy and clawing at his arms.

"AHHH!" Wielund shouted in pain. "No! please no! Let me be!"

"How many more of your men will have to die, until you give me what I want?" She sneered. "I will ask once more. Have you or your men come across anyone else upon my lands?"

"A girl!" Wielund cried out, tears and snot running down his bleeding face. "We saw a girl! Out there in the Wreath!"

"Smithy!" Seig shouted, but the ravens released the crying man and flew obediently towards the governor.

"And what have you done with this ... *girl*?" she asked as her birds swirled about him.

"Leave her alone! She is innocent!" Wieland shouted. Before he could protest further, the sorceress turned around and sent a horrible blast of magic into his chest, silencing the blacksmith forever.

Seig raised his hands to cover his face, palms out, splayed in a show of surrender. "I have done nothing with her!" he shouted back, his words wounded and defiant. "It was those damn woodcutters. They set her free."

"And where are these woodcutters you speak of?" she said, all too pleasantly. "Besides the one that I have fed to my birds."

"There!" he pointed over his shoulder. "Out there, on the edge of the forest, and more than double your number," he replied.

"That was not so hard now, was it?" she cooed. "Your cooperation will have its benefits, dear Governor. So bring me those men. Bring them here to our little stronghold, and let me tell *them* of the great gifts I have to offer. Let us see if they might more willingly assist me in my cause. If they choose to do so, I will let you become an aide to their kind, serving those who chose to serve me first, just to show you that I am not heartless." She laughed, amusing herself with her twisted cleverness.

"I will ... I will never..." he sputtered in outrage.

"*Or,*" she reasoned coldly, "you and your men can serve me, and I will make sure that both your loyalty and your leadership are rewarded. Either way, you will bring those woodcutters to me." She turned back to look at the sniffling, bleeding blacksmith. "And ... I would very much like to hear of this *girl*, and how it is that she has found herself free in my lands without first taking my gift."

Seig thought on it as the ravens still swirled and raged around him. It was both the arrogance of this woman and the impotence of his own strength against her witchcraft that became all too much for him to consider. "What is the girl, this savage... this *Wreather* to me, anyway?" he said, his gaze still fixed on the fire-lit ground. "Pyrrhus," he ordered.

"Yes, my lord," the fire knight said nervously.

"Bring Yasen to me. It would seem that..." he looked up with a sneer of disgust, both for these circumstances and for his own fear. "It would seem that the *Raven Queen* would like to have a few words with him."

"My lord?" Pyrrhus asked. "If what she says-"

"You saw the dragons," Seig interrupted. "King Jhames bent the knee to her, and we him. Now unless you would instead like to pledge your fealty to those woodcutters out there, I suggest you follow through with my orders."

Pyrrhus kept the rest of his protest to himself, knowing full well that it would fall upon deaf ears. "Yes, Governor," he answered at last, swinging his leg over the saddle of his own mount.

Seig didn't so much as look at the knight; his thoughts were otherwise occupied. "And be quick about it."

Pyrrhus saluted and wheeled his horse about, ready to ride out past the stronghold and then on towards the braziers at the forest line. He caught sight of the blood-streaked eyes of the dead smithy as he did so, and the fear that had made its mark upon Wielund's face planted its very seed in his own resolve. He spurred his horse, kicking up sand and shell as he did so. "You better know where that girl is, Yasen!" he growled into the darkened dampness. "Or we will all be a feast for her ravens!"

Nogcwren surveyed the scene about her. Although she had not the full might of her Nocturnal strength with her here, both she and the men of Haven knew with grave certainty who was indeed the lord of this land. She smiled, her yellow eyes aglow with both a satisfaction and an insatiable hunger, all at the same time.

"Men of the dead tree, thank you for the safe passage," she said as she stroked the silver hull of the beached *Determination*. "There is glory still to be won, only... you will not need to bother yourselves with the toil and tedium of timber. Follow me, take my *gift...* and you will need no fickle light to find your glory by. Not with me."

Seig looked up and met her lustful gaze. "If you have no more need of timber, then you would have no more need of woodcutters to harvest it for you. If not a colony, if not timber to harvest," Seig asked, "What then?"

"I need an army," she said as she strode towards him, nearly gliding across the sandy shore. "And I will need someone to lead this army for me. A captain, perhaps?"

His eyes shook off the haze of wounded pride, and focused now on the pale, poisonously persuasive face before him as she spoke.

"No, not a captain, a *general!*" Her voice nearly hissed as she let the idea linger. "Why be a governor, when you could be a general?"

The tall, dark-haired governor thought on it, looking at the lifeless, bloody heap of his woodcutter, remembering the image of the winged serpents. He turned, looking back to the stronghold that he and his men had carved out of the wilderness here. He had been so proud of it, and believed in his heart that this would just be the beginning of his glory. Now, in the sickly light of these unforeseen circumstances, it looked shabby and crude to him.

"A general, one who knows how to lead an army..." he said without emotion.

"Would be rewarded, high above all my servants," she said, finishing his thoughts. "Yes, and when the full might of my strength has arrived ... you will command a power the likes of which the *mighty kingdom of Haven* has neither the imagination nor the wit to comprehend!"

"I see," Seig replied.

"I was told that there was a great leader, a mighty warrior across the black waters of the Dark Sea. I only assumed that this great man was you. Though I could, if you prefer, wait to see what these woodcutter underlings of yours might propose; that is, if you are not agreeable to my offer."

"No!" he growled. "Do not waste your time with those fur-clad timber men; their wit is not half as sharp as their dullest blades. It is easy enough to fell a host of trees when soldier pines haven't the will to fight back, but if you are going to lead an army ... a real army ... you are going to need a man with a keen edge on both blade and battle."

***

Pyrrhus rode hard towards the flickering, amber braziers of the woodcutters. His mind was troubled at all that he had just witnessed. "I knew that girl was trouble, the moment I laid my eyes on her," he told the dark air about him. "Though this new woman ... I like her even less."

His thoughts raced in rhythm with the pounding of his horse's hooves upon the timber trail. He was so occupied with worry that it wasn't until he was but a hundred paces from the timberline that the unsettling realization crashed into the forefront of his mind.

"Do you hear that?" he asked his horse as he pulled back on the reins, commanding a hasty halt. "Shut up now, quiet yourself!" he growled to his snorting steed. "I don't hear a thing; not a damned crack of bark! What in the damnable dark is going on here?"

He frantically scanned the forest before him, looking for movement or shadows dancing in the flickering amber of the woodcutter braziers. He saw nothing but the dark, empty canopy of the Greywood. "Yasen, you bastard, you'd better be where I can find you!" he said, now more nervously than before.

With that, he angrily spurred his mount, racing off towards what he already knew in his heart he would find.

Chapter Seven

The onslaught of the Raven sentries crashed into the dwindling and diminished ranks of Marcum's remaining guardsmen. Bows were loosed, and for every white-plumed arrow of Haven that found its mark, the ugly black bolts of the Nocturnal marauders downed yet another of these last, brave guardsmen who fought valiantly at the foothills of the Hilgari.

"Fire at will, men!" Johnrey shouted from across the road. "There is no surrender left. We either fell them, or they fell us!"

"Keily!" Marcum shouted down at her from his position on the hilltop just above. "Get them out of here! Get them to safety while you still—"

His words were cut short as a spray of blood washed over his face. The guardsman next to him had taken a raven-fletched arrow right through his throat. Marcum wiped his face, then quickly caught the bleeding young man as three more bolts pierced the guardsman's body.

"Dammit all!" the lieutenant shouted, as he laid the dying man on the ground in front of him. "Get them out of here, now!" he shouted down to her.

"Come on! Come on now, hurry, they can't hold the line much longer," Keily ordered the women and children as they grabbed whatever they could to carry with them. She slung her own bow over her shoulder and cinched tight the scabbard to her belt, for she needed her hands to help shepherd those who were stumbling in the darkened hurry of it all.

The horrible sounds and screams of battle clamored overhead, and though her heart longed to aid the guardsmen and to loose a quiver of arrows in the hearts of these raven invaders, she knew that she was the last defense this fleeing remnant could hope to have. The clank of metal and the thud of dirt cleared her thoughts at the sound of another of her kinsmen tumbling end-over-end down the hillside to their hiding place.

Keily was brave, and she herself had felled scores of these raven enemies, but in that moment, she thought of Yasen, wishing that he were here to help protect these people alongside her. She brushed the thought of him aside and motioned for the group to follow her. Without any other need of persuasion or prodding, Keily led them off towards the northwest, the same direction that the young boy Roshan had fled.

Marcum looked back over his shoulder to see the barmaid leading the women and children as far away from here as she could. He steeled his resolve and shouted his orders as his last arrow loosed and buried itself in the helm of a raven soldier.

"To arms! Draw your blades, men ... we've got to fight them back by hand!" the lieutenant shouted.

The sound of sliding metal rang its deadly tone upon the symphony of battle as the remaining guardsmen of Haven drew their blades and prepared to put up one last fight, futile as it seemed, for the hope that someone, anyone might survive this hellish night.

"Corporal!" one of Johnrey's men shouted to him as he fired an arrow into the fray. "I think there are more coming! Do you hear that?"

Johnrey turned quickly, squinting off into the darkness beyond towards the sound of heavy hooves and rusted wheels. "More?!" he growled. "Come to finish us off, are they?"

Just then, a wash of amber firelight lit up the field of battle. "What in the damnable dark?!" he wondered aloud.

Six torches seemed to blaze to life on the back of an ox-driven timber cart that was barreling down the North Road into the heart of the battle.

"Is that...?" the guardsman began to ask.

"The woodcutters!" Johnrey yelled. "Thank the THREE who is SEVEN! All is not lost lads, we are not alone!"

At the reins of the twin oxen sat Brádách, the wounded woodcutter. A large, wooden shield was lashed to his arm and he laughed a maniacal laugh as nearly a dozen woodcutters fired their bows upon the hoard of Ravens.

The team of oxen was enraged, and though the barbs of the enemy pierced their hides, their madness carried them through the enemy's lines. Horns gored and heavy hooves trampled the raven soldiers. At the sight of the welcome chaos, Marcum signaled for his men to charge.

A shout came out from behind the cleft of the hilltop and a dozen guardsmen came issuing forth, blades brandished, bloodlust in their eyes. Not a moment later, Johnrey and his handful of guardsmen did the same, all converging on the Nocturnals.

"Attack!" came the shout of Črotmir, the Raven commander. "Bend them to her will!"

Arrows flew, and swords were buried deep into flesh. What was mere moments before a hopeless endeavor, became now a small chance for victory for this final army of Haven.

"Back from whence you came, foul servants of darkness!" shouted a young Priest as he loosed arrow after arrow into the fray. His bloodstained tunic and bandaged head made him quite the irreverent sight to behold, far from the piety and decorum expected of his order. Nonetheless, he joined the few wounded woodcutters, cooks, and the northmen's smithy, to do what they could in the face of so much wrong.

"Am I glad to see you, woodcutters!" Marcum shouted amidst his thrusts. "I thought we were all but dead and gone from this world."

"Aye!" Brádách bellowed as he buried his axe in the helm of another Nocturnal. "We thought we were all that was left!"

The guardsmen and woodcutters began to carve their way into the confusion, and one by one, the Raven soldiers began to fall.

"Do not let them retreat, lads!" Johnrey shouted as his blade blocked and then bit into the green-eyed enemy. "No quarter would they give you, and no chance for report shall we give them!"

Marcum dodged one of the crude blades, and in return he swept the legs of his foe with a powerful kick of his own, sending the Nocturnal flat on his back with a clank and a thud of metal upon dirt. He wasted no time and used two hands to drive his sword into the exposed underarm of the fallen enemy. His notched blade caught on a bit of bone or armor, and though he pulled at it, it refused to come free. Distracted by the inconvenience of it all, Marcum did not see the mighty Črotmir approaching from behind. The Raven commander stepped over the bloodied bodies of guardsmen and ravens alike, his black spear turned crimson with the blood of his kills. His sights were trained on the unaware lieutenant.

Marcum twisted and turned the arrested blade until finally it gave way. He pulled hard and spun round to see the field of battle, when an explosion of pain erupted in his shoulder. The lieutenant looked and saw a vile black spear piercing his mail and buried violently in his own flesh.

"You will bend to her will, one way or the other, men of the dead tree," Črotmir taunted as he retrieved a fallen sword and leapt towards the kneeling lieutenant in one swift motion. "Either by dragon," he raised his blade high above his own head as he spoke, "by fire, or by my very own hand—"

His bullying words were stopped short as a bright arrow of Haven stuck halfway out of his rotten-toothed mouth. Črotmir's eyes went wide in disbelief as he stumbled and fell, first to his knees and then flat upon his pierced face.

Behind him stood the young Priest, holding his bow in one hand, and kissing his flint in the other.

It was not much longer then, that Johnrey, Brádách, and the rest dispatched the remaining company of Nocturnals from this unfortunate field of battle.

"Marcum!" Johnrey shouted as he wiped the black blood off of his tired blade and motioned for help to come. "Hurry, he is wounded."

"I am alright," Marcum said through gritted teeth and with great labor. "See to the others; perhaps we might use our brother woodcutters' timber cart to help them."

"You are not alright, Marcum," Johnrey argued. "A damned spear has nearly run you clean through."

"I'll be alright soon enough," the Lieutenant persisted as he tried to stand to his feet, then wobbled and knelt back down again.

"Easy there, guardsman," Brádách bellowed. "We'll get you back to our camp soon enough, but first let us be rid of this barb, huh?"

Johnrey held his lieutenant steady as Brádách grabbed the shaft of the Raven spear. "Alright, be done with it already," Marcum said as he braced for the reprise of pain that was sure to come. The woodcutter yanked with one bloodletting pull, freeing Marcum from his deadly burden. "AHH!" he grunted against the pain, his fists clenched in a fury.

"Alright then. Priest!" Brádách shouted. "If you've got any bandages, the lieutenant here is going to be needing some mending before he bleeds out like a stuck boar."

The young Priest came over to him, and with no bandage to be had, tore the cleanest portion of his tunic that he could find, and bound the large shoulder wound as best as he could. "We will see about a proper dressing for it when we get you all to our camp," the Priest assured him.

"I am indebted to you, woodcutter," he said with a grimace as he took the large hand of the limping man. "But how are you alive? And how did you find us?"

"We are here because we couldn't fight when my brothers needed us to," Brádách told him as he helped him up into the seat of the cart. A cloud of shame and sadness fell over his battle-stained face. "All of them are gone, you know. We are all that are left, a sad bunch of cripples and cooks, and, well ... one slightly less-useless Priest."

"Lieutenant!" came the shout of a guardsman off in the distance. "They are gone! All of them, all the women and children! They are gone," he said breathlessly as he ran over to the ox cart.

"Did you see them, Brádách?" Marcum asked. "Our women and children, did you see them?"

"No," he said, shaking his bearded head. "We saw no one. They must have run off to hide, but there is not going to be much out there to sustain them, and certainly no safe shelter."

"We have got to find them," Marcum grunted as he pulled himself up to his feet, the fresh pain of the wound ever-present in his words. "How many of us remain, guardsman?"

"Thirteen, Lieutenant," the man reported.

He raised his flint to his lips and kissed it in an effort to ward off the evil of that most foreboding of numbers. "That is not a good sign there," he said warily.

"Well, it could have been a far worse number, and old omens be damned already!" Marcum dismissed. "We haven't the time for superstitions, as you can plainly see. Where is the Corporal?" Marcum asked.

"He is over there, sir." The young guardsman bowed his weary face and saluted with his response.

Marcum quickly turned to look for Johnrey in the direction his guardsman had pointed, praying to himself as he searched the field.

"Is he alright?" The lieutenant asked as he peered into the darkness before him.

"Yes, lieutenant," the guardsman answered him. "Only he is ..." His voice caught in his throat as he tried to convey the happenings.

The corporal was kneeling before one of his fatally wounded guardsman, his battle-worn hands holding tight to the failing grip of the bleeding soldier. "You fought brave there, lad." He spoke in a fatherly whisper. "You did us all proud."

The guardsman blinked against the darkness, tears filling his fading sight as he clung to the hand of his leader.

Johnrey looked up, met Marcum's gaze, and shook his head as the final breath of the dying man escaped past his grey lips. He kissed his own two fingers and whispered the ancient words.

Amidst all the destruction and death, all the hunting and madness of these last dark days, it was Johnrey's small kindness that toppled the dam of emotions that had been ever growing in the hearts of the guardsmen of Haven.

"Twelve," Marcum said solemnly as he watched Johnrey close the eyes of his fallen compatriot.

"Twelve, sir," the guardsman answered. They waited there in a moment of silence in the wake of the sobering loss around them.

"Aye, thirteen does seem like better luck now to me," Brádách said, nodding his head in somber sympathy.

"Corporal," Marcum finally called out to Johnrey. "Gather your men, and whatever aid you can find on the bodies of our fallen. Do it quickly, for the rest of our remnant needs us now."

"Yes, Lieutenant," the white-bearded corporal agreed. He and his men hurried themselves with finding blades and bows, and gathering as many spent arrows as they could manage.

"Brádách," Marcum said. "We have got to find them, and they can't have gone too far on foot. The barmaid is with them, so their peril may not be as great as we have feared."

"Barmaid?" Brádách asked. "You don't mean Hollis' niece, do you?"

"Yes ... I do," Marcum said as he used his good arm to lend a hand to the wounded still climbing up onto the ox cart.

"Ha!" Brádách laughed out loud, shaking his head in wonder as he did so. "This is a most lucky moment indeed. First we find you all, and save you from doom, I might add. And then ... then we learn that Keily is still alive!"

"That woman can cook, you know!" Brádách said, elbowing Marcum as he cracked the reins on his team of oxen. They began rolling off in the direction of the fleeing remnant. "Though I wouldn't cross her if I were you."

"And she is mighty fine with the bow, at that," Marcum praised. "As brave as any of my seasoned guardsmen."

"Oh, is she now?" Brádách said, raising his bushy, red eyebrows in wonder. "All the more reason to pay her mind. I remember this one time, the chieftain had brought a few of us into Piney Creek for stores and supplies, and one of the old lads had got a little too *liberal* with his greetings." Brádách laughed as he remembered the story.

"Oh?" Marcum said with a knowing smile as he wiped at his tired eyes.

"She nearly picked the lad up by his ear and threw him clear outside with the dogs. Then she turned and told the whole Knob, 'If you want to act like an animal, you are welcome to eat with the animals too!' Ha! That girl ... I am glad she is one of us," Brádách said with genuine gratitude replacing his jovial laughter.

"Me too, woodcutter, me too," Marcum agreed.

The twelve guardsmen and the eleven from the cutter camp made their way northwest in search of Keily and the rest of the women and children.

Chapter Eight

"What is this place?" Soma asked his chieftain as they both surveyed the mad markings and repeated writings on the walls of the prison tower. "And just who do you think it was that was held here?"

"It is some kind of prison hold, alright. Cal told me about it," Yasen answered. "And I doubt you would believe me if I told you who he said was once here."

"I don't know, North Wolf ... the world has became a rather strange place as of late, and I just might believe you after all." His eyes were a mix of both shock and wonder, all at the same time.

"Our groomsman says that it was Illium, or at least Illium's men, if you believe that sort of thing," Yasen told him, though his own wonder overshadowed the skeptical tone he tried to embody. "Though I am not as certain as to how he came up with that story."

"Illium or not, what do you suppose this means?" Soma said, pointing to the strange word jaggedly carved into the stone wall.

"Shaimira," Yasen answered. "That, brother, is where Cal was headed. That's where he believed he would find what it is he was looking for."

"And just what was that, do you suppose?" Soma asked.

"Something, I guess, we have all been looking for. Only he believed we were all a bunch of damned fools, looking for it in the wrong place," Yasen said as he tried to wipe the weariness of uncertainty from his tired eyes. "He is looking for the light, Illium's light."

"Huh," Soma grunted. "He is looking for it in the North, then?" His fingers traced the very same arrow that Cal had not so long ago found.

"Aye," Yasen agreed. "And I think it's time that we be quick on his heels."

"Aye," Soma said. "Seek the light, huh? Well, whoever it was that was held here … I hope they found what they were looking for."

"Me too, brother, because if they did … maybe they will have room there for us, too."

"Maybe so," said Soma.

Together, the two woodcutters made their way down the treacherously aged stairs, all the way to the moss covered floor of this long forgotten tower. They walked silently through the heavy canopy of the Greywood, their torch light dancing in the cold easterly wind, as they made their way back to the timberline of their once great efforts.

"What do you suppose it is?" Soma said, breaking the long silence. "The thing … the … that storm we saw?"

"I do not know, brother, but whatever it was, I don't think its intentions were peaceful."

"Aye," he said. "Neither do I-" Soma's words caught in his mouth as he saw the eyes of the fire knight catch his own gaze. "Damn it all!" he growled.

"Pyrrhus!" Yasen spat. "What in the damnable dark does he want out here? Doesn't he have his captain to welcome back?"

Pyrrhus spotted the two woodcutters inside the mouth of the forest and spurred his mount, riding hard after them. "Yasen!" he shouted into the trees. "Yasen! I have been looking all over for you and your woodcutters. The governor has requested your attendance."

Yasen read the fear and the dishonesty in the voice of his rival. "My *attendance,* is it? Who then, do you suppose, will be cutting down these trees for our countrymen if I am off, heeding to Seig's every whim? Huh? No Pyrrhus, I have a job to do, and I intend to stay and finish it; that is, of course, unless you would rather take my place."

"Shut your mouth, woodcutter!" Pyrrhus demanded. "I've neither the time nor the patience for your insolence. Where are your men?"

"My men are *my* concern, *knight*, not yours!" Yasen argued. "And for whatever errand I have set them upon, they are mine to command."

Pyrrhus looked back over his shoulder towards the raven-infested beach. "Whatever errand you have given them, you had better pray that it is far enough away from this place," he whispered.

"Are you threatening me, Pyrrhus?" Yasen said as he stepped closer to the agitated knight.

"Consider it a warning," he growled exhaustedly.

"A warning?" Soma chimed in. "A warning of what?"

Pyrrhus looked back again, more nervously now, and then to his own hand that held the reins of his mount. "The governor has requested your attendance." He swallowed dryly as he spoke. "And I cannot return without *you* coming back with me. Whatever errand you have your men attending to, that is not of my concern. But you will *come with me.*"

Yasen studied this shortsighted bull of a man. There was no love shared between them, and yet something different was in the words he spoke, something almost brotherly.

"What will I find when I return to the stronghold?" Yasen asked. "What was that storm upon the beach, Pyrrhus?"

Pyrrhus looked down, his mind a mess of self-interest and fear as he tried to sort between the gale for the right words. "That is why *you* have been summoned," he said as he met Yasen's gaze.

"Soma," Yasen said after he mulled the words over. "Find the others, and make sure that they find what we were looking for."

"If you are going to see the governor, then I will ride with you," Soma argued.

"No!" Pyrrhus shouted almost before Soma could finish his thought. "It was Yasen that was summoned, not you."

The North Wolf watched his foe, sensing the unspoken plea that was hidden, folded into the words of his demand.

"Soma," Yasen ordered him. "You tell the men to seek the light. Tell them to turn their axes northward and *seek the light.*"

Soma searched the face of his chieftain and saw plainly the meaning of his words. "But Yasen-"

"I am not going to keep the governor waiting any longer now, not while his dog is still hungrily begging for table scraps." He turned towards the still-mounted knight, mistrust plainly written upon his face. "I'll see what our fearless leader would have of me."

"We will find it, Yasen." Soma promised him quietly. "We will find this Shaimira, I swear it."

Yasen winced at the mention of the word, hoping against all luck that Pyrrhus had not heard it spoken. "You tell the men to get to work. Just because I am called back for a conference does not mean their blades can stop their biting." He spoke almost too sternly as he squeezed the shoulder of his brother, trying to cover the mention of Shaimira with his heavy-handed authority.

"Aye, alright then," Soma said warily, understanding the folly of his words. "We will get to work, alright. Axes pointed northward."

Yasen watched as his friend threw his leg over his white-coated Percheron, crossing his arm over his chest as he spurred the onyx colored beast towards his brothers.

"Come on then, Yasen," Pyrrhus ordered weakly, anxiety stealing the wind from his once fiery bellows. "I do not want to keep her-" Yasen's eyes caught his own at the slip of the word, "*Him* ... waiting. Now is not the time for that kind of treason."

Yasen climbed atop his own mount, fingering the hunting knife he kept sewn into the lining of his fur-clad boots. His mind, wary and mistrusting, could not help but think of his auburn-haired bar maiden, who sewed for him the very patch that he wore so proudly on his scarred face and useless eye. As he started towards the ominous stronghold off in the too-near horizon, he prayed for her protection, and that he may yet see her again.

Yasen looked back over his shoulder towards the abandoned braziers on the tree line, knowing full well that he had not a friend left in the colony at the shore. He swallowed back his nerves before he spoke. "Tell me what this is about, Pyrrhus. What was so important to our governor that he would take me from my task and my men?"

Pyrrhus rode in thoughtful silence, the clomping of his horse's hooves filling in the tension of the question. "It is not my place to say, woodcutter." He released his exhausted breath, then turned his head to look at the target of his errand, and Yasen could see fear etched plainly upon his wiry face.

"Alright then, knight of Haven ... take me to him." Yasen said.

Chapter Nine

After packing up their small encampment, Cal and Astyræ mounted their two horses in search of the ancient path of the White Stag. Northward they rode, eager to find just where these mysterious holy markings might lead them.

It wasn't long, less than a league from where Cal had first spotted the glowing white markings at the base of the large pine, until they saw the next marker of their journey. Though to both Deryn and Astyræ they were nothing but the scratches and scars of a rutting beast of the forest, Cal's new eyes could see the magic amidst the ordinary.

"There!" Cal shouted to his friends. "I see another one! Right there at the base of that great cedar!"

"Are you sure?" she asked him timidly. "I can't see anything at all ... every tree is beginning to look the same to me, Cal."

"Yes, my lady," Cal assured them. "I can see the markings clear enough; they glow for me ... for us. Come on!" Cal clicked his tongue inside his cheek and in an instant the mighty silver courser sprung to life.

"Will they all be like this, Deryn?" Astyræ asked as she watched the groomsman fly across the forestland. "Will they all be so easy for him to find?"

"I cannot say for certain, my lady," Deryn answered her, trouble clearly coloring the lines of his tiny, furrowed brow. "He has been given a gift of sight, and I do not believe that this gift will be wasted." Deryn paused as he chose his words amidst his ponderings. "He will be able to see the markings of the Stag, however plain or hidden they might be. Only..."

"Go on, then," she urged as she watched him labor over his words.

"Only ... he will still need to *look* for them. It will be nearly impossible to see anything, magic or otherwise, if he forgets or fails to look for them in the first place."

"Well then," she said with a kind smile, "if we are going to remind him ... we will most certainly need to keep up with him."

By the time his friends reached him, Cal was kneeling at the base of an enormous cedar tree. He ran his fingers over the scarred bark. Each line seemed to have been made a dozen lifetimes ago.

"Thank you," he whispered to the cold, dark air about him. "Thank you for this, for making a way for us."

"Does it say anything?" Astyræ shouted to him as she reined her chestnut mount to a halt. "Does it give you any direction?"

He looked at the markings, examining, searching for a sign or any possible clue. "No," Cal told her with a sigh. "It doesn't say anything at all, but neither did the last one."

"How do you suppose we will find the next one, then?" she asked, nervous at the possibility of missing it altogether.

"I suppose I will just ... see it." Cal said, a bit unsure himself.

"Cal," Deryn said as his charge mounted the back of the silver coated Farran. "Your sight is a gift from the mighty cervidae; but ... please ... in your seeing, do not become blind."

"What do you mean?" Cal said, rather confused.

"What I mean is," Deryn said as he flitted up to meet the gaze of his friend, "these lands have for too long been under the tyranny of the Sorceress and she will care not for ancient paths, nor for groomsmen who can see them."

"He is right, you know," Astyræ agreed.

"Just keep an eye out for other things too, the dangerous and the devilish things, lest we fall prey to them," the Sprite said.

"Alright then, my Sprite guardian," Cal said with a disarming smile. "I will be mindful enough. Now come on you two; our destiny might just lay at the end of the Stag's path. I have waited and wanted my whole life to find this new light ... and do not wish to wait a moment longer than I must to finally find it!"

"I know, Calarmindon Bright Fame," Deryn said in a fatherly tone of voice. "Just mind that you are seeking in a strange and hostile land."

"I will," Cal assured him. "Are you ready yet?"

"Yes, groomsman," Astyræ said playfully. "We are ready."

Her smile caught his attention, and her beauty momentarily overshadowed the brilliance of their shared quest. He could not help but to smile in response.

"What?" she asked him. "What is it, groomsman? What are you smiling about?"

He swallowed his nerves back and shook his head in jovial astonishment. "I have never noticed before just how ... how bright these wilderlands can be when you ... when you smile like that."

Her grin grew all the more sincere at his compliment. She stared at her hands as she felt the warmth begin to color her cheeks. "And I have never known a groomsman to be so ... I don't know." She huffed out a breath of frustration at the words she couldn't seem to grasp in the unexpected moment. "Thank you, Cal," she said timidly, her eyes raising to meet his.

An unspoken energy passed between the two of them. "Aye," he said, finally.

Deryn looked back and forth at the two of them, shaking his small, silver-haired head at just how quickly the moment had shifted. "Come on, then. I fear we still have quite a long road ahead of us."

"Aye," Astyræ said in reply, her violet gaze sparkling in the torch light.

Cal nodded and lightly spurred Farran with the heels of his boots. And with that, the three of them set off, riding North in search of the next marking.

Days passed as they followed the hidden trail, led only by Cal's gift of vision. Seeking the light was foremost in the groomsman's mind, though the smile of the lady Astyræ did its best to rival it.

"Cal!" she shouted from behind "Cal!"

The groomsman reined in his iron-grey horse, wheeling Farran around to see just what was the matter.

"My lady?" he asked.

"Can't we stop? Can't we rest now?" she pleaded. "I want to find Shaimira too, but we have been riding for days and it still seems no closer than when we first began. Perhaps it is time that we rest."

"I see it ahead," he told her. I can see the next marking like a beacon in the night, as bright as the Maris Tower in the Bay of Eurwen."

"But if we ever want to reach it with enough strength to seek the next one ... we still must rest."

"She is right, Cal," Deryn said in agreement. "The seeking heart, so driven as it may be ... still needs rest."

Cal looked about, frustration and resignation mingling in the forefront of his thoughts. He searched in the violet glow that colored his vision for some place to make their camp and shelter them from the wilderness. The terrain of the journey had changed over the last few leagues, from the thick undergrowth of the mighty Greywood forest to the sandy, rock-strewn floor of these northern marches.

He exhaled his acquiescence. "Alright then, my friends, I could do with something to warm my belly, and perhaps a place to rest my eyes for a bit."

"I could use a place to rest my backside, if I am honest," she said with a laugh in her words. "I haven't ridden this much since, well … since before I had reason enough to find myself locked in the heights of Enguerrand."

"And just how long ago was that my lady?" Cal said, returning her laughter with his own playful question.

"Long enough, groomsman," she told him with a look in her eyes that suggested this story was indeed done with its telling.

"Alright then, there is a cleft up there a bit," he said, pointing slightly westward. "We can tie the horses off, and perhaps make our shelter up there upon the ridge if that suits you two."

"At least this way we will have stone to our backs, and whoever might wish us harm will have to make their way uphill to get to us," she agreed.

Deryn flitted about, surveying the wild lands about them, listening and straining his ears for any sign of danger.

"Deryn?" Cal asked. "What do you think, my Sprite guardian?"

Deryn looked deep into the forest, and though he could neither see nor hear anything or anyone, a wariness colored his thoughts. "Yes, let us make our camp in the cleft of the rock, but do not trust this place, my friends."

"Do not trust it?" Astyræ asked him. "You don't suppose there is another wizard or beast out here too, do you?"

"My lady, the things that make their home in the dark reaches of this world are beyond my supposition. There is not one place, while darkness abounds, that will ever feel truly safe." Deryn said, his azure eyes still scanning the thickly shrouded tree line about them.

"What are you saying, Sprite?" she said, a nervous grit now coloring her voice. "Speak plainly."

"I am saying that though we need our rest and our recovery, be ever mindful that it is we who are the strangers, the trespassers in these shadow lands."

Chapter Ten

"Shhh! Shut it now ... I hear someone coming!" Oren said to his woodcutting brother.

"You couldn't hear a tree fall if it was your own thick head that it crashed into!" Alon retorted. "I still don't know why it was you they set to keep watch—"

Alon's words caught in his mouth as he too heard the pounding of hooves upon the forest floor. "I hear something ... quiet now ... shh!"

"I told you!" Oren said as he slammed his elbow into his brother's side. "Someone is coming."

Soma rode hard, looking intently for his brothers, peering into the thick, black haze that covered every league, limb, and leaf in these parts of the Greywood. "Goran!" he shouted in a whisper.

"It's Soma!" Alon said excitedly.

"Aye, it's Soma alright, but it's only Soma." Oren said. "Not Yasen."

"Are you sure?" Alon asked.

"Aye. Just one horse ... just one rider," Oren told his brother.

"Soma!" Alon called out as he sparked his flint into the darkness about him. "Over here! Over here, brother."

"Thank the THREE who is SEVEN that I found you!" Soma said as he leapt from his panting steed. "Where are the others?"

"Where is Yasen?" Oren asked pointedly.

"That's what I need to speak with you all about," Soma countered.

Alon and Oren looked to each other, worry beginning to color their faces. "They are at the cave over there, waiting for you, I suppose."

"Come on then, we have much to discuss," Soma said.

"Have you seen Rolf?" Alon asked him.

"I was going to ask you the same thing," Soma replied. "He has not returned?"

"No." Oren said solemnly. "No one has seen him yet."

When the three of them reached the mouth of the cave, the edge of the forest was washed in the glow of the woodcutter's fire. Some men rested, others fiddled with and sharpened their blades as they all waited for their chieftain to return and tell them what to do next.

Goran spotted Soma first. "They are here, brothers! Yasen and Soma are back!"

Everyone turned their attention towards Soma as he rode closer to the camp. "Where is he?" Goran asked. "Where is the North Wolf?"

Soma took a deep breath to steady himself. "He is with Pyrrhus."

"What?" Goran shouted in befuddlement, the rest of the camp following suit.

"What in the damnable dark is he doing with that one-armed pig?" Gvidus shouted in disgust.

"What is he doing there?" Goran shouted. "I thought it was decided that we—"

"Of course it was decided." Soma cut him off.

"Then why? Why are we not looking for this place that Cal spoke of? Why is Yasen back at the stronghold with the governor's dog?" Goran argued.

"Yasen and I found the tower, the place where Cal said he found the girl," Soma started.

"I don't care about some damned tower!" Oren blurted out.

Soma shot him a look, and Oren shook his head in aggravation.

"Aye!" Alon agreed. "What good is a tower if our leader is left here with Seig? Is he not coming with us?"

"Whatever it was that rode upon that storm might take issue with our going anywhere at all," Oren said ominously.

"Will the lot of you shut your gullets for a moment?" Gvidus said as he walked his large-bellied frame into the center of the commotion. "Let the man tell his tale."

Soma took a deep breath before he spoke again. "We found the tower... the one Cal believes Illium was held prisoner in."

"Illium?" Alon asked aloud as a throng of whispers began to roil around them.

"Aye, that is what Yasen told me," Soma said.

"Go on, brother. What did you find there?" Gvidus said.

"We found a word. I think it is the name of the place Cal is looking for, and we know he is looking for it somewhere north of here."

"What was the word?" Goran asked.

"Shaimira," Soma answered him quietly, looking nervously to the trees.

"Shaimira? What does that mean?" Alon asked bluntly.

"Hush! I don't know what it means. But I know it's what we are looking for. And let's not let the whole forest know about it either!" Soma chided. "Yasen and I had made our way back to the tree line when Pyrrhus rode up to greet us," he continued on. "He looked more nervous and agitated than I've ever seen him."

"What did he want then?" Goran asked, rather impatiently.

"He wanted Yasen. He said that it was urgent that the governor see him that instant." Soma blew out an anxious breath before he spoke again. "Something is not right, brothers. I feel it in my bones. Something very wrong is about to happen."

"If it was *just* Pyrrhus, why didn't Yasen bury his axe in the bastard and be done with it all?" Oren said, disgusted.

"I think … I think he wanted to give us a chance to get as far away from this place as we could before whatever it is that is over there comes looking for us, too," Soma told them.

"Well, I am not leaving him!" Alon said brashly. "No sir … I can't in good faith abandon him to the likes of Pyrrhus."

A shout of agreement rose up from the gathered northmen.

"You don't understand, brothers!" Soma tried to reason with them. "He made me swear to tell all of you to point your axes northward and seek the light!"

"Point our axes northward?" Oren said, not fully understanding the meaning. "Why would he say that?"

"Because, brother… he wants us to find Cal, and he wants us to get far away from here while we still can," Gvidus answered.

The cutter camp was silent at the realization. Worry and frustrated anger fell upon them all like a damp fog.

"I don't like it either, brothers," Soma told them as he looked back over in the direction of the stronghold. "I don't like the feeling I have in my gut right now … something is very wrong indeed."

"Aye, but our chieftain has given us our orders," Goran told the men. "And it is high time that we point our axes northward and see if we can't find that damned groomsman."

"Shaimira, then," Gvidus replied.

A grumble of agreement rolled through the gathered woodcutters. Knowing glances, worried looks, and ultimately nods of understanding were given before they spoke again.

"May it be so!" the men agreed.

Chapter Eleven

Michael and the others caught up to Fryon and his brother. Hidden in the rock and shielded from the glowing fires below, they warily watched whoever it was that camped on the side of the black rocks of Cair.

"What word, Fryon?" Michael asked his friend. "Have you seen anything?"

"Aye," Fryon answered. There was no fear in his voice, though there was a great deal of mistrust.

"What, then?" Celrod asked, still wincing at the festering wound in his rather sizable leg.

"A dozen shadows or so, walking in and out of the glow of those fires over there," Fryon answered.

"Shadows?" Margarid asked warily.

"Aye, shadows," he confirmed. "Of people."

"Well, that is a relief," Timorets said. "We know they aren't the damned Raven soldiers?"

"Don't be so sure, master brewer. Those Raven soldiers looked like men, too," Celrod replied. "Or at least they looked as if they might have been men, once before."

Timorets agreed with a shrug of his weary shoulders and an exhausted breath.

"The Ravens had no use for natural fires," Fryon observed. "These are people, alright. What *kind* of people? Well … that I cannot be sure of just by counting their shadows."

"There!" Fryon's younger brother whispered as he pointed. "There they are again."

"They are people, aren't they Margarid?" Georgina exclaimed a little louder than any had wished.

"Aye … so it would seem, girl," she replied. "But keep your voice down, lest they hear us before we wish them to."

"Have you seen any blades? Any weapons in their shadows?" Michael asked as he studied the moving figures against the walls of the mountain.

"It's hard to tell," Fryon said. "Could be a broom, could be a spear … I am not certain."

"Alright, then," Michael said, taking in the responsibility of the moment before he spoke. "We will meet them together, blades sheathed and hands open. I would hate to scare off any chance at a warm bowl and safe rest, just because we are uncertain."

"Blades sheathed?" Harmier said, aghast at the thought. "But what if theirs are not? What then?"

Michael looked again into the glowing shelter there against the rock. "It doesn't much look like a trap, nor a band of Raven soldiers, now does it? See, over there." He pointed further along the rock line. "There are more shelters, more faint fires. They are probably cooking fires for this … this village, I suppose. And we can't be the first strangers to come upon them unawares like this—"

The distinct sound of a bowstring being pulled taut stalled the words in his throat. First one, and then another, and then again the chilling sounds of three more bowstrings were heard by all. Michael raised his finger to his lips, and reached his hand for the hilt of his blade.

"Unawares, we are *not*," said a dry and unamused voice behind them. "Do not be mistaken … we have been watching you far longer than you have been watching us."

"Please," Michael said, turning his head in the direction of the voice. "We mean you no harm, we but seek refuge with your people."

"Refuge?" the man replied gruffly. "Refuge from what? From this darkness?" He laughed with angered joviality. "You have sought in the wrong place, for there is no refuge here from that."

Michael stood to his feet, catching the glow of the fire in the eyes of the archers about them. "We seek refuge from those who hunt us, from those who have destroyed our homes and our city."

The hooded man stood there, staring at them from beneath the shadows of his cloak.

"Please, we mean no harm," Margarid added.

The archer pushed back his hood enough to reveal a look of disgust upon his face. His long, dark, braided hair hung heavy on his right shoulder, and his eyes flashed in wary repulsion. He walked right up to the standing groomsman and without warning slapped Margarid with the back of his hand. He snarled his reply at the gasp of the huddled remnant before training his bow once again at Michael's chest. "Maybe not, that is not for me to decide. But I, Hildræd, will not suffer a woman to speak to me, not now … not ever."

Margarid let out a wounded whimper as her soft hands clutched at her burning cheek. Her friends tightened their grips on their spears and swords, bracing themselves for a fight.

Michael held his hands up, willing the deadly tension away from the moment. "Alright, Alright! She will be quiet now … won't you?" he said to her, his eyes pleading, his countenance covered in worry.

She nodded her humiliation, then lowered her eyes from him.

"You said it was not for you to decide, then please, Hildræd, tell us whose place it is," Michael asked.

"Lord Æsc will judge you worthy or not of refuge here. But it is not his *hospitality* I would be worried over." He laughed a disappointed laugh. "For it is *Ragnarr* who might cause you to stay ... indefinitely," Hildræd said gravely.

"I don't understand." Michael said.

Hildræd looked with disgust at Margarid and spat on the dust before them. "You will. Soon enough, you will."

The remnant looked worriedly back and forth, while Michael did his best to stand bravely as their spokesman. "Will you take us to him then? To Æsc? Please ... we have no home."

Hildræd looked him over from boots to brow with a loathing gaze. Then, without a word, he walked past him, the full force of his inconvenienced weight slamming into Michael's shoulder as he strode towards the fire light. "You can keep your blades, if you like," he said with a taunting laugh. "They will be of little use to you, for they are but tinder in the presence of an angry warlock."

Michael watched as Hildræd continued on past them, unsure whether they were to follow after him or not, and even more unsure if they now wanted to do so at all.

"You heard him. Up with you ... all of you," came the snarling voice of another sentry. "We *Walha* do not suffer strangers or trespassers, let alone the dogs of *Haven* on our doorsteps. It's time to get the judging over with before your fleas have time to hatch in our homes."

The men grabbed Michael's shoulders and pushed to get him moving. The rest of the remnant rose to their feet and followed suit, moving towards the flickering shelter at the base of the black rocks. As they came closer to the fires, they could see more and more of the hooded figures, staring at them from the shadows.

Margarid grabbed Portus' arm, squeezing her worry to the tall tanner. He nodded in silent understanding as they wound their way past the rocky, black outcroppings of stone and the scores of staring eyes.

"Who are these people?" Georgina whispered to Harmier.

"He said they were the Walha," the merchant whispered back.

"Outliers. I have never had dealings with them myself, but a trader I know from the upper borough used to get juniper from them."

"And what did this trader friend of yours have to say about them?" Celrod asked in hushed nervousness. "I, for one, would like to know what kind of hornet's nest we are walking into."

"They are a harsh people, not very hospitable at all ... and women ... well, just be as quiet as you can is all," Harmier pleaded with them.

"We are here!" Hildræd shouted in annoyance. The band of captives halted their marching descent in front of a level clearing, a plateau in the black rock of the mountainside. On the edge of the clearing were curved little structures, comprised of a mix of mud and stone, with rounded, smooth rooftops that were no doubt finished and refined by the sandy wind that whipped down from the great heights above. Small fires were lit in the hearths of each of these homes, and at the center of the community rose a large, oval-shaped hall.

"Wait here," ordered Hildræd. "For your sakes, let us hope that Æsc is even willing to receive an audience this day." He turned to his sentries before he swung open the large, wooden door adorned with the white skulls of some massive beasts of old. "Watch them, and I'll go see if our liege and his *wizard*," Hildræd grimaced, then spat to ward off his trepidation, "will be willing to meet our guests."

The sentries grunted their acknowledgment, and Michael was shoved back into the group. "I do not believe we will find much welcome here, let alone refuge," he said rather worriedly to his friends.

"I've never even heard of this place, let alone the Walha!" Celrod exclaimed. "I thought that these mountains had long since been barren of civilization."

"Well ... there doesn't look to be much that is *civilized* here, if you ask me!" Timorets said with a nervous laugh.

"Aye," Fryon agreed. "Outliers. Their homes are governed by their own laws, and not many, if any, have much affection for our kind."

"Our kind?" Georgina asked.

"Yes, girl," Harmier answered her. "Our kind ... our people ... Haven."

"But why? Our city is beautiful, and our people are peaceful. I don't understand," she murmured.

"Yes, we are peaceful … to our own kind," Fryon told her. "But strong cities like ours barter and trade and rein with different kinds of rules."

"Different rules?" she asked.

"Strength is not always strong enough to protect the interests of anyone other than its own, and in turn it becomes the bully who takes, rather than the neighbor who shares," Margarid said warily.

"She is right," Harmier replied. "Long have we leveraged our high-walled strength to—" His words were interrupted by the abrupt slamming of the hall's large door.

Hildræd nodded to his men, and Michael, Margarid, and the rest of the remnant were corralled towards the ominous opening. "My liege will see you, if but only to rid our people of you!" the large, dark-haired man grunted to them.

Michael reached out and took Margarid's hand, squeezing his wordless soothing to her worried heart. She squeezed her reply in return and with a nervous exhale they passed through the darkened threshold into the large, mud-covered chamber before them. Braziers lit the rounded walls, and vine-like patterns scrolled from floor to ceiling, covering the black and brown room with vibrant veins of green and spots of pale blue.

The cold, granite floor was covered in the furs and skins of animals foreign and terrifying to look at. At the center of the room stood a rounded, stone-lined hearth and spits of iron-skewered beasts, dripping delicious smells of roasted meat into the amber coals below.

Celrod's belly let out a large, awkward rumble that echoed off of the rounded walls, and Timorets elbowed him in reply. "Keep it quiet, lest you want one of us to end up on the wrong end of that spit!"

The group had not eaten a true meal in what seemed like days now, save the strips of dried meats and fruits that Elmer had so lovingly thought to pack for them. The delicious smells here in this most inhospitable chamber were utter and complete torture to the road-weary remnant of Haven.

At the end of the hall, seated at the head of a large, wooden table, sat a tall, strong man. His long, dark hair was braided with strands of fine gold, and his face was clean of hair, save the long braid that descended from the point of his chin, which too had woven into it the same finery as the rest of his dark hair.

"I could sense your hunger the moment you stepped foot upon my lands," the large man said, without so much as raising his gaze from the roasted foul his large hands were buried in. "How can it be so that the fat *princes of Haven* show up on my threshold, famished and gaunt like stray dogs?"

Michael looked to his friends, not quite sure if he were to respond, or if silence was the best option. Just then, a heavy, gloved hand struck hard the back of his head. "My liege, Æsc, has asked you a question, *dog*! Do not further insult him with your ignorant silence," spoke the voice of Hildræd.

Michael rubbed the bruised and throbbing part of his head, his eyes clouded over with the pain of the assault. "I'm… I'm sorry, Lord Æsc," he said through gritted teeth. "I did not mean to insult—"

"Enough sniveling already," Æsc replied, cutting off his apology with his full-mouthed annoyance. "Answer the question I asked of you. How do these *princes of Haven* find themselves here, bedraggled dogs on *my* threshold, begging at *my* doorstep?"

"Our city is taken," Michael said without further pause. "Overrun and sacked, Lord Æsc."

"Ha!" He laughed, choking on his food as he did so. "You mean to tell me," he coughed and sputtered, "that the great walled city of Haven, with its mighty gates and its maddened high pass, is in *ruin*? Overtaken? Ha! Ahhargh!" He laughed and coughed again before taking a deep draught from a large, clay goblet.

"If my father could only hear these words, huh?" Æsc said. "Ealhstan would surely have loved to see the ruin of Kaestor's fortifications, his mighty highways gone, especially after what that damned king did to him ... did to all of us."

"The tree of Haven has lost its fire, my liege, but I am not so inclined to take the word of these runaways as evidence of the city's ruin," Hildræd said warily.

"It is true, Lord Æsc." Celrod spoke up. "Three, maybe four days ago, though I am not quite sure now, as we have lost count ... our journey—"

"You expect him to believe this?" came a slippery, thin-sounding voice from within the shadows of the hall. "That Kaestor's mighty city has fallen?"

At the sound of this strange voice, the room went cold, though no breeze had blown in through its lone door.

"I barely believe it myself," Michael said, his eyes peering into the shadows and searching for the stranger in the dark.

"Who then?" Æsc demanded. "Who has that kind of strength, boy, to break those high, white walls?"

"I do not know *who*, Lord Æsc ... but I do know... *what*," Michael replied, his gaze still fixed on the shadows. "I saw it with my own two eyes. I saw the burning and the breaking, I watched the guardsmen cut down the attacking forces ... and... I saw my friend torn limb from limb by the demons themselves." His voice no longer carried the air of fear, rather, anger had hardened the road-weary edges of his tone.

"Speak plainly, boy," Æsc growled in reply. "My patience for strangers and strange tales has already run thin enough. Do not test me further with your riddles."

"No," came the sound of the cold, slippery voice. "He speaks the truth ... I have seen it." A pair of yellow eyes flashed sickly in the corner as a man walked out from the shadows and over to the tableside.

"Margarid?" cried Georgina.

"Silence, girl!" Æsc shouted as he pounded his fist against the table, sending a mound of crab apples rolling and skittering onto the floor. "I will not suffer a woman, no matter her age, to speak in my court! My grandfather made that mistake once. He and my father fell victim to the poisoned words of that witch, and sent our people into unending exile!"

His angry eyes drilled into Georgina, and she began to cry.

"Dragons," Michael shouted back, drawing attention away from the girl. "It was dragons that took Haven."

"Lies!" Hildræd said, enraged now. He kicked Michael's legs out from under him, and the groomsman fell hard upon the stone floor. Hildræd grabbed him by his hair, holding his stunted blade menacingly close to Michael's face. "There are no such things as *dragons*. Do you know what we Walha do to liars and false-speakers? We rid them of their tongues!"

"No, please!" Margarid shouted into the storm of offenses. "You must believe him, he is speaking the truth! Cut his tongue out, cut all of our tongues out … but if the dragons fix their gaze upon these black mountains, you will be the fool who refused the warning of the dogs of Haven!"

"Greater women have died for lesser words than these!" Hildræd growled as he threw Michael to floor and stood to his feet, hands clenching with rage.

"He speaks the truth … twins they are, moving in mirrored unison," Ragnarr mused aloud, his pale, spindly fingers flicking and waving at the air about him as he spoke. "Winged justice, my liege!" he said as a yellow-toothed smile grew upon his bearded face. "I have seen them, and their green fires."

"Truth or no truth, Father!" Hildræd reasoned. "You cannot be taken by *her* words! Do not repeat the folly of Ealhstan, and do not suffer these runaways an audience any longer."

Æsc looked to his councilor and then back again to the frightened group from Haven that stood before him. "If what you say is true, wizard, then what is there to say that these *dragons* won't turn their gaze towards us?" He looked contemptuously at the gaze of the auburn-haired woman who had dared to address him so brazenly.

Harmier held Georgina close, willing her to keep her fear and her tears to herself. Portus, Fryon, and the rest clenched their fists and gripped their blades with hardened resolve.

"There is nothing that any of us can do, Lord Æsc," Margarid said calmly and defiantly. "If these dragons want to raze your homes, I doubt that your arrows have any more strength than the thousands of Haven's bolts that were loosed and defeated."

"She is right," Celrod, the schoolmaster, said humbly. "Our city and its armies could not keep those damned beasts at bay, and I fear that unless you have a magic greater than the strength of their talons, teeth, and green fire ... hiding might be our only salvation."

"That is all we are good for, isn't it, Father?" Hildræd grumbled.

"Do not disrespect your liege, young sentry," Ragnarr seethed aloud. "Wise council is not always as rash as young men hope it to be."

"Aye, but it is not always as fearful as old fools presume!" He retorted. "Our people have been banished, hidden for almost a century, resigned to lead shame-colored lives in the black, barren rock." He spat as he spoke.

"That is *enough*, Hildræd." Æsc demanded.

"And for what?" he said, ignoring his father's command. "Because your father fell in love with a king's daughter? And foolishly thought he could make her his own!" He laughed. "We are nothing but outliers. But now, look! Don't you see? We have been given a gift. Justice has come for our people, and these long, meager years will now grant us the spoils of war, if we but *take it for ourselves!*"

"You don't understand!" Michael pleaded. "Haven has been conquered. It is not just dragons, there is a whole raven army that occupies the citadel. You can't ... I mean there is ... we have to flee for our lives!"

"Who will be left to stop us, Father? Huh? A bunch of birds?" Hildræd reasoned. "Haven is ripe for the taking. Just look at your sons, your people ... don't we deserve the prize your father never had?"

The hall went silent for the moment, save the crackling of the brazier fires and the pop and spittle of the roasting meat over the large hearth. The lord of these black hills thought on all that had been said, and finally spoke. "What do you say, Ragnarr? Do you liken your council to that of my war-mongering son, or do you say we choose to run and flee like these mongrels of Kaestor?"

The wizard looked to the huddled remnant, his yellow eyes aglow with something sinister. "These dragons will not abide here long, my liege, for something ravenous compels them westward." He looked deep into what seemed like nothing at all, his face glowing with the satisfaction of his clairvoyance. "I see it … her … she commands them!"

"Did you hear what he said, Father?" Hildræd spoke up. "Something compels them westward? Once they leave this place … all of it will be ours!"

The remnant watched nervously as this battle of wills raged uncomfortably before them. "I just want to be done with this place," Fryon whispered to his brother.

"Aye, me too," Timorets replied.

"We must not move too soon. We must wait for our moment, bide our time!" Ragnarr whispered.

"And scavenge the leftovers like rats, like the exiles they treat us as?" Hildræd argued. "We have the chance to be the new kings of this world! We Walha are strong, Father. This is justice! Ravens or not, dragons or not … this moment is ours!"

"Better to be a huddled and humbled rat who lives, than a foolish warrior who bleeds out on the stoop of his pride!" Ragnarr retorted.

"Enough!" Æsc shouted. "The lot of you! Enough!"

The room went quiet in the wake of the liege lord's fury. It was Michael who broke the silence with his rather bold request. "Lord Æsc, whether you choose to claim our broken walls as your own or not is of no consequence to me and my friends." He looked back over his shoulder towards the huddled mass of the remnant. "Our time in Haven has come to an end. All we have known and loved in Haven is lost. Our families, our friends … dead, or worse. There is nothing left there for us but heartbreak. We ask only for a bit of hospitality as we continue on our way."

"You, a stray dog of Haven, are asking the Lord of the Walha for the scraps from my table? Ha! And where do you presume to be headed, dog?"

"I am not sure," Michael replied humbly. "But somewhere to the north."

"Father!" Hildræd begged, his annoyance at this audience evident to all.

"Shut your mouth, lad!" Æsc growled at his son. He took a deep breath, pondering all the choices and tales that had unexpectedly stumbled upon his threshold. "If you flee northward, the only refuge I know is the Halvard, and it has long since been in disrepair. Even before my childhood it was but an echo, a ghost of ages past."

"But a strength still runs through the mountain door," Ragnarr commented mysteriously. "A strength which is not unopposed."

Æsc looked at the warlock, confused and rather uninterested in his words, before continuing to speak to Michael. "Our people will not show hospitality to your people, for we were exiled from our homes by one of your mad kings. But although you will find no rest within my walls and no warm hearths from my people, I will not be like your king. I will not sentence you to die in the cold of your banishment. I'll see to it that you have a skin or two of the juniper wine, and furs enough to keep you from freezing over... and here," he said as he flicked his fingers and then returned his gaze to his own supper. "Some salted meat and a loaf of black bread for each of you, but that's it."

Æsc nodded at his attendant and within a few long moments he reappeared with the promised provisions.

"Thank you, Lord Æsc," Michael said on behalf of his friends.

"Those furs are moth-eaten and molded, but from one exile to another, I hope you find a land to start over again," Æsc said as he drank deeply from his clay goblet.

"Aye," Michael agreed.

"Ahhh!" The wizard gasped happily. "Movement, my liege! The dragons! She moves them!"

"Father!" Hildræd interrupted. "Now is the time! Even your wizard sees it ... justice has finally come for us!"

"Show them to the foot of these black rocks, and I will consider your plan to take the broken city. But be quick about it, lest the warlock see some unfavorable change in the wind."

With that, Michael and the others bowed in gratitude and donned the old furs. Timorets and Harmier slung the two skins of juniper wine and the sack of vittles over their shoulders, and the remnant followed the sentry down past the rows of homes until they at last arrived at the base of the black-rocked mountains.

"If north is where you are going, there is only one road that will get you there," Hildræd said begrudgingly. "The River Ithelum will cut off your way, save for the Meinir at the center of it. Cross the land bridge if it still stands, and be gone with haste from our lands."

"Thank you, we will find it," Michael replied. "Do you know what is beyond it?"

"With that, I cannot help you," Hildræd said smugly. "I have a city to claim."

Chapter Twelve

After several days of searching, Marcum, Johnrey, and their group of surviving soldiers and woodcutters passed the fens of the Abonris. "I found their tracks again!" Johnrey reported back. "They have come by this way, and in a hurry at that."

Marcum listened intently to the corporal's report, scanning the darkened horizon for any sign of Keily and the women and children. "Do you see signs of distress? Were they chased?"

"Not that we can tell, but wherever she was leading them, she wanted them as far away from that road as possible," Johnrey added.

"Come on, lass," Brádách moaned out loud. "Just slow down and wait for us already."

"Where are you taking them, Keily?" Marcum wondered aloud.

"The best we can tell," Johnrey answered, "Is that she is leading them west along the foothills here. And thank the THREE who is SEVEN, she looks to have gone completely unnoticed by the ravens."

"That is good enough news for so dark a day," Marcum replied. "Thank you, Corporal. We will follow where she is leading us."

And with that, they made their turn west along the base of the Hilgari Mountains. They walked slowly but deliberately, their ears and eyes peeled for signs of their friends and their foes.

"Lieutenant!" came the whispered shout from the front of the caravan. "Lieutenant, I think we may have found them. The tracks stop just ahead."

"Alright now, lass, take it easy," Brádách said under his breath. "There are no ravens here, keep your bow to yourself."

Marcum looked at the old woodcutter, amused at his mutterings but also reminded both of the dire situation Keily had fled from and her skill as an archer.

"Light your torches!" Marcum shouted to his men as he labored to sit up straight.

"Lieutenant?" Johnrey asked.

"We are friend, not foe. Friends will show themselves, foes will not," Marcum replied.

Understanding quickly registered, and the white-bearded corporal relayed the orders to all of his men.

"Keily!" Marcum shouted into the darkened outlands of Haven. "Keily, it's us! It is Marcum ... we have been tracking you for days." He winced at the sharp pain in his shoulder. "We found help, my lady. We are not alone."

Off in the distance, hidden behind an outcropping of stone and juniper bushes, came the flashes of three sparks. Johnrey signaled his reply with seven flashes from his flint, and eruptions of joy rang out from the silent dark before them. Gabriel, Annsley, Huckston and Ryder, the remaining children of their company, squealed in elation as they ran towards the guardsmen and called out to them. "You're here!" "You've found us!" "We are safe now!" Their voices sounded in a chorus of hope against the darkness.

The remaining women and the elders came out from their hiding, smiles spreading across their faces.

"Lieutenant?" Keily spoke as she lowered her bow. "Is that you? I thought ... I thought for sure you were lost. All of you."

"Some unlooked for friends found us, and came to our rescue," Marcum answered her with a warm, albeit wounded, embrace.

"Woodcutters!" she exclaimed. "But I thought ..." She trailed off as grief washed over her face. "I thought you were gone from this world."

"Only the bravest of us, lass," Brádách said as he made his way down from the timber cart, limping over to behold the fiery barmaid.

She smiled and hugged him with genuine gratitude and surprise. "Oh, Brádách," she said with matronly sternness in her voice. "Tell me that I am not going to have to make you eat with the dogs ever again, am I?"

"I thought you said it was one of the old lads?" Marcum asked, grinning as the truth of the story came clear.

"Easy there, lass!" he said, holding his hands up in surrender. "That was many years ago, and I have repented of my waywardness. And I am truly glad to see that the niece of my chieftain is alive and in one piece." He squeezed her shoulders tight.

"I saw him, Brádách," she said, her smile fading. "Hollis ... his lifeless head was flung upon the battlements of the North Gate in a wash of green fire. I don't know if I can ever rid my thoughts of that horrible memory."

"He was the bravest of us all, lass; braver than I'll ever be," Brádách replied gently, his voice catching in his throat.

"Keily?" Marcum said, interrupting their reunion. "Are you, are they ... is everyone alright?"

She turned and looked at the wounded lieutenant. "Yes, we are all safe. Except ... except for Roshan." Her eyes fell as she mentioned his name. "We ran as fast as we could, and I was trying to find him. I wanted to make sure he was safe," she said worriedly. "But that horse took him, and I don't know where they went. We've been hidden here for days now, and there is no sign of him."

"There now, lass," Brádách said kindly. "I'm sure the lad is alright. Come on now, we can't be chasing ghosts out here in the cold north."

"He is right, Keily," Marcum answered. "He could be anywhere now. Besides, we have got to find shelter and mend our wounded."

"Aye," Brádách agreed. "Our camp is now a half a day's walk back eastward, and we have some provisions and some shelter, enough for all of us ... enough for now, at least."

"But we can't turn back ... he is just a boy!" Exhaustion colored her protest. "He is just a lost boy with no light out here in the darkness."

Just then a flash of light came from the edge of the perimeter, one of the guardsmen signaling a warning. "Did you see that?" Brádách asked nervously.

"Yes, I did," Marcum answered. "Corporal?"

"Right away, sir." Johnrey answered.

Marcum motioned for his men to surround the ox cart, while the women, elders, and children climbed inside or hid underneath, seeking shelter and preparing for whatever was out there to meet them. The guardsmen drew their bows and held their blades at the ready.

Three flashes came then out from the western darkness, and Marcum answered it with his seven. "What is it? What do you see?" Came Marcum's whispered demands.

"Lieutenant," came the breathless response of the guardsman runner.

"What is it? Tell me, quick," Marcum ordered.

"It's ... it's an old man." the guardsman replied.

"An old man?" Marcum said. "Out here? All by himself?"

"Well ... in a way," said the guardsman incredulously. "He is in a mule-drawn cart, only ... only he is not by himself."

Marcum looked off into the west, and Keily and the rest followed his gaze. What they beheld captured their hearts with wonder. A small light was held aloft, swaying back and forth with the rhythm of the mule cart, and yet the glow that emanated forth was not of candle or torch. Rather, it lit the mountainside with a deep, violet glow.

"What in the damnable dark is that?" Marcum asked.

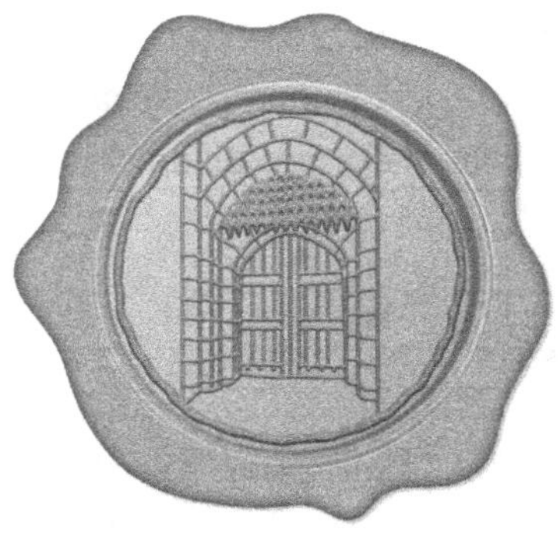

Chapter Thirteen

Michael and his remnant made their way northward by walking east through rocky lands at the base of the black mountains. They were tired, and their weary feet were in much need of rest, but their hearts were grateful enough to have left the lands of the Walha with as little injury as they did.

The torches of the remnant brightly lit the way, though their violet hope allowed them to see well enough to traverse the inhospitable landscape.

"A bridge, he said?" Portus asked aloud.

"A land bridge," Celrod replied through grunts of pain. "And let's all of us hope that this River Ithelum has not washed it out. I for one would prefer a shortcut right about now, and I doubt I have the strength to swim another river."

"Ah, you would find a way," Timorets said jovially. "Somebody has to torment me each leg of this journey, and it would seem that you have been doing a right good job of it already. I would hate to see someone have to take it over for you."

"Ha!" Celrod laughed. "Well, I would like to see them try!" the large teacher said with a pained yet sincere smile.

"Michael?" Georgina asked curiously. "What is a land bridge? Is it made of stone and metal like the King's Bridge?"

"I do not rightly know what it is made of," he said to her. "I imagine it is a pass that stretches out across the river. I suppose it could be made of stone ... but as our *kind host* pointed out to us, it is very old, and it might not even be there anymore."

"Oh," she said in thought. "I hope like Celrod hopes too, then. That it is still there at all. I am ready to be wherever it is we are going."

Michael mussed her hair before he spoke. "Me too, girl, me too."

He looked over to the auburn-haired maiden and felt the heaviness of the brash exchanges of the Walha still looming upon her countenance. "Are you alright, Margarid?" he said cautiously.

She nodded, though she kept her gaze focused towards the darkness before them.

"I am sorry that they hit you, and that they spoke to you like they did," he told her apologetically. "I wish I could have done something."

"You did what you had to do, Michael. I am not sore with you." She looked him in the eye. "I am sad, and hurt, that there are still people like that in this world; holding on to ancient offenses, blinded by bitterness and hatred."

"I know, my lady," he spoke softly to her.

"This world is dark enough. If we ever have the hope of starting over in a new land ..." she paused, collecting her words in the midst of her frustration. "I just think that those of us who are still left will have to shine what light we have *together*, instead of clouding any brilliance with selfishness or ignorance or hatred."

Michael let her words hang there in the tension. A swell of pride washed over his heart for her. "You are rather remarkable, you know."

"What?" she said in confusion.

"Here I thought you were upset about the way those angry fools treated you, and yet you are more concerned as to how we all would treat each other." He smiled deeply at her as he reached for her soft hands. "Engelmann would be proud of you, Margarid."

A tear rolled down her dirt-smeared cheek as she thought of the murdered sage, and then she smiled, laughing a humble, knowing laugh. "I hope so, Michael. I truly hope so."

"Water!" came the shout of Fryon's voice from the head of the group. "I hear water! I think it is the river that the Walha talked about!"

"Ithelum?" Michael asked.

"I think so!" Fryon replied. "I have never been this far outside the walls of the city before."

The remnant walked hastily towards the sound of the rushing water. Their hearts were hopeful at putting more distance between themselves and those who had destroyed their city. Ahead of them, coming into view by the faint glow of their violet hope, they saw the rock-strewn banks of the river.

"Ithelum!" Celrod exclaimed. "This must be the river they spoke of! What other body of water this grand, save the mighty Abonris herself, would cause one to name it? Surely this must be the river."

"Aye," Timorets agreed. "For once I think you are right, schoolmaster!"

"I've never in all my days seen water this majestic!" Portus mused aloud. "It must be three, no ... at least five times as wide as the Abonris!"

"How will we cross it?" came the nervous questioning of Georgina.

"We will have to find the land bridge that the Walha spoke of," Margarid said as she pulled her closer to her hip. She too was overwhelmed with the sight before them, "It has to be here."

"Aye," Fryon agreed. "It looks as if this river could go on for leagues and leagues in either direction. I wonder if the Raven soldiers crossed here?"

"He is right!" Michael exclaimed. "I'll bet they did, but those Ravens couldn't have crossed by swimming. It has to be here, the land bridge …. the *Meinir,* they called it. We must keep our wits about us so our eyes can be keen to its beginning."

"Agreed," Harmier said. "We were on a path. It has to lead to it somewhere. Do you see any markers about?"

They all split up in twos, each of them with a torch in hand and hope in their eyes. They began to comb the banks of the raging waters in search of a way across. Many long minutes passed with no progress, and it wasn't until Georgina's voice rang out in a squeal that any of them believed they would find their way across.

"I found it!" she exclaimed. "I found the Meinir!"

The rest of the remnant hurried over to the shrieking excitement of their youngest companion. Their hearts leapt at what they beheld along the riverbank. Granite rocks extended out into the depths of the rushing waters, from each bank and all the way across the river. On top of the granite slabs was a torn and trodden path of green, mossy carpet, wide enough for three horses to pass together.

What was most impressive about this passage was not its dark stone, nor its thick matted carpets, but that the rushing waters of the Ithelum flowed not more than a handsbreadth over the top of their passageway.

"Amazing!" Celrod exclaimed. "I would have walked past this a hundred times over, never thinking to look into the water for our way through. Well done, girl! Well done indeed!"

"You don't suppose that the THREE who is SEVEN fashioned this bridge when he sung the whole of Aiénor into being, do you?" Portus asked his friend and leader.

"I do not know if he fashioned it by his own hand, or if he fashioned it into the mind of those who came before us," Michael answered reverently.

"I am not worried as to who made it or when it was made!" Timorets said. "I, for one, am just grateful that we don't have to hold our breath over perilous heights just to reach the other side this time!"

The lot of them laughed a nervous, relieved laugh.

"True enough," Michael said with concern on his furrowed brow. "Easy as it may seem, though, let's not forget to use caution when we cross. There are strange things in these even stranger lands, things we may not see at first glance."

"He is right," Fryon agreed. "The water is cold, and it moves rather swiftly."

"And I wouldn't doubt that the moss might be as slick as a newborn foal," Michael agreed.

"We should all still keep hold of each other," Margarid chimed it. "We have gotten this far together... let's not forget that part now." She reached down for the small, slender hand of the youngest member of their tribe, taking it with a motherly squeeze as she spoke. "You will walk with me, alright?"

Georgina squeezed her hand in reply and nodded an excited smile to her friend and protector. "I will, Margarid. I will."

"Fryon?" Michael asked without needing to.

"Aye," he answered. "Come on, brother ... you and I will take the van again."

The two brothers held their torches and cinched their packs tight upon their backs, setting out upon the land bridge ahead of their friends. It was a sight to behold, the two flickering flames of the fearless scouts, floating ghostlike above the cold, rushing waters amidst the violet haze of their seasoned hope.

"How far do you think it is, Michael?" Margarid asked as she leaned into his strong shoulder. "I can't see the other bank."

"I am not sure if that is just because the Ithelum is that large, or if the damn darkness is just this ... well, *dark*," he replied.

"As long as the path stretches ahead of us," Georgina replied, eavesdropping on their worried conversation, "it doesn't really matter if we can see the other side or not. Does it?"

Michael reached down, and with a surprised smile he patted the wise child's messy hair. "I suppose it doesn't."

BOOM.

The sound of something solid and heavy colliding with the ground beneath them echoed into the darkness. The eyes of the remnant went wide, and the two flames of Fryon and his brother disappeared.

"What was that?" Portus asked.

"Did you hear where it came from? Which direction I mean?" Celrod asked nervously.

"Is it the dragons?" Harmier asked, the chill of fright frosting over his usually confident voice. "Are they coming for us? Did they find our trail?"

BOOM, BOOM, BOOM!

Three more massive blows rang out, like a mighty hammer upon an anvil.

"I can't make out the direction," Timorets worried aloud.

"Come on then, let us not tarry a moment longer!" Michael urged his friends. "We need to get across this river, now!"

"But what if the sound is coming from the other side?" Timorets asked.

Michael looked behind them at the black mass of inhospitable mountain lands, and back in the direction of the desolated city that once thrived in its protective bosom. He weighed the danger ahead against the devastation they had left behind.

"There is no life for us on the ruined bank behind us and yet there still may be life for us on the other side of these unknown waters," he whispered to them in a passionate, hushed voice.

BOOM! The rumbling reverberation sounded again.

"Michael?" came Margarid's frightened voice.

"We know what monsters hunt us, do we not?" he asked the group. "We are no match for dragons and ravens."

BOOM, BOOM, BOOM! The same, nerve-rattling rhythm shook them yet again.

"And over there, Michael?" Harmier pointed across the cold rushing waters of the kingly river. "What monsters wait for us?"

"We know nothing about over there, Harmier, monstrous or otherwise," Michael said as he pulled tight the leather straps of his pack.

"And that is what I am afraid of, Michael!" Harmier argued.

"Aye," the groomsman acknowledged. "There is plenty to be fearful of, but there is also some to be hopeful for. The unknown isn't always the enemy." He took his first step upon the water-covered pathway. "It *could* also be our refuge from the monsters we have been so afraid of."

BOOM! The pounding came again.

"Come on, then!" Michael said, braver than he felt. "Let's see what lies on the other side of this unknown."

"Come on, then," Portus echoed, clasping a heavy hand on the schoolmaster's shoulder. "He is right."

"Aye," Celrod agreed as he swallowed back his own reservations.

Hands were held in eerie similarity, a poetic reflection of a not-so-distant passage. And though their peril this time was not in them falling into the doom of an abyss below, danger swirled about each soggy step, a fearsome current threatening to snatch them from their passage.

They came upon the brothers, still somewhere in the midst of the land bridge, waiting on their comrades. "How much further do you think?" Margarid called to them atop the sound of the water.

BOOM, BOOM, BOOM! Three beats, again.

"I would say we are halfway, maybe a bit more than that." Fryon surmised. "Is everyone alright?"

"Aye," Celrod agreed. "Almost *too* alright."

"Seems too easy," Timorets mused.

BOOM!

"Agreed!" Harmier said. "Like we are walking right into the jaws of the monster itself."

"I, for one, will not argue with an easy passage, we have had more than our share of treacherous ones!" Portus argued.

"We are not done yet, though," Michael said. "Can you see anything out there? Any movement? Any idea where that sound is coming from?"

"No," Fryon answered. "It is too dark to tell. And the sound ... it bounces off the water, so I can't make any sense of it."

Michael squinted hard, peering out through the faint violet glow into the unknown beyond, desperately willing something, anything to come into focus.

BOOM, BOOM, BOOM!

"It's in a pattern," Georgina said thoughtfully. "Once, then thrice, over and over again."

"She's right," Margarid said. "What could that mean? It must be something … on purpose!"

"Let's not wait like a school of huddled fish for whatever net is being readied to catch us," Timorets said. "I say we be quick about this crossing! At least that way we can run and hide if we need to."

"The brewer is right you know." Harmier said as he kissed the flint that still hung from his neck. "We decided to go. Let's get on with it."

Torches were held aloft, and hands were held tight as the sound of boots slogging through the cold wet of the Ithelum accompanied the nervous rhythm of their beating hearts and the ominous sound of whatever pounded against the ground.

"There!" Fryon shouted in a hushed whisper. "I see the bank, just ahead!"

"I told you it would stretch!" Georgina said as she squeezed Margarid's hand.

"That you did, love … that you did indeed," the lady replied with a guarded smile.

It wasn't long before the whole of the remnant had made it to the pebble-strewn bank of the kingly river. The sounds of the booming had ceased for the moment and the silence of their arrival unnerved even the bravest of their lot.

"Do you hear that?" Celrod asked in a whisper.

"Hear what?" Timorets asked his large friend.

"Exactly," the schoolmaster answered. "I don't hear a damned thing!"

"Is that bad?" Georgina asked innocently.

"That is hard to say," Margarid spoke honestly. "It could mean that there is nothing here to make a noise."

"And that would be good, right?" she asked.

"Or it could mean that whatever is here is lying in wait, ready to fall on us unawares!" Harmier said fearfully.

"It doesn't have to mean either," Michael said without emotion. "But it does mean something—"

His words were cut off as Fryon raised his finger to his lips. He pointed to the ground before them, and they glimpsed the traces of hundreds, thousands of footprints that had disturbed the terrain around them.

"They came this way? By way of the Meinir?" Margarid asked.

"Who came?" Georgina asked.

"The Ravens did," Portus answered. "See, look there!"

Not a hundred paces from the entrance to the land bridge were broken helms, shields, and the black-blooded, decaying bodies of the fallen enemy.

"What happened here?" Harmier asked. "Who would have fought them this far from the city?"

"Surely Armas and his men did not venture so far from the Northern wall," Timorets mused.

"No. It wasn't our guardsmen who fought them," Fryon replied.

"He is right. There are no remains of their bodies, no green cloaks or cloven helms," Celrod agreed.

"And no horses ... no fallen horses," Michael said as he bent down to closer examine the ground below.

"Could it have been the Walha?" Harmier asked.

"No, I don't think so. They seemed genuinely surprised to hear of the enemy," Celrod said.

"Who then?" Margarid asked excitedly. "Who would have fought them out here? Maybe they are friendly; maybe we could take refuge with them?"

"I don't think it is a *who* that fought here," Michael said as he beckoned Fryon over to examine what had just caught his eye.

"What do you mean, groomsman?" Timorets asked gravely.

"I think the question is *what* fought them here," Michael said as he pointed down to an enormous footprint that spanned the entire, broken body of a fallen raven warrior.

BOOM! The sound came again, this time louder and closer.

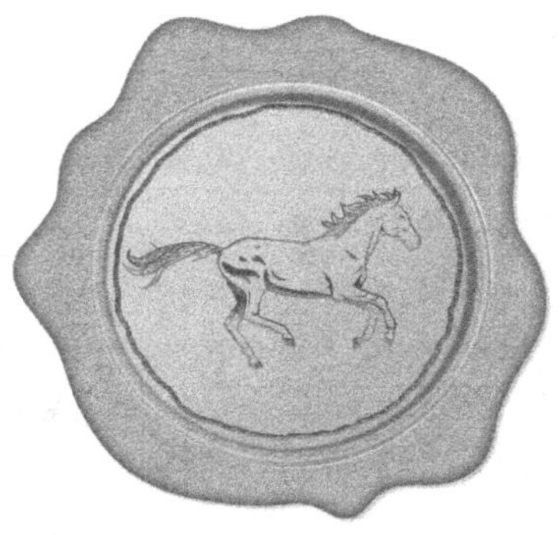

Chapter Fourteen

"Cal!" the worried whisper of his Sprite friend woke the groomsman from his rest. "Cal! Wake up, my friend."

Cal rubbed the sleep from his eyes with one hand while reaching swiftly for his sword, Gwarwyn, with the other. "What is it, Deryn? What troubles you?"

"I hear a voice upon the wind, there to the east, beyond the thicket," the Sprite pointed off into the distance.

"What kind of voice?" Cal asked, now standing to his feet.

"A young voice, or so it seems to my ears. I don't sense danger, yet I am wary of it," Deryn told him.

"Aye," Cal said as he looked out into the distance. "I cannot see anything. Should we go look?"

Just as the words came from his mouth, a deep, guttural growl stole the air from his very lungs. Astyræ woke at the menacing sound, her violet eyes immediately searching the faces of her two companions for assurance or warning.

"You let me alone!" came a voice from the darkness. "Be gone, get rid of you!" The sound of breaking bramble and thudding stones told the story of the moment to all who would hear. "No! Let me alone!" and then again, the thud of thrown rocks punctuated the plea.

"Well, come on then," Cal told them. "We can't just let whoever that is be eaten by whatever *that* is out there."

"But we don't know who or what they are!" Astyræ argued.

"And I didn't know *who* or *what* was crying in that old tower cell of yours either, did I?" Cal said, his sword held at the ready. "And look just how well that turned out."

"Stop it! Let me alone!" came the cry again. "Please!"

"Come on," Cal said, the playfulness all but gone from his eyes, replaced with the urgency of rescue. He leapt atop Farran, and Astyræ atop her chestnut, and they rode off in search of the frightened voice.

As soon as they had crested the bramble-laden mound, Cal beheld a young Wreather woman, whose braided hair was pinned close to her head and whose basket was brimming with roots, herbs, and mushrooms. She was picking up the large stones about her feet and throwing them with great haste and with great force at the small pack of green-eyed timber wolves that circled hungrily around her.

"Astyræ!" Cal shouted over his shoulder.

Without any other word, she notched an arrow in the mighty bow Arianrhod and loosed its fury upon the encircling beasts. Cal spurred Farran on and charged into the assault before them.

A bolt of the Silver Moon found its mark in the breast of the first wolf just as Cal swung Gwarwyn, carving a swath of flesh and blood into the hide of the second. The next bit at Farran's legs, growling with agitated fury. The wild-eyed horse kicked at the hulking timber wolf, and Cal swung his blade to defend his mount, but the beast did not relent. A hoof found its mark and sent the wolf reeling in a tumble of fur and fang, but in an instant it sprung again to its paws; mouth foaming with hatred for those that stood in the way of its prize.

Astyræ loosed another arrow, but the wolf leapt towards Cal and evaded the deadly bolt. Teeth barred, he bit into the foreleg of the silver courser as Cal swung his blade with a protective vengeance.

Farran snorted and cried, rearing up on his hind legs. The wolf yelped in pain and lost his bite, falling to ground. Cal jumped from the back of his mount and turned to face the beast himself. The hilt of Gwarwyn glowed violet and silver, beauty and power in juxtaposition to the hungry hatred found in the eyes of the timber wolf.

Another arrow buried its biting point into the matted brown fur as Astyræ halted her chestnut mount beside Cal. The dog growled and whined, and then the green light went out from his menacing eyes.

"Are you alright?" Astyræ asked him breathlessly.

"Yes, my lady," Cal told her. "But I am not so sure about Farran."

The horse whinnied, shaking his head in anger and pain as he hobbled towards Cal.

"There now, Farran." Cal whispered, eyeing the raging red gashes that streaked his wounded foreleg. "There now, my boy. I am here, and Astyræ took care of that wretched beast of a wolf. Shhh, easy now boy, we are safe … safe enough for me to get a look at you."

Cal walked up to his steed, his hands splayed out, willing the mighty courser to calm himself down. He began to sing, right there in the dark madness of this wild land, with a pack of slain wolves about his feet; his compassion and care for his silver friend overcame his heart. "There now Sigrid's son, you bright silver prince," he cooed in a lilting voice. "Lend me your leg, let me see what damage has been done."

Farran snorted with contempt at his woundedness. His eyes conveyed his fear that perhaps a doom had befallen him, a doom that may come to any noble steed, a doom that may stop him from delivering his rider to whatever destiny called him forth.

"This is not your end, my friend, but a gash and a scrape is all. Come now, let me mend you," Cal whispered.

"I'm sorry for your horse," came the voice of the young lady whom they had just rescued. "I'm sorry if it was my fault. I didn't mean it, you know."

"We know," Astyræ assured her. "They weren't your wolves, were they?"

"No," she answered quickly. "They weren't mine."

"What is your name?" Astyræ asked as she relaxed Arianrhod and extended her hand in friendship. "And how is it that you are out here in this wild, dark wood all by yourself?"

"I am Delilah. My father used to call me Dilly ... but that has been quite a long time ago now," she said shyly. "I was looking for herbs. My little brother Mahlah is ill."

"Oh, what I wouldn't do for a bottle of the stable warden's liniment right now," Cal said to himself in frustration as he held the wounded leg of his horse.

"May I call you Dilly, too?" Astyræ asked her.

She offered a polite smile, and then, as if the severity of the moment struck her right between her eyes, her brows furrowed, and her smile vanished. "Who are *you* two? And just what were you doing, riding so freely out here in the Queen's wood?"

Astyræ looked sharply over to Cal, but he was too worried about Farran to notice her gaze. He grabbed a skin of wine from the satchel tied to his saddle, and he prayed that it could clean the wound well enough.

"Well?" Dilly asked, rather petulantly. "Who are you? I mean I am grateful and all ... but this land does not lend hospitality to strangers, no matter if they saved you or not."

"We ... um ... we are travelers," Astyræ told her as she looked back and forth from Cal to this sable-haired girl, wary to say too much. "We are looking for our friends, only, we don't know where they have gone."

Cal poured the skin of wine over the wound, and though the blood and the dirt washed away clean, the wound showed itself to be roiling with something vile upon the flesh. "Easy now, boy," he cooed, his worried hand stroking the silver neck of his wounded friend.

"Your friends?" Delilah asked suspiciously. "Out here? This is not a place for *travelers*." She eyed the golden-haired woman for a moment. "And tell me ... what is *that*?" She pointed to the glowing, azure-colored Sprite that hovered near Astyræ.

"This is ... Deryn," she said matter-of-factly. "He is ... well, um... he is a fairy, and a friend of ours. He is helping us find our other lost friends out here."

Deryn scowled at the mention of the word fairy, his tiny blue eyes lit with the fire of indignity. "*My lady*?" he said incredulously.

"I don't know," Delilah said as she inspected the flying companion. "I've never seen a *fairy* before ... though you do have wings, don't you?"

"Astyræ?" Cal said, oblivious to the conversation happening around him. "He is wounded badly. It looks ... poisoned, almost. I need to clean the wound better." His worry for Farran had nearly caused him to forget why he was wounded in the first place, but when his eyes met the young lady, hope arose in his worried countenance.

"Friend, do you have some liniment? Or some kind of spirits I might use to clean my horse's wound? That timber wolf got him pretty bad, and I'm not sure he will be much for the journey if I don't help him, and soon."

"I don't have any of the like, but I was out here looking for herbs, the healing kind," she told him. "My brother Mahlah has come down with a fever, and we haven't anything to—"

She stopped mid-sentence, catching herself from saying too much to these strangers.

"Say ... what friends are you looking for, huh?" The tone of her voice grew guarded and wary. "And how do I know that you are not spies for *her*?"

"Spies?" Astyræ said, rather taken back. "Do we look like spies?"

"That might be something that a spy would say," Dilly argued as she busied herself, filling her basket with the fragrant herbs at her feet. "Besides, I don't know who you really are, and my brother needs me!"

"Please, my friend needs me too," Cal said, willing his request to compel her heart. "And besides ... the only reason he is wounded in the first place is because we came to rescue you."

She looked the three of them over and surveyed the angry, red wound on Farran's leg. "Alright then, I'll give you some of my herbs. There is a creek up ahead, a short walk from here. You can wash him and bind him there, but you can't follow me, and I can't help you after that."

"Agreed," Cal said as he tore a piece of his tunic and wrapped the wounded foreleg of his friend. "Lead us, then, and let us both be about mending those that we love."

"Alright then," she agreed. "This way."

And with that, the young lady began to lead them further north and ever slightly to the west. The ground beneath their boots turned from the rich loam of the thickened forest into the sparsely treed, rock-laden ground of the river lands.

"Can't you just ask your fairy to do something about his wound?" she asked, both curious and annoyed at being waylaid from her duties to her own brother. "They are *magic,* aren't they?"

"Fairy?" Cal said, the laughter nearly blurting out of his mouth as he walked beside Farran. "He is not—" Astyræ elbowed him in his side before he could protest any further. Cal coughed, his words catching in his throat.

"Well?" Dilly asked earnestly.

"Well, of course he is magic, but he doesn't have ... healing magic, you might say," Cal said, his eyes apologizing to his offended friend even as he spoke the words.

"Oh?" She asked. "What kind of magic does he have, then?"

"I don't know all of his magic, but I have seen him make fire before with not much more than a song."

Delilah didn't reply. She was deep in thought, pondering what sort of rabble would travel in the company of *fairies.*

"I am sorry, my friend," Cal whispered to Deryn as he flew right beside him. "Don't be cross with us."

"It is a good thing I like your horse," Deryn said in mock offense. "Otherwise, I might be forced to defend the honor of all my Sprite-kind."

Cal smiled his saddened thanks, and reached up to pat and sooth his limping mount. "Let's get to the creek, and I'll wash it for you, and I'll bind it with herbs, alright?"

Farran snorted his understanding, but the pain of his travels could not be hidden from his face.

"Are there many of them out here?" Astyræ asked. "The timber wolves I mean? Should we be wary?"

"Aye," the young lady answered. "And her spies are everywhere, all around us. Hunting and seeking and doing her green-eyed bidding." She spat to the pebble-laden ground for emphasis.

"What are they looking for?" Cal asked. "Who are they hunting?"

Dilly stopped. Her hands balled into fists, her lovely face furrowed and scrunched in anger at so ignorant a question. "Do you not know? Do you *truly* not know? The Sorceress ... she hunts every single one of us who has managed to not succumb to her will!"

"I am sorry," Cal told her earnestly. "I am not from here – the Wreath, I mean. I am just now learning of all its trappings."

"Not from the Wreath?" Dilly asked, her voice both curious and suspicious at the same time. "Where then?"

"I came across the Dark Sea, not more than a few months ago, from the city of Haven ... my home." As he told her, a wave of homesickness washed over him. He thought of his cousin, and his Poet friends under the mountain, and he longed to see them again.

Astyræ watched the conversation unfold, and though she had no real reason not to trust this young lady, her heart told her to be cautious.

"What for?" Dilly asked.

"What do you mean?" Cal said absently as he led his limping friend along with a gentle hand upon his neck.

"What did you leave such a city for?" she continued. "Why come all the way out here, into the dark woods of the Sorceress?"

"Well ... that is a long story there, Delilah," Cal said with a hopeful smile. "You see, I am seeking a new light—"

"Cal!" Astyræ blurted out, awkwardly interrupting his story. He looked at her, confused at first, but her eyes explained her caution and he understood her meaning.

"We are here … at the creek, I mean," Astyræ continued. "Don't you think you should tend to Farran first? Who knows what kind of evil the fangs of those wolves held!"

"Aye," Cal agreed. "Come on then," he whispered to his horse.

Cal and Farran waded out into the stream of water. It was a creek, but it was flowing much too fast and sure to be from some lazy spring nearby. He squatted down to wash the cold, clean water over Farran's wounded leg, and as he did, he heard something that he had not noticed before. There, off in the distance, he heard the distinct sound of rushing water.

Farran snorted and breathed heavily as Cal did his best to rid the wound of whatever evil lingered in the raw, open flesh of his leg. "Shhh, there now boy. I'll have you running through these woodlands in no time."

Delilah stood on the pebble-strewn shoreline of this northern creek, her mind overrun with a stampede of unanswered questions about these three strangers.

"Delilah?" Cal asked her, though she was too lost in thought to notice. "Delilah?" he asked again.

Her eyes blinked away her thoughts, and she shook her head and turned her attention again to him. "I'm sorry," she said apologetically.

"This creek … where does it lead?" Cal asked her. "It sounds like there is a river nearby, doesn't it? Does this lead to something bigger?"

"What? Oh, yes. Back that way." She pointed westward. "All of these little creeks flow into the Argiñe."

"The Argiñe?" Deryn asked her.

Cal followed her gaze, and as he did the faint glow of the Stag's marker shone off in the same westward direction. "There it is!" he whispered in exhausted delight.

"You really are not from here, are you?" she said, shaking her head. "It is the hidden river. Well … not so much *hidden*, rather, no one knows where it flows from."

"What do you mean, girl?" Deryn said as he flitted up to meet her gaze.

"What does it matter?" she said defensively. "I mean that this creek and a dozen others all flow into the Argiñe, and the Argiñe flows from the white-peaked Itxaro Mountains, but no one knows just where it begins. It's hidden, don't you see?"

"It just disappears?" Deryn asked her carefully. "Into the mountains?"

"Well... not just into the mountains," she said, annoyance coloring her tone of voice. "It goes over the falls."

"The falls?" Astyræ said. "Would you show us?"

Dilly looked at her basket of herbs, remembering her sick brother. "I really must get back to Malhah, mother will need these to tend to him. Besides, there is nothing to see after the Falls of Ammon."

"Alright then," Cal told her. "But could you spare some of those herbs for Farran here before you leave? His wound seems to be getting worse, not better."

She reached into her basket and handed him a small bunch of flatleaf herbs whose stems crested into tiny white-and violet-colored flowers. "This is called *Osane*. It grows only in these rocky highlands. My mother will boil them into a tea to help with fever, but maybe they could help here, too."

Cal reached out and took the herbs, grateful for something, anything, that might aid in his friend's healing. "Thank you, Delilah. We will ask the THREE who is SEVEN to bring swift healing to your brother."

She looked at them, grateful for their aid and yet still mistrusting of their intentions. She turned to leave, but curiosity got the better of her. "Have you seen it?"

"Seen what?" Cal asked her.

"The light. I mean ... it's *source*, you know... where it comes from?" Delilah stumbled over her question.

"Yes, I have," Cal told her as he rubbed the herbs in his hands, breaking the leaves and releasing a pleasing fragrance.

She thought for a moment before she spoke. "Is it beautiful?"

Cal held the herbs against the wound and tied off a piece of his torn tunic on Farran's wounded leg. "Aye, it was once ... though I think it is gone now."

"Be wary of spies," she said, after a brief pause, her voice going flat. "I must go now." And at that, she dashed off eastward along the fens of the Argiñe towards wherever it was that she called home.

"That was strange," Cal said once the young woman was out of earshot.

"There are not many left on this Wreath worth trusting, groomsman," Astyræ scolded him. "She was trying to protect both herself and her family. And we are not much more than strangers to her."

"Alright, alright," Cal said, urging Farran to walk alongside him as they continued to follow the creek westward.

"You haven't tried to survive out here very long yet, Cal," she continued. "There is not much hospitality left in this darkened world of ours. There are those who still have refused the offer of the Sorceress, whatever their intentions may be. And though she deems them enemies to her cause, they do not call themselves friend to many others, save themselves."

"Well, I can't rightly understand the reason for that," Cal argued as he held the long, silver head of his four-legged friend in his rough hands. "Why don't they band together and oppose her? Wouldn't it make more sense for them all to stand united?"

"Of course it would, groomsman," she said as she clicked her tongue and urged her chestnut along. "But fear does deeper harm than what can be seen on the surface of things. It clouds the air. It strangles vision and casts a perilous shadow on the paths that might otherwise seem clear." She looked into his eyes, her expression weighted with an all-too-familiar and burdened gravity. "They are too afraid to oppose her."

Cal laughed to himself as he listened to the words of this Wreather woman, shaking his head and smiling at a not-so-long-ago memory.

"What?" she said with embarrassment. "Did I say something wrong?"

"No, my lady," he said gently, kindness coming into his clouded eyes.

"Well, what is it then? Huh?" she said with a slight growl in her voice.

"You remind me of an old friend is all," he said. "He used to speak just like that to me ... to anyone who would listen, really. Always poetry and riddles, mostly of the sagely sort."

"I don't understand what you are saying to me, groomsman." She turned her head westward, keeping her eyes on the bank in front of her. "I am not giving you riddles or poetry."

"Still ... you have the heart of a Poet, lady Astyræ. I am trying to pay you a compliment in saying so." He laughed as he spoke. "You are both beautiful and wise, and I am grateful to have you with me on the journey."

She thought in silence as they led their horses further west. A smile slowly crept across her soft face as his words found their mark on the center of her heart.

"Cal, do you hear that?" Deryn said, the sound of his bright voice interrupting the cadence of hooves and boots upon gravel. "The river must be close; I can hear its music upon the wind."

"Aye," Cal agreed. "I remember the last time I followed a river. It brought me to the halls of Petros, and to the great bowels of Islwyn. How I do wish for some similar hospitality for us on this journey ... for at least some liniment and perhaps a fresh bandage for Farran."

"I would gladly sail across the Dark Sea all over again to see that prayer answered, my friend," Deryn told him as he flew next to his charge.

"I know you would, Deryn." Cal replied. "You must miss your home very dearly. Let's just hope that our return will be a happy one, one of brighter circumstances."

The three of them traveled like this for what seemed like leagues, ever upward and inward into the highlands of the Wreath, following the banks of the fens of the Argiñe until at last the waters merged into a mighty river before their very eyes.

"I don't understand something," Cal mused aloud. "We can all hear the sound of rushing water. The falls ahead must be massive, but I still don't see it anywhere before us; the water must be going in some other direction." He glanced at the Wreather beside him. "Have you ever been this far North before?" Cal asked her.

"No, I haven't, though I have heard stories of the realm. The cities of Asier and Clarus were both here in the Northern marches of the Greywood. My grandfather told me of how Clarus and its people were mighty mariners of old; their city was the color of the foam of the waves upon the sea. He used to say that the birds of the sea first led them to the springs that fed their lands."

Cal stopped suddenly, and his friends slowed their march and followed his gaze. They beheld a once-ornate stone bridge, carved with runes and markings that had become overgrown with ivy and moss.

"Clarus," he said as he walked warily towards the ruined bridge, taking in the broken statues that flanked its entryway. "Did their city and its people dwell this far inland? These are chariots, not ships, that mark these ruins."

"I am not sure, but I don't suppose so," Astyræ told him. "Perhaps the Asierians ... they were the brave and the learned. Grandfather used to tell me of their city made of redstone, with palaces that climbed into the sky."

She came closer to see the markings for herself, while Cal brushed the dust away and splashed a handful of the cool water upon the stone bridge

"It is redstone! Or at least it was once," Cal said with a self-satisfied smile. "It is rather faded and weather-worn now, I would say."

"This must have been built by the people of Asier!" she wondered aloud. "Maybe their city was nearby?"

"Whatever happened to them? The cities, I mean?" Cal asked.

"Clarus fought for a time, but most of them finally left upon the wings of their mighty ships. They refused to bend the knee to the Sorceress but forsook their homeland in the process."

"And what about Asier?" Cal asked. "What happened to them?"

"That is a mystery in itself, groomsman," she told him, her face alight with some nearly forgotten memory. "Legend tells it that one day everyone in the city *vanished*. They all just disappeared into the darkening mist."

"Disappeared?" Cal said as he led Farran over the redstone bridge and on to the northern bank across the river. "How does a city full of people just ... disappear?" Did *she* have something to do with it?"

"No one knows. One day they were here, and the next ... they were not."

"Has anyone ever heard of their whereabouts?" Cal asked, his curiosity growing.

"No," she said as she followed him. "And that is why they say she hunts them, those who have escaped her rule. She is always looking, always plotting to subdue all of Aiénor, and to those who oppose her or evade her, she bends her wrath and pours out her vengeance. "

"I would like to know what happened to them ... that would be a story to hear, of that I am most certain," Cal said as they made their way closer and closer to the distant stag markings.

"There are many stories in Aiénor, Calarmindon Bright Fame, many whose deeds have put quill to parchment and words to song; many whose tales have long been forgotten," Deryn said mysteriously into the pale violet gloom.

They walked and talked for leagues along the northern banks, sharing histories and poetry, and at last they came to a fork in the river. The Argiñe split, its main source coming from the north, and yet a branch of it forked off south and westward away from the shores they had just traversed.

"Well, there is your water music," Deryn said as he flitted high above to take in what lay before them. "There are some falls just ahead."

"Aye, I can hear it," Cal replied. "And I see more markings, there, just on the other side of the bank between the fork of the river."

"Do you see where it leads?" Astyræ asked him.

Cal whirled around, spinning in search of something, anything that might point him in the right direction. "No, I can't see any other marking."

"What does it mean?" she said nervously.

"I think it means that we ought to reach the destination that we *can* see before we worry about the path beyond," Deryn said to them both.

"Alright then," Cal said as he surveyed the depths of the waters of the river. "It doesn't seem too swift over there!" He pointed a few dozen paces north. "In fact, it looks rather shallow."

"Well come on then, let's be about it already," Astyræ said.

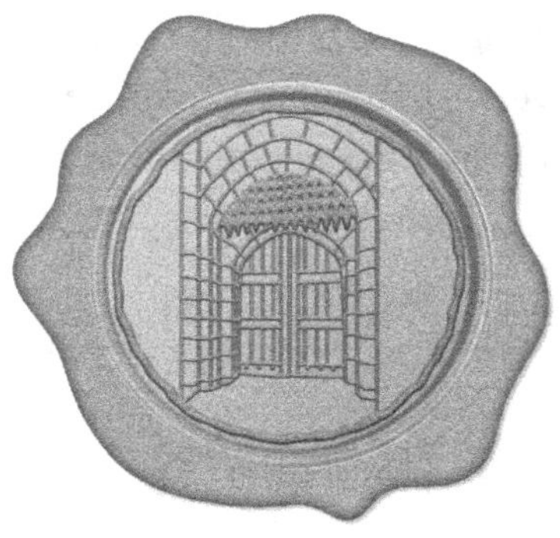

Chapter Fifteen

"What in the damnable dark," Celrod shouted in a whisper, "is *that*?"

"Do you not know, schoolmaster?" Timorets said grudgingly as he gulped back the rise of bile in his throat. "Have you never seen a footprint before?"

"Aye. I have beheld many boots' markings in my day, brewer," Celrod replied. "Though not once have I seen one span the entirety of a man."

"What does it mean, Fryon?" Margarid asked as she held Georgina closer to herself.

"I can't be sure," he said as he examined this impossible mark upon the foreign shoreline.

"I didn't know men could be so large," Michael said as he frantically surveyed the wilderness about them.

"Over here!" Fryon's brother beckoned. "There are more ... many more. They seem to be coming from all directions."

BOOM, BOOM, BOOM! The sound continued, hammering against

their already frayed nerves.

"Whatever it was that made these tracks did not welcome the Raven Army to an easy passage," Portus said nervously.

"That's a good thing, right?" said Harmier. "If it, this … *whatever* it is, is not a friend of the Ravens, then maybe it will be friendly enough to us."

"I don't know," Fryon told them. "But I don't think we should wait out here in the open to see what hospitality it might offer us, unprotected as we are."

"He is right. Come on then, all of you; we have to keep moving," Michael ordered.

"But where to?" Margarid asked.

"North," he replied. "That is all we know, so we have to assume that we will find our way there, no matter what lies before us. Come on then, let's be gone from this river."

"Aye," Celrod agreed.

The remnant huddled close, hands upon hilts and eyes keenly sharpened as they made their way north and east through the valley before them. Rising high on both sides of their passage grew the craggy, granite, black mountains, and littering the valley floor was the unmistakable disruption of an army's worth of footprints, and the broken bodies of hundreds of their makers.

They walked what must have been nearly a league of hesitant steps, following the path of their great city's intruders in reverse, when the valley took a sudden turn towards the north.

"Do you feel it?" Margarid said as she squeezed Michael's strong arm.

"Aye," he replied, straining to listen into the darkness before them.

"We are being watched," she continued in a whisper.

He turned and met her worried gaze, fear present upon his weary face. "Wait here; take the girl and the rest, and hide here against these outcroppings."

"And what do you plan to do?" she asked him.

"Find out what we are walking into," he told her.

"Celrod, Timorets!" he called in a hushed voice. "Stay here with the rest. Fryon, his brother, and I will scout what we can. If something happens, keep them safe!"

"And then what?" Celrod said.

"I don't know. Just ... keep them safe," Michael ordered. "Please."

"Alright, groomsman." Timorets agreed for them. "Just don't be a fool if you don't have to."

They clasped arms in agreement, and Michael and the brothers took their torches and blades and made their way past the bend in the valley.

"Do you think the giants are friendly giants?" Georgina asked innocently.

"Giants?" the schoolmaster asked, dumbfoundedly.

"Well, what else would you call them?" the child replied. "No one ever thought there were such things as dragons either, but we saw them with our own eyes," she reasoned. "Why shouldn't there be giants, too?"

"I don't ... well ... I mean, I can't say, girl," Celrod shook his head with a smile. "We have seen quite a lot these last days, haven't we?"

"Yes," Timorets said, almost willing the childish thought to be true. "And why shouldn't they be friendly giants?"

"Well, you could look around you and reason that out for yourself," Harmier said doubtfully.

Georgina scrunched her face up as she tried to find words for her reasoning. "Well, yes. But ... " She let out a frustrated exhale. "But maybe they were just not friendly to those who were not friendly to them!"

"I do hope you are right, child," Margarid said as she looked out behind her hiding place.

BOOM, BOOM, BOOM! The ominous sound came again.

"It's getting closer, isn't it?" Portus asked.

Nobody dared to lend credence to his observation.

Michael and the brothers had not gone more than two hundred paces past the bend in the valley before their blood went cold as ice. He lifted a finger to his lips, motioning for them to halt and watch.

They crouched low behind a smattering of broken rocks and

boulders, and what they beheld seemed just as impossible as all the other events they had lived through.

A giant, nearly the size of four grown men, raised a massive, black, iron hammer and struck the side of the mountain with violent rage. They heard rocks splinter under the weight of its fury, then crumble and crash to the valley floor below. The giant reached down and gathered, in a single armful, what would have taken a team of oxen two cartloads to carry. Then he moved his harvest into a single pile at the center of the mountain pass.

"What is he doing?" Fryon whispered to Michael. "Why the rock? Is he trying to block the way?

"I don't know. But I've never, in all my days, seen such strength before," Michael whispered in return.

The giant set the stones onto a heap of rubble in the middle of the pass with surprising care. He bent down and picked up the mighty hammer, growling in what seemed like grief, and then he angrily strode off to strike the mount again. His braided and metal-bound beard reached clear to his belly, and his arms were clad in massive leather vambraces, giving him a fearsome and wild look as he raised the hammer high over his head and poised to strike again.

But before the hammer struck the stone, he froze, mid-swing. He sniffed the cool, dark air about him. His enormous head turned sharply northward, towards the pile of his rubble, and then suspiciously southward in the direction of the hiding scouts.

They were close enough to him that the sound of his sniffing was something akin to the growling and snorting of an army of wild hogs, or like a terrible beast, and the three brave scouts felt their bodies shake involuntarily with worried reverberations. Without warning, and with his hammer still frozen in mid-swing, he spun in a gracefully horrible motion and flung the hammer not twenty paces from where the three of them had taken cover to watch.

"Have you come for me now?" the thunderous voice bellowed. "I will NOT BE TAKEN UNAWARES!!!" he screamed in outrage. The giant leapt towards them and the ground shook as he collided with the rocky floor. He ripped and tore at his leather tunic, beating his enormous chest as he shouted into the valley. "Do not hide like the carrion fowl, do not linger in the shadows like cowards! Show yourself to Vŏlker, and be done with it!" he roared.

Hilts were gripped tighter, and blades were unsheathed as Michael and the brothers prepared themselves for unimaginable violence.

"I will not suffer you passage a second time, *crows*! Not without vengeance being taken first!" the giant bellowed.

"He thinks we are Ravens," Fryon whispered as he kissed the flint that hung from his neck.

The giant reached down to retrieve the massive hammer, then stood tall and angered, rage blazing in his wild eyes. *"Show yourselves!"* he screamed against the darkness. Then he hurled his hammer a second time against the cleft of the valley, a mere thirty hands above their hiding place.

The side of the mountain exploded in a torrent of rock and dust, and the three of them ran from their cover out into the pass, coughing and straining against the aftermath of the monster's rage.

"Ravens!" Vŏlker shouted.

"No!" Michael shouted, still coughing against the granite dust that hung in the cold angry air about them. "We are not Ravens! We are not who you think!"

"LIES!" Vŏlker shouted, enraged all the more.

"We are not liars, Lord Giant!" Michael pleaded as Fryon and his brother held their blades at the ready.

"Do you think I will suffer the dark birds passage on my road a second time?" the giant bellowed angrily as he grabbed a massive rock and hurled it just above the heads of the three scouts.

Michael, Fryon, and his brother dived to the ground, barely eluding the missile that was sure to have unburdened them from their heads if they had not acted so quickly.

"LIES from SPIES!" Vŏlker spat in disgust. "Where are the rest of your kind? Where is your God-forsaken murderous army? Did they send ye out here again to see firsthand the wrath of we Măgąn?"

Michael stood warily back to his feet, his hands held out and open before him, willing for his calm display to disarm this mighty giant. "We are not spies, and we are not Ravens either, Lord Giant!" Michael swallowed to steady his shaking voice. "Please, my friends and I mean you no harm or offense."

Vŏlker stood menacingly over them, impossibly tall, with a mountainous piece of granite in his hands. His bushy, grey brows pinched in on themselves as he weighed the words of these strangers before him. "If ye not be Ravens ... then who are ye?"

"My name is Michael," he managed to say, his hands still open before him. "My friends and I are just strangers in this strange land," he said, with resignation in his voice.

"Strangers!" Vŏlker shouted as he raised the rock above his head. "Let me show ye what *strangers* are to we Măgąn!"

"No!" Michael begged. "We are not your enemy! We mean you no harm! We are—"

Michael's words were stolen from his voice as the sound of skittering stones echoed from behind their hiding place. Vŏlker turned his mighty head with a surprising quickness towards the origin of the small sound, as his dark eyes surveyed the path behind them with feral intent.

"LIES from SPIES!" Vŏlker growled under his breath.

"We are not! I assure you ... please believe me!" Michael begged. Fryon eyed his brother, then glanced at their blades upon the road before them.

Vŏlker's eyes shot back to the three scouts and then again to the sound of footsteps, echoing a few hundred paces behind them.

"This is lies, I can feel it. I can feel it in me bones," Vŏlker mumbled. "The same lies, the same Ravens that cut down me *Hlíf*. I know your kind!"

"No, please," Michael tried again. "I don't know who your *Hlíf* is, but I do know the Ravens, and they are not our friends, either!"

The steps came again, soft and muted in the wake of the giant's booming voice. Vŏlker hurled his massive rock towards the small sound, and Fryon and his brother darted for their fallen blades.

"No! Wait!" Michael called to his friends.

As their hands grasped their hilts, a child's scream froze them in their places. Vŏlker turned his head curiously, like that of a herdsman's dog who caught wind of a curious scent.

"No," Fryon whispered.

"Georgina?" Michael managed as he peered hard into the darkness behind him.

"What kind of trickery is this?" Vŏlker said warily.

"Let me go to her!" Michael begged.

"Michael?" came the voice of the child.

"Spies," Vŏlker said as he bent to pick up another of the massive stones. "Strange spies, indeed."

"Let me go to her, please! She is just a child, just a small girl!" Michael shouted at the giant, his protective nature outweighing his trepidations.

"Lies from spies." The giant muttered the words again and again, but his mantra had begun to seem like more of a question than an enraged fact.

"We are not spies!" Fryon shouted. "Why won't you listen to us?"

"Georgina?!" Michael called again.

"Michael?" she replied, her voice seeming closer than before.

"Lies from spies," Vŏlker continued.

"Please, let me go to her! Please!" Michael demanded.

A glint of amber and yellow flickered out from behind the rubble at the bend of the mountain pass. Vŏlker raised his huge, ink-embroidered arms back up and over his head, taking aim at the coming glow.

"Georgina!" Michael shouted. "NO!"

Fryon and his brother charged the giant's legs, swinging their blades at the iron greaves. Sparks flew as metal clashed with metal, and the giant tore his gaze from the bend and diverted his attention to the skirmish at his feet.

"Run, girl!" came the shouts of Fryon and his brother.

"Stop it!" called the soft, girlish voice upon the wind.

Völker growled at the men and shook off their attack, but when he turned his head back towards the voice, the vengeance melted from his eyes.

"Lies from spies?" he asked, without conviction.

"Stop it, please, sir!" Georgina begged as a trickle of crimson ran from the corner of her brow. "They are not lying, and we are not spying ... well, not like you say we are at least."

"Georgina, no!" Michael said. "It is not safe ... please run from here!"

Völker kicked the two brothers and sent them sprawling in a heap with just one sweep from his large, wool-lined boot.

"We are not Ravens, sir." Georgina continued. "The Ravens took our homes, broke our city ... killed our friends."

"Then ... what are ye?" Völker asked in an almost remorseful tone as he peered down at her.

"I am a girl. A girl from Haven, is all." She walked closer to the mighty giant.

Völker dropped the stone, and it shook the very ground beneath their boots. "How do I know for true that ye are not a Raven spy, telling me Raven lies?"

"I can't prove it, sir. But maybe you could trust me?" Her steady gaze seemed to humble the great creature before her. "We mean you no harm. Michael was right when he told you so. Our home is gone ... stolen and burned, and we ..." She trailed off as tears began to fall. "We don't know where to go," she finally whispered.

Margarid breathlessly appeared from the darkness behind her and wrapped her arms around the child, the others now following close behind her.

Völker's countenance broke behind the rush of his own sorrow. His bearded lip began to quiver, and tears the size of ripe grapes began to form in the corners of his eyes.

He knelt, then sat hard upon the valley floor; the ground shook as the weight of his weariness overcame the mighty giant. "I, too, have lost me home, me *Hlíf...* me wife." Völker wiped his tears on the sleeves of his tunic.

Georgina left the safety of Margarid's arms, overcome with empathy, and bravely made her way to the weeping giant. "There, there ... I am sorry for your loss, master giant." Her tiny hand reached up to pat his large leg.

Völker reached into his pocket, and with a rather alarming rush of sound he blew his sadness into a sodden rag. "Völker is not one for tears, girl," he managed as sternly as he could muster, surveying the dumbfounded gazes of these woebegone strangers. "But now ... me is all alone."

It was an odd moment for Michael and his remnant of friends. So much desolation and loss, so much destruction and death had befallen all of them these last long days. And yet, it was here in the valley of the wilderness, in the presence of a stranger's honest grief, that they all surrendered to the sadness that they had not had time to truly feel. It weighed heavily upon them all as their eyes clouded with tears of their own.

"If I may ask, Lord Giant?" Celrod said, breaking the quiet of the moment. "Your *Hlíf,* your wife... is that where she fell?" He pointed to the mound of rock and rubble there on the pass before them.

"Aye, there she lay," Völker said as he turned his bearded head to gaze at the grave pile. "The ravens!" He growled as he pounded the ground with his mighty fist. "They cut her down. They pierced her beautiful body with their ugly black bolts," he said as he dabbed at a lingering tear.

"What was she doing out here?" Margarid asked him. "In the middle of nowhere, I mean?"

"This is not nowhere, girl. This is Halvard! We Mågąn have guarded its pass for generations," the giant told them. "Me father, and his father, and his fathers before him – all of our kind, at that – we have been stewards of this place for far longer than me can hope to remember."

"What happened, then?" Timorets asked him.

At that question a guttural sob began to well up inside the mighty giant. "It's all me fault, all me fault!" Võlker bellowed. "Me saw a Stag, a mighty White Stag, out beyond the keep. And we was hungry! Ever since the light started to fade, strange things have been happening ... and the game ... well, they have been all too scarce, you see."

He snorted and blew his veiny nose into his rag. "Me thought, me thought me would catch us something tasty to eat for supper; and so me went out for a hunt ... and ... me left the Halvard gate *wide open!*"

He sobbed against his embarrassment, growling in hatred both of himself and of those who had stolen his wife. "Me such a failure, such a shame. Her would still be here if it were not for that damned Stag, and those double-damned Ravens. And if it not be for me."

Georgina patted his leg again, and Võlker sighed. "By the time me had come back, it was too late. I saw the broken bodies, the mangled feathers. They had walked right through that gate and me *Hlíf* was the only one to stand in the Ravens' way. And her was gone. Dead and gone."

Michael sheathed his sword, looking compassionately at the giant. "Have they come back this way? The Ravens, I mean," Michael asked him. "Is that why you thought we were Ravens too?"

"No," he grunted softly. "Though me wish they would! Give me my hammer and the chance to revenge me *Hlíf!*" His angered voice now rose upon the wind of his words.

"But," Georgina said matter-of-factly, "but then you might die too!"

"Me would like to see them try!" Võlker growled.

"She is right, Lord Giant," the schoolmaster said. "We have seen them, thousands of them! There are far too many of them for one giant!"

"And dragons," Harmier said. "They have dragons."

"It is better to stand and fight and fail, than to fail to stand and fight," Võlker said obstinately.

"More death!" Margarid shouted. "More death? Is that really the answer? We have all lost, we have all failed, we have all seen honor overrun by cruelty! Do you really think another dead man or woman or child or *giant* is going to change the appetite of evil?"

The group stared at her for a moment, the tumult of her emotions resonating within all of them.

"No, it won't!" she blurted out desperately.

Völker furrowed his bushy brows as he pondered her words. "What would ye do then, woman?"

"*Live,*" Margarid told him resolutely. "We have watched everything we have loved crumble. We have seen those whom we have trusted and followed, destroyed by the Raven devils. And yet, here we are! All of us, here, now together in this ... this Halvard Pass. And for what?" she asked them. Emotion, bridled by pure clarity, pulled against the reins of her heart. "To die, and make their loss and sacrifice meaningless? No! We must fight death and destruction with life itself."

Völker stared at her for a long moment, then surveyed the ragtag remnant before him. At last his eyes fell upon the tiny hand of the girl at his side. "Me not so sure about choosing to live. But ye ... ye might need some food, and some rest, and mayhapse some mead to start with." He looked longingly back to the grave, and then again to the group of travelers.

"And a fire?" Georgina asked as she shivered against the cold, northern winds.

"Aye, a fire too," Völker agreed. "Come on then, all of ye. Me is not gonna die today; and neither are ye."

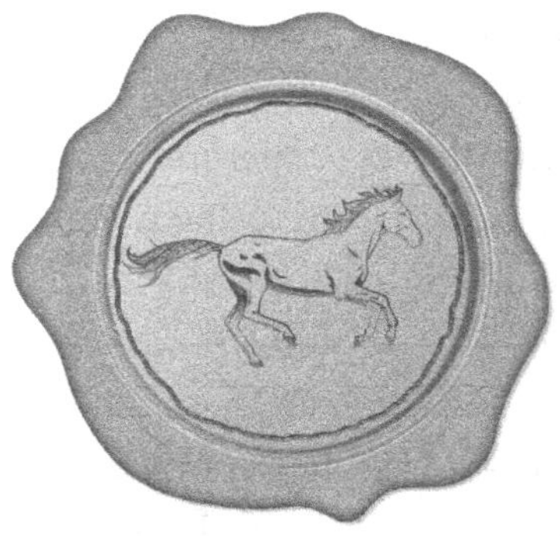

Chapter Sixteen

Cal held tightly to the leather reins of his wounded friend, Farran, leading him through the rushing water. Astyræ followed atop her chestnut, both taking cautious and exploratory steps in the cold waters of this unfamiliar river.

The Argiñe was wide, but at this fork in the river, the main body of its strength flowed eastward; out into the black waters of the Dark Sea. This path they had chosen to follow led them across the western branch of the river, whose waters noisily began to gain speed towards the treacherous Falls of Ammon.

"Come on now, boy," Cal whispered into Farran's ear. "If we are ever going to find out just where the Stag is leading us, we are going to have to get across."

"Cal!" Astyræ called out against the rush of the river's chatter. "Cal, it is getting deeper, the water is nearly up to your chest now."

"Just stay atop your chestnut, she will carry you across well enough," he reassured her. "We haven't got much more to go."

"Deryn?" Astyræ called out. "Can you see the falls? I can hear them, but I can't tell how close we are?"

"They are not far at all," he reported as he flew back towards his river-sodden friends. "Not even half a league from here, the toothy underbite of Ammon crests the river and sends it plummeting below."

"Cal," Astyræ said worriedly as she watched him and Farran struggle against the sweeping current.

"I heard him!" Cal shouted over his shoulder at her.

"You should mind your step, groomsman," Deryn offered.

"Thank you, I will ... take that into consideration," he spoke with barely veiled annoyance.

Cal felt the sole of his boots slide against the boulder-laden floor of the riverbed, the ancient stones slick with ages of silt. His feet lost their purchase, and he slipped down into the rushing water.

"Cal!" Astyræ yelled in panicked surprise.

He kicked against the rushing water, his hand still tightly wound in Farran's leather reins, and he pulled against the current with all his might. Farran whined against the awkward strain, but the weight of his body shifted as he braced his equine strength on his wounded leg. Cal breached the surface, his blonde hair soaked brown, as he gasped for breath.

"I'm alright!" he blurted out as his feet frantically searched for safe ground.

Farran snorted with both worry and pain, but sighed in noticeable relief when both the weight and the concern dissipated at Cal's surfacing.

"Are you alright?" she called out from atop her chestnut. "I thought I lost you over the falls."

"No ... yes, I'm alright," he said as he wiped his dripping hair out of his eyes and then reached up to thank Farran with a pat to his neck. "I've taken a perilous ride down some treacherous falls once before," he said, smiling back at the violet-eyed beauty that worried for him. "I'm not looking to take another trip like that anytime soon."

"We are nearly there, Cal," Deryn told his sodden friend. "Perhaps you should mind your step the rest of the way."

Cal laughed good-heartedly, then shook the water from his hair as he pressed on through the cold rush of the river. "Come on, then! Not much further now, and besides ... I've already found the slick spots."

The small band of friends finished fording the river, but as they reached the stony, western shore, the worsening of Farran's wounds became all too apparent to Cal. The mighty horse limped and snorted with great effort as he climbed out from the water and up the steepened bank. Although Cal had cleaned and bound the wound with herbs, it was clear that an infection had set in.

"Oh, Farran," Cal whispered as he bent low to see the fingers of angry red spreading beneath the grey coat of his friend and steed. The groomsman began to shiver as the air chilled his soaked clothes. Although the wind was cold, it was something more that chilled him all the way down to his bones.

"Do you see the markings?" Astyræ said as she laid a hand on his shoulder, redirecting his attention to the darkened highlands.

"Th-there!" the words shivered in time with his chilled body. "Th-the t-t-t-tree, over there." He pointed to the base of a massive cedar, two dozen paces from the bank of the river.

"We've got to make a fire, and soon, Calarmindon," Deryn said, the playfulness gone from his voice. "I'll not have my charge dying of a chill, not when we have come this far."

"I-I couldn't agree with you m-m-more, my Sprite friend," Cal managed with a smile. "Bu-ut I don't feel safe lighting one out here in the open."

"Not in the Queen's wood," Astyræ agreed.

"My lady, these trees and this place ... these are not *hers*," Deryn scolded. "Not even if she inhabited them with a legion of dragons, for a century of time, would I acquiesce to her the ownership of so divine a space."

"I'm sorry, I didn't mean..." she fumbled over her apology, taken aback by his unforeseen wrath.

"Just because those who walk upon these lands have resigned themselves to her rule, does not mean that the world itself has given up as easily," Deryn continued.

"I—" she tried to apologize again, but Cal interjected with excitement.

"There!" he exclaimed. "The next marking!"

Astyræ and Deryn halted their discourse and whirled about to see where the groomsman was pointing. "Where is it?" she asked him.

"Right there, next to the top of the falls, less than half a league away," he told them. "They are getting cl-closer together!" He took one of the packs off his saddle and hoisted it upon his own back. "Come on then, it could be a safer place to make a fire!"

"What do you think it means?" she asked him. "The markings getting closer together, I mean."

"I hope it means that we are getting cl-closer too," he said as he patted Farran's neck, leading him by the reins down the rocky path towards the next Stag marking.

As they reached the edge of the mighty falls, Cal spotted yet another marking down at the base of the falls, near a calm pool of water below.

"Down here!" Cal called triumphantly. "I see it."

Deryn flew out in front, leading the way downward and doing his best to illuminate a course for his friends. The way was steep, though not impassible, and the two dismounted riders led their horses slowly and cautiously back and forth down the rocky hillside.

Farran labored harder than did his chestnut friend, and a white froth began to gather in the corners of his mouth. Although Cal was mindful of his steps, Farran stumbled and tripped, tearing open the already worsening wounds on his foreleg.

"Almost there, boy," Cal whispered as he watched tendrils of red blood and yellow puss soak through the fabric of his tunic and ooze down onto the massive hoof of the courser. "Easy now ... take your time.

I'm not going to fre-freeze just yet."

The weary whine of his four-legged friend pulled at his heart, and he wanted nothing more than to be off of this cliffside and back home in his stable yard with real medicine and fresh hay for Farran to rest in.

"He needs to rest!" Cal shouted out to Deryn who flew out in front of them. "Are we close to the bottom yet?"

"Nearly there!" Deryn called as he flew up high enough to see the worry in Cal's eyes. "Nearly there."

Farran touched his nose to Cal's forehead, but it was dry as dust, and that worried the groomsman all the more. The exhausted horse sighed, and as he did splatters of blood flecked Cal's hands and forehead. The groomsman held his hands up for a closer look, and what he saw made his heart sink.

"I don't know what kind of damned venom breeds in the mouths of those vile wolves, but I don't for one moment doubt that it comes from that damned Sorceress," he grumbled to himself, worry giving way to hatred.

When at last they had reached the valley floor, Cal quickly set about unburdening Farran of the saddle and supplies that were still tied to him. He laid him down on a bed of soft green grass that grew serendipitously along the banks of the massive pool.

"Please, can you get a fire going?" he asked his friends, no longer caring to hide his worry.

Cal took the wounded leg and placed it as close to the cold, clear water as he could manage. He cupped his hands and scooped the water, then poured it over the infected wound.

Farran winced, raising his head up off the grass in pain, then laying it defeatedly back down again. "I'm sorry, boy," Cal whispered, washing and rinsing and washing the sour smelling gashes again.

The sounds of the fire popping and crackling behind did little to distract him from his task, and the comfort of its warmth seemed almost sinful to think about as his friend lay in such pain.

"Look there!" Astyræ called out. "The herb, the same herb that Dilly found. It's everywhere, growing all over the walls of the cliffside."

"Aye, but they haven't seemed to do much for him, have they?" Cal said defeatedly.

"Yes, but she said they would boil them into some kind of tea," Astyræ told him, desperately wanting to help. "Maybe we could do that, too?"

"We don't have any pots or kettles," Cal mumbled.

Astyræ, determined to help her friends, was not content with so easy a resignation. "There has to be something about!" she insisted as she stood to her feet to survey the area around them. "A shell, or a bone … something! There has got to be something we can use." She walked over to him as he was kneeling by the edge of the pool, fussing over Farran's leg. She laid a soft hand on his shoulder, and her tenderness temporarily overcame the anxiety of the moment.

"Please, will you help me look?" she asked him. "There has got to be something out here."

He nodded his agreement. Gently patting the side of his horse, he stood to search the banks of the pool. His clouded eyes scanned the reeds and grasses that grew along the rocky boundaries, following the lazy current of the river as it departed from the spacious pool and continued on into the wilderness of the Wreath.

He kicked at stones and picked through the reeds, looking for a tortoise shell or some other long-forgotten treasure on the floor of the pool. "Nothing," he said. "I don't see a thing, not even fish to catch and cook on the fire."

"Keep looking, there has got to be something," she told him from further down the shoreline.

The amber light of the fire cast its shadows, and Cal looked up to take in the fullness of his surroundings for the first time. What had seemed like a valley from the high grounds turned out to be not much more than a grotto, a grassy relief, probably carved out by the river long ago. Now, the swollen river had subsided, allowing the cedars and grasses to reclaim this land back from the intruding river.

"It is beautiful, in its own way," Deryn said as he flitted over to see about his worried friend. "It feels both hidden and forgotten all at the same time."

"I am sure the falls would detour intruders," Cal replied. "Though I am not sure why the markings led us here ... there is nowhere else to go that I can see."

He surveyed the surroundings, his eyes searching the small grove of stunted and crooked cedars, tracing the lines of the grasses and the white and violet flowering herbs towards the cascading waters, when something bright and glowing caught his eye.

"What in the name of the THREE who is SEVEN?" Cal said aloud.

"Did you find something?" Astyræ called out.

"What? What is it Cal?" Deryn asked, flitting up to meet his gaze and see whatever it was Cal could see.

"I found it," Cal said, the wounds of Farran momentarily forgotten.

"What did you find?" Deryn asked excitedly.

"The way."

Chapter Seventeen

Days passed ever-so-slowly in the dark silence of the prison hold. Very little love did the guardsmen of the colony have for Yasen and his men, and even less love did they show him these last days, now that *she* was here.

Yasen reached up to touch his bloodied and swollen lip, his fingers gingerly surveying the damage of this past day's beatings.

"Oh, if Hollis could see you now," he grunted and winced against the pain. Just then, his stomach roiled and growled angrily. He could not rightly remember when last he had a proper meal, let alone a crust of bread to assuage his unhappy hunger. He spat fresh blood onto the cold floor of the cell, when he heard a commotion of voices out from beyond his prison.

"She is not happy with this lack of progress, Pyrrhus!" Seig said in a growl as he held the fire knight by the threads of his tunic. "And I will not have *her*, my queen, *our* queen, dissatisfied."

"Yes, my lord," Pyrrhus said apologetically. The anger and rage that had earned him his name were all but ashes now in the light of this new power that had come for them. "But he won't speak. He won't tell us anything about where his men went off to."

"Well then, *apply pressure*! Or do I need to demonstrate again what it is I mean by that?" Seig growled.

"No, Governor," Pyrrhus said.

"The Raveness will return any day now from Aerebus, her reserved strength marshaled from the bowels of the Hekate' to usher in this gift of a new light," Seig reminded him. "And what did she ask in return for such generosity?"

"Only our colony's complete loyalty and allegiance, my Governor," Pyrrhus replied.

"Our *complete* loyalty, yes exactly," Seig went on. "But let me ask you this," he released his grip on Pyrrhus' tunic and turned in a dramatic fashion to survey the square at the center of the stronghold. "Does it look like our colony has delivered her request?"

"No, my lord," Pyrrhus admitted.

"No, it does not!" Seig seethed. "In fact, the only woodcutter that we have even seen in these last dozen days is locked behind the bars of the prison hold and leading us *nowhere*!"

"I know, my lord, but he won't tell me where they have gone off to," the fire knight argued.

"Do you think she will care to hear your excuses? Do you think her dragons, who have devoured nearly all of our livestock and horses, will be stayed by our failed attempts and poor efforts?" Seig said, his finger pressing violently into the mail upon his guardsman's chest.

"No, my lord," Pyrrhus said as he stole a wary glance at the ashen faces of the company of her guard that stood there in the center of the square.

"She will return any day now," Seig concluded. "Get him to talk before her dragons have a taste for something other than oxen and horses." With that the governor strode off angrily in the direction of his own quarters, bowing in exaggerated reverence to the twin serpents as he left.

Pyrrhus wiped the sweat from his brow with his remaining hand, embarrassment boiling over into rage at the belittlement he felt. He marched deliberately towards the iron bars of the prison hold, and as he arrived he slammed the hilt of his blade with a loud clang against the metal of the bars.

"It will not be me she feeds to those monsters," Pyrrhus growled. "I will not pay for your insolence, woodcutter."

"I am not asking for you to pay for anything," Yasen said as he rose to his feet, "but, I won't tell you … because *I don't know.*" Yasen looked into Pyrrhus' eyes and said the words as if he had spoken them a thousand times already.

"You know, alright," Pyrrhus argued. "I was there that day, remember? That day her ravens dragged that damned ship upon these damned shores. I saw you and your man talking about *seeking the light*, and all the while none of your *brothers* were anywhere to be seen."

"What do you want me to say, Pyrrhus?" Yasen asked as he held a hand to his swollen side. "I don't know where they went, and even if I did, I wouldn't turn them over to you, or Seig, or the *Raven Queen,* as you call her. She is not my queen, and I would not, for all the timber in all the land, bend a knee to her will."

"You don't know what she is capable of," Pyrrhus said, his face ghostly white in the firelight of the braziers. "I have seen her command her carrion, as they tore one of your men into a thousand bloodied pieces at the flick of her vile finger. Do not believe that these soldiers of hers are the pinnacle of her strength. She will return, and God help us all when she does."

"We have all seen our share of witches, Pyrrhus, or do you not remember the Isle?" Yasen said in mockery. "And we escaped both her wrath and her snare. What is one more witch upon our journey, huh? Are you bullied into submission by a few birds and a dozen soldiers? I thought you were a knight of Haven."

"There is no more Haven, *woodcutter*," he said in exhausted, lifeless defense. "There are only those who are for the Raven Queen and those who are against her. And mark my words, Yasen ... all will bend the knee to her; if only half of what she boasts is true, you will not be the last to do so."

Yasen lowered himself gingerly to the dirt floor of his cell. "I think not. But in any case, I don't know where the woodcutters have gone, so you can leave me be and go about your finding them another way."

"You do know," Pyrrhus growled as he leaned his oily, angered face into the bars. "You said it before, that day ... only I can't remember the word. I know it is north. You didn't think I was paying attention, but a man can remember much when he puts his mind to it. "

Yasen looked up, his eyes showing his alarm at this sudden revelation.

"I am right! Your face betrays you, woodcutter," the fire knight said with a studying stare. "I have not guessed far from the truth, and that is *something*."

"Do you really think this *queen* of yours is going to be happy with such a vague answer as 'north'?" Yasen argued.

"Oh, I'll remember it alright. I've remembered this much, haven't I? I am sure the rest will come to me in due time." Pyrrhus said, gloating at the prospect of both pleasing the governor and distressing Yasen all at the same time.

The air erupted with the sound of a low, soul-chilling horn blast; once, twice, and then six horrific times in a row. "What in the damnable dark is that?" Yasen said, laboriously rising back to his feet.

"She has returned," Pyrrhus said, swallowing his fear against the bile that churned in his stomach. "God help us all, woodcutter, she has returned," the knight whirled about, his tattered, green cloak catching the air about him. He barked orders to his fellow guardsmen, and their faces betrayed their own fear.

The few dozen Nocturnal soldiers in the courtyard rose to their feet, their faces ashen and emotionless, shadows of their former humanity.

Their sickly-green eyes were aglow with the obedience they offered to her.

"Do they not see?" Yasen said to the darkness about him. "Were they not men once? With hearts and minds of their own? How do they not see the brightness they have forfeited to gain the sight of her world?"

Her soldiers marched in formation towards the timber gates of the stronghold, and Yasen watched in horror as they broke their line to receive their mistress. Seig and the rest of his guardsmen stood upon the platform of the square, the banners of the colony and the braziers of the watch fires dancing in the chilled, wild winds of the Wreath.

Rank after rank of the raven army poured into the timber walls. Their standards, lit with the sickly-green torch light that crowned the bannerman's pole, pictured a white raven on a black field.

Her soldiers snapped into formation, their unpolished armor and blackened blades held in a stoic salute as a storm of green-eyed ravens drew a chariot upon their winged wickedness into the center of the parade line.

The driver, the very same who held the helm of the hijacked ship, screeched out his command in a soul-chilling voice to the murder of crows. With that, the obsidian-wheeled chariot came to a halt.

Nogcwren stepped gracefully down from her transport. The dark, onyx train of her feathered dress gave her an almost floating quality. Her black-steeled bodice clung to her frame while a crown of ravens' feathers encircled the ever-changing ink markings that writhed and morphed upon her slender, pale neck.

Yasen saw that there was a yellow in her eyes, one reminiscent of the lady of the Isle Dušana. And yet, this was not an evil veiled; it was scorn on full and defiant display, and he shuddered in fear at the very sight of her foreboding presence.

Seig rose to his feet from his seat upon the platform, a lord turned vassal in the presence of her intoxicating power. He spoke loud enough for all to hear, "My Queen." He bowed his head and splayed his arms in a dramatic gesture, "We are delighted for your return, and my colony welcomes you, yet again."

She looked at him, not with malice but rather with triumphant pity. "My dear Seig, have you forgotten already?" she said, her voice as seductive as silk upon bare flesh.

"My Queen?" he asked, rather confused by her question.

"This is not *your* colony; this is but an outpost of my Nocturnal kingdom." With that, she raised her scepter and pointed it towards the governor. The air about them cracked with her witchcraft as she forced him to his knees.

Seig dropped, his large hands barely catching the ground before he fell to his face. "Forgive me, Raveness, I did not mean—"

"Good," she silenced his stumbling apology.

The guardsmen looked wide-eyed in horror, though not in surprise, for they had seen her display of malice there upon the shoreline before.

"My Queen," Seig managed, breathless from her powerful blow. "What would you have of me?"

She seemed to glide upon the ground as she strode triumphantly towards her now-humbled servant. "Arise," she purred as she beckoned him with a ringed finger.

He leapt up from his prostrated position, as if some marionette master had yanked upon hidden strings, until he stood tall before her.

"Have you brought to me the rest of *your* colony, like I have asked you to do?" she said, examining the gathered forces around her. "It looks as if our reception is rather poorly attended."

Seig swallowed hard against the fear that threatened to steal his voice. "I have found and sequestered one of the woodcutters, Raveness."

"*One*?" she asked, her thin, black eyebrows rose. "Just one?"

"Yes… but he is—"

"I did not ask for *one* of your woodcutters. Not five, nor a dozen," she said, cutting him off. Her voice was cold, but it was not without decorum. "I asked for *all* of them, Governor. If one intended to rule all of Aiénor, wouldn't it stand to reason that all of Aiénor would need to be presented to their new ruler?"

"Yes, Raveness," Seig managed.

"Then bring them to me!" she railed in anger. "This was your first assignment." She came closer to him, her black-nailed hands tracing the collar line of his shirt. "Was it not?"

"Yes."

"Then you have failed, Governor." Her voice grew colder by the moment.

"Yes," he stammered his response. "But ... we have their chieftain." Her eyes brightened at his words. "And I am quite sure he will point us towards our quarry. That is, if we ask the right questions." His confidence was beginning to return as her attention turned away from him and towards the woodcutter in the prison hold.

"Pyrrhus," Seig called.

The fire knight stepped forward, his remaining arm crossing his chest in salute. "Yes, Governor," he answered warily.

"Tell us of the fruits of your interrogation. Our queen is eager to know of the woodcutters' whereabouts." Seig dusted the dirt from his tunic as he spoke condescendingly to the knight.

"Of course, my lord," Pyrrhus answered nervously. "He ... he said they went north."

Her head snapped in his direction like the strike from a serpent. "North? Where north, *fire knight*? My Nocturnals have patrolled these lands for years. It would be *helpful* if you could be a little more specific as to *where* exactly north they might have gone?"

"He wouldn't say, Raveness," Pyrrhus replied.

"Perhaps I should have asked a man with two arms to do this kind of job," Seig interjected.

"I asked every way I know how, but he won't loose his tongue." Pyrrhus shot back, fear and disgust roiling in his eyes. "He is there in the prison hold if you would like to ask him for yourself."

"Captain Durai," Nogcwren ordered. "Bring the woodcutter to me."

"Yes, my Queen," the green-eyed captain responded. With that, he and three others of his company broke their ranks and headed off in the direction of the prison hold.

Yasen watched as the small consort of Raven soldiers marched deliberately to where he sat in irons inside of the wooden cell. "Oh, Keily girl," he exhaled with resignation as he thought of his love. "God help us all."

"Woodcutter?" came the throaty, creaking voice of the large captain. He was dressed in a grey tunic, with an armored breastplate that was as black as the surrounding darkness, and his skin seemed as ashen as the spent coals of a long-forgotten fire.

"Aye," Yasen said matter-of-factly. "I am one, yes."

"Your presence has been requested by the Queen of Aiénor," Durai ordered.

"The Queen of Aiénor?" Yasen argued. "I've never heard of such a person."

The captain nodded to his escort and, with the swift clang of a sword hilt, the lock that had held him both captive and safe released its hold. "She is waiting."

Two soldiers rushed into the small cell and grabbed the bruised and beaten woodcutter under his arms, dragging him to his feet. Yasen winced, taking in a painful gasp of air as his aching ribs protested the movement. "What does she want with me?" he growled.

"We will all find out soon enough, won't we?" Durai said with a sinister grin.

They dragged him halfway across the square of the stronghold, at a pace he could not keep up with, until with labored breath and sweat-soaked brow he stood before the gathering of guardsmen and guests alike.

"My Queen," Seig said with a flourish, "I present the woodcutter you have requested."

Yasen turned his head and met the gaze of the former governor, his eyes asking the confused questions that his lips dare not.

"I see," she said, studying Yasen for a moment. "No wonder he told you nothing, Governor. His spirit, unlike yours, has not yet been broken.

Tell me, woodcutter, do you always stand with such disrespect in the presence of power?"

Durai came up from behind Yasen and swept his legs out from underneath him with a violent swing of his spear. Yasen grunted in wounded protest as his knees crashed upon the ground, his hands still bound in irons.

"Your Queen is addressing you, woodcutter," Seig said quietly. "Pay her the homage she is due and let's be done with this charade."

Yasen raised his head, his lone eye meeting the yellowed fire in her own. "You are no queen of mine," he told her.

"Yasen!" Pyrrhus shouted in a whisper. "What are you doing, you fool!"

"Yasen, is it?" Nogcwren cooed. "My governor here tells me that you are the chieftain of your people, mighty with an axe."

Yasen just stared, refusing to take whatever bait it was that she was looking to trap him with.

"Are you not?" she asked, an edge ever-so-slightly coloring the tone of her voice this time.

He stared defiantly, all the while praying in his mind.

Her sickly, yellowed gaze never left his for a moment, and so it was without warning that the thunderous clash of mail-covered fists upon the tender side of his ribs sent an explosion of pain through his already weary body.

Yasen coughed and sputtered, doubled over in the dust, a sticky trail of saliva and blood clinging to his battered face.

"Are you not the chieftain of these woodcutters?" she asked again.

"I am," he managed as he coughed against the pain. "What do you want with me? Let's be done with it already."

"What do I want with you?" she asked as she tore her gaze from the crumpled woodcutter and fixed it now upon each and every man of Haven. "I want the same thing that I have always wanted." She paused and let her gaze rest again upon the tall and still proud governor of Haven, before she spoke. "Aiénor."

"Well then, take it already," Yasen said as he struggled to rise to his feet. "You've taken Haven, or at least that is what Pyrrhus tells me. You've got more blades than we do, that is plain enough. What do you need a broken, one-eyed woodcutter for?" He spat the blood from his mouth and wiped tentatively at his lip with a sodden sleeve. "Looks to me like there aren't many who could stand in your way."

"My Queen," Seig tried to apologize, motioning at Pyrrhus to enforce the homage this woodcutter refused to display.

"Enough," she said with a sick sense of amusement. "It is much more satisfying to put rivals in their place than it is to tame mere beasts. Is it not, fire knight?"

Pyrrhus was flushed with sweat, his hair clinging to his reddened face. His chest heaved from both adrenaline and exhaustion. He glanced in surprise to the Raven Queen when she addressed him, then turned his attention back to Yasen, laying there in a heap. A shameful smile twinkled in his eyes for the briefest of moments before he blinked and met her gaze again. "My Queen?" he said, and the weight of her words sunk into the forefront of his mind.

She smiled at him, causing his heart to leap and his blood to run cold almost in the same instant.

"I said I wanted Aiénor, woodcutter," she told Yasen as she bent down to punctuate her message.

He looked up with a bloodied and swollen face, the lines of his scars angry and red, his good eye not much more than a slit. He saw her for what she was: greedy and insatiable. The runes of her dark, hellish magic swirled and floated upon her pale skin, and the swell of her breasts heaved with excitement as her black-lined lips spoke her truest intentions.

"Not part of Aiénor, nor most of Aiénor," she continued in a sultry, toxic whisper. "Not just its lands, nor its cities. I want *all* of Aiénor; every beast of the world and every son of Ádhamh." She rose, and the air about her began to move violently. The feathers that crowned her inked shoulders began to dance in the wake of the wind, and a smile, deep and satisfied, crept across her dangerously beautiful face. "And I will not rest, woodcutter, until every soul has been taken from Him, and until all of His once-bright world is subject to my great darkness."

"Madness," Yasen said through labored breaths. "There will always be those who refuse to bow to your wickedness."

"Oh, dear woodcutter," she began to laugh, the sound of her cackles more ominous than ever amidst the whooshing of the soul-chilling wind. "They will bow!" The joy and hatred in her voice chorused in unharmonious fanfare. "They will bow, indeed!"

As if to punctuate the moment with fearsome flair, crushing reverberations from the two winged beasts sounded on either side of the timber walls. Their massive forms dwarfed the defenses of the colony as torrents of their green fire lit the night sky above them.

"ROARH!" came the furious announcement.

"Run! God, help us!" came the shouts of the frightened guardsmen as the hulking, winged serpents circled the stronghold of the first colony with violent delight.

The men of Haven dropped blades and banners alike, falling to the ground and away from the flames. Panic washed over them as terror threatened every last ounce of their waning resolve. Pyrrhus shielded his face with his one remaining arm, while Seig stood alone, his face drained of any remaining pride.

"What in the damnable darkness?" Yasen whispered to himself as he swallowed back bile, his stomach threatening to empty itself against his will.

"The people of Aiénor will bow before their queen, or I will feed them to my children," Nogcwren said, delighted to be reunited with Abaddon and Angrah.

"Why?" he asked, wincing in pain with each labored word. "Why does it matter?"

"Tell me, woodcutter," she said, without hesitation. "What happens to a god when he has no souls left to subjugate?"

Yasen just stared at her, trying to understand the depths of her meaning.

"I would very much like to find out," she told him with a wicked smile.

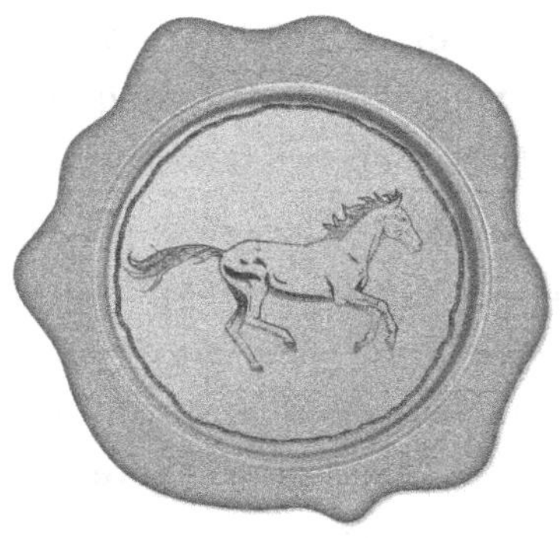

Chapter Eighteen

"Where?" Deryn said as he flew to meet the gaze of his kneeling friend. "Where is the way?"

"Cal?" Astyræ said as she eagerly came up from the bank and ran over to him.

"It's there, right there," he said, pointing into the crashing waters of the falls.

"I don't understand," she protested.

"It is hidden, isn't it, Cal?" Deryn confirmed. "Guarded by the rushing waters?"

"I think so," Cal said as he rubbed at his eyes to be sure. He rose to his feet, walking towards the spray of the clear, rushing waters and forgetting the mission he had, not moments before, thrown himself into.

"I can see the markings glowing behind the water," he told them excitedly as he pointed. "Right there, to the left."

"How do we enter? Do you see a path, a break in the water?" she asked him.

"I don't quite know yet," he said, his clouded eyes turning up ever so boyishly at the corners. "I've only just now found it."

She reached out for his hand and took it. "You've done it groomsman! You've really done it!" She pressed his hand to her lips and kissed it as she squeezed with her own tender grasp.

"I haven't done anything yet, my lady," Cal said with every bit of caution he could manage to muster, though he wasn't quite sure he believed his own tempered words. "For all we know it could be a cave, like the one you and Goran were nearly lost to."

"But then, why would the Stag lead you here and mark this as part of the ancient paths?" she argued, her own joy and wonder coloring every inflection of her hopeful voice.

"Well, that is true, isn't it?" The groomsman looked at his two friends in disbelief. "Shaimira!" he whispered.

The three of them stood there, staring at the falls in reverent wonder.

"Thank our Great Father, for He has indeed made a way for us," Deryn postulated his gratitude.

"May it be so, my friend," Cal agreed. "May it be so, indeed."

A pained whinny and desperate snort broke their reverie and, just like a wave upon a sandy shore, the sound of their wounded and suffering friend caused their momentary elation to crumble.

"Farran," Cal said guiltily. "Oh Farran, I have not forgotten about you," he cooed as he walked back over to the wounded horse. "We are nearly there, boy. And maybe... maybe there are people there, with liniments and medicines! I'm sure of it, Farran ... help is not far now."

The horse picked his head up off the ground to nuzzle his friend. A flicker of hope shone in his weary eyes, but it was drowning in a bog of pain and poison. Cal held the grey courser's head in his calloused hands as he spoke to him.

"Oh, mighty steed of Haven, we have one more leg of this journey. Can you find the strength enough to come with me?" he whispered.

Farran stared into Cal's eyes, a lifetime passing in mere moments. Farran snorted his agreement, and with great labor he began to rise to his feet.

"There now," Cal said, his voice swelling with pride and love for the brave horse as he settled him back down onto the grassy lawn. "Rest a bit more first. We need something to eat, and you need to be off that leg of yours so I can try to clean it proper."

Cal finished tending to Farran while Deryn spoke life into the fire they had set nearby. Astyræ had used her mighty bow to spear a few brightly speckled river trout, and with great skill had cleaned and skewered them on broken branches to roast over the open flame. Cal found a broken shell of a turtle, and though it did not hold much water, he was able to place it near enough to the fire to heat the water and to steep the herbs they found.

When they had eaten their fill and the tea had grown potent enough, Cal placed the head of his friend in his lap, stroking his mane and singing to ease Farran's mind. Astyræ took the makeshift pot and poured the hot elixir upon the gruesome wound. Farran tensed, his massive muscles recoiling at the searing pain of the liquid, but he subdued his protest at Cal's calming touch. Astyræ tied a piece of her own tunic around the angry wound and said a prayer for the herbs to do their best against the poison of the timber wolves, and Farran closed his eyes to the sound of Cal's voice.

They made a camp for the night, each doing their best to get what sleep they could manage to find. Although they all felt safe here in this hidden place, their worry and anticipation could not give way to real rest.

It was Farran who woke first, nudging the sleeping groomsman with his nose.

"Are you alright, my friend?" Cal asked him eagerly. But when he arose to examine their efforts upon the wound, his heart sank all the more. "Alright then, let's not tarry here any longer."

He woke the rest of his companions, and they packed up their belongings, all the more eager to follow the path set before them.

"Can you see a way?" Cal asked Deryn as his Sprite friend flew in and about the falling water.

"I see an opening behind the water," he replied. "But I think we are going to have to get wet; I don't see any way around it."

"I was afraid of that," Cal said, looking back at Astyræ and the horses. "But a little water will be a small price to pay for the life beyond this, huh? Will you be alright?"

"Well, our Great Father did not intend for His fruited children to swim, but if you will carry me, I will go with you."

"Alright then," Cal said with a chuckle to his words. "Twice now it will be that I have been baptized into such unknown adventures. I'll keep you as safe as I can, my friend."

With that, he took Farran by the reins, and opened up his tunic for Deryn to shield himself against the crashing waters. Surprisingly, the pool was not at first as deep as he feared, so both he and Astyræ led the horses out deeper and closer to the falls. Finally, his foot felt the rocks beneath them give way to the deeper waters.

"Alright then, hold your breath and dive as deep as you can," he told them all. "We are going to have to swim until we pass under the falls. Beware that you don't stop too soon."

"Will the horses be alright?" Astyræ asked worriedly.

"They will follow, and they are strong. And at least Farran won't have to walk for a moment or two." He patted Farran's neck and stroked the mane of the large chestnut.

"Are you ready, Deryn?" he asked playfully. "Time for your first swim, my friend."

"Just don't you forget that my lungs are not as large as yours, groomsman," Deryn said nervously.

"Alright," Cal laughed as the music of the pounding waters filled their ears. "Deep breaths now, here we go!"

Cal leapt from the safety of the shallows and plunged into the waters before them. They dove deep, horses in tow, and as they did they could feel the force of the falling river pushing them downward. He kicked and pulled, one hand on the reins and one hand stroking through the waters in front of them, willing them to move towards the other side.

Cal opened his eyes, searching the riverbed for purchase, and to his surprise the clear waters were lit in a faint, violet glow. He kicked and fought, resisting every urge to let the river take them back downstream. His lungs burned, and panic threatened, but it was the chestnut that caught his eye. The large horse had fearlessly followed, and then with great strength pulled Astyræ forward past the churning danger above.

Farran, following the bravery of his fellow horse, finally turned the tide of the moment and swam hard towards the safety beyond the falls. Cal's head broke the surface of the water, cresting with a loud gasp for breath. "Deryn!" he shouted as he pulled back his coat to free his friend from the watery stranglehold. But Deryn did not reply.

"Astyræ!" Cal shouted in a panic. "He is not breathing!" He kicked, searching for a foothold.

"Give him to me!" she shouted back against the roar of the water. The chestnut had made her way up onto the stone ledge of the cavern, and Farran was pulling him closer towards them with each moment.

Cal reached into his cloak and pulled out his Sprite friend, handing him shakily over to Astyræ. Quickly she bent Deryn's small body over her hand and began to pound his back, willing the water to release from his lungs.

Cal and Farran finally found their feet again enough to slip and then climb up the rocky slope and onto the landing before them. "Deryn!" Cal shouted.

"Come now, my half-brother!" Astyræ whispered her prayer as she continued to work on the Sprite's soaked lungs.

"Is he alright?" Cal begged. "Please, Deryn, breathe!"

A small but violent cough, and then a wretch, came as the most welcomed sounds that either of them could have ever hoped for. Deryn expelled the water from his lungs and gasped desperately for air. His eyes fluttered open, exhaustion and relief swirling in the brightness of his eyes. He took in his surroundings as the rush of the falling water woke his sensibilities to life.

"He's alright!" Astyræ said as her pink lips smiled away her worry. "You are alright, my little friend," she told him sweetly.

"I do thank you, my lady," he coughed with a raspy scratching to his voice. "But if you would be so kind as to put me down ... you are squeezing the life out of me."

"Oh!" she blurted quickly. "I am sorry, Deryn." She placed him gently on his feet on the wet stone beneath them.

"Pretty exciting for your first time under the water, huh?" Cal teased.

"Thank you for your enthusiasm," Deryn said in mock offense as he shook out the water from his azure-colored wings. "But if it is all the same to you, I would prefer to spend my days above the ground, not swimming beneath its surfaces."

"Well, you might have to delay your preferences for the time being," he said, taking in the immensity of the cavern. "It appears that we will be well beneath the surface of the ground until we find our way out again."

"I think you know what I was trying to say," Deryn continued. "But, yes, it would seem so."

Cal walked over to this new set of the Stag's glowing marks, touching their rutted lines. "You don't suppose it's another hidden grove, like Islwyn, do you?"

"I don't rightly know what it is, or where it will lead us, though I doubt it is as beautiful as Islwyn," Deryn said. "But I do believe it will still be worth finding."

"Quite right, my Sprite friend," Cal said as he rose to his feet. "Well ... should we be on our way? Astyræ, are you alright?"

"Besides being a bit soaked through, we are just fine. My chestnut here was a brave one, huh?" She ruffled the horse behind the ears. "I couldn't fight the current on my own, so she just dragged me along after her. When we find our way out of here, I'll make sure you get a carrot, or an apple, or something sweet to show you my thanks."

"Now look who is talking to the horses, huh?" Cal said with a wink and a smile.

"Do you see the next marker, Cal?" Deryn asked, taking in the massive cavern. "I don't see much in here, just stone and wet."

Cal looked about, squinting into the blackness before them, trying to extend the reach of his violet vision. "No, I don't. But this marking here is as plain as the silver fire on the once burning tree ... so this must be the path."

"Ok then," Astyræ agreed. "We should be about it, then."

"Through the bowels of the wilderness we will go," Deryn said solemnly, placing his tiny, azure hand upon Cal's broad shoulder.

Cal smiled at these friends of his. Never, in all his days in Westriver, would he have dared to dream of such an adventure with such unforeseen friends. As he took Farran by the reins and began the journey into the cave, he wondered if Michael would ever believe the tale. He hoped that his cousin would not be too cross with him about missing out on the whole thing, then smiled at the thought.

"What are you grinning about, groomsman?" Astyræ asked him playfully.

"Just my horse-faced cousin is all," he said without any further explanation.

She tilted her head in curiosity as she continued forward, one golden eyebrow cocked as she considered this *tree man*, this foreigner, this ... love of hers. "Well," she said finally and with great playfulness, "I, for one, am rather relieved to note that you must only slightly resemble him, then."

"Ha!" Cal blurted out, his laughter so welcomed and yet so out of place in this endless cavern of stone and dankness. "You are now, are you?"

"As relieved as one can be." She gave him a wink and sweet, kind smile. "You know, that is the first time I think you've even mentioned your family to me. And yet ... I've told you nearly everything there is to know of mine."

Cal walked, considering her words for a moment before he spoke. "I suppose you are right, my lady."

"Would you tell me of them?" she asked.

He smiled, remembering what he could of his family. "I wish they could have seen all of this ... my parents, I mean," he told her wistfully. "We would have had to try to keep up with them, you know, not the other way around."

"Oh?" she encouraged.

"Aye. They never stopped expecting that the THREE who is SEVEN would reveal His new light for all of us, and so they never stopped searching for it. Even when it became dangerous, or treacherous, to do so."

She thought on his words, enchanted by his longing for his lost parents and his pride for who they once were. "It sounds as though they were very much like you."

He looked into her eyes with gratitude. "I hope so."

And so they walked, for leagues it seemed, through the cavernous path underneath dirt and mountain. They talked of their families and lives now long displaced in the wake of the ravenous evil. Deryn listened patiently to their exchange, busying himself with flying out ahead of them any time a bend in the tunnel turned them down a blind, unexpected path. A subtle sound began to grow ahead of them, but they could not discern it just yet.

When their feet and hooves could walk no further, they sat against the dank, dark walls of stone. They passed a skin of wine between them and longed for a dryer, softer place to make their rest.

Cal laid his head against Farran's flank, his own heart sinking as he heard the labored breaths and the wheezing, sodden exhales of his hurting friend. He stroked the horse's neck and prayed for relief as Deryn came close.

"He is worsening, isn't he?" the Sprite asked.

"He sure sounds that way," Cal said sadly. "I would have thought the herbs and the water would have washed that damned venom from his wound by now, but it only seems to have traveled deeper inside."

"He is strong," Deryn said reassuringly. "He walked the whole day, with barely a protest."

"I know," Cal agreed. "I had almost thought that last bit of doctoring had worked. But it doesn't seem so, Deryn."

"No, it does not," Deryn sadly agreed.

Their rest was not comfortable, but sleep came upon them quickly and with little resistance. When they woke with renewed energy, they paid a bit more attention to the faint, rushing sound within the tunnel.

"Do you hear that?" Astyræ asked them.

"Is that...?" Cal stood, stretching and straining to make sense of the sound. "Is that water? Is that falling water?"

"You don't suppose we've been walking in a circle this whole time?" she said fearfully as she rose to her feet.

"Deryn?" Cal asked. "You don't think so, do you?"

"No," he said. "I mean ... yes, it is water. And no, I do not believe we have gone wandering in circles."

"Then what it is?" she asked, a bit lighter now. "What could it be, I mean?"

"I am not sure," Cal said as he peered into the darkness before him. "But I know I am not going back to sleep, not now. So I say we go find out."

"Agreed," Astyræ answered.

"Let me go ahead of you while you ready the horses," Deryn told him. "If it is danger before us, I doubt anyone is going to be expecting a Sprite to happen upon them here in the dark of this tunnel."

"Very good, then," Cal replied as he tightened his scabbard belt and packed up his supplies. "But don't go too far ahead of us."

Deryn nodded his agreement and unsheathed his tiny, azure blade from its scabbard. In a wisp of blue light, he darted off down the cavernous pathway.

Cal knelt beside Farran, whose breath was still labored and weary. "Come on, boy, I don't think it is much further now." He stroked the worried face of his friend.

Farran opened his eyes, and Cal could see that the love he shared with his rider was as real as the rock beneath their feet. With great determination and muted anguish, the horse rose once again upon his weakened legs.

"Thank you, my friend," Cal whispered into his ear. "I'll get us there soon enough."

"Are you ready?" he asked Astyræ.

She smiled a guarded smile, exhaling her worries and nodding her golden-haired head.

With one hand on the leather reins and the other at the flowering hilt of Gwarwyn, Cal led them forward, towards the sound of falling water. Despite the faint, violet glow in the tunnel, no markings or signs of life could be seen.

"Do you see Deryn?" Astyræ asked.

"No," Cal said, scanning the dark before him. "I don't see him at all. I just told him not to go too far..."

"Shhh," she hushed him as she held her slender finger to her lips. "If someone happened upon him, we should do our best not to announce our presence, too."

He nodded and drew his sword from its white sheath. "The water," he whispered after a few paces of silent steps. "It is getting louder."

Farran snorted, agitated by something before them. "What is it, Farran?" Cal asked without taking his eyes off the black before them.

They continued like this for a hundred more paces, the tension nearly strangling the breath from their very lungs.

"I still can't see him," Cal whispered to her. "Where in the damnable dark did he go?" He felt worry rise within him as they wound around another bend in the tunnel.

"Wait, Cal!" Astyræ said in an excited whisper as she pointed ahead. "There, what is that?"

"It ..." Cal paused, trying to make sense of what he saw. "It looks like water, like ... a waterfall of some sort."

"Yes, but why ... why is it *glowing*?" Her voice rang of both confusion and curiosity.

He walked closer, holding his ancient blade at the ready. "It ... is that ..." he tried to connect his words to the image in front of them. "There is *light* behind it ... yes! It's glowing because there is a light behind it somehow!"

"But how?" she said, her mind still swirling in a tumult of thoughts.

Cal smiled a knowing, wide smile; his clouded eyes came alive with excitement. "Come on, my lady!" he said as he placed his blade back in its scabbard. He reached out and took her hand in his own. She tore her gaze from the view before them and met his own with her still-searching eyes. "It's here," he said, his voice catching with emotion. "We found it, my lady."

She looked to the glowing falls and then back again at him. "I hope you are right, tree man."

With a steady breath, they walked together towards the light until they passed through the small, rushing falls of glowing water into the hopeful unknown before them.

Chapter Nineteen

The realization of the magnitude of the Raven Queen's power fell upon Seig's mind with such force that he nearly doubled over. He slumped, hands upon his knees, eyes wide with amazed terror at the two impossibilities that flanked his small outpost here on the wild shores of this wild land. The air was silent, save for the sounds of the dragons breathing, but a storm of panicked words and frightened thoughts raged with unprecedented volume in the minds of guardsmen and governor alike.

Pyrrhus reached for his blade as his men dropped theirs, but the Nocturnal soldiers of the Raven army stood resolute and unmoved by the twin serpents of Nogcwren.

Yasen's heart sank, for he knew that these two beasts of war were responsible for the fall of his city and the desolation of his home. If he were honest with himself, he also feared that these two abominations might have brought something terrible upon his Keily. Yasen looked upon the Sorceress as he got gingerly to his feet, and hatred entered his heart at the very thought of all that had been destroyed by her hand.

Just then, a duo of voices sounded inside the minds of the colonists.

Men of the dead tree.

Behold, your Queen has come to liberate this world from the chains of darkness and the slavery of your impotent god.

"Where is that voice coming from?" came a panicked cry of a guardsman.

"What kind of devilry is this?" shouted another. "Make it stop!"

Yasen looked back towards Seig, gauging his reaction. He saw both wonder and resignation there in the once-strong eyes of the governor. Pyrrhus stood next to him, fear plain as day upon the face of the fire knight.

Do not be troubled, for she offers a gift to all who are worthy to receive it.

The dragons continued, their words toxic yet dripping with a compelling sweetness.

Your kinsmen have taken her at her word, and no longer do they toil and labor in the merciless darkness of a dying deity. Behold, a new light has come to Aiénor.

"My Queen," Seig said, his voice cracking under the strain. "What would you have of me and my men?" He knelt as he spoke, this time of his own accord.

"I've asked you for the whereabouts of this chieftain's woodcutters," she replied brusquely, her eyes alight with a feverish yellow. "But have you given me what I have asked for, Governor?"

He dropped his eyes from her gaze, knowing that he had already failed. And although shame was brooding, wrath quickly rushed into the forefront of his mind.

"No, you haven't," she said coldly. "So, what would make you believe I would waste another moment of my illumination on you, dear Governor?"

"I ask your forgiveness, my Queen," Seig said quietly, hardly able to keep the growl out of his voice. "But my only failure was to entrust the fool Pyrrhus with the task of gathering the information." He pointed accusatorily at his former confidant, then rose angrily to his feet, a desperate madness raging in his eyes as he marched towards the one-armed knight and the bloodied woodcutter.

Nogcwren smiled, ever-so-satisfied at the display of frightened hubris and the violence that was sure to come.

"Governor, what would you have had me do differently?" Pyrrhus shouted in protest. "I have beaten this man for days, I have starved him half to death, and you can't tell his right side from his left for the amount of swelling and blood that covers his face!"

Seig reared back and, quick as a snake, backhanded the fire knight across the face with a tooth-jarring slap. "I would have had you never let his men out of your sight in the first place!" he growled.

"That is not what you ordered me to do!" Pyrrhus said, his remaining hand raising to comfort his now-aching face. "You said to bring Yasen here, and that is what I did."

"I knew I should have sent you with the *Determination* and not Tahd. He is a true captain and would have known how to follow the heart of my orders! Your foolishness ... look what you have done!" He landed another slap with his left hand and then punched the knight's stomach with a crushing right blow.

Pyrrhus coughed and groaned, spitting blood. Confusion and hatred were ablaze and uncontrollable now. He straightened himself with great labor and limped closer to the bound woodcutter. "You," he seethed at Yasen, spittle and blood frothed upon his lips. "This is *your* fault."

The dragons laughed, a sinister accompaniment to the clash of wounded wills.

Oh, blame!

Their voices seemed to gloat in delight.

How easy it is to assign, when your own failure is too ghastly a reflection to endure.

"Tell me where your damned men went!" he tried again, but Yasen just breathed through his bloodied nose and stared at his accuser, silent.

Without warning, Pyrrhus kicked the legs out from under the woodcutter, and Yasen fell, his bound hands doing very little to break his fall. "Your fault! This is all your fault," Pyrrhus shouted again as he reared back his leg and landed his boot in the woodcutter's face. It hit Yasen with such force that the patch Keily had made for him flew from his face and landed in the dirt before him.

Seig drew his sword from its sheath as guardsmen and Nocturnals alike watched in both horror and delight. "You are a waste of a knight, a shame, a shame of a knight!" He swung his blade wildly, and Pyrrhus managed to stumble out of its reach. "A shame of a knight," he yelled. "I should have left you on the Isle! I should have let those men with the mirrors cut you to ribbons!" He swung again, drunk with embarrassed rage. Pyrrhus danced away, backing into the stone-like body of Durai.

Pyrrhus heaved, his mind reeling. The words of the governor rang in his mind. *Shame and mirrors, shame and mirrors.* There was a connection there, and something began to take root in his mind.

Durai pushed him forward. "Meet your justice, dog of Haven," he said lifelessly.

Pyrrhus looked at the heap of a woodcutter on the ground nearby, and then at the raging bear of a man who held his two-handed blade with deadly intent. The words of the governor raced through his mind over and over again until his eyes suddenly shot open in a brilliance of understanding.

"I know where they have gone!" he managed to say as he tried to catch his breath. "I think I remember now! I heard them say it!"

Yasen raised his head from the dirt, willing Pyrrhus to be wrong. His face was a mess of blood and dust, his eyes nearly swollen shut.

"Shame-era... sham-," the knight tried to cough out before the Sorceress interrupted him.

"Shaimira?" she seethed. "Is that what you are trying to say?"

"Yes ... I think that's what he said. Shaimira, I am certain of it," the fire knight replied to her with a greedy hope.

"Where is this Shaimira?" Seig said warily. "I've never heard of such a place."

Yasen dropped his head in defeat, exhaling a bloodied, defeated breath. Nogcwren's eyes went wide with understanding and her captain turned to meet her gaze.

"It was Soma, or one of his damned bearded brothers; I can't remember." Pyrrhus said stumbling over his words. "That day I brought him to you. He said they were off to find something... I've just now remembered that word... Sham- Shaimira."

"If you are lying," Seig growled as he grabbed the collar of Pyrrhus' shirt and pulled him in close, "I'll rid you of your other arm, and both of your legs, and leave you to fend off the ravens with nothing but your own lying beak."

Seig pushed Pyrrhus aside and stole a contemptuous glance at Yasen as he turned to face the Sorceress. "My knight seems to have remembered something he should have never forgotten to begin with," he said respectfully, bridling his wounded pride for the moment. "Does Shaimira mean anything to you?"

She stood there, the temperature of her displeasure quickly coming to a boil. The yellow in her eyes turned sickly and vile, the beauty of her facial features beginning to harden as the discoveries of the moment sank in. "Does it mean anything to me?" she asked in a menacingly exasperated voice which escalated into a roar of contempt. "Does it *mean anything to me!?*"

The men of the colony clasped their mailed hands over their ears, the sound of her rage threatening to burst their eardrums. A mist began to roil about her feet, and a tempest of lightning and thunder lit up the sky and threatened the stronghold with its cumulous wrath.

The dragons shifted as they too became uneasy in the wake of her displeasure. She tilted her head and looked to the gathering sky before she spoke. "*Shaimira* is the last stronghold of those who remain *willfully unenlightened!* The last of an ungrateful and insolent people who spurn both my generosity and my will!" She turned her gaze to meet the eyes of the governor. "And now, because of your foolishness, dozens of armed men have gone to join the ranks of their resistance!"

"Why not just go to them and present them with the light of your generosity, my Queen? Show them the might of your strength, the graciousness of your offer, and be done with them for good?" Seig blurted out, trying to deflect her wrath.

"Oh, my dear Governor," her voice went sickeningly sweet once again. "If it were only that easy. You see..." she raised her scepter, pointing it at Seig. Fingers of yellow lightning shot forth through the air and into the governor.

Seig writhed, his body lifting from the ground, suspended by her malice. Currents of sorcery wound themselves over his entire body, searing him with a burning pain. He twisted and screamed, the very veins threatening to burst straight through his skin.

"I have been looking for the Asierians for nearly *a century of time*, and still they elude my grasp! And *your* men, *your* charges, *your* fools have allowed these woodcutting traitors to find them, right under your imperceptive nose!" she raged aloud.

She lowered her scepter and the torrent of magic ceased. Seig collapsed to the ground like a beaten dog, as she walked towards him with the forcefulness of great power. Just then, a commotion rose up from beyond the gates. The Nocturnal army parted as two raven sentries dragged a bound man into the entrance of the stronghold. Yasen lifted his head and leaned upon one arm, working laboriously to get to his knees so that he might have a better view of what was happening. Nogcwren paused her stride and gestured to her captain.

Durai met the sentries at the gate. Within moments, he had turned back to address his queen, pleasure upon his ashen face. He spoke as he approached her. "It would seem that favor has shifted in our direction. We have finally caught the miscreant who has been skulking about the grounds." He motioned to his men and they brought a man, a woodcutter bound with irons, toward the Raven Queen.

Yasen saw his friend, and his heart plummeted. "Soma?" he

whispered.

"So, you know this man?" Nogcwren asked, delight returning to her countenance.

Soma looked at his beaten brother and then to the yellow-eyed woman who lorded herself over all who had gathered. "What ... what do you want with me?" he managed, trying to keep the fear out of his voice.

She smiled, the delight in her eyes like those of a barn cat who toyed with its prey just before devouring it. "I have a gift for you, dear woodcutter," she said as sweetly as she could. "Sight in the darkness. No more need for watch fires and felling timber ... this new light I offer you is my gift to all of Aiénor."

"Yasen?" he said, tearing his eyes from her and looking pleadingly at his friend and chieftain. "Forgive me, I was just trying to rescue you."

"I but ask one small token in response to my enormous generosity," she cooed.

"And what is that?" Soma said bravely. "You want me to do your bidding? Or what, I'll end up like him over there?"

"No, dear woodcutter," she said, amused at her own malevolence. "I simply want you to follow the will of your chief, this broken dog that you have put your trust in."

"I ... I don't understand," Soma said, looking back and forth between Yasen and the gathered ranks of Raven soldiers.

"I only ask that Yasen be the first of your kind to take and receive my gift. And then that all of you who give your allegiance to him would but follow his wise and noble example."

"Never," came the grunt of the wounded woodcutter as he rose to his feet in defiance of her suggestion. "I'll never bend my knee to your will, never."

"Oh, Yasen," she said as if she had lived this exact moment a thousand times before. "You will, if you are any man of valor, if you have wisdom left in that poor, swollen face of yours ... you will take my blessed gift."

Almost on cue, both dragons lifted their enormous heads and

stretched their inky, scaled necks in over the all-too-short palisade walls of the stronghold. Their massive talons reached for purchase upon the battlements, only to crush them beneath their immense weight. They leaned down towards Yasen, and their green eyes, alight in a sinister glow, came within a handsbreadth of his face.

Yasen could barely see through the swelling of his beatings. When his eye focused on the twin terrors that loomed before him, true fear gripped him in ways that none of the beasts of the dying forests had ever done before.

"What? Will you have them eat me?" he said, doing his best to muster some semblance of courage. "And then what? How will you find the woodcutters then?"

"North Wolf," she said sadly. "That is what they call you, isn't it? It is not you I will have my children eat."

The dragons let out a torrent of green fire in ferocious unison, their fiery breath lighting the dark sky with the intensity of their power.

Let us be done with this parlay, for we have flown long across the waters of the dark sea and still have a hunger that must be satisfied.

They opened their mouths, displaying row after row of sharp, yellowed teeth. Then, slowly and tauntingly, they turned their heads to Soma and reached out their forked, black tongues to lick at the bound man.

"Yasen?" Soma asked, his body quivering. "Yasen! Help me, please." With that, a trickle of urine soaked the front of his pants and ran down into the dirt.

"Soma!" Yasen said, bile threatening to rise beyond the boundaries of his churning stomach. "Wait! Please!"

Nogcwren watched with familiar delight, for this was not the first strong man she had watched beg her for her gift.

The jaws of the twin dragons opened wider, and he could see, even from where he stood, the evil fire that grew in their foul bodies. "Wait! Wait ... I'll take your gift. Spare him, and I will take your gift."

The twin dragons smiled ominously and closed their jaws so that they might make way for their Queen.

Yasen reached down and took the patch that Keily had made him, holding it in his hand, a last token of a love he was sure he would forfeit in the light of this sorcery.

"He is not taking it before me!" Seig shouted in wounded defiance. "I am the governor of this colony, and I will be first to bend my knee and take your gift, my Queen ... not some dog of a woodcutter."

"Gentlemen," she cooed in mock exasperation. "I have light enough for all of Aiénor. But very well, Governor, I suppose your time has come. I will let you set the example for your men."

He brushed the dirt off of his large, black tunic, then settled his collar so as to make himself presentable for such a moment. "Thank you, my Queen."

Come and kneel, Seig. Receive your Queen's gift.

The dragons spoke the command in unison, and Seig kneeled before the mighty serpents, bowing his head in exaggerated reverence.

A blast of green fire issued forth from the nostrils of the dragons, enveloping the wide-eyed governor in a cloud of green flame. His men flinched at the sight of it, but when no screams were heard, and no smells of burning flesh could be smelled, they let out a collective sigh of relief.

Seig rose to his feet once the cloud had dissipated. His eyes had turned green like the surrounding hoard. He held his hands aloft, examining them almost as if for the very first time.

"Amazing!" he shouted. "Truly amazing! I can see!"

"And you, woodcutter," she directed.

Soma met Yasen's gaze. He watched the North Wolf place his eye patch on his wounded and bruised face, covering his left eye with the small token of Keily's love. Then Yasen silently walked the fifteen paces forward to where the dragons stood waiting.

"No, Yasen ... wait," Soma protested.

"It's alright, Soma," Yasen said sadly. "I am so tired, so very tired of all of this."

Yasen knelt without fanfare, though he kept his head held high.

"Your gift, woodcutter," the Raven Queen whispered as she gestured to her dragons. A torrent of vile magic erupted once again and washed over the bloodied body of the woodcutter.

"Yasen, I am sorry!" Soma muttered.

The fog dissipated and the North Wolf bowed his head, holding his face in his hands. It was a long, uncomfortable moment before he rose to his feet and examined his hands, much in the same way that Seig had done.

"I can see," he said as he looked into the face of his friend. "I am alright, and soon you will be, too."

Soma looked at him, his expression wrinkled with questions.

"Wait a minute!" Pyrrhus blurted out. "His eye... why is it not colored like the Governor's? Like those of your army?" His voice was wary with suspicion and hatred for the woodcutter.

"Willingness," she said with a flit of her rune-covered hand. "I've seen it a hundred times. The more willing the subject, the more evident their *blessing*. However ... willing or otherwise ... my gift has made his will subject to my own."

Pyrrhus nodded his understanding as she continued.

"His eyes will turn soon enough." She laughed a satisfied laugh as she thought on the many whose strength and kingdoms had now become her own. "The more reluctant the man, the more ruthless they seem to become."

"My Queen," Yasen said, turning to meet her gaze. "I have held up my end of the bargain. Set him free."

She looked at Yasen for a moment before a smile crept across her face. "Abaddon, Angrah ... free the woodcutter."

And in an instant, the dragons lashed forth and buried their yellowed fangs into the body of Soma, tearing him into two ragged pieces. Yasen watched in horror as they gobbled and swallowed his friend without so much as a second thought.

He wanted to scream in protest, but he knew that he no longer could.

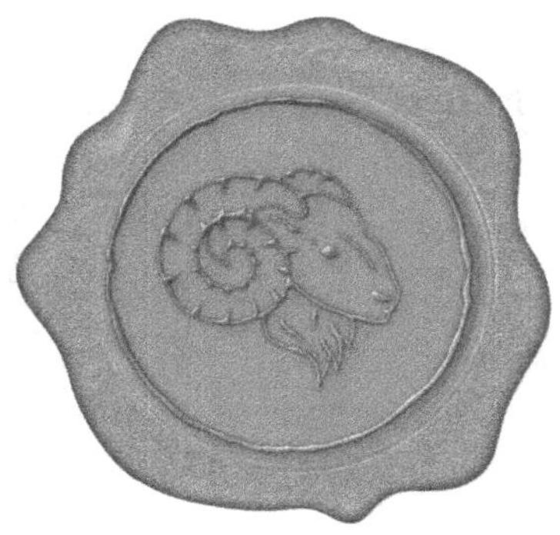

Chapter Twenty

The water fell quickly upon Cal and Astyræ, though it was but a fraction of the strength of the Falls of Ammon. They passed with only a light soaking of their cloaks, and as they wiped the water from their eyes and swept the plastered hair from their vision, what they beheld captivated them in a way they could not have begun to imagine.

"Not a step farther!" came a commanding voice from the van of a group of guards. "Not one more step if you value your life."

"Please," Cal said as he held his empty hands out before them. "Tell me where we are … tell me we have found it at last!" He took an impulsive step closer, despite the guard's threats.

"This is your last warning, stranger." A man stood before him in a deep blue tunic and bright, brilliantly adorned armor. He motioned towards the score of bow strings that were drawn taut, pointing at Cal and Astyræ.

"I'm sorry!" Cal said, working to bridle his elation and pay the guard his due respect. "I mean you no harm, forgive me. But please … you must tell me the name of this place."

"I am Sendoa, keeper of the Pass of Kemen. You are now at the mercy of the Lord of the Amaian realm," he said, his authority unwavering. "You, unwelcomed strangers, might do well to mind your place before you begin demanding answers."

"He didn't mean anything by it … we don't wish any offense, my Lord keeper," Astyræ said humbly. "We have been searching long for you, is all … and we are just so happy to be here."

Sendoa studied her, his eyes narrowing at the sight of her violet and amber flecked eyes as he proceeded to place restraining irons on both her and Cal's wrists.

Cal allowed his gaze to wander to the line of the majestic mountains that hemmed in this hidden city of splendor. Spiraling towers made of stone, many arched windows on granite battlements, and a mightily fortified wall with but one small gate were just the beginnings of the ornately sculpted, stone works that flooded his sight.

"Tell me this, strangers," Sendoa brought his attention back to the moment. "What kind of strangers travel with the ghosts of beauty's long-dead offspring?" He forcefully held out a small birdcage taken from the nearby rookery with an azure-winged Sprite captive within.

"Deryn!" Cal shouted. "Are you alright?" The intoxication of their discovery was finally surrendering to the sobriety of the moment.

"I'm fine, Cal," Deryn said calmly, "other than suffering from the smell of the messenger bird who inhabited this cage before me. Just tell him your story."

"That is my friend," Cal said, wary of the many pointed arrows aimed at him and his friends. "His name is Deryn, Sentinel of the house of Iolanthe who is Queen of the Sprites." Cal answered him with a measure of his own authority. "I ask that you please let him free from that cage. We are not your enemies, not in the least."

"And you? Who are you two?" Sendoa pressed. "Why would we presume to take orders from you, stranger?"

The groomsman spoke humbly. "My name is Cal. I am just a groomsman from Haven, the once-shining city from across the Dark Sea. And this ... this is Astyræ, daughter of Dardanos. Her father, Aius, was once the king of that place, or so I am told." Cal bowed slightly to the tall man before him. "Please, Lord keeper, we mean you no harm. We have been sent on a quest to find your people. Please tell me ... is this ... *Shaimira?*"

Sendoa tried to mask the surprise on his face at the secret word. He stared into Cal's eyes for a moment longer as he surveyed the strange assembly before him. The legend of Aius' daughter had not been hidden from the ears of the Amaians, for some of the Dardanians had wandered far enough north, bedraggled by sorrow and road-weariness, and had come into the keeping of the Lord of the hidden city.

He shook his head. "You had best be ready to give account for where it was that you heard that word, groomsman of Haven." Slowly, he lowered his white leather gloved hand, signaling to his guardians to lower their bows. "In all my years as keeper of the pass, I have never seen a company quite like yours."

Cal and Astyræ both breathed a sigh of relief. "Well, never in my wildest of fantasies would I have imagined a boy from Westriver would find himself on the Wreath."

The keeper nodded, his countenance softening ever so slightly, though he still kept one hand upon the hilt of his sheathed blade. "I will suffer you entrance through the pass, though it will be with little hospitality until the lord of the hidden realm grants favor upon you."

"Will you take us to meet your lord, then?" Cal asked hopefully.

"Yes, I will take you," Sendoa agreed. "Though I will ask for your weapons until favor has been permitted."

Cal's bright and hopeful face fell at the idea of relinquishing Gwarwyn to this stranger.

"It will be alright, Cal," Deryn said wisely. "This will not be the first time you have been a stranger in a strange land, and I do not believe it will be your last either."

Cal reached to unbuckle the white leather scabbard, but before he did, he spoke with an authority beyond his station or his age. "Before I give you, a stranger to me and this ancient blade, keep of so mighty a weapon, you must confirm to me the name of this hidden realm."

Sendoa raised an eyebrow. It was plain to see that these travelers were no rabble from the Greywood seeking shelter and handout, nor were they spies of the Sorceress. It seemed that both doom and magic were woven about their fellowship. He looked to examine the strange, flowering hilt of the white-sheathed blade.

"Were I to speak to you the name of this sacred place, our home, you would be bound, welcome or not, to its laws," Sendoa said gravely, rubbing his greying, neatly trimmed beard with his gloved hand. "Though if my gut tells me true, your strange arrival here has already bound us to you."

Cal took a deep breath. "Very well, then. This is Gwarwyn, and its silver-mooned sister is Arianrhod, both born of the mind and the craft of Blodeuwedd, the ancient Sprite Armorist." Cal wrapped the leather thongs of the scabbard around itself and beckoned Astyræ for the bow and quiver. "They were gifts from the THREE who is SEVEN to us. Do not dishonor the Giver with negligence."

Sendoa removed his helmet, whose sculpted rams' horns peaked at the comb and came together to encircle the head of its wearer in fierce, silvery elegance. He bowed his head in respect to these out-of-the-ordinary strangers before he spoke.

"Garaile will see to their well-keeping, and I will accompany you myself to the heart of our city." He signaled Garaile, his second-in-command, who came with an open, reverent hand and took the weapons as they were offered. The keeper turned and faced the gate guards at the wall, signaling with the high-pitched twill of a small wooden flute.

The sound of metal and gears straining let out an ominous rumble.

"But you did not-" Cal started to protest.

"Welcome, strange travelers," Sendoa interrupted him. "To ... Shaimira."

They stood in silence for a moment as the truth of his words washed over them.

"I told you we would find it," Astyræ whispered as she elbowed him playfully.

"You told *me*, huh?" he said with a deep, satisfied smile.

The line of guardians moved into column formation with Cal, Astyræ and their horses at the center, hemmed in as they marched beneath the only entrance to the hidden city.

Farran was sounding worse and worse with each passing step. His uneven gate and wheezing breath were giving Cal more and more unease. Although they had finally passed through Shaimira's lone gate, they still had far to walk.

Beyond the battlements there lay an open field before them with row after row of vegetation, farms and fields, and small streams of waters. The surrounding borders at the foothills of the enormously high Itxaro Mountains were covered with great forests of all kinds of trees. The road before them was paved in shining, granite stone, and along its way were high lamps lit with fragrant oils.

"In the name of the THREE who is SEVEN," Cal prayed under his breath as he patted the flank of his wounded friend. "I had hoped for a stronghold, a band of brothers, maybe even a tribe or two of woodsmen or something," he told Astyræ. "But this ... never in all my days did I imagine such a place beyond the walls of Haven."

Tears flowed from Astyræ's eyes, both hopeful and sad. "It reminds me of my home too, groomsman."

The city of Shaimira sprung forth from the center of the encircled valley. Mansions and spired stables were surrounded by flowing fountains of crystal-clear waters; it seemed there were too many to count. At the heart of the hidden realm, a mighty, spiraled tower loomed over the open city before them. Astyræ gasped as she pointed at it, compelled by its sheer size and grandeur.

Sendoa spoke. "*Kelila*, we call it. A symbol of victory over the cruelty of the Raven Queen."

Cal and Astyræ nodded solemnly.

As they passed along the roadway, a pair of massive, sculpted chariots flanked either side of the passage. Teams of armored horses, frozen and carved in stone, held these monuments of power in sedentary battle.

"You are passing the *Oroitz Guardia*, the pride of our long-forgotten home," Sendoa said with a tilted bow to his head. The wheels alone were the height of three, maybe four men, and the chariots and riders dwarfed the passersby with their enormity.

"These statues remind us of who we once were … and who we have been saved to become," he told them. "Our pride was once in the open field, and our chariots were many, but this," he gestured to the encircled city before them, "is no place for chariots. Our strength has become the mountain itself. And the mightiest on the mountain is the ram, not the horse."

"Chariots?" Cal said aloud. "Yes … we passed over a bridge days ago, with carvings of chariots, that must have been of your people."

"That is impossible," Sendoa said as he escorted them through the grid of the city. "My people abandoned our city over a hundred years ago."

"I am sure of it," Cal said excitedly. "The work looks very similar, though it was carved upon red stone not the granite you use here."

Sendoa smiled, his eyes betraying his growing kindness towards these strangers. "Thank the Giver of Light, then! Perhaps her cruelties have not devoured all of our ancient efforts."

As they walked into the city, thousands of people peeked out from windows and over garden hedges. They gathered in the squares and the markets and turned their attention to the parade of guardians and these new strangers. Children chased after each other, laughing and playing more freely than Astyræ had ever seen of any child. "This place," she tried to put into words, "I've … I've never seen anything like it before."

The pace of their marching had echoed in rhythm together since the mouth of the tunnel, but the sound of something out of place stole Cal's wonder and hijacked it with worry. He tore his eyes from the majesty of it all and turned to look at Farran, whose eyes were turning a pale, spoiled color, and whose mouth had begun to froth and foam. His hooves clumped awkwardly and unsurely upon the paved roadway.

Cal reached up to steady his friend. "Astyræ!" he shouted. "Astyræ, help me! It's Farran ... something is wrong."

Cal stopped in the midst of the procession, not sure what else to do. He took Farran's head in his hands and spoke in a soothing voice. "Hang on now, boy. We are here! We made it! I'm sure they will help us now. Please, hang on!"

Farran swayed unsteadily, and Cal fought against the seasick motion of the mighty courser, willing him to stay upright and sure-footed. "Help me, please!" he begged, but the horse could no longer hold himself upright. Farran's knees buckled, and in a painfully ungraceful manner, he collapsed to the road in a heap.

"Farran!" Cal shouted, and threw himself down to comfort his friend. Farran sighed an exhausted, congested, bubbling sigh. "Come on, stay with me," he cooed to his friend. "Help him, please!" he shouted to the guardians of the realm. "He was wounded, poisoned by some green-eyed, damned beast of the Sorceress! Please! He needs medicine!"

The column of guardians had halted their parade, and Sendoa watched the wounded horse and its worried rider with true pity in his eyes, though his mind was still wary of some unlooked-for treachery of the Raven Queen.

"Please, I need medicine!" Cal said as he stroked the mane of the fallen horse. "A healer, somebody, anyone who could help him."

The keeper knelt down and looked into the sickened eyes of the horse. What he saw there did not give him cause for hope.

"Luken," Sendoa called out to the young man at the end of the column. "Send for Aysa, the healer, and have him see to the wounded animal. Tell him what you know, what the groomsman here has told us, and be quick about it."

The young guardian bowed with a tilt to his head. "Right away, sir," he replied. Wasting no time, he took off through the streets toward the house of the healer.

"Thank you," Cal told Sendoa, his eyes welling at the struggle he could feel that Farran was enduring.

"Luken is fast, and his family knows Aysa well enough," he assured him. "They will be here shortly, but I cannot permit you to wait."

"But-" Cal tried to protest.

"You are still a stranger to our people, and we still have laws we must abide by," the officer said sternly. "Your horse-"

"He is more than just a horse!" Cal shot back, fear and anger boiling over. "He is my friend, my family."

Sendoa took a deep breath to quiet his own outrage over the lack of understanding and respect from this young man from Haven. "Your ... *friend*," he said with steeled diplomacy, "is in the best hands he could possibly be in, stranger. And thank the Giver of Light that it was my watch at the pass this day, and not Zuzen's, for *you* are also in the best hands that you could possibly be in."

"I'm not leaving him," Cal said, tears beginning to spill over in defiance.

"Cal," Astyræ said as she knelt and placed her hands upon his shoulders. "We are still strangers here, Cal, and they are not some wandering tribe or band of peasants huddled in the Greywood," she reasoned sweetly with him. "We need to trust them. We need to go with them."

"But, my lady!" he tried.

"They have sent for a healer, and the sooner we meet the lord of this realm, and gain their favor," she said, her voice more firm now, "the sooner you will be able to go back to him."

Cal looked deep into her eyes, considering the wisdom of her words, and then down to his suffering friend. "They are sending someone for you, boy," he cooed as he stroked Farran's face. "I have to go. I don't want to, but I have to ... and as soon as I can, I will find you."

Cal kissed his horse between his weary, sickly eyes, and Farran sighed his gurgled understanding. The groomsman stood to his feet, wiping his face with his hand. "Alright, keeper," he agreed quietly, "take me to your lord, then."

Sendoa examined him and nodded his agreement. "To the Palladium," he ordered his men.

The guardians resumed their march, and Cal and Astyræ followed their escort deeper, past rows of stone-carved houses and gardens, shops and stables, until at last they stood before an elevated stone building, whose many carved columns supported an open-air colonnade. Pools of reflecting water surrounded the Palladium, ushering all who would need approach this house of wisdom and law towards the massive set of steps that led to its only entrance.

Atop the steps, centered between two massive, copper braziers, stood a woman in white flowing garments. The wind caught the wing-like sleeves of her gown and fanned her dark-brown hair, which cascaded down her shoulder. A crown of gilded ram's horns, with a single sapphire set in woven silver, adorned her brow.

"Weary travelers," she welcomed in gracious authority. "I am Johanna, Lord of the hidden realm, granddaughter of King Julen, and Queen of the Amaians." She met each of their gazes with her own, her strength and compassion unveiled for all to see. "Welcome to Shaimira."

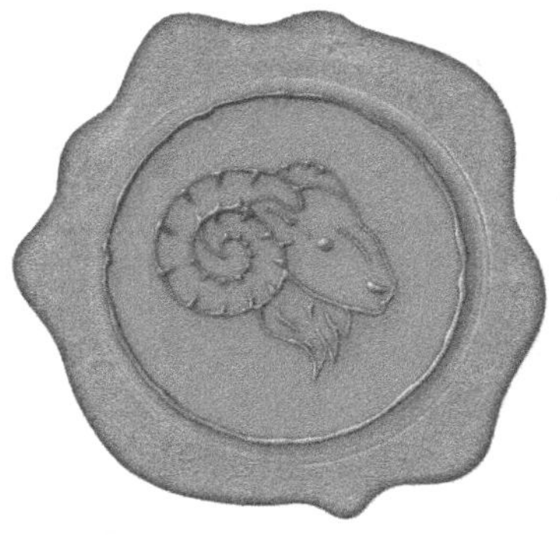

Chapter Twenty-One

They were escorted inside the Palladium, past ornately carved columns and flowing fabrics. Dozens of leaders and lawmakers moved throughout the annex, all busy about their duties here in this place.

She led them to a large hall. Row after row of wooden tables and woven tapestries lined its perimeter, and at the very center of the room was a massive, brick lined hearth whose coals and embers lit the chamber in welcoming warmth.

In the corner of the hall was a high seat. Though the chair was humbly carved and upholstered in sheep wools, it held authority over all who took court here. Behind the queen's chair was a statue carved in white stone, the likeness of a mighty horse, with massive wings that appeared to nearly take the relic of stone to flight.

Johanna approached the dais, bowed her head before the carved image, and took her seat, inviting these strangers to stand before her.

Sendoa had gently placed the birdcage that held Deryn captive down upon the table nearest Cal and Astyræ. Flanking the seat of power were two pairs of the lord's guardians, whose white capes were broached with the same sapphire jewel that adorned the Queen's horned crown.

Sendoa tilted his head as he bowed before her, and at her bidding he told her all that he had learned from these strangers. He spoke of who they claimed to be and of the fallen, wounded horse.

"How is it that Illium's kind, Aius' daughter, and a Sprite brought back from beyond the grave have made their way to my kingdom?" she said, her eyes examining their intentions. "How have you come beyond the hidden pass and into the Itxaro?"

"Please, Lord Johanna," Cal said, his cheeks stained with tears. "My friend ... my horse, is badly hurt. I need your help, please. May I go to him?" he asked, not bothering to answer her questions.

"Cal, is it?" she said, compassion not altogether lost amidst her sternness. "It has been a very long time since we have had strangers in our midst. And it has been even longer since an equine creature has graced our presence. I, too, wish nothing more than for your friend to heal fully. But as the Lord and protector of my people, my duty first is not to the glories of our people's past, but to their future. And if I am to look brightly upon their future, I must first determine if there is an enemy or a threat that has found its way into our kingdom."

"Of course ... thank you, Lady Johanna," he said, remembering his place. "We are no enemy, I assure you." Cal's voice still carried his worry. He looked to Astyræ and then again to his winged guardian, determining that he had little to hide and that truth and speed might get him to Farran all the sooner.

"I sailed across the Dark Sea, leaving the colony of my people for but one reason ... to seek the light," he said. "When Deryn and I found Astyræ prisoner in that tower, I saw the markings of our long-lost king etched upon the same prison wall. One word was there, and I knew that my quest for the new light of the THREE who is SEVEN would lead me to follow in his footsteps."

Johanna listened intently; her wonder at the bright, magical threads still woven through this ever-darkening world could not be hidden from her face. "And what was this word, light seeker?" she asked him quietly.

"Shaimira," Cal replied. "I've been looking for you ever since."

Johanna smiled deeply, and she exhaled a sigh of satisfaction at Cal's story of Illium. Then she turned her attention to the golden-haired woman who stood next to him. "And you, Princess Astyræ?" She spoke the title with honor, bringing the attention of the room to the exiled royalty of Dardanos. "What is it that you seek here?"

Cal turned his head to look at Astyræ. Although he knew of her past, he had never paid much attention to her nobility. He felt somehow surprised to hear her addressed in so formal a way.

"I seek revenge," Astyræ said coldly. "I seek justice, and the destruction of that evil woman and all her kind." Her violet-eyes burned with hatred for the Sorceress. "I want my people back, I want my city returned to life ... and I want my father... if he is yet somewhere, to be found."

"Yet you align yourself with this light seeker, who has made no mention of the Sorceress?" Johanna asked.

"My grandfather told me stories of your people, of a hidden strength and a growing rebellion," Astyræ told her. "He said that one day, you would be strong enough to stand against *her*." She looked at Cal, her affection for him clear on her face. "Cal is seeking a new light, and that seeking has led me back to the hope I have held onto since I was a little girl. If his light wipes out her darkness, then I will follow him as long as I may."

The Queen thought on her words, measuring Astyræ's intentions. The hall was quiet, save for the pop and crackle of the burning coals in the hearth behind them, and although the mood was deep, there was little malice to be felt.

"And you, fruit of the forgotten trees?" She turned finally to face the small, caged Sprite. "What is it that you seek?"

Deryn bowed in exaggerated reverence, used to the pomp and circumstance of royalty, for he had spent most of his bright days in the court of another queen. "Queen Johanna, I am here as but a guardian and a servant to my own Queen; Iolanthe of the Sprites, Lord of Islwyn, the grove under the mountain." Deryn stood tall in his prison, pride and love beaming from his glowing face. "Calarmindon Bright Fame was given to me as my charge, to watch over and aid him in his seeking. For the darkness that has befallen Aiénor is driven by a magic more ancient and much deeper than mere dragons and ravens. True victory shall come only at the hand of our Great Father."

"Calarmindon Bright Fame, is it?" she said as she glanced back to Cal, speaking with both respect and a touch of amusement. He nodded to her and she tilted her head in acknowledgement.

Then she looked back to the Sprite. "So … you believe that your charge is seeking a light that will be the weapon we use to defeat her evil, once and for all?" Johanna asked.

"No, I do not," Deryn said with all sincerity. "This light is not a weapon, Queen Johanna."

"If you are speaking in riddles, master Sprite, I shall warn you that I do not enjoy them." She gazed at him directly, "Speak plainly."

"The light is our *victory*," Deryn obliged. "The heart of our Great Father is not a trinket or a tool to use as we see fit. Rather, it is the very firmament our dying world will be rebuilt upon. In that light, darkness cannot exist. And evil? Evil will find no welcome."

She thought long on the Sprite's words. When she had finally finished pondering on all that these strangers had told her, she whispered a command to her guard. He walked over to the cage of the Sprite, his bearded face betraying no thought or emotion. He placed his hand upon the cage and turned to face his queen.

"Wait, my Queen!" Cal blurted out, nervous that this guard meant to harm Deryn. "Please."

She ignored Cal and nodded her approval to the guardsman. Both Cal and Astyræ held their breath, fearful of what injustice may befall them all. Then the guard took a small, silver key from the leather pouch upon his braided belt. He placed the key in the small, inset lock upon the cage, and with a quick turn of his gloved hand, he released the mechanism and set the Sprite free.

The door swung open and Deryn stood there, proud and noble, one hand upon the hilt of his tiny blue blade, and the other crossing his chest. Cal and Astyræ breathed a sigh of relief as they listened to the queen speak.

"My people came here to escape the tyranny and malice of one who dared to name herself ruler of these lands. We forsook our homes, our great city, our pride, and our strength to crawl through the bowels of the mountain and begin again here." She told them as she, too, rose to her feet. "For over a hundred years in this blessed valley, we have built up a strength to withstand the bite of evil. My father died knowing that his people were safe, protected and at the ready to fight any who would threaten our strength, our peace, or our freedom."

"And yet, we have existed to be a refuge for any that the Giver of Light might lead to our door," she continued. "Hundreds, over the decades, have found and made this place their home, too. There are those from both of your cities that have found refuge amongst us here. But never once, in all my days, did I dare to dream that I might behold the fabled fruit of forgotten beauty ... here in these hopeful halls of ours." She walked over to the stone table to give her hand to the Sprite.

"Please, receive my welcome, and please, forgive my prudence at your arrival. Captain, release them from their bonds." She looked each of the travelers in the eyes. "For you are no longer strangers to Shaimira. You are our honored guests. And never again, dear Sprite, will I subdue you within the confines of a cage."

Deryn bowed in reverence as he spoke. "Thank you, Queen Johanna. If it pleases you," he said as he looked over to Cal, "my friend would dearly like to tend to his horse."

Cal smiled a weary smile at the request of his Sprite guardian, and the queen could not help but understand the affection that passed between them at this simple gesture. "Very well," she told them. "My guards will take you to the home of the healer that Sendoa summoned on your behalf. May your feet swiftly lead you to your equine friends, and may the Giver of Light grant Aysa the strength to mend every wound."

"Thank you," Cal said. "We are honored to be your guests here and hope to learn much about your people soon. My friends will stay here and heed your counsel for as long as you like. But yes … for now I am quite grateful to be off to tend to Farran."

She nodded to her guard, and without further conversation Cal left, off in a hurry to see about his horse. The room was still in the wake of his leaving, and long moments passed as she considered all that she had been told by this unexpected group of travelers. Finally, she broke the silence. "Tell me then, daughter of Aius, what news can you give me of the Sorceress?"

Astyræ spoke of the desolation of the Wreath. She told her of the marching of great armies through the north, and of the hunting for the hidden refuge of Shaimira.

"And what of this new colony of Illium's kind?" the queen asked her. "It is absurd to think that she would allow such an outpost to thrive upon these shores."

"I would say," Astyræ replied as she considered the words of the queen, "that it is only a matter of time before she insists that the Tree Men accept her as their Queen."

"That is also my thought," she said in agreement. "I am grateful that the Giver of Light has granted us these mountains of hope, to keep us safe and to shield us from her lust."

"And how is it, Queen Johanna, that her dragons have never espied this place?" Astyræ asked. "In all their ravenous searching, have they never turned their attention to these mountains?"

"These mountains are larger than one would think, stretching leagues into the north. And they are more and more inhospitable the higher they climb into the cold air," the queen answered. "Our hidden city is but a torch hidden beneath a stone cleft. The light cannot reach the sky above."

"Queen Johanna," Deryn said as he flitted up to meet her gaze. "If I may be so bold as to speak … do not put your trust in these mountains alone, for though they have been your cleft to rest in, they are not your salvation."

She listened to the words of the magical creature, and although she wished him to be wrong, she did not disregard his winged wisdom.

"Your strength has been preserved, and it has grown and flourished here, but only at the will of our Great Father." Deryn continued. "Do not forget that it has been preserved for a purpose."

"I hear your warning, master Sprite, and I will consider it with due gravity," she told them. "But while we have these mountains to hope in, they will afford you and your friends the rest you will need. So please, accept my hospitality and rest easy."

The queen nodded at her attendant, a tall dark-haired young man whose beard had just begun to come in, and gave her command. "Alexio here will see to it that you have what you need: clothing, food and drink, but most importantly... rest."

"Yes, Lord Johanna," Astyræ said gratefully. "Thank you."

"He will see to it that there is room enough for Cal as well," she continued. "Now, go, and I will find you on the morrow."

With that, the young attendant led the lady and the Sprite out, beyond the flowing curtains and down the stone steps, past the portico and into the heart of this strange and beautiful city.

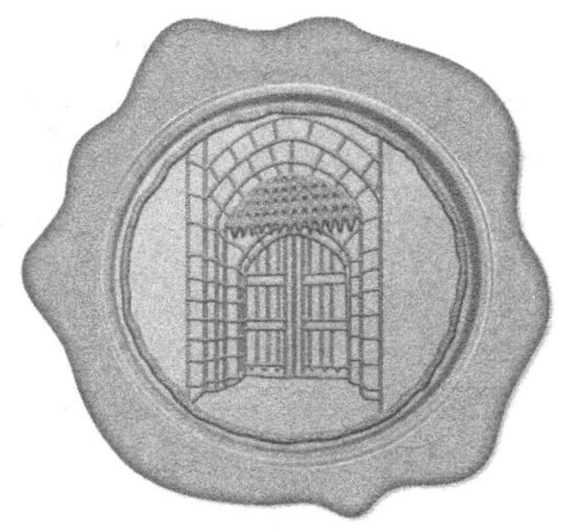

Chapter Twenty-Two

The remnant followed in the footsteps of the giant, Vŏlker, though Georgina had eagerly ridden upon his right shoulder. The winding, mountain road turned to the northeast until a massive grey-stoned keep halted their passage.

The stronghold spanned the breadth of the roadway, and its walls seemed to be carved right out of the mighty mountains that stood high on either side. At the very center of the façade stood an enormous portcullis. The black iron of the gate was pocked and aged, but with no sign of rust or decay. It stood taller than four grown men, while walls bereft of banners and pageantry, rose over a hundred hands high into the cold, blowing night.

"What in the damnable dark is this place?" Portus asked aloud.

"It looks as if it grew right out of the mountainside!" Georgina exclaimed.

"Vŏlker?" Michael said warily. "What is this place? I have never heard of castles in the mountains, nor of anything of much significance out beyond the walls of our city."

"Never heard of castles in the mountains?" Vŏlker said, beside himself with amazement at the notion. "This is the most famous of all the mountain castles!" His large hand made a great show of display. "Well," he said, scratching his head as he thought longer on his own words, "that might not be rightly true; though it is the most important one to me, it is."

"Why is that, master giant?" Celrod said with great interest.

"Well ... this is me home!" Vŏlker told them with a sad smile. "This was me and me Hlíf's home."

Georgina patted his scarred, bearded cheek, doing her little girl best to soothe his grieving heart. "Does it have a name? This place, I mean?"

"It looks as if it has been here for ages," Timorets said in wide-eyed wonder.

"Have you ever in all your days seen such a design?" Celrod marveled.

"Aye," Vŏlker answered. "Halvard it is called, the *Guardian of the Rock*... that is what me father said it means." He surveyed the keep he had spent all of his life taking great care of.

"Did you build it?" Georgina asked innocently.

"No, girl!" he said with a deep, echoing laugh. "Mågąn have not the skill for such finery, ha. No ... Halvard was built by the king of long ago."

"The king?" Michael asked. "Which king do you mean?"

"Ha!" the giant said with comedic disdain in his voice. "The first king! The only king that Vŏlker and me father ever served. Æðelric was his name, the high king of Terriah he was called." He spoke with a reverent whisper. "His sons, Faramund and Ermendrud, Vŏlker had little love for. But Æðelric was a good king ... was friend to Mågąn."

"Terriah?" Celrod said in wonder. "Then ... then it must be a thousand years old, this place."

"Four hundred and sixty-three years old," the giant answered proudly. "That is if me remembers rightly. It was built by the first king, and he told me father's father to care for it, and to keep a sharp eye for all who wanted passage through its gate." The giant sighed a deep, saddened sigh as he continued. "And that's what me father's father, and me father, and me did … until those Ravens stole their way through."

"What was it for?" Michael asked. "I mean, why … why did the King of Terriah build this place out here in the midst of these mountains?"

"Why … to guard against the wilderness is why, boy," Völker said matter-of-factly.

"The wilderness?" Michael asked sincerely.

"Are ye daft?" Völker said incredulously as he lowered Georgina to the ground. "Just beyond that gate is the only stretch of land in all the world that connects our part of it to their part of it."

"What are you talking about, master giant?" Celrod asked in earnest.

Völker sat down and furrowed his sizable brow, confused at these strangers who did not know the makeup of their own homelands. "Out there," he said as he pointed to the west, "is nothing but the black waters of the Dark Sea, for as far as ye can behold; but there is… this one strip of land that connects the wilderness of the west to this, me home."

"So the Ravens, then … they came from the wilderness?" Fryon asked.

"Aye, murdering me Hlíf," Volker growled.

"And burning our city and killing our brothers," Timorets chimed in.

"Me swears by the bones of King Æðelric, that when those *damned* Ravens turn feather and head for their home, vengeance will be mine!" The giant pounded the ground below him.

"They are coming back?" asked Georgina, frightened at the thought.

"Völker?" the lady Margarid asked, kindly trying to discourage this kind of conversation as she walked closer to the seated giant. "Is there a fire inside, some place for us to warm our tired bones and rest our tired feet? We have been walking for days upon days and have not received the slightest bit of hospitality from anyone."

"She is right," Michael agreed. "We would be grateful if we could rest a bit, at least until we gather our strength for the rest of the journey."

Vŏlker thought on their words as a sad smile broke out upon his bearded face. "Me sad that me Hlíf is not here to meet ye; she always wanted to have a visitor or two." He rose to his feet and dusted off his large pants. "Aye, there is a hearth inside, big enough to roast a whole bull on a single spit, it is … if there were still bulls in these rock lands to hunt. Ye all can rest. And then, when yer bones are less weary, ye can tell me where it is ye are journeying to."

"Aye," Michael said as he placed a friendly hand upon the leg of the giant.

"Thank you, master giant." Margarid said. "My friends and I are grateful, indeed."

"Alright, then," he said, blushing at the gratitude of this tiny, auburn-haired woman. "Warm yer bones and rest yer feet."

The giant led them through a tall door opening just to the left of the large, iron gate. They walked up a flight of steps that ran parallel to a few enormously deep steps, which Vŏlker ascended with little effort. Finally, he led them into a massive hall with a roaring fire burning in its oversized hearth.

"Oh, it's wonderful!" Georgina exclaimed as the warmth met the coldness of her cheeks.

"It is, indeed," Michael said, feeling the strength returning to his road-weary body.

"Aye," Vŏlker said as he surveyed these strangers. "Me have a blanket, maybe two that ye can use; but we are all out of straw since the animals are gone."

"Thank you," Margarid said with a smile.

"Ye can sleep here if it suits ye," He piled the old, patchwork blankets near the hearth. He looked into their eyes and knew that indeed these were the good kind of people in this darkened world. "Alright then … get some rest."

And with that, the giant left the hall, walking up the back spiral stairs into his bedchamber in the tower above them.

"Do you think this is safe?" Harmier asked warily.

"He could have killed us a hundred times over already," Fryon said.

"Agreed," said Celrod. "We are not his enemy."

Margarid looked about, her eyes tracing the beautifully carved stone, the craftsmanship of the cobbled floors and ornate masonry about the roaring fire. "Can you believe this place? I do wish Engelmann could see it. Do you think he knew someplace like this existed in the world?"

Michael came over to her, and took her slender frame in his arms. "I think he knew a lot more about Aiénor than we could even begin to guess."

"Margarid?" the little girl asked.

She lifted her head from Michael's shoulder and found the worried eyes of Georgina. "Yes, dear?"

"What happens if they come back?" she said nervously. "The Ravens, I mean."

"We will be safe here, girl," Michael tried to intervene. "These walls are big, and besides, we have a giant that is looking out for us now."

"It wasn't safe for his Hlíf, was it though?" she said as tears began to stream down her face.

Margarid looked up at Michael, telling him with her eyes that she would handle this from here on out. She walked over to the little girl, laying down beside her and holding her close. "You are right, but things are different for us here."

"Oh?" Georgina asked through muffled tears. "How so?"

"The giant has us looking out for him, too," Margarid said as she kissed the top of her head. "Now, don't worry. It is high time we all get some rest."

The remnant of Haven slept deep and well, their bodies far beyond the point of exhaustion. There, in the hall of the Halvard, by the light of its great hearth, they found peace.

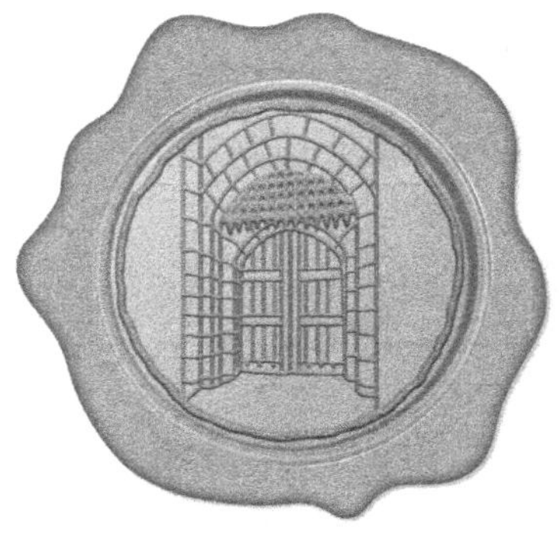

Chapter Twenty-Three

Michael woke with a startle, fully expecting to have slept long past his appointed watch at camp. When his eyes acclimated to the warm glow of the room, he let out a relieved breath and wiped the sleep out of his eyes.

"Me trust ye slept well, Michael." Vŏlker said as he tended a delightful smelling cauldron by the fire.

"Huh," Michael said with a lilt to his voice. "That is probably the first real sleep any of us has had in far too many days. Thank you, Vŏlker, for your hospitality."

"Me Hlíf would have had it no other way," he said, his eyes still red with fresh tears in them. "Besides, a friend can be found if our enemies are the same, aye?"

Michael patted his enormous back as he peered over to look into the fire at what the giant was stirring. "That smells good. What is that, there?" he asked hungrily.

"There is not much meat here in the Halvard, not much by way of food really at all; just some dried corn and beans and some fish that me salted some time ago," Vŏlker told him. "But what we lack in vittles, we more than make up for in wine. See, the first king had a great cellar filled to overflowing with barrels upon barrels of it."

"Wine?" Michael asked excitedly.

"Aye, good wine at that," he said with a wink. "And with a few of me Hlĺf's tricks and spices, well ... me thought this would warm ye and yer friends right to yer toes. Besides ... it seems like such a waste to dirty her mulling pot for just meself."

"Thank you, Vŏlker. I thank the THREE who is SEVEN that my friends and I happened upon you; though I am sad for the circumstances of it all," Michael told him as he reached out his hands to accept the horn of mulled wine that the giant offered him.

"Circumstances, indeed," the giant said as he wiped his sniffling nose on the woolen sleeve of his tunic.

"Tell me this," Vŏlker said after a long, silent moment between them. "Where are ye and yer kind headed to? Hundreds of years have gone by since we have seen a single soul out here in the pass. And now, since the whole damn world went dark, there is not much friendly in these parts."

Michael took a sip of his steaming wine, color and life coursing through his body with the fantastic, fragrant flavors of this small gift. "North," he said with an unsure sigh.

"North?" Vŏlker tried to understand. "Just ... north?"

"A friend, a teacher really, died saving us from the Ravens," Michael began to tell the giant. "A great magic was in him, and it is by that same magic that we are alive today." Michael heard the room stirring as his friends began to wake from their much-needed sleep. "The last thing he told us, before the magic left him, was to go north. And so, we have gone north."

Vŏlker thought on his story as the rest of Michael's friends came towards the sweet, warm smells of his Hlĺf's mulling pot. He smiled and poured horn after horn of the warm drink, receiving the gratitude of these strangers. For the first time Võlker could remember, this great hall of his home felt alive and full and vibrant with laughter, just as he thought a great hall should feel.

"Thank you, master giant," Georgina said with a wide smile as she took the smallest of horns to drink from.

"Indeed, little one," Võlker said with a smile in return.

He let out a decided huff and rose to his feet, towering three times over the tallest of them. "Me don't know yer friend and teacher, but me doesn't think there is much more beyond these walls that is worth risking your necks to find."

The remnant looked at one another, curious as to what this giant was trying to say.

Võlker grumbled to himself, frustrated that his point was not being understood. "Halvard is big enough for me and the whole lot of ye, too. This may not be North enough for ye ... but ... ye can make it home for as long as ye like."

Margarid gave him a grin and a grateful nod of her head. "That might be the happiest news any of us has heard in months."

The remnant and the giant spent the better part of the day sharing stories and touring the inner chambers of the mighty stone keep. In what had once been a great kitchen, Fryon discovered a fountain where cool, clear water spilled over into a stone carved pool. It stood in front of a row of bricked ovens that, in their former glory, had baked bread for the men who had once been stationed here.

Barracks and washrooms, now mostly empty storehouses, were all found on the opposite side of the large gate, but it was the small stable that filled the remnant with the most hope.

"Goats!" Portus exclaimed when he happened upon it. "All is not lost after all!"

"Aye," Võlker said with pride in his eyes. "And there be a hog or two; though they are too skinny these days. Me Hlíf milked the goats and managed to make cheese after a while... but Me is ashamed to say it; Me don't rightly know how to do much more than feed 'em and eat 'em."

"Well, don't you worry then master giant," Michael said with a hopeful smile. "We will tend to them for you; we might even find a way to fatten them up a bit."

Their spirits rose over the next days. The women tended to the few animals and saw to the arranging of the supplies and beds within the old castle; the men brought what wood, roots, berries, and brambles they could scavenge from around the surrounding land.

Timorets was especially pleased when he came upon a great hive of bees hidden within the rotting trunk of an old gnarled hemlock tree, just beyond the north side of the great gate. He clothed himself from head to toe and with great effort he managed to remove a sizable piece of the comb from the angry swarm of bees. "Mead!" he told his friends through a swollen smile, punctuated by the stings he had received for such a prize. "I'll make us the finest mead this keep has ever seen!"

Laughter and hope were nearly palpable in the air about them as they all explored and worked hard through the glow of their violet hope. Singing could be heard throughout the halls, and even Vŏlker joined in on the unexpected merriment.

Celrod found a small room at the top of the eastern tower, its shelves lined with scrolls and tomes from the people of Terriah. He spent his time pouring over the ancient words, fascinated to learn of all that had befallen them.

"Did you know that this place was first meant to guard against the Mågąn, Vŏlker's kind?" the old schoolmaster explained. "The first king thought them too hostile, and was afraid they would indeed wage war upon their settlement out here in the mountains. But after years of peace, he opened its leagues to befriend the giants."

"I can see why they were afraid at first," Harmier said, still rather uncomfortable with the notion of giants living in this previously uncomplicated world of his. "But I am glad they are the peaceful kind of giants."

And so it was that as the days went on, the hospitality of the first king was still beating true within the heart of this outpost as the ancient friendship was rekindled between Mågąn and men.

"Michael," Vŏlker said one day, happy to have these people of Haven living in his home. "Me would like to show ye something." He led Michael and Fryon up the spiral stairs, past his own bedchamber, and into the lowest room of the western tower.

"Me can't rightly fit in there, but... me never really had a need to. But ye and yer kind might could use some of it." He pointed to an iron-clad, wooden door.

Michael and Fryon looked each to the other, curiosity dancing upon their hopeful faces. "What is in there, Vŏlker?" Michael asked.

"Go on, then, and see for yerselves," the giant urged.

Fryon pulled hard against the iron hinge that had been little used for ages, and as the door swung noisily open, what they beheld filled their hearts with promise.

"I was wondering, you know," Fryon said to Michael as the two of them entered the armory of the ancient keep. "Though I was afraid to ask, being that we are guests and all."

"Can you believe it?" Michael asked as the bronze colored armor caught and reflected the light of the flickering torches. "Vŏlker!" Michael shouted back through the opened door and into the stairwell. "There must be a dozen suits of armor and nearly twice that in spears and bows." He removed the oiled skins that covered their deadly points.

"Aye!" Vŏlker replied. "Though me doubts that any would have fit me or me Hlíf!" he said with a laugh.

Fryon had found nearly a dozen quivers of arrows, with faded fletching that had once been dyed a brilliant yellow.

"I have seen this kind before," Michael said to Fryon. "There, look... the armor. It looks like folded, bronzed feathers. Cal was wearing the very same kind when he and I rode to Abondale, before the fall. I thought it looked strange, nothing like the armor of Haven's guardsmen. It felt odd, peculiarly out of place ... now I know why."

"You don't think he was here before, do you?" Fryon asked.

"No, not here," Michael mused. "But surely he must have found this other place Vŏlker spoke of."

"Come on, we had better tell the others—" Fryon's words fell short as an all-too-familiar sound stole the excitement from his mouth.

BAROOM.

The loud, sickening bellow sounded: the horns of the Raven Army.

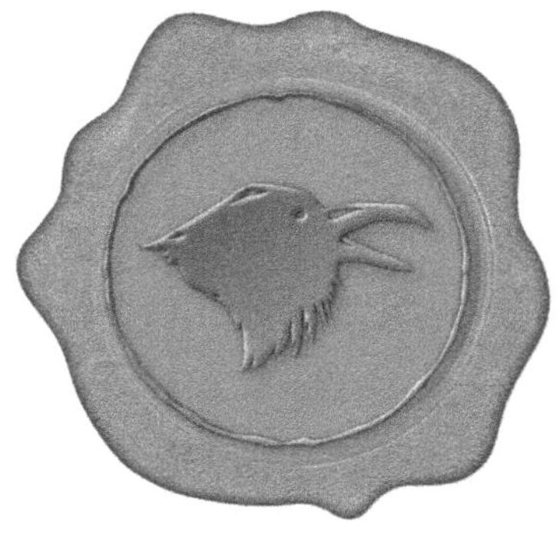

Chapter Twenty-Four

Ever since Pyrrhus had watched the two dragons rip the woodcutter in two, he had not been able to manage to keep much more than bread from churning violently in the restless bile of his worried bowels.

He rode with a few of his knights and Yasen as they searched the wooded wilderness, searching along the tree line of the woodcutter's vanguard.

"Captain!" came the shouted excitement of one of Pyrrhus' mounted guardsmen.

"What is it?" the fire knight said, with little excitement in his voice.

"We have found something," the guardsmen offered.

Pyrrhus looked over to Yasen. The face of the North Wolf showed little emotion since those damned dragons breathed their witchery over him. He mistrusted Yasen, the Raven Queen, and this whole unsettling business; but he knew he too had much work to do if he was going to fall back into the good graces of the lot of them.

"Does this look familiar, North Wolf?" Pyrrhus said with exasperation.

Yasen looked about and saw the mouth of the cave where once the girl and Goran had been sent to hide. "Aye, it does," he offered blankly.

"Well, well ... now the dog has the scent, huh?" the fire knight quipped. "Come on, let's be done with this already. I don't know why my men and I are the ones who have to retrieve before we get our reward. You are the damned dog who let them loose to begin with." He growled as he spoke, still wounded in more places than his flesh.

They rode cautiously up to the inhospitable cave, its blackness extending into the depths. "Do you see that?" one of the guardsmen said with frightened awe. "The torch light ... it just *disappears* in there. No shadows, not even the hint of a flame."

"They are not here," Yasen said matter-of-factly.

"Oh, is that so?" Pyrrhus said as he puffed out his chest and bumped Yasen with the stump of his arm.

"Aye," Yasen said as his one eye met the maddened gaze of the fire knight. "And no, I don't know where they are, but I do know they are no longer here in this cave."

"And just how convenient is that?" Pyrrhus jabbed. "For all we know they could be lying in wait, right there beyond the mouth of the cave itself. "

"By all means, please feel free to explore and waste our Queen's precious time," Yasen said flatly. "Ah ... but then, you have not been given this gift of sight yet, have you?" he said with contempt in his voice. "Who is the dog here, fire knight? The one who does his master's bidding, or the one who still begs for scraps from the table of her favor?"

"We could run you through right now, and say that the beasts got you," Pyrrhus spat as he seethed in anger.

"But then, who would help you see, when you haven't the sight to see on your own?" Yasen retorted as he bent down to finger the prints in the ground. "They are not here, because they have gone North. Their trail leads that way." He pointed off into the wilderness.

"To your mounts," Pyrrhus growled again. "The dog has found the scent of the other mongrels."

The small scouting party left in pursuit of the fleeing woodcutters, though they were not alone in their mission. Perched high in the trees above them sat a murder of Ravens, whose glowing, green eyes beheld the progress of the men who did their Queen's bidding.

"Caw!" came the cry of a black bird as it flew back towards the stronghold on the shore. It flew past the tree line and traversed the plains till its wings carried it over the palisade walls and it landed upon the shoulder of Nogcwren herself.

"Well there you are, my pet," the Sorceress cooed as she sat in the court of the colony, at the head of a nearly empty table. "As loyal a servant as any queen could hope for."

The mood of the colony was dark, and though fires still burned in the braziers for the men who had not been given the gift of her un-light, it was plain for all to see who it was that ruled this stronghold. The dragons lay curled in the center of the square, their massive, inky bodies guarding the entrance and the exit of the gate. All who dared to pass must do so under the watch of their hateful, glowing eyes.

"My dear Governor," she said with great delight in her voice. "It would seem that this North Wolf has found the trail of these woodcutters of yours."

"Your Raveness," he said with an exaggerated flourish of his hands. "All of my men, the enlightened and those still stumbling in the darkness, aim to serve you well."

"*My* men," she replied.

"My Queen?" he asked, confused at the notion.

"You meant to say, *my men*, did you not?" she said, her yellowed eyes a tumult of rage.

"Of course, my Queen," Seig said humbly.

"Captain Durai," she said, her eyes not moving from Seig's as she spoke. "Make ready the whole of my strength ... the might of Aerebus must be ready to march! For when Governor Seig's men find the misplaced woodcutters ... I am quite *confident* that they will have led us to the last stronghold of our enemy."

"Yes, my queen," the hulking captain said with rueful obedience as he turned and walked past the sleeping dragons and out into the encampment of his Nocturnal army.

"I suppose it would do you well to muster the rest of your own command, Governor," she ordered him as she drank deeply from a chalice of steaming wine. "I do expect these men of Haven to fight quite bravely for my cause ... that is, if they hope to receive the gift that I have so graciously given you."

"Yes, my Queen," Seig said. "We shall indeed fight more bravely than you have ever seen before, and I'll be there, sword in hand, leading the charge." He rose from the table and left her to her own thoughts and pleasures as she brooded over the battle that was soon to come.

***

Yasen and Pyrrhus followed the trail through the Greywood for days, finally coming into the rocky highlands. "They might be days ahead of us, but your woodcutters did not travel as stealthily as they may wish they had once we find them," Pyrrhus said with determination in his eyes.

The fens of the river Argiñe began to reach cold, wet fingers into the hard ground about them as the riders continued to move northward.

"Captain!" came the whispered voice of a sentry who held his hand high.

"Do you see them?" Pyrrhus asked.

The guardsman shook his head and pointed at a group of trees a hundred or so paces to the east.

As they looked into the distance, the smell of fire and stew carried upon the thick fog. Whether these were aromas from the woodcutters or not, Pyrrhus still had an intuition that whoever was here would know where to find the ones he sought.

The fire knight dismounted, and Yasen and the rest of the riders followed suit. "What do you see, North Wolf?" Pyrrhus asked.

"It is too hard to tell for sure," Yasen answered as he peered into the darkness before them. "One stacked chimney, maybe more—"

"You have the gift and can't even use it properly," Pyrrhus cursed and spat.

"I can see in the dark, but I still haven't the eyes of an eagle," Yasen argued as he made his way closer and closer, his hand at the handle of his axe.

"Stop, right there!" came a shout from somewhere in the clearing.

Yasen signaled to Pyrrhus. The guardsmen fanned out to surround the clearing.

"We mean no harm," Pyrrhus said as his hand gripped the hilt of his blade.

"How do I know that?" a man shouted back. "Five riders near the Argiñe? I don't trust it, not at all."

"We are looking for some lost friends of ours is all, good sir," Pyrrhus continued as he and the rest of the company closed in their circle with measured steps.

"What friends would five riders have all the way out here?" he continued.

"Puppa!" came a shout just off to the right, followed by the unmistakable sound of a drawn bowstring.

"We do not mean you harm," Yasen said, his voice even. "We are looking for our friends and would like your help in finding them."

"How do you know they came this way?" the man shouted nervously. "Be off my land now, before I fill you full of these arrows!"

"We know because I tracked them here," Pyrrhus said, his eyes alert. "Put your bow down, old man, before you do something you won't live to regret."

Just then, guardsmen came crashing out from behind the trees and charged the small cluster of thatch-roofed homes. Arrows went zipping through the air, most flying wild against the onslaught.

"Delilah! Mother!" the man shouted out. "Get back inside!"

The guardsmen came in closer, surrounding the lone man who stood at the center of the clearing with a great huntsman's bow drawn taught.

"There are no friends of yours here," he growled at the intruders. "It's just me and my family, and you are not welcome. Off now ... begone with you!"

One of the guardsmen took another step forward, his boot crunching against the twigs and rocks of the ground. Without warning, an arrow discharged from across the clearing and buried itself into the shoulder of the now-bleeding guardsman. In an instant the scene boiled over, and the rest of the guardsmen rushed the man with the bow, swords brandished and voices shouting. Another arrow was loosed, barely missing Yasen's face. Screams and the sounds of struggle could be heard off in the shadows.

"Do not kill them!" Yasen shouted at the two guardsmen who had just tackled the man with the bow. "We need them alive!"

Pyrrhus and another of his guardsmen held a boy, maybe fifteen or sixteen years of age. The bow that had loosed the first arrow lay broken at his struggling feet.

"Now, are there any other sons of yours out here in the trees?" Pyrrhus said as they dragged the boy to the center of the clearing.

The father just shook his head. His face, pressed into the dirt, was a mash of fear and hatred as the guardsman held him pinned to the ground. "Please," he said through gritted teeth, "he is just a boy. He didn't know any better."

"Tell that to my man over there who is bleeding from his wounded shoulder," Pyrrhus said as he spat.

"My wife," the man in the dirt said. "She has the touch of the healer about her. She can mend him up, good as new. Only... don't hurt the boy."

Pyrrhus glared, then nodded his agreement. "Go on then, call for her."

"Dani!" the man called out. "Mahlah shot one of the men in the shoulder. Come quick, and see to the wound."

A skinny woman, whose once-dark hair had been run through with shocks of grey and white, peeked her head out of the humble doorway. She held the shoulders of her daughter and looked on with fright in her eyes at the sight of her husband and son bound by the strangers in armor.

"Are you alright, father?" the young girl asked worriedly.

"I won't be if you don't help these men," he scolded.

The guardsman pulled him up to his knees as the woman nodded her agreement and went to fetch her tools.

"Are you alright?" Pyrrhus shouted over to his wounded man.

Before he could begin to answer, he was interrupted by the frantic bustling of the woman. She removed the arrow and packed the wound with a poultice of herbs and oils, and within moments had the man's shoulder wrapped and cleaned. When she was done, she let out an exhausted, frustrated sigh and turned to address these strangers.

"There ... he will mend, though he will need to change his bandages when you return to wherever you came from."

"We thank you for that, however ... we won't be heading back to *anywhere*, not until you tell me where we can find our *friends*," Pyrrhus told her.

"Like I told you before," the man said, his eyes pleading now. "We haven't seen anyone out here for quite some time. It's just us."

"And how is it you and your family live out here on your own?" Pyrrhus pressed. "This is the Queen's land, isn't it? And it doesn't appear to me that you have taken her gift, either."

The woman's face went white as she looked to her husband and then again back to her children for sign of what to do.

"It is simple, really," Yasen chimed in. "We know that our friends came this way. If you spotted the five of us before we spotted you, I'm sure that you spotted nearly forty large men."

"He said we didn't see 'em!" the boy shouted.

"Out of this, boy!" the man growled back. "You've made enough mess for now."

"We know you have seen them, because that axe right there, buried in the flesh of that pine stump, came all the way from across the Dark Sea." Yasen spoke dully as he walked over to the pile of freshly chopped timber. "Now is the time when you tell us what it is that we need to know."

"Who are you?" the man said, the fire of his resolve diminished. "I've never seen your colors, nor your sigil. And you don't have the eyes of the Sorceress?"

"Never you mind," Yasen said sternly as he picked up the axe and in a single fluid motion launched it at the old man.

"Father, no!" came the cry of the woman, but the blade of the axe buried itself not a hand's breadth from the crotch of the kneeling man.

"They went that way, along the Argiñe River towards the falls!" Delilah blurted out, not caring to protect the strangers who got her into this mess in the first place.

"Girl, shut your mouth," the father said half-heartedly.

"Why?" Yasen pressed. "What were they seeking, did they say?"

"They were looking for the man and the woman, Cal was his name I think," she told them willingly. "And they had a fairy, too."

"Have they come back this way?" Pyrrhus asked.

"No," she said with a scowl on her brow. "Fools probably got swept up in the river and went over the falls."

"We've told all we know," the old man argued. "Now let us be ... please."

"*She* has told us what we asked *you* to tell us," Pyrrhus corrected the man, and with a flip of his head he signaled one of the guardsmen to bring his torch over to him. "Now you will get your reward for treachery against the queen."

With that he tossed the torch onto the roof of the main house, and a roar of fire erupted as the flames greedily licked the dry thatch. Screams and shouts of protest could be heard from the whole family.

The guardsmen shoved the boy into the dirt and then turned to mount their horses. "Be warned," Yasen said coldly. "The Queen and her army will be soon upon these lands. Take her gift, or hide somewhere else."

With the house of Delilah ablaze, and the light of the fire stretching out before them, Pyrrhus, Yasen, and the guardsmen rode out in the direction of the river.

"Can you manage?" Yasen asked the wounded and bandaged guardsman.

"I will be alright," he replied through grunts of wounded exhaustion.

"Sir," came the voice of another guardsman. "You should send him back to the stronghold to tell the governor what we have found."

"I am not sending a wounded servant to report such news, and I am certainly not reporting it to the governor." The fire knight's contempt seethed on each word. "My report will be for the Queen and the Queen alone. You three ride to the falls and track the bastards down. When I return, it will be with the Queen's army!"

Pyrrhus kicked his horse and with a loud, "Yah!"

He and the wounded guardsman rode south, back towards the stronghold. Yasen and the others continued on their way along the southern back of the Argiñe, tracking the trail of the woodcutters.

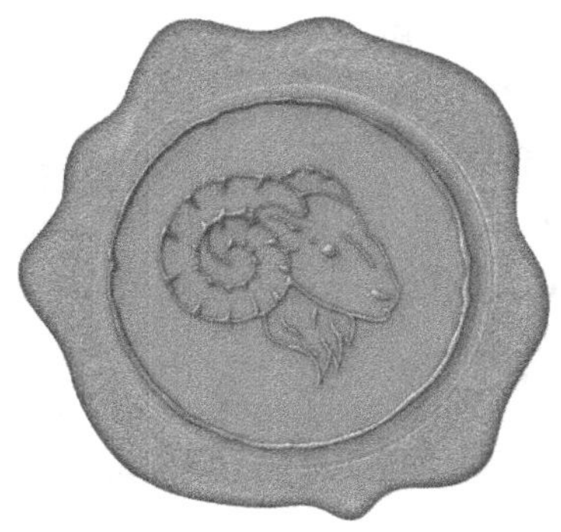

Chapter Twenty-Five

"He has been like this for far too long now," Astyræ told the queen. "He hasn't left that place except to sleep and to eat, and just barely at that."

"He is grieving a terrible loss," Johanna reassured her with a soft hand upon her shoulder.

"I'm worried for him," she said, her violet eyes misting over in grief for the groomsman who held her affections. "He can't just waste away like this. Farran's death will be in vain if he just gives up like this."

"I wouldn't say that he has given up, my lady," Deryn kindly disagreed. "I have seen grief befall the bravest of warriors, and I think—"

"He is lost," Deryn's words were interrupted by the Queen. "Finding this city but losing a friend in the process would make even the stoutest of heart unsure of the next step."

"Will you talk to him, Queen Johanna?" Astyræ begged." I feel as if I am just making it worse."

"Yes," she answered. "I will speak with him." With that Johanna strode eastward, on past the outskirts of the city's clearing to the Weeping Woods in the shadow of the mountains. She saw Cal there, just inside the tree line, his back against a great elm. His golden-haired head was staring straight ahead at the carved, white, stone marker atop the mound of a gravesite.

"I should have been there," he said flatly as she approached. "I should have been with him, he was my horse, my responsibility."

"There was nothing else you could have done for him, Cal," Johanna reasoned.

"I should have been with him, instead of answering a bunch of questions just to appease your laws," he continued.

"The mightiest of our healers employed her greatest craft, and still your Farran succumbed to the Sorceress' poison," she argued. "What would you have done, son of Haven, that would have been greater than what Aysa could do?"

"I would have told him, *thank you,*" he said, his tear-streaked face turning to meet her gaze. "I would have made sure that he knew how deeply I cared for him. I would have at least kissed his head and told him goodbye before he passed."

Cal rose to his feet, his swelling grief beginning to boil over into anger.

"I did not kill your friend," Johanna said as she stepped closer to him.

"But you did not allow me the chance to honor him as he died!" Cal nearly shouted. "Did you?"

Johanna was not afraid of the tumult of emotions behind the eyes of the young man, and she held his gaze. The mercy and grace of this true queen was unrelenting, even in the face of accusation.

"Do you know why he is buried here?" she asked.

Cal didn't answer, but he refused to hide his indignant eyes from hers.

"Walk with me," she ordered kindly as she began to walk deeper into the forest before them. "Of all the peoples who have found their way to this refuge city of ours, the most mysterious to our kind were the sons of

Haven. The *Tree Men,* as the young lady friend of yours calls them. They dwelt with us for a time, though they themselves were never wholly Amaian as we are; they sought after the very same legend that you, Cal, seek even now."

Cal followed her footsteps, past the carved image of the white stone horse, and into another small clearing surrounded by a forest of trees. He saw grave markers all about them through the mist that clung to the forest floor, adorned with swords, ships, and even an image of the great tree of Haven.

"So, when these sons of Haven passed out of this darkening world and into the realm of the Giver of Light, we saw it only fitting to lay them to rest among their own." She continued to speak as she stopped before a marker of the great tree. "I was but a young girl at the beginnings of womanhood when your King Illium was laid to rest here in the *Zuhaitz Dolu,* the mourning trees. All of the sons of Haven are buried here, at the easternmost part of our hidden kingdom, closest to their homeland."

Cal's eyes went wide at the story she was telling him. "Are you saying that Illium the light seeker, the lost king of Haven, is buried here?" he asked, hardly believing that this could be true.

"Yes. Yes, I am, Cal," she said with a gracious smile. "Though I would not say that he was lost in the slightest."

He turned his head back towards the grave marker and let his trembling fingers trace the long-ago etched runes.

The seeker of light, Illium. King of Haven, Lord beyond the waters of the mighty Itsaso.

"Is it really you?" he said to the old grave marker, his grief momentarily overwhelmed by wonder.

Cal spun round in a whirlwind of excitement as the boyishly hopeful thoughts crashed into the forefront of his mind. "What about his men? Were there others? Did they make it here with him?"

"Have you not been listening?" she said kindly. "All of these markers are the sons of Haven... and some are the wives and children of the sons of Haven."

Cal looked back at the markers and then again at Johanna, confusion wrinkling his brow. "They were the daughters of Shaimira, whose hearts and fates became interwoven with your kind," she told him.

"Are they all gone?" he asked.

"Illium's men? Yes. They have long since been laid to rest," She told him. "But there are still those with mingled blood in the city. "Navid, grandson of Payam, is chief of the Ramsguard, and there is Gelinda, granddaughter of Barkas, who has been tending to you and your friends. Everard had many sons, and so did Dacain-"

"Did Illium?" Cal asked, interrupting the Queen. "I mean, did he ever take another wife from among your people?"

She smiled softly at the young man. "No, he never did. My father always told me that when he asked the King why not, Illium would always respond with the same answer."

"And what was that?" Cal asked.

"That he already had a wife, and if he could be about finding this light he sought, he hoped to get back to her," she told him.

This made Cal's heart both happy and sad all in the same moment, for he knew that Evande had not waited for Illium. She gave herself over to the black waters of despair and ended her waiting.

Silence hung there between them for the moment as the thoughts and implications of all that was said weighed heavy on his mind.

"I am sorry for the loss of your friend, Cal, and I am truly sorry that you were not able to say goodbye to him," she told him with sincerity in her dark eyes. "This is why we chose to bury him here, amongst the sons of Haven, alongside those who so bravely sought Illium's light."

Cal sighed a surrendering breath, the anger he had tried to hold onto exhaled at the understanding of so many things. "Thank you."

"It has been long since my people have seen the equine. We were once a proud people whose greatest delights were the braided manes of our horses and the gleams of our gilded chariots," she told him. "For us to see and care for a horse, a horse as beautiful as he was, was an honor for both me and my people."

One of the Queensguard approached them, his white cape trailed behind him in the swirling mist. "My Queen," said Mezulari with a bow of his head. "Navid has sent word from Sendoa's men; there are strangers near the pass."

She turned her head slowly, thoughtfully, to meet Cal's eyes. "Are there more of your friends that I do not know about?" she asked him, her kindness quickly replaced with a weighty caution.

"No ... none that were with me," he told her. "We left them all at the colony."

She studied him, her dark brown eyes blazing with a hundred unasked questions. She turned to speak to her guard and then thought better of it as a question formed on the tip of her tongue. "Could you have been followed?"

Cal thought on it, remembering the green-eyed ravens, the band of Nocturnals that had found their camp, the timber wolves that had attacked them, and the little girl they had rescued along the way.

"It is possible ... though we have been traveling for a very long time, and—" He tried to explain, but she had already turned her attention to the messenger.

"Have the Ramsguard at the ready behind the wall, half held in reserve," she ordered with a quick and deliberate cadence to her voice. "And have Sendoa and his guardians beyond the gate armed and ready to protect it at all cost."

Mezulari bowed his obedience, turned, and quickly faded back into the mist of the forest as he left to deliver his queen's orders.

Johanna turned her attention back to Cal before she left to see about her people. "Let us hope that you were not followed, Cal," she said as she let out a worried sigh. "I pray that these strangers are not of the Sorceress, but if they are, and war is what she seeks ... then war we will give."

"How will you fight?" he asked. "If it is her, I mean?"

"For over a century, my people have been preparing for this moment," she told him, without a trace of wavering in her voice. "Our hiding has not been without purpose. If the Ravens wants Shaimira ... it will have to contend with the host of the Ram."

It was with those words that Johanna bowed her head graciously and then left Cal there in the forest with the graves and the histories of Haven.

Chapter Twenty-Six

Cal prayed that it wasn't an attack as he walked between the graves in the misty woods, reading the names of the heroes of Haven. He thought long on all they must have endured, and hoped that he, too, might continue the quest they had set out on so long ago. He stopped again to look at Illium's grave as his pulse quickened at the unbelievable sight.

The sound of a horn in the near distance rang out, bouncing off the encircling mountains and finding his ears. "Astyræ, Deryn." He startled from his reverie. "I've got to find them."

The groomsman of Haven started to run towards the carved horse that marked Farran's grave, but as he did the hairs on the back of his neck began to prickle. A flush washed over him like a fever, though he did not feel ill. He slowed his pace and continued cautiously, the mist making it hard for him to see beyond the reach of his violet gaze.

Cal instinctively reached for Gwarwyn, though it wasn't quite fear that had alerted him. He heard the sound of feet on the ground before him, but the mist clouded his vision from seeing who it was.

"Hello, there," Cal said as calmly and friendly as possible.

No response came. He walked past the large elm that towered over Farran's resting place, scanning the darkness all about him.

"Astyræ? Queen Johanna?" he asked the mist. "Sendoa, is that you?" No response came but the sound of heavy feet upon on the mossy floor. He flexed his hand and gripped the hilt of his sword. "Please, show yourself. If you are friend, you have—"

The sound of a snort caused his words to falter right on the tip of his tongue.

"What in the damnable dark?" he said aloud, but the only response was the heavy stomping of impatient feet and another exasperated snort. "Farran?" He asked in confusion. "Is that you?"

As Cal walked past the marker, the mist began to part. What stood before him there in the open space was the most beautiful beast he had ever seen. "Dear God," he whispered to himself.

"No, you are not Farran, are you?" he said calmly to the massive white horse, whose deep blue eyes threatened to peer into Cal's very soul. Cal raised his hands, his fingers splayed as he approached the magnificent creature.

The horse snorted and stamped his hoof upon the mossy dirt while Cal continued to speak soothingly, singing his words as he approached the horse. "How did you get here?" he asked curiously. "The queen said there were no horses left here in Shaimira?"

It was almost as if this horse understood the question being asked of him. All at once he took a step toward Cal and shook out two glorious, white-feathered wings. Cal stopped, his hands still splayed before him, his mouth agape in wonder. "In all my days," he said to the beast as he kneeled before the winged horse. "I have cared for and tended to hundreds of horses, but I would have never believed this … what are you?" he asked with great reverence in his voice.

The horse snorted and then bowed his own head. Cal's clouded eyes drank in the magical form of this mighty, winged horse, as a man thirsty for water after wandering long in the dry, barren land.

"My name is Cal," he said as he stood to his feet, close enough to feel the breath of the mighty creature on his face. Then he heard a word whispered in his mind.

Uriel.

"Is that your name?" Cal wondered aloud. The horse just stared at him, his large, dark eyes both fierce and kind in the same moment.

Cal reached out for him, placing one of his hands upon his soft pink nose. He felt the warm exhale of the creature's assent. "Beautiful! You are absolutely magnificent, you know that?" he said as his hands stroked the soft, white coat.

"What are you doing here, Uriel?" Cal asked as his hand slid from behind the horse's ear and onto his strong neck. As his hand found the horse's throatlatch, a surge of energy passed between them, and he began to hear the voice of the magical animal all the more clearly.

The waters of evil are rising, the time of darkness draws nigh. But do not dismay, for the faithful and the true will bring the dawn. Put not your trust in the strength of man, nor the kingdoms he has built, but seek the dawn above all else.

And with those words, the winged horse bowed its magnificent head. An explosion of power and wind erupted as Uriel unfurled his wings and climbed into the darkened sky. Cal's eyes were wide with wonder as he watched the mighty horse take to the sky before him. "Please, don't leave me!" he shouted to the ascending horse. "Please!"

But Uriel flew away without another word, and Cal was left without comfort for his wild and racing thoughts. Just then, the sound of another horn blast cut through the wonder of the moment, and Cal remembered the words of the messenger and the warning of Uriel. "Astyræ, Deryn!"

Cal took off in a sprint, out through the Weeping Woods and back into the heart of the city. He reached his room at the house of Gelinda, but found that Deryn and Astyræ were no longer there.

"The gate!" he said aloud as he fastened the ancient breastplate of Terriah over his chest and cinched his sword belt tighter about his waist.

He took off running as soon as he was armored, praying all the time that his friends were safe and that the warning of Uriel was not yet upon them. As Cal drew closer to the entrance of Shaimira, he saw hundreds of soldiers gathered in rank and file, whose ram's horned helms and bright mail over blue tunics presented a formidable greeting to whomever may have found the passage under the falls.

A blast of the horn rang again and Cal's heart began to beat wilder and more frantically in his chest. He ran through the ranks of the Ramsguard, finally spotting the golden hair of Astyræ and the tiny blue glow of Deryn there upon the battlement of the lone, stone wall. "Astyræ!" he shouted as he ran, his chest heaving with worry and exhaustion. "Astyræ, are you alright?"

His words found her ears, and both she and Deryn turned to see him running towards them.

"We are alright, Cal!" she shouted down to him.

"But the strangers!" he shouted back. "It's the Sorceress' men! The white horse told me!" he yelled without explanation as he ran closer and closer.

The Queen heard his words and turned her head in the most curious of manners as the portcullis creaked to life before him.

"No!" he shouted back. "Why are you opening the gate?"

Horns sounded and the Ramsguard began to shift their formation into two columns of men on either side of the entrance to the stronghold. "No!" Cal tried to shout above the noise, but it was of no use. The iron gate began to raise, and the guardians locked into formation with spears brandished. The keepers of the pass appeared beyond the gate, escorting the strangers they had found.

Sendoa entered first and Cal ran up to him in a panic. "Sendoa! What are you doing? This is not safe!"

"Orders of the Queen," he said, his voice and his face stoically resolved.

"But why?" Cal tried to argue. "She doesn't know what she is doing!"

"Are you saying that you have found this place, but you haven't the room or the hospitality to share it with the likes of us?" came a jovial, dramatic voice.

"What?" Cal said as he spun around to see where the familiar voice was coming from.

"Or are you just afraid that we are going to embarrass you in front of your new friends, eh?" Goran said with a wry smile.

"*Goran?*" Cal asked incredulously.

"Aye, brother," the woodcutter said. "Not just me. It's the whole lot of us here ... or at least, almost the whole lot of us."

Chapter Twenty-Seven

"Lower your weapons," Marcum ordered in pained speech.

"What do you think that light is?" Brádách said, his eyes wide with wonder. "I've never in all my days seen something so ... so, well ... pretty."

Keily just stared, her mind whirling with questions as she thought of Roshan.

"Corporal," Marcum ordered. "Take two of your men and go see if he is as friendly as we are hoping he is."

"Yes, lieutenant," the white-bearded corporal agreed.

"Keily?" came the worried voices of the children who hid underneath the ox cart.

"It's alright, children," she told them as she bent down to catch their worried gazes.

"What is that purple light?" Gabriel asked.

"Is it some kind of magic?" Annsley wondered aloud.

"I hope it's the good kind," Gabriel replied.

"Me too," she said with a smile. "Though my heart is not troubled by it. Now stay put until I tell you otherwise. Alright?"

"Alright," the children said in unison.

As the cart drew closer to the huddled remnant, Johnrey and his men went out to greet it and its driver. Marcum could see plain enough by the glow of the violet light that the corporal had removed his hand from the hilt of his sword and had reached out in greeting to the man atop the cart.

"Sheath your blades now, lads" Marcum said with exhausted relief. "The THREE who is SEVEN has sent us a rescuer ... we are going to be alright."

Johnrey returned to the remnant first, running out ahead of the cart with tears streaming down his face.

"Corporal?" Marcum asked, his brow furrowed with question.

"I've never ... never even thought to imagine," the old corporal tried to explain.

"You never what?" the lieutenant asked impatiently.

"I never imagined that anything like that ever existed in this world of ours. And here, now, of all times and places, we find something like this?" Johnrey said as tears of joy fell uncontrollably down his face.

"Pull yourself together, Corporal," Marcum said as his own eyes contagiously misted over. "I still have no idea what it is that you are blubbering about."

"Lieutenant, is it?" came the voice of the driver.

Marcum looked over the shoulder of the corporal, meeting the kind eyes of the wild-haired, old man who drove the cart. Then his gaze shifted from the unexpected driver to the violet glowing light that emanated from a creature his eyes had never dreamed to behold. There, perched atop the back of the seat of the wagon, was a silver-winged warrior whose brilliant armor looked as delicate as fishbones and as fierce as lightning flashes.

"What in the damnable dark!?" he exclaimed as the whole of his company turned to see the incredible sight.

"Lieutenant?" the old man asked again, his patience not hindered by the bewilderment of these soldiers.

Marcum swallowed, unsure of what questions he even needed to ask anymore.

"Lieutenant, my name is Elder John," he said with kindness in his aged, wrinkled face. "And this ball of brilliant light," he chuckled as he spoke, "is Faolan, Captain of the Sprite Host, commander and servant to Queen Iolanthe herself."

"What?" Marcum said with a dry, parched mouth. "Sprites?"

Faolan stood to his feet, the crystalline armor reflecting his own violet brilliance. "Lieutenant," he said with a respectful nod of his head. "I understand that my appearance may be startling to you and your people. But may I suggest we speak of lineages and long stories once we have reached safety, and not when the enemy is still at large?"

Marcum rubbed at his eyes, then turned to make sure that he was not the only one seeing this mythical creature alive and present before them. "Yes," he managed clumsily. "Yes, of course, Captain. My name is Lieutenant Marcum, and these are all that is left of the company of brave guardsmen that were under my command."

Faolan flitted up and out of the seat of the cart and flew over to meet the lieutenant face to face. "You have fought and sacrificed bravely against an enemy who knows no valor and who has earned our vengeance. Now you must rest and recover your strength; for though your battle may have finished ... the war for Aiénor has just begun."

"And what will you do, Sprite?" Marcum said, the weariness of these last days weighing heavily upon him. "What can any of us do to thwart that army of darkness whose vanguard is held by dragons?"

"Alone?" Faolan said. "Nothing. But by the power of our Great Father, and for justice and the memory of Éimhear, the slain High Queen," Faolan's face hardened, "and for all our people, both Sprite and man ... together we will strike a brilliant blow to her darkened heart."

The captain unsheathed his silver blade. As he did, a note pierced the darkness about them, and without warning the back of the mule cart exploded in a wash of violet eruption as a dozen more Sprite warriors came out of hiding. They drew their own blades, small and terrible, and the song of their vengeance echoed against the mountains to the north.

Marcum raised his wounded arm across his chest in salute to this unlooked for friend. "Are there more of your kind?" he asked.

"Many more, Lieutenant. I will escort you and your people to Petros, whereby the skills of the Poets and Eógan our healer, we will see to it that you are mended."

"Thank you," Marcum said as relief flooded his eyes.

"But what about the Ravens?" Keily blurted out. "Who is going to find them and stop them? We can't just let them go, unopposed, wherever the bloody hell they will it! Not while there may still be more of our people alive and scattered."

Brádách limped over and put a hand on her shoulder. "There now, lass." He tried to comfort her, but she slumped off his kindness and stared deep into the violet eyes of the Sprite captain.

"They will not go unopposed, Daughter of Ádhamh," Faolan replied. "Though recklessness will never produce the victory that your heart seeks."

"It is not victory that my heart seeks," she said as angry, tired tears pooled in her eyes and fell down her face. "It's vengeance. It's ... payment ... retribution for the hell they have brought upon all of us."

"Arthfael," Faolan commanded.

The large Sprite flew over to his commander and knelt before him on the damp dirt, placing the point of his blade against the ground and bowing his head to receive his orders.

"Take your company and scour the lands about the Hilgari," he ordered. "But do not reveal yourself unless no other option is present."

"Yes, Captain," Arthfael replied.

"Where did you encounter the army of the Sorceress last?" the captain asked Marcum.

"East of the North Road," he replied. "Nearly a league."

"You won't find any of them left in that heap of bones, laddie," Brádách said with a laugh. "My band of cripples, and the Priest here, we dispatched the last of them."

"He tells the truth," Marcum said, his head feeling dizzy after so much blood loss.

"They were patrolling eastward," the corporal said, interrupting the conversation. "We attacked them, not the other way around. They were marching out from the city, to only God knows where ... but it was east, alright," Johnrey said with conviction.

"Start there, Arthfael," Faolan commanded. "The city has already fallen, and though our brave woodcutter friends have aided in dispatching some of these Ravens from this world, the whole of their army is still at large. We must find them, and their dragons, and uncover their intentions if we are to stand and fight them."

"Yes, my captain," the large Sprite bowed his head and addressed his company. In a whirl of silver and violet, the twelve shot to the sky in search of the Raven army.

"They are beautiful, aren't they?" Annsley whispered beneath the cover of the wagon.

"Yes, but are they big enough to make a difference?" Gabriel asked.

"I sure hope so," she replied.

"My dear lady," Faolan addressed Keily with all the sincerity in his violet eyes. "Once we find them, we will not let their evil go unrequited. Of that, you may rest assured."

"Now, if you don't mind me interrupting." Elder John spoke up, inserting himself into the conversation. "We still have quite a distance to travel yet before we are safely inside the halls of Petros. And there is quite a number of you that could use a good tending to."

"He is right," Marcum said exhaustedly, turning to Elder John. "The THREE who is SEVEN has smiled down upon us with your kindness, and we would be fools not to heed it."

"But Marcum?" Keily protested.

"Gather the children and the wounded and see to it that they make their way into one these carts," he told her sternly.

Her eyes found the children under the woodcutter's cart, and when she saw them, the fire of her revenge cooled in the weight of her duty to them. "Sir?" she said to the Poet atop the cart. "There was a boy, it must have been days ago now ... I put him on a horse and sent him westward. My friend told me once of the Poets in the mountain, and I took his word to—"

"Roshan?" Elder John said.

Her eyes went wide with amazement at the very mention of his name. "You found him?"

"Well, no," Elder John replied.

Her face fell, confused all over again.

"Rather, he found us! Ha!" His laughter seemed so out of place here in the treeless outlands at the foothills of the cold Hilgari. "That boy ... well, he is the reason that the Sprites and I were even out here looking for you."

"God bless you, Roshan!" she prayed under her breath.

"Is he alright?" Ryder asked hopefully.

"Well, look here now," Elder John said with great happiness in his eyes. "Aren't you a brave little one to have traveled all this way."

"I'm brave too," Gabriel said, climbing out after her. "I have a sword that one of the guardsmen gave me. Well, it's a knife, really. But I can use it against the Ravens if they come back."

"Haha!" Elder John laughed again. "Oh ... and you must be the bravest of them all, young lady?" he said to Annsley as she put her arms around the other children's shoulders. "Keeping watch over your friends."

"But sir?" little Huckston asked. "Is Roshan alright? Did he get hurt?"

"Come see for yourself, my boy," Elder John said as he patted the seat next to him. "All of you, hop on. I have much to show you, many bright and beautiful things. And yes, your friend Roshan will be delighted to see you again."

The remnant of guardsmen, woodcutters, cripples, cooks, and the

Priest saw to it that the wounded were carefully loaded into the two carts. Those that were able walked alongside, with bows at the ready and hands upon hilts. They were grateful for the hope of someplace to rest and recover, though not trusting the passage there would be wholly safe.

As the wagon traveled the rocky paths and pitted roads of the foothills, Keily couldn't help but think about Yasen. "Oh Yasen, I hope that you are greeted by unexpected strangers ... and I pray that the hospitality you find keeps you safe enough to return home to me."

They traveled slowly, so as not to add further insult to the injured, when the ground beneath their boots began to change. The same flagstone road that Cal had traveled so long ago now took them along the base of the mighty Hilgari, up amidst the pillars and the carvings of the faded highway.

"This must be the palace that Cal was talking about," she said aloud.

"Cal?" Elder John said. "Did you say, 'Cal'?"

"Do you know him?" Keily asked the old Poet.

"Ha!" Elder John said. "Symmetry ... all the good stories have symmetry, my dear."

"I am not sure that I know what that means," she said sheepishly.

"The first time I met Cal, we rode this very same cart, drawn by Ransom, my mule, along this very same road!" Elder John said as he fondly remembered that very first encounter. "And neither he, nor any of us, for that matter, had any clue as to what we would all be getting ourselves into."

"So, it's true, then?" she asked. "This place, this ... um, Petros? It is a palace?"

He thought on her words for a moment before answering her. "It was. Well, now that I say it ... it still is. Only, it is so much more than that."

Chapter Twenty-Eight

The reunion of Cal's woodcutter brothers was both unexpected and deeply needed. "Goran!" Cal said as he embraced his old mountain of a friend. "But how? How did you find me? How did you find this place?"

"Well, it was not *that* hard, brother," said Oren.

"Aye, we just followed the stink of horses without any difficulty at all," Alon said as he came over and made a show of smelling his groomsman brother. "That's how we always know where to find you!"

Cal laughed, overjoyed to be amongst such friends and in such a place. "But tell it true, how did you find me?"

Gvidus lumbered to the front of the group to see how his watercart stowaway had faired all this time in the wilderness. "Ah, not too much the worse for wear now, are you brother?" The large-bellied woodcutter smiled, the creases in his round face punctuating his gladness at the reunion.

"You told us you were headed north, groomsman. So, when the evil storm landed upon the shores of the colony..." Goran's words trailed off as he pictured the fear that had befallen all of them that dark, damned day. "Yasen sent us off after you. Told us to find you, or if not *you*, then to find this Shaimira you had been looking for."

Cal's eyes looked at the thirty or so woodcutters, scanning their faces in search of Yasen.

"He is not with us, brother," Gvidus said sadly.

"Aye," Alon agreed somberly.

"What?" Cal said, confused about his absence. "Why not? Did that damned Pyrrhus do something?"

"What could a one-armed flicker of a knight do to the North Wolf, huh?" Oren said mockingly.

"Not if he valued his last remaining arm, that is!" came a call from the crowd.

"Aye," Goran agreed as he thumped his fist against his own chest. "It wasn't Pyrrhus; at least I don't believe it was." He rubbed his hand over his tired, road-weary face as he collected his words. "Something has happened, brother. Something bad, I fear, though we can't rightly say what."

"Something evil," Gvidus agreed. "Yasen was summoned by that fool of a governor right after the black storm crashed in on us. He told us to make for the North, but we couldn't just leave him there."

"So, Soma decided to follow after him." Goran continued, worry aging his face. "We waited for him to return and tell us what he saw... but he never came back."

The sadness of the moment was interrupted as Astyræ ran up to the largest woodcutter and wrapped her arms around his broad shoulders. "Goran!" she exclaimed, overjoyed to see the man who had watched over her in the bowels of the cave. "I am so glad to see you!"

He blushed as he hugged her back. "Ah, it's good to see you too, little sapling."

"I can't believe we finally found you all," Oren said happily.

"Aye!" agreed Alon. "But who is in charge of this place? It's... well...

it's unbelievable really."

The keepers of the pass snapped into formation, bowing their helmed heads as the Queen of Shaimira approached these strangers. She met Cal's eyes, suspicion and curiosity unrelenting in her stare.

"I am Johanna, Lord of the hidden realm, granddaughter of King Julen, and Queen of the Amaians." She stood tall and proud before these men of the woods, her guard flanked on either side, hands upon hilts and eyes fixed on these strangers.

Gvidus was the first to kneel, and then Goran, then the others. Alon made an elaborate show of a bow and Oren punched him in the arm, motioning with a roll of his eyes for him to kneel like the rest of them.

She smiled at their awkward formality, intuiting that it was genuine if not even a bit noble for the bearded axe-wielders.

"It has been long since we have had strangers enter beyond the Pass of Kemen, and yet, in not much more than a few days, the men of Haven have found our home for a second time," she said cautiously. "Tell me, how did you come to find this place?"

"My Lord," Goran said, stumbling over his words as he beheld the beauty of the Queen. "I mean, my Lady."

She raised an eyebrow as she watched him compose himself.

"We have been traveling for a very long time, it's hard to tell anymore, you know. We started out north, trying to find traces of our groomsman friend. A while into our journey we saw lights off in the distance. Not the amber flames of torches, or of campfires. They were *white*. Pure, burning white. We thought maybe it was Cal. Maybe he finally found the light he had been looking for all this time."

Astyræ looked at Cal, her gaze curious and dumbfounded. "How can that be?" she whispered to him.

So we followed the white lights, and they lead us past league after league of elm and oak, spruce and pine," Goran continued.

"We even saw an old sailing ship out there," Alon interjected.

"Aye, right smack in the middle of a clearing!" Oren exclaimed. "I wouldn't believe it if I hadn't seen it with my own eyes."

"Even then, it doesn't make much sense," Alon agreed.

"What he says is true," Goran said apologetically. "There was a ship out there in the forest, but the light was beyond it, and so we kept following it. It lasted until we came to the strangest of camps, where we saw a handful of slain men. Well... I'm not sure if they were still *men* anymore."

"How do you mean?" she asked.

"I've seen dead things before, my Lady," he went on. "I've seen dead men before too; their skin was far too grey, and whatever it was that oozed out their wounds was no longer blood."

"Aye," came a chorus of agreement.

"It was black," Goran continued. "The strangest part of it all is that their bodies were undisturbed. I've spent most of my life in the wilderness of this world, and it doesn't take long for the scavengers to come for anything dead. But no wolves, no carrion; not even a fly buzzed about these bodies. Their flesh was too foul even for the flies to eat."

"That is when we saw the tracks," Gvidus grunted as he labored to his feet. "And we knew we were headed in the right way."

"Aye," Goran said, nodding his bald head. "We tracked you then, following your footsteps along the bank of the river. When they disappeared, we guessed that you had either been swept away downstream somewhere, or that you had found a place to take shelter."

"We searched that bank for the better part of a day, and we came up with nothing," Alon interjected. "Sure, we found the tracks of a few dogs, and what looked like a large stag ... but they all led into the water; not a boot or horseshoe print to be found anywhere else along that bank."

"So we followed them right into the river," Goran continued.

"And what a comedy that was!" Oren blurted out. "You should have seen these brothers of yours trying to swim! It's a wonder we are all still not half-drowned!"

Alon elbowed Oren in the side, and shook his bearded head in embarrassment.

"That's when we found your camp," Gvidus added. "We all made camp ourselves and dried out a bit, but most of us couldn't sleep. Something just ... I'm not rightly sure how to make sense of it. It felt too close, I guess," the large woodcutter tried to explain.

"Those falls," Goran tried. "It was like they were singing to us. Your tracks went back into the water and nowhere else. I watched that never-ending, white water cascade down for a long while. I stood on the bank throwing rocks, thinking hard about this whole damn mess, when I threw a right good size stone into the falls. And wouldn't you know, it went clean through."

"That's when we jumped in the pool and found the path behind the falls," Gvidus finished for him.

"And so, here you are?" Johanna said. "Two, maybe, three dozen of you? Caravanning through the forests, tracking these travelers ... were you seen along the way? Did you leave evidence of yourselves behind you? Did you spy any more of her Nocturnals, dead or otherwise?"

"Nocturnals?" Goran asked, unsure of the term and nervous at the edge in her voice.

"The Sorceress' soldiers," she told him. "The fouled bodies you found along the way. They are hers, her army of men who exchanged their souls and their wills to see in the dark. Did you see them? Did they see you?"

"We saw some people, but we don't know anything about a Sorceress," Alon offered. "They were no army, just ordinary people, in need of a good bath and a warm meal, I'll wager."

"Aye, he is right," Gvidus agreed. "There were some, hiding in the scrub and the brush; children, some of them. But they seemed afraid of us, not a threat."

Johanna listened, and as she did a doom she could not seem to shake held onto her thoughts. "Though you may be friends of Cal, and though you may oppose the Sorceress, your arrival is, at the least, unsettling."

The woodcutters all stood to their feet, exchanging worried glances, bracing for a fight if need be.

"Long have my people been safe here in the cleft of the encircling mountains," she told them. "I fear that, though guided by whatever light brought you, your arrival will not have gone unnoticed by our enemy."

The weight of her words settled over all those gathered at the gate of Shaimira.

"Sendoa," Johanna ordered after a moment of silence. "See to it that these woodcutters are given back their weapons, and find them a place to make their rest and regain their strength."

The keeper of the pass bowed his understanding and ordered Garaile to release the weapons back to their owners.

"As for longer than that, I am not certain how long our hospitality can prudently endure," she said addressing the woodcutters. "I will convene with my council, and will address you on the morrow."

"My lord?" Cal asked, confused by the tension in her voice.

She looked past him, ignoring his interruption. "But for now, you are welcome here, and whatever food or aid we can offer, however brief it may be, you have but to ask."

"Thank you," Goran said, his voice a mix of emotions. "If I can ask a question of you before you leave?"

"Very well," she agreed. "What is your question?"

"If you have been safe here all this time, time long enough to build all of this," he said, gathering his thoughts as best as he could, "I doubt anyone would be stupid enough to march an army though a narrow cavern to try and take your mighty gate as a thousand arrows rain down upon them."

"What is your question?" she said, her patience beginning to run thin.

"What has you so worried then?" he said as respectfully as he could.

"I am not worried about the gate, nor futile efforts to funnel an army though it," she told them. "I am worried about her dragons."

The woodcutters stood silent, stunned by the revelation of the Queen. She nodded to her guard, and the column of white capes began to usher her back towards the heart of the hidden city.

Cal had just turned to speak with his friends when the column of guardsmen halted. A lone voice rang out, and its tone caused worry to begin to rumble in his belly.

"Cal," Johanna said with little love in her words. "Would you please escort me for a moment?"

"Go, brother," Goran whispered to him. "And see what you can do to lengthen our stay here a bit, huh? Besides, the lady Astyræ will show us around." He smiled gratefully at the violet-eyed woman.

"Alright then," he said, embracing his old friend. "I have so much to tell you all."

Astyræ smiled a worried smile at him.

"Don't worry my lady; I'll find you later." With that, Cal ran to catch up with the column of the queen. Two of the guardsmen parted and let him into the center of the formation.

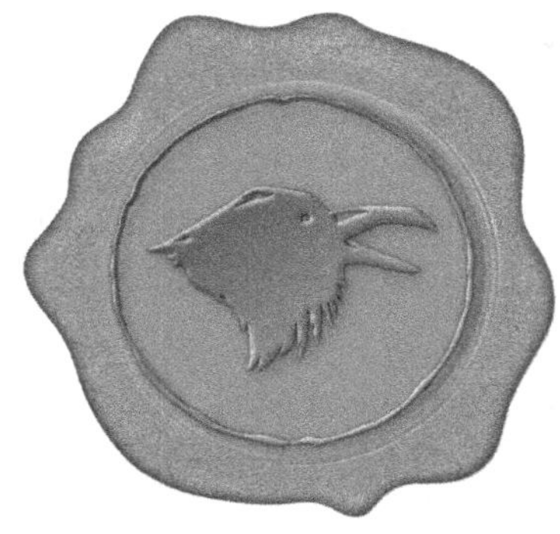

Chapter Twenty-Nine

The bright brass sound of the guardsman's trumpet woke the whole of the colony's stronghold to frantic life.

"Open the gates!" Seig ordered as he rose excitedly from his place at the table, looking to see if the fire knight had returned with good news.

The one-armed knight and the wounded guardsman rode in through the gates, past the soul-chilling eyes of the twin dragons, and right into the heart of the square. Seig moved to greet them, looking to impress his new mistress with the obedience of his underlings.

"My Queen," Pyrrhus said without so much as an acknowledgment of the governor that stood before him. "We have found them!"

"Well done, Pyrrhus," she said, not wholly trusting his words. "And where would you say that *they are*? For that matter, where is the rest of your scouting party? I do hope the North Wolf was not harmed on your journey?"

"We tracked them north, a few days' ride through the Greywood and all the way to the banks of the Argiñe," he said proudly.

"And…" she said, imploring him to continue.

"I rode as fast as I could to come and report to you, my Queen," he replied.

"What did they tell you when you confronted them?" Seig asked. "Did they fight?"

"No, they—" Pyrrhus stumbled over his words, understanding now the folly of his ways. "We did not confront them, sir."

"So, you didn't actually *find* them?" she asked, her gaze narrowing as the ink marks on her arms swirled and writhed in agitation.

"No, we didn't see them, but we know where they are headed. Yasen and the rest of my men are tracking them as we speak!" he said excitedly, hoping his enthusiasm would convince all who listened.

"And where, pray tell, is that?" she said coldly.

"North, along the river," he said proudly.

"Let me understand you correctly," Seig interrupted. "You were given a command to find the woodcutters, so they would lead us to the hidden city of Shaimira. And instead, *you* felt the need to ride home to tell us that you *found their tracks*?" He stepped down from his platform and strode angrily over to the fire knight before he placed a massive finger in the center of his chest.

"What happens when those tracks disappear, and there is no trace or trail left to find them?" the governor screamed in frustration.

Pyrrhus searched his mind, desperate for anything to appease their anger, furious at himself for not seeing the folly of his actions. "There is only one place where it could be, only one place a city could hide!" he argued back desperately.

"And where is that?" the Raven Queen growled. As she did, the attention of the twin dragons was piqued, and they unfurled their massive necks and narrowed their malevolent gaze upon the man in question.

"The mountains! I am unsure of their name … but that is surely the only place it could be," he reasoned.

"Do you not think that my faithful Raven soldiers have not searched the Itxaro before?" she hissed as she spoke. "I have combed every step on the face of them, and my twins have circled their highlands, without sight of even the smallest moving creature!" Her voice was now fully enraged. "And still they are hidden!"

Pyrrhus stumbled backwards to the ground against the force of her rage.

"They are north, I know it. The girl, she said she saw Cal, and that the woodcutters were following him," He blurted out. "Yasen is tracking them as we speak, and I know that he will find them and give them over to you: the woodcutters, that damned groomsman, and the whole hidden city!"

Her chest rose and fell, heaving against the wrath inside her, her yellow eyes ablaze in frustrated fury.

"Angrah and Abaddon," she said with utter coolness to her voice. "Find the North Wolf and aid him in his search. Prepare a place for my army to gather." Her stare went through the very heart of Pyrrhus. "If the fire knight is correct, then we will scour every inch of those damned mountains, or we will raze them to the ground. And if he is wrong, he will experience the very meaning of his name before all of my kingdom."

With a bow of their heads, the twin dragons roared and then shot high into the darkened sky in obedience to their queen.

"Durai, prepare my Nocturnal army," she ordered. "If these *Tree Men* have found Shaimira, then its people will most certainly be expecting us. Let's drive these rats from their holes and be done with these vermin once and for all."

"As you command," Durai said.

"Pyrrhus, there is one thing that I am quite unclear about," Seig said as the fire knight rose to his knees and began to dust himself off. "How is it that your guardsman over there was wounded and then mended again?" he continued. "Those bandages don't resemble any from our stores."

"The woman who told us of the woodcutters," Pyrrhus said. "She told us what we needed to know, after a great deal of persuasion, she then saw to the mending."

"And were these people enlightened?" Seig asked. "Did they serve our Queen?"

"No, Governor," Pyrrhus said, lowering his eyes and bracing for what would come next.

"And you didn't think to bring them?" he pressed.

"No, Governor."

"My Queen, what say you in this matter?" Seig asked.

"I would say that you need a more competent captain to do your bidding," she said almost without thought as her attention had shifted. "This dog of yours is better suited in a kennel than on the field of battle."

Pyrrhus' eyes went wide in disbelief at the very thought. "I have served you well!" he protested. "I have lost my arm for you, Governor, surely that has to count for something." His voice had turned to a desperate growl. "I deserve to be on the field of battle, with you and my men. You need my sword!"

Seig nodded his head as the fire knight groveled. The displeasure the queen felt towards Pyrrhus was undeniable, though obedience and loyalty had served him well so far. "I do not *need* your sword Pyrrhus, for there is an army of swords gathering as we speak," he said coldly. "Neither do I need your command. No longer will you be captain to me, and no longer will these men be in your company, for you have none."

Pyrrhus' face went crestfallen; he could not fully understand what he had done to deserve this disfavor.

"But you can fight, I will grant you that," Seig offered. "Now, pick yourself up, and either hide in the kennels like the mongrel you have become, or grab your sword and fall in rank."

"Men!" Seig shouted proudly as he turned to address the rest of the men of Haven. "We will join our queen and bring forth a new victory for all of Aiénor!"

The men let out a nervous cheer, not sure where their loyalties were best placed, afraid to be found on the wrong side of the Sorceress' wrath.

They took up their swords and spears and fell into formation with the whole of the Nocturnal army.

And so it was that with a loud blast of a deep horn, the thousands in the company of the Ravens began their march northward to unleash their might upon the city of Shaimira.

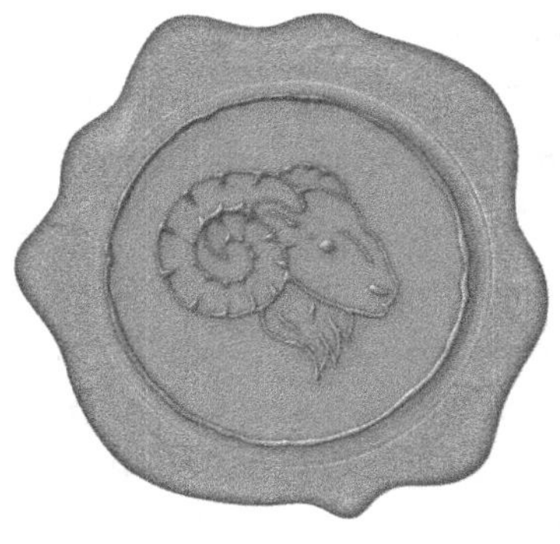

Chapter Thirty

"Dragons?" Cal asked without prompting. "What dragons are you talking about?"

The queen did not change her stare, but looked straight at the road ahead as they walked and spoke. "The Sorceress, or the Raven Queen as she calls herself ... she has dragons, Cal."

"I... I didn't..." he tried to reason aloud.

"It has never been about the size of her armies, nor the strength of Aerebus; rather it has always been her dragons that have caused cities to lay down their banners without so much as a single loosed arrow or drawn blade.

"Dragons," Cal said again. "How are we to withstand dragons?"

"For over a hundred years my people have been hidden from her ever searching eyes. The Itxaro Mountains have encircled us and have kept our secret safe," she continued. "But if they flew over the peaks of our shield, and glimpsed our city and its people," she turned to meet his gaze, "it would bring ruin upon us."

"That's why, isn't it?" Cal asked, the picture of doom coming into focus for him. "That's why it matters if we were followed."

"The Pass of Kemen could be held indefinitely, by less than a hundred men, if need be," she told him as they approached the streets of the city. "The bodies of our enemy would pile so high that the pass would be dammed. But, if an assault came from the sky, where would we run, Cal? Where would the thousands of my people flee?"

He thought about this beautiful refuge in the mountains, about its strengths and its people, and he understood the peril ahead.

"If I've brought this upon you—" he tried to apologize before she could chastise him, but she cut him off with her own question.

"What did you say to me, when you came running up to the gate, before the woodcutters were given passage?" she asked him.

"I'm not sure I understand," he said, confused.

"You were afraid," she told him as they walked between the mirrored reflecting pools in the garden of the Palladium. "You were afraid, I could see it all over your face. Panic, fear, desperation." She turned to meet his eyes. "But why?"

Cal was silent for a moment; the dread he had felt had all but been eclipsed with the joyful reunion of the woodcutters.

"What words did you try to tell me?" she pressed him.

"Not to open the gate," he told her.

"Why?" she asked again. "What cause of fear would you have had at that moment? You were grieving at the mourning trees moments ago, and then you came forth, adorned in mail, demanding that I stay the opening of the portcullis?" She narrowed her gaze. "Why?"

"Because the winged horse gave me a warning," he said, his eyes searching hers for meaning.

She breathed a steadying breath, exhaling anger and wonder both in the same moment. She turned, and without a word climbed the steps of the Palladium with great haste.

Cal watched as she went, unsure what had angered her so. "Is that all you wanted from me?" he called as she continued up the steps and past the curtained entryway. He shook his head in confusion, and then followed after her. "Lady Johanna?" he shouted for her again. "What is the matter?"

Her guards swung open the doors to the great hall, the light of the hearth revealing her already gathered council. She strode deliberately past them, marched right up to the dais, and fixed her attention on the massive, carved image of a horse in flight.

"The winged horse?" she asked him, her voice cold with distrust. "I don't rightly care if you are the very son of Illium himself, statues of stone do not speak to the living."

He looked up at the statue as if he were seeing it for the very first time. His eyes went wide as the likeness of the image registered. "Uriel."

"What did you say?" the queen asked.

"It does have a great likeness to him," Cal mused.

She stood there for a moment, considering the implications of his words. "A likeness? Do you even know what this is?"

Cal looked to her, waiting for her to go on.

"This is the *Anahiera,* the salvation of my people, creature of legend," she told him as she looked reverently up at the great statue. "The beast who bore away my great grandfather's grandfather from the cruel slavers in the south to our home north of the Falls of Ammon."

She turned her gaze to meet his own. "None, save our first king, has ever seen the *Anahiera* before."

"I don't know about all of that, my Lady," he said quite apologetically. "But as I was in the Weeping Wood, a white horse, with great feathered wings just like this, came to me."

A collective gasp could be heard by all who were gathered, and Cal looked about, nearly forgetting that they were not alone. "His name is Uriel, and he warned me of a great evil that is coming for this place," he told them all. "When I heard the horns of your people... I feared the doom was upon us."

"He *spoke* to you?" she asked with guarded wonder.

Cal thought as to how he would try to explain the nearly unbelievable ways in which all manner of creatures had spoken to him. "Yes, though not in the way you might think."

"This is madness!" came the exasperated shout of an elder councilman. "This *stranger* has been here for only a few days and is already exploiting our lineage to turn our sympathies!"

The offended grumble of the gathered council members began in response.

"I heard him clear enough!" Cal demanded, his conviction silencing the din. "He spoke of a great doom for this place, of an evil crashing in upon it." Cal sighed his own exasperation.

"The *Anahiera* just so happened to find you, there among the sleeping sons of Haven, and chose to speak to you? A foreigner?" came the reply of the long, white-haired councilman. "I find that rather impossible to believe!"

A roar of agreement erupted yet again, but Johanna just watched the exchange unfold before her.

He looked at the queen longingly, his eyes pleading for understanding. "I sailed across the black waters of the Dark Sea and forsook the walls of our colony, all because the *impossible* was told to me," Cal said, ignoring the grumbling council members and aiming his words towards the heart of the queen.

"It was Oweles that first whispered the quest to my heart. Since then, I've found Poets living in ancient halls and Sprites thriving beneath the mountains. I have encountered witches, and monsters, shadow cats, green-eyed ravens and timber wolves." As he spoke, his mind replayed each impossibility of his journey over again.

"I found the name of this city, this very place, carved into the stone wall of a tower in the middle of the vast wilderness, and unknowingly rescued a princess from its prison. My very eyes are clouded over because the White Stag himself wanted me to see the path that led here." Cal turned and looked to the gathered council.

"So, it did not alarm me to find that Aiénor was still filled with mysteries and magic that I had not yet imagined to exist in this world. And when the winged horse spoke to me there in the forest, I did not doubt his words, nor question why he chose to speak them to me. "

"My Queen," the elder pleaded. "You can't possibly begin to believe these ... these fantasies of this stranger! We have been safe here for over a hundred years, hidden from the sight and the reach of the Sorceress! Why would we listen to these absurd tales? And besides, who here has even heard of such things as Oweles?" he mocked.

The rumble of agreement was less boisterous now, though a few did lend their voice to the elder's.

"Councilman Iker," the queen said with a tone that signaled his time for speaking had indeed come to an end. "Just because we have never heard of such things or of such creatures does not in fact mean that they do not exist. There is much in this world that I myself have not yet begun to imagine."

Cal breathed a sigh of relief, glad to see that she did not wholly discount him.

"As for the *Anahiera*," she continued, "though I do not understand why he would show himself to you and not one of our own kind, I do not mistrust his warning. If it is as you say it is, Cal, then peril must be nigh. For Asier himself believed that the *Anahiera* came for the purpose of salvation alone. Perhaps such a warning, no matter how it was given, is a mercy we should not be so quick to discredit."

A rumbling of whispers echoed through the great hall as the men and women of the council began to consider the queen's words.

"Lady Johanna?" Cal leaned in to address her more privately. "What would you have of me and my friends? If the Sorceress and her dragons are to come, we will assist you in defending this place." The desire to help welled up in his chest as he spoke to her.

"I do not know why the *Anahiera* chose you, dear Cal, but if you will choose us ... salvation might find us yet," she said, kindness returning to her eyes. "Now go, and see to it that your friends are well fed and well rested. We might call upon your strengths soon enough."

Chapter Thirty-One

Much time had passed as the council of Shaimira debated their recourse and defenses. Cal relished in the shared moments with his woodcutter brothers, and strength gradually returned to each of them as they rested and refueled together. Cal was grateful for the return of his comrades, but was continually unsettled in the wake of his encounter with the *Anahiera*.

He sat with Deryn near the mirrored pools of the Palladium, considering how they could possibly help the people of Shaimira. Without warning, a snort and then a stamp sounded as Uriel folded his mighty, feathered wings against his luminously white body. The sight of the winged horse caused Cal's heart to leap to his throat.

"Bless our Great Father," Deryn said in wonder. "It is one of the *Tarrthála*!"

"You know of these creatures?" Cal said as they walked closer to the magnificent beast.

"Yes, in tale only though," Deryn replied as he flitted next to his friend. "A gift from our Great Father."

"His name is Uriel," Cal told his companion.

Deryn did not seem surprised by this revelation, for he knew Cal and his quest; both seemed to summon all manners of intervention, divine or otherwise. "Uriel," Deryn said in reverent wonder.

The two friends approached the majestic creature, Cal's hand upturned and out before him, inviting the horse to receive him as a friend. Uriel bowed his head to meet Cal's hand, his thick, white mane so lustrous that the firelight of the braziers reflected in its sheen.

"Hello there," Cal spoke kindly as he began to stroke the soft, white neck. "It is good to see you again, Uriel. Though I will say, your presence here has caused quite a commotion."

"Hail *Tarrthála*, lord of horses," Deryn said in a show of reverence. "Cén fáth a bhfuil marcaí mór an aeir á lorg anseo?" he continued in his native tongue.

Cal's hand stopped just behind the white ear of the great horse, his fingers finding a familiar spot upon the throatlatch, and his own skin connected with Uriel's. In an instant, a vision arrested his sight and his movement. Cal's clouded eyes blazed white and his body went completely rigid.

Deryn shouted, worried at first for his friend. But as he stared into the bright light flooding from the eyes of Calarmindon Bright Fame, he calmed himself and allowed the lord of horses to speak to him.

The vision was terrifying.

Cal saw legion after legion of a Nocturnal army, carrying banners of black with a white raven. He saw the machines of war they transported, and the murderous clouds of green-eyed ravens above them.

"What does it mean?" he shouted against the rush of wind and the sound of their marching, though none save Uriel could hear him. "Where is this army going?"

Do you not guess, Calarmindon Bright Fame?

"Not here!?" he shouted in reply. "Not Shaimira! They will never find it!"

The vision shifted from the marching armies of darkness to the winged, twin terrors of the sky. Cal's mouth went dry and his blood went cold as the serpents barred their blood-stained fangs in greedy anticipation.

"What in the name of the THREE who is SEVEN!?" Cal shouted in awe. As he spoke, the vision vanished. His arms recoiled reflexively and his breath rushed in like a desperate, crashing wave.

"Cal?" Deryn asked worriedly "What is it? What did you see?"

Cal whirled around, his eyes frantically taking in the hidden realm: every home and market, every garden and every citizen. "I saw them, Deryn," he whispered, unnerved and shaken. "They were countless. I saw them marching. I saw... the dragons."

"What do you mean? Where did you see them?" his Sprite friend asked.

"I am not sure," Cal told him, his face wrinkled in uncertainty. "Uriel?" Cal turned again to the winged horse at his side. "Will you show me? Please, I have to know."

Uriel bowed his white head, and Cal understood the invitation that had been granted him. He reached his hand for the white mane of the horse and with a strong grip he swung himself atop the back of the lord of horses.

"Cal?" Deryn whispered.

"Warn them," he said with dire gravity. "Please ... make sure they are ready!"

With that, Uriel shot up into the air with a blast of wind from his mighty wings. His white feathers beat against the dark sky as Cal clung to his majestic mane. The horse flew higher and higher, gaining speed as he went. The walls of the Itxaro climbed high in the northern lands of the Wreath, and so it was with great labor that Uriel fought to soar above and beyond their encircling crown. The air about them turned colder and colder with each pounding of his wings, and by the time Cal had crested over the great heights of the hallowed range, he could see the snow-covered stone along its rocky peaks.

"Uriel!" Cal shouted in wonderment. "This is amazing!" His elation momentarily eclipsed the worry that had sent him into the heavens of Aiénor. "I've never in all my days dreamed I would see the world from this vantage."

Uriel snorted his understanding and then banked to his left, eastward and away from the Itxaro. "Where are you taking me?" Cal shouted into the rushing wind, but even as he spoke, he could see the River Argiñe coming into view, past the Falls of Ammon, near the bank where Cal had crossed.

Uriel continued along the river's edge, deeper into the forest lands. They came upon an outcropping of stone and dense forest, and Cal saw a small village, a cluster of huts, that still smoldered in the aftermath of a recent desolation.

The winged horse circled the ruined clearing three times before he deemed it safe to land. "Why have you brought me here, Uriel?" Cal asked, confused at what seemed like a detour to more pressing things.

Look, Calarmindon Bright Fame. See the answer to your unasked riddle.

Cal didn't understand, but he looked nonetheless. As he took in the sight of this ravaged place, a haunting doom pressed in all about him. Homes and small animal pens stood burnt in the wake of green fire. Ten, maybe twelve bodies lay scattered, pierced with dozens of raven-fletched arrows.

A haunting feeling washed over him as he stared at the familiar image. It was just like that day when he had first come across the empty outlier's village just beyond the gates of Piney Creek. "The arrows," he said, looking back at the white horse. "They are the same here as they were across the sea! The very same arrows that pierced my brothers in the north!"

Uriel snorted his own anger and disgust.

"It is the same enemy? All of this death and destruction has all been her doing?" Cal asked.

There has always only ever been one enemy, though she has worn many faces. And her deeds have always born her ravenous mark.

"But why?" Cal said as he walked to each one of the mangled and massacred bodies that lay strewn and blood-soaked on the chilled ground. "What did these people have? How could they have possibly drawn the attention of the Sorceress?"

Uriel did not answer him, but stood erect, his blue eyes blazing with a luminous intensity as he watched.

"They are nothing to her! Not a threat, no great riches or power or strength—" Cal's words caught in his throat as he recognized the face of one of the slain. "I ... I know this one." He turned to meet Uriel's gaze as he knelt beside the bolt-ridden body of the young girl. "I know her face."

His hand reached out to brush the dirt and the hair from her face. "Delilah," he whispered sorrowfully. "Dear girl ... why would they—" Cal stopped mid-sentence as an avalanche of understanding washed over him. "She knew which way we went!" Cal looked frantically back again to Uriel. "Goran said he had met someone who had seen us! No!" Cal brushed his hands through his golden hair. "Oh Delilah ... what have you done?"

A monster does not care for the means by which he hunts his prey.

Uriel's solemn voice felt heavy in Cal's mind. His eyes went wide as he guessed closely at the turn of events that befell these innocents. "They must have tracked the woodcutters here, and then... then murdered these people until they told them where they had sent the men from Haven."

You are not far from the truth, Calarmindon Bright Fame.

Cal surveyed the darkened forest about them, and the nape of his neck prickled as his nerves sensed they were not alone. "Do you feel that?" he asked the winged horse.

Uriel stamped his hooves upon the blood-sodden dirt and snorted his agitation.

Just beyond the small, broken barn, in the thick of the trees, appeared a half-dozen pairs of green, glowing eyes. "There!" Cal said as he drew Gwarwyn from its sheath. "In the forest."

The sound of feet upon leaves and the snapping of broken twigs rang loudly in the unsettling quiet of these violated homes. A growl could be heard as the green eyes began to move closer towards them. Cal whirled his head about, making sure that they were not about to be taken unawares. For the moment, the immediate danger was the pack fanning out before them.

"Timber wolves," he said, his words dripping with vengeance, fear all but fleeing as he remembered Farran. "You will meet no mercy here," he growled into the darkness.

Calarmindon. Why do you wrestle with the tail of the serpent whilst the head pursues?

"They killed my friend!" he shouted at the encroaching timber wolves. "They killed Farran because we dared to protect that little girl, and now they've killed her too."

These wolves will not decide the outcome of this war, Bright Fame. Not unless you give them the opportunity to.

Cal held his blade out before him, his grip resolved and his muscles ready to strike. "You would just have me leave them? No justice for Farran? For Delilah?"

The enemy is not far, and guesses all the more closely at Shaimira's hiding place. You asked to see for yourself this enemy that we fight. Do not waste your time on such mongrels, for their master is nearly upon us.

Cal looked at the wolf pack, his teeth gritted in revenge, but the words of the winged horse found their mark on his heart. With a great sigh of resignation, he sheathed the blade of the dragon slayer and mounted Uriel. "Let's be gone then!"

The lord of horses took to the air in a great gust of power and might. They flew above the tops of the mighty oaks and soldier pines, following the path of destruction and disregard that the army of Nogcwren had carved against the forest. When the bank of the river Argiñe came into view, the sight of Cal's horrific vision came into full focus. There, thousands upon thousands of Nocturnals waited in anticipation as others of their kind fell into formation to cross the ancient redstone bridge of Asier.

Horns blew their sickly, ominous notes, and both the banners and the green light of the torches flickered in the wake of the cold winds. "What in the damnable dark?" Cal whispered against the rushing wind. "The dragons?"

There, on the north bank of the Argiñe, the twin dragons stood watch over the crossing army. Each of their massive, green eyes peered into the lands about them, relentlessly searching for signs of their enemies.

"We have got to warn them," Cal whispered to Uriel. "Come on ... faster, my friend."

Without a word, Uriel banked southward, back over the forest, so the distance and the trees would hide his passage. His mighty wings beat harder and harder against the sky and soon, when he felt that they had climbed high enough, he made his way northward again towards the hidden kingdom.

"What will they do if they track them to the entrance at the falls?" Cal asked worriedly. Uriel did not answer him, though Cal's own imagination gave him a sickening idea of the disaster that would befall his friends if indeed the Raven army and the winged serpents were to find the hidden stronghold.

"Uriel!" Cal said, inspiration and determination now clear in the light of imminent war. "Please, take me to the Palladium, show yourself to the Lord of the hidden realm, and help me persuade them."

Persuade them of what? What do you hope to accomplish, Calarmindon?

"For the queen to lead her people from behind those walls ... and to ride out to open war," he said resolutely.

The request hung there in the silent, cold air between them as Uriel crested the peaks of the Itxaro Mountains.

Very well. Now hold tightly, this will not be the easiest of descents.

Cal dug his hands into the luminous, white mane of the mighty horse as Uriel brought his wings tight to his frame. The cold rush of air bit and stung his face, his blonde hair whipping in the wake of such speed, as the winged creature shot like an arrow from the bow of a hurried hunter. As they descended faster and faster into the sanctuary of the encircling mountains, the ground began to race towards them, and horns began to ring out. Cal could barely hear them for the roar of the wind in his ears. "Uriel?" he shouted in fear.

Trust in me, Calarmindon Bright Fame. You need not worry.

With these words, he unfurled his magnificent wings and caught the air in the grip of his strength. Uriel circled three times around the great heart of this hidden city; drawing all who had eyes to see that the *Anahiera* had returned.

Torches were lit, and braziers burned brighter as the Amaian people poured out of their homes to see this beast of legend with their very own eyes. "Well," Cal said with laughter in his voice as he did his best to swallow back the stomach that had crept its way into his throat not moments before. "You do have a way of drawing a crowd, don't you?"

The queen approaches. Do not tarry or muddle your words, for this is the moment of action, lest great evil befall us all.

Cal saw Johanna, her councilmen, and the Queensguard alike come running past the muslin curtains that whipped in the wake of Uriel's wings. People gathered by the thousands, surrounding the reflecting pools of the Palladium with awestruck faces.

"Cal!" he heard Astyræ shout as she nudged and wormed her way through the gathering throng towards him.

He smiled as his eyes caught her own. "I'm alright!" he shouted back to her.

Cal threw his leg up and over the back of the great horse and slid down his soft, white flank, somewhat relieved to be back on solid ground again. He placed a hand on the neck of his new friend, patting him affectionately.

"Lord Johanna," Cal said, tilting his head in the manner of the Amaian to show reverence before their lord. "This is Uriel, Lord of the

Anahiera." A collective gasp rang out from the masses surrounding them. Then, almost as if they had practiced their whole lives for this moment, the people of Shaimira knelt in unison at the sight of legend come to life.

Johanna would not meet the gaze of the horse as she spoke. "Lord Uriel, we are not worthy of such a moment as this one. Whatever you ask of me, it will be granted freely, and with great honor."

Uriel snorted his understanding, and bowed his own majestic head in acceptance of her offer.

"All hail Uriel! Lord of the *Anahiera!*" shouted the voice of the herald. The people responded with great exuberance, tears filling their eyes as their smiles displayed their wonder.

"Hail Uriel!" came the collective voice.

"Queen Johanna," Cal said, walking hurriedly towards her. "I must speak with you now."

"Can it not wait a moment?" she said as her eyes drank in the sight of the winged horse. "We are in the presence of splendor!"

"My lord!" Cal persisted. "It cannot. What I have to ask of you must be heard this moment!"

Uriel snorted, agitated by the lack of attention to the urgency of their message. He reared up, hooves pumping the air and eyes a bit wild, punctuating Cal's insistent tone.

A murmur of voices rolled through the ranks of the people, and Johanna blinked as if warding away a deep and magical sleep.

"Johanna!" Cal said with greater authority than he held.

"Speak then, man of Haven," Johanna said, taken aback. "What is so urgent that you have to tell?"

"Not here," he said, surveying the masses about them. "We must speak privately."

She nodded to her Mezulari, and the Queensguard formed a column and escorted Johanna and Cal up the granite stairs and into the cover of the portico.

"Tell me, Cal," she said with less formality here in the cover of the Palladium. "The *Anahiera* has chosen you as his rider. Why?"

"My lord," he said as he swallowed back his nerves. "The Raven Army approaches. They are gathering on the North bank of the river as we speak, thousands upon thousands of them, gathering for war."

"The woodcutters," Johanna said solemnly after a moment to take in his report. "She followed them, didn't she?"

"It seems so. And soon enough those dragons might rain fire down upon this place, turning these mountain walls into a hearth to cook us all in," Cal told her.

"Is this why the *Anahiera* brought you to me?" she said, wounded. "To foretell our certain death?"

"No, my Queen," Cal said with compassion in his eyes. "The Sorceress only guesses at the location of the hidden realm. But she will certainly find it once she finds the gate beyond the falls. It is certain that her scouts and her spies are growing closer to finding it with each passing moment."

"What would you have me do?" Johanna asked earnestly.

"We must ready the army of Shaimira and meet them out beyond the Pass of Kemen," Cal said definitively. "We will draw them away from the passage under the mountain and the gate at the falls. If we ride east and then north, we can meet them in the shadow of the mountains."

"You would have my people leave this stronghold that they have carved out with their own hands?" she asked incredulously. "And for what? To march to their death, to declare war upon the Sorceress herself?"

"Did not your grandfather, faced with the very same fate, abandon the city of their home and lead his people to safety? Even at the protest of those he labored to save?" Cal countered. "If you stay here, this very stronghold will be the ruin of all who abide in it." Cal took the queen gently by the shoulders as he spoke.

Her guards reached for their spears and pointed the ornately carved blades at a dozen spots on Cal's body. Johanna raised her hand slightly, signaling them to wait.

"Ride out to meet her, draw her attention away," Cal continued, paying no mind to the guards. "Those too weak, or too young to fight, might remain hidden here behind the safety of these walls, and Shaimira could remain secret."

Tension hung there between them as she measured the words of this stranger from across the dark waters of the Itsaso. His hands still rested upon her, and one word from her could end his life in an instant. She considered his plan, the arrival of the *Anahiera,* and her love for her people. But mostly she thought about her grandfather, Julen, and what bravery he had shown to lead his people far from their home, with naught but hope that they could make for themselves a new one amidst these high mountains.

"Mezulari," she ordered her captain. "Have your men lower their spears, and bring to me Commanders Navid and Sendoa; we must prepare for war."

Chapter Thirty-Two

The war council of the queen convened within the great hall of Shaimira.

Cal watched the brave woman as she rose from her high seat, there upon the dais of the great hall, resolute in what she must do now for the safety of her people. She strode past the line of guards and councilmen, taking the hands of her commanders one by one and blessing each in turn with words of her confidence.

Sendoa, with his horned helm under his left arm, gladly took the hands of the queen, bowing his head in both obedience and awe. "I have a thousand bowmen at the ready, and another five hundred spears waiting for you, my Queen."

"Very good, commander," she said with a sad smile. "And see to it that the supplies and the stores are ready as well."

"Of course," he said with a bow. "Garaile will see to it that the caches of supplies and weapons will be made ready along the battlefield."

"Thank you, Sendoa," she said, dismissing him to be about his assignment.

He turned to leave the great hall when she called out to him one last time. "Commander!" Her voice was both embarrassed at her forgetfulness and saddened at the need to speak her request.

"Yes, my Queen?" the keeper of the pass replied.

"Please see to it that the healers are made ready, and that they have as many to help as they can find," Johanna ordered.

"I'll speak with Aysa right away," Sendoa agreed. He searched her eyes for any remaining unspoken requests, and seeing none, he made leave to be about the city's defenses.

"Navid," she said, now turning her attention to her other commander.

"I have two thousand mounted Ramsguard at the ready, my Queen," the shorter, dark-haired warrior said, his breastplate adorned at its center with a massive, silver ram's head.

"Ride quickly then and secure our fortifications at the base of the mountain," she ordered.

"Yes, my Queen," his deep voice answered in reply. "With both the river and the mountains between us and them, we should be able to give them quite a fight."

"Let's pray so, commander," she replied with a bow of her own, dismissing him to his duties.

Johanna then turned to the two gruff northmen standing to the side of her council. "We will need all the bravery and all the strength of citizens and strangers alike, men of Haven," she said in a carefully measured tone. "Cal invited you to the war council, and I trusted his judgment. But the question is, do you fight for Shaimira or for yourselves?"

"We fight against the darkness, Queen Johanna," Goran said respectfully. "If Cal is fighting for Shaimira, then we are with you. But where? Where will you want us? Yes, we offer our bravery and our strength, but more importantly, our axes!"

She stood still, silent with his question hanging there between them.

"Wherever you would be willing," her face filled with a sad kindness as she spoke, "to fight this battle with us, I would be grateful."

Goran looked to Gvidus and nodded his satisfaction with her request. "My Lady, we are not many, but we have felled tens of thousands of trees. Our swing is true, and these green-eyed devils still owe us all a debt."

"Oh?" she said, confused at this revelation.

"Aye!" Goran agreed. "Back across the Dark Sea ... they ambushed our camp and murdered our brothers."

"And not one of us has forgotten that night," Gvidus said.

"Thank you," she said, the weight of their commitment overwhelming her stoic gaze with tears of gratitude. "I will see to it that the armorist gets you all anything you need."

"Aye, that would do nicely," Goran replied. "Being that the trees we have been fighting these days on the Wreath ... well ... they don't do much fighting back."

She smiled, the levity a welcomed guest in so tense a house. She turned and nodded to one of her attendants, giving the order for the assistance.

The two woodcutters crossed their arms over their massive chests and gave their salute as they left the Palladium to inform the rest of their brothers.

"And what about me?" Cal asked as the great hall had emptied of all, save the council and the queen. "Where would you have me fight?"

She looked at this blonde-haired stranger from across the leagues of dark waters, the one who had found his way into the heart of their hidden city by means of hallowed legend. "Cal ... the *Anahiera* has chosen you, but for what I cannot say."

"What do you mean?" Cal said, his words guarded.

"You are not mine to command, son of Haven. Go where the spirit of the Giver of Light leads you."

Cal thought on her words, a mix of relief and duty washing over him as he stood in this secret, holy place. "I have been searching for this place since the moment my feet set upon the shores of these darkened wilderlands. How could I dare not defend the very thing that I have sought?"

Johanna smiled at the passion of this young warrior, grateful for his convictions. "Thank you, Cal, but if I am not mistaken," she said as she walked closer to him, placing her hand upon his strong shoulder, "it is not this place that you have been led to seek. Why would the *Anahiera,* lord of the horses, salvation to Asier himself, reveal himself to one who had already fought and found his prize?"

Cal shook his head in disbelief, stunned by both the wisdom and authority of this woman of Shaimira.

"Seek the light, Cal," she told him, patting his shoulder as she walked past him towards her next task of importance. "And may it truly be a salvation to us all."

He smiled his understanding, and without looking back, he walked towards the dancing, linen curtains of the Palladium in search of his friends. He walked down the great steps and past the reflecting pools of the portico, and there, waiting for him near a pair of braziers, he saw Astyræ.

"Well ... what did she say? What is to be done now?" the violet-eyed woman asked earnestly.

Cal looked about at the hustle and urgency all around them, of those making preparations to hide and of those readying themselves to fight. He saw warrior upon warrior in the bright blue and the horned helm of the city, kissing their loved ones goodbye and then hurrying towards the gathering ranks near the pass.

"Cal?" she asked him.

His eyes swept over the action of the moment before they found hers again.

"War, my lady," he told her as he reached up to caress her pearl-soft cheek. "They are preparing to ride to war."

"War?" she said, her brow furrowed in concern and confusion. "Against the Sorceress and her army? Against her dragons?"

"Yes." Cal said, his thumb tracing the line of her cheek bone.

"But, the dragons!" She pushed his hand from her face.

"Astyræ," Cal said, trying to calm her.

"Did you not hear what I said, groomsman?" her voice bordering on belligerence. "She has a pair of fire-breathing winged serpents! What army in all of this damned, darkened world can stand against dragons?"

"Astyræ," Cal said, taking her by the wrist and pulling her focus back from the edge of despair. "They all know about the dragons."

"Then why?!" she exclaimed, unbelieving. "Why would she send her people to certain slaughter? Not one city in all the lands has withstood —"

"To save them, my lady," Cal said, interrupting her.

The horns of the guardians rang out as the host began their march out beyond the Pass of Kemen. Sendoa's men donned their horned helms and brandished both bow and spear as the blue standard of this hopeful people whipped and danced in the chilled breeze.

"Where are they headed?" Astyræ asked as she watched them march in solemn formation.

"To the base of the mountains," Cal said as he pointed south of the lone gate. "Just on the other side of these rocky walls. They will take the passage out to the falls and pray the river gives them shielding enough 'til they can fortify in the foothills at the base."

The sound of another horn blast rang out, though it seemed to come not from the gathered host before them but rather to the east. "What in the damnable dark?" Cal said as he took in the unfathomable sight before him.

"What are they doing?" she asked in confused wonder.

"They are Navid's men," came the answering authority from behind them.

They both startled at the sound of the unlooked for voice. "Queen Johanna?" Cal exclaimed at the sight of this woman who had abandoned her linens and gowns for mail and metal and the horned helm of her people.

Astyræ bowed her head as she caught her breath, but the queen felt no offense at their words. "These are the Ramsguard. My ancestors' pride was in horses and chariots, and in their day, the Asierians had no equal. But horses cannot ascend the mountain, lest the road is made before them."

"Ascend the mountain?" Cal asked aloud.

"The ram needs no road or cut path to find its way, and so we have never had to risk such signs of our whereabouts upon these hallowed hills. For it is the Ramsguard alone that has been able to traverse the rocky ascent up and over the Itxaro Mountains."

"And you?" Cal asked as he saw her guards, adorned in white, mounted upon the armored rams of Navid's company. "Will you ascend the walls, too?"

She placed her golden helm upon her head, sister to the crown she wore moments earlier. "No, son of Haven, I will ride with the host of Sendoa and your woodcutter brothers." She smiled and motioned with her head towards the approaching woodcutters. "I must go now, the elders are seeing to it that our people will be hidden, and the pass shut against the Raveness." She mounted a mighty, grey-wooled ram. The sharpened points of its horns were dipped in metal, and its breast was armored in the same gilded fashion of the queen who rode him.

"Seek the light, dear Cal, and may the *Anahiera* watch over you as you do." She nodded her head towards her captain and without further word, the queen of Shaimira rode off to join the host of her warriors.

"So will you too be joining us, then?" came the jovial words of Alon.

"Of course he will be joining us!" Oren said as he smacked his brother upside his large head. "I don't think he fancies a long, bumpy climb on the backside of one of those lesser beasts."

"Ah, good," Alon said. "We did just find you, you know. We don't mean to be losing you again already."

Cal smiled and put his hands upon the shoulders of these brothers, but there was a pause to his reply and a weight in his stare that caught Goran's attention.

"No … I don't think he is coming with us, brothers," Goran said, with no malice to his words.

"What?" Oren said, incredulous at the very thought.

"Goran, Gvidus … brothers," Cal said, meeting their eyes and pleading with his own for them to understand. "I have got to find it! That is why I am here. That is why I sailed across the world."

"The light? Illium's light?" Goran asked.

"Aye," Cal said. "Though it's not Illium's light. He was just the first one to choose to go seek after it. It's *His* light, the THREE who is SEVEN. And that, my friend, is the only thing that will ever truly dispel this damned darkness."

"Is that why your horse up and sprouted wings then?" asked Gvidus.

Cal looked back toward Uriel, his eyes still filled with wonder at this magnificent beast before him. "He is not—"

"I know, I know," Gvidus said, his hands raised in mock surrender. "He is not *your* horse."

"No, he isn't," Cal said, the weight of the moment resting on his earnest brow. "But you *are* my brothers, and her soldiers are countless. So please, be safe. When this is all said and done, when the Sorceress and her foul beasts have finally been felled..." Cal trailed off, emotion catching his voice.

"And the new light shines?" Goran added gently.

"Yes," Cal said, his eyes welling with compassion for these men of the North. "When the new light shines, I would very much like to see you in it."

"Alright!" Alon said as he honked his nose into a kerchief. "Enough of that already, you're gonna make my brother start weeping like a little babe."

Oren punched his large brother in the shoulder, wiping away a rogue tear that caught in his bright eyes.

"Goran?" Astyræ said as she looked up at the mountain of a man.

"Aye?" he replied.

"Thank you. Thank you all for protecting me, I know what it must have cost you to do so." She stepped up on the tips of her toes to plant a soft kiss on his bearded cheek.

Goran's bushy eyebrows went high, and the points of his cheeks flushed a bright red. "Oh ... I ... I mean," he stammered, caught off guard by this display of affection. "You are most welcome, lass."

"What about me?" Oren said. "I protected you too!"

Goran smacked him on the back of his large head. "Come on, brothers," he said with a wink to the violet-eyed lady. "Let's make sure our axes are extra sharp today. We've got to show these mountain people that we Northmen can do more than fell timber!"

"Aye!" came the collective cheer of the thirty or so woodcutters as they raised their fists high in the air and then strode off towards the host of Shaimira.

"Cal!" Goran shouted back over his shoulder. "Find it ... and find it soon, brother."

Cal nodded, crossing his arm over the feathered armor of Terriah that he had found so long ago in the mountain halls of Petros. He watched as the woodcutters disappeared into the throngs around them, then eased his arm around Astyræ's waist as they walked toward the winged horse.

"And what about you?" he asked her as he moved to cinch the leather straps of Farran's old saddle around the flank of Uriel. "Will you ride to war? Or will you stay here and see to the people of Shaimira?"

"Is that it?" she asked him, offended at his assumption. "Is that what you expect of me? To fight or to hide?"

"What else would you do?" Cal said, unsure of her offense.

"I have come this far, groomsman, because of *you*, because of your search for this light of yours. So if Uriel can bear me ... well, I would like to continue my journey with you." She offered her hand towards the lord of horses, hoping to receive his blessing.

Uriel snorted his agreement and placed his soft, pink nose in the palm of her slender hand.

"Besides, the blade and the bow have only just now found their way back together. Perhaps it is for reasons yet unknown to us. I would hate to be the cause of their separation again."

Cal stopped what he was doing and turned to meet her violet stare. He smiled, his eyes filled with gratitude for her companionship and her fearless spirit. "Alright then," he said as he leaned in and kissed her strongly before he donned his feathered helm. "Our journey, my lady... seems to have only just now begun."

He reached out his hand for hers and helped her swing her leg up and over the back of the winged horse. There was just enough room in the dark leather saddle, if she rode close to him, though there was no place to secure her feet.

"Here," he said as he handed her a small lashing of braided leather. "Tie this about your waist, and then to the back of my belt. The last thing I want is for you to lose your hold, and fall to your death," he said matter-of-factly.

"Oh well... that instills me with such confidence, groomsman," she said nervously as she followed his directions. Just then, a flash of blue light came screaming towards them from the direction of the pass.

"And where do you think you are going?" Deryn scolded.

Cal laughed aloud at the feigned offense of his Sprite guardian. "Nowhere without you, I can see."

Deryn took in the sight of the two riders upon the back of the ancient horse lord, concern and pride smoldering in his azure eyes.

"If the great *Tarrthála* will permit me passage, I will ride with you; if none is granted, I will fly beside you," Deryn said with a bow.

Uriel bowed his head in agreement and spoke without speaking to the three companions.

I will bare you three for as long as my wings will permit it. But though I have been summoned to lend aid to your cause, no secrets or hidden wisdoms have been granted to me to shorten the distance of your journey.

Astyræ's eyes went wide and her breath caught in her chest as the words of this magical creature permeated the sanctuary of her thoughts. She squeezed Cal in nervous reverence. "Th-thank you..." she swallowed.

"Thank you, Uriel."

Cal reached down and stroked the neck of the mighty, white horse. "But that is where you are wrong, my friend," he said with an earnest smile. "For the grace that you have already granted us, to ride upon the wings of the lord of horses, has revealed many unlooked for secrets and has imparted wisdom for our decisions."

The horse snorted his understanding. Cal gestured to his Sprite friend to find his place at the head of the saddle. "Uriel, take us high … we have got to find the light of the THREE who is SEVEN if our friends ever have a hope of surviving this doom."

Chapter Thirty-Three

Astyræ tightened her grip about Cal's waist, and Cal secured his hold upon the reins. With a blast of power Uriel sprang into a gallop, beating his mighty wings against the cold air.

"Cal?" Astyræ said nervously against the rush of wind.

"Hang on, my lady!" he reassured her as he moved a hand to comfort hers.

The winged horse began his ascent upwards, circling the Palladium of Shaimira. As he did, the marching host of woodcutters and warriors let out a cheer that raised the spirits of all who had found themselves caught in the web of this war. Soon they were climbing higher, up past the roof tops of the hidden houses on the mountainside, and higher still past the watch towers and spires of the Palladium. The air grew colder as they soared up and finally over the peaks of the encircling mountains, until at last the great, darkened expanse of the Wreath opened up before them like a panorama.

"Cal!" Astyræ exclaimed, her fear supplanted quickly by wonder. "It is beautiful! Never in all my days would I have dreamed of seeing this world from such great heights!"

The violet glow of their violet hope seemed to permeate the sky about them, and though they could not take in the full scope of Aiénor's splendor, their wonder was not diminished.

"How will we know where to look?" she asked him.

"I suppose it will be just like before, when the markings of the White Stag led us to the gates of Shaimira," Cal shouted back to her. "Though I am not quite sure where we are supposed to begin our search."

"Cal," Deryn said gravely. "Look there!" He pointed to the ground ahead of them.

"Dear God!" Astyræ said, her words laden with dread. "There are so many of them. There is no chance that the warriors of Shaimira will stay them! We are outnumbered three, maybe four to one!"

Cal's stomach churned at the sight of rank after rank of Nocturnal soldiers marching towards the Falls of Amon. Uriel circled high above the gathering forces, beyond the sight of the enemy below.

"There, do you see them?" Cal shouted at his friends. "In the valley below! Its Sendoa's men... marching northward to the base of the mountains."

"I see them," Astyræ said worriedly. "Hurry now, good men of Shaimira. This is no time to tarry."

"Do you see anything else?" Deryn asked his friend. "Do you see any markings?"

Cal tore his gaze from the two converging armies. He scanned the horizon before them, and when he saw nothing, he spoke to Uriel and doubled back towards the mountains.

"No ... nothing yet." He told them, hope not altogether absent from his voice.

"You will, groomsman," Astyræ told him as she drew her arms tighter around him. "You will."

Before them, descending the craggy, rock face of the Itxaro, rode thousands of Ramsguard, down from perilous heights and into the fortifications they had prepared along the southernmost point of the encircling mountains, readying to meet their fellow warriors who were progressing north from the Pass of Kemen.

Hidden stores and concealed weapons had been positioned both out of reach and out of sight from any who gathered in the valley below. The men of Shaimira worked quickly and diligently as they armed a dozen ballistae scattered and entrenched in the cracks and outcroppings of the mountain face.

"It's amazing, really, how they can descend the crags and boulders of this place with such ease," Cal said aloud as his eyes scanned the mountains for any sign of the Stag's markings.

Uriel turned again and made his way southward. Cal scanned the highlands where his friends were moving in the relative protection of the valley below. His eyes traced the horizon for signs of the approaching enemy, praying and hoping against all odds that Johanna would reach the shelter of the mountain fortifications before the Sorceress and her army crested the sightline of the highlands.

The company below was still nearly a league away from the covering of the Ramsguard, when Cal saw something that made his blood run ice cold in fear. There, far above the highlands, two pairs of enormous, green orbs were sweeping back and forth.

"Cal!" Astyræ whispered in shock and fear. "Are those…"

Cal swallowed hard and looked fiercely for his friends below, but it was plain to see that whatever ground he had willed them to make in the last moment had not been enough.

"Astyræ, Deryn!" Cal said desperately. "They are out in the open! Those dragons…"

"They will consume them with fire," Deryn whispered.

"We have got to do something, Cal! We have to warn them or … I don't know, *something!*" Astyræ pleaded.

"They are following the tracks of the woodcutters, and they are expecting to find them." Cal said, leaning back to be heard over the rush of wind about them. "But they are not expecting us!"

"Cal?" Deryn asked. "But what about your quest to find the light? And what about my charge to see you through it safely? I don't—"

"I am not abandoning our quest, but if we don't do something … there won't be anyone left to quest for," Cal interjected, cutting off Deryn in determination as he placed a hand on his Sprite guardian's shoulder. "I am not saying we fight them, but perhaps our unexpected arrival could be the distraction that Johanna and Goran need."

"Alright then," Astyræ agreed. "Let's go—"

Her words caught in her throat as a glint of violet and silver caught her attention. She looked closer and saw vivid colors beginning to radiate out from Cal's left hip. "What is that?" she wondered aloud.

"What is what?' he asked, turning his head to see her face.

"Cal, your sword … it's … it's glowing," she said.

"What do you mean?" he asked. Then he looked down and saw the lights that mingled there around his scabbard.

Deryn bowed his head in reverence. "The sword of Caedmon was once drowned in sorrow, and languished in cold, deep water... its brilliance forgotten and believed dead." He looked up to meet the eyes of his friend. "But now … sorrow has been replaced with hope, and the languishing has been replaced with a faith in something greater. The waters have been dried up in the light of your love for your friends." He beamed with a mix of awe and pride as he stared at the sword. "The *Beautiful Dawn* has been reawakened!"

Cal gripped the hilt of this blade that had traveled a lifetime of journeys with him. This heavy, tarnished sword had become more and more brilliant as he sought the light; and as his hands held firm to the weight of his calling, he could not help but know what it was that he must do. Leaving the blade sheathed, he placed his hand on the neck of Uriel, and without so much as a spoken word he felt the rhythm of the horse lord's heart upon the palm of his hand. With a simple sigh, Uriel agreed to Cal's request.

"Hang on!" Cal shouted to his friends, his clouded eyes alight with the fire of destiny.

Uriel sprang forth in a display of strength that his riders had not expected. The winged horse began to climb higher and higher, the wind roaring in their ears as they flew above the hovering dragons. Then, without warning, the mighty horse pulled back his wings and began to dive directly towards the twin serpents.

As they approached, Uriel unfurled his great, feathered wings like newly loosed sails catching the north wind. Their plummeting descent halted in an unmistakable display of power.

The dragons, whose gazes had been relentlessly searching and scanning the ground below, were startled at such an assault from the sky. In their arrogance, they had not given heed to the wind and the air above them, considering themselves unmatched in this realm.

And yet, the moment of surprise wasn't enough to pull off an attack. The dragons pulled back, halting their pursuit of the armies below, their inky wings beating the sky as they hovered in place. Their glowing eyes examined this unexpected foe, and their amused malice spread across their fanged smiles.

Who is it that dares to approach us?

The serpents spoke in sickly harmony.

And upon the wings of the hidden horses no less? Is there only but one of your kind left, Tarrthála?   A pity you were not ten thousand, then it would seem more satisfying to destroy you.

Their mockery seethed inside the thoughts of Cal and his friends.

Uriel reared up, his anger at their insolence fueled a burning in his deep, blue eyes, and a froth of wrath in the corners of his white mouth.

"Silence, serpents of the Sorceress!" Cal shouted. "How dare a slave speak so to a lord!"

The twin dragons narrowed their gaze and showed their yellowed fangs as they focused their malice on the young rider.

Do not dare to address Abaddon and Angrah, foolish offspring of Ádhamh! For the wind is ours, the darkness is ours, and even the very breath you breathe will soon be ours!

"Leave this place! Be gone and never return!" Cal demanded, the authority of his words coming from some place much deeper and more ancient than himself. "Lest justice fall swiftly upon your venomous heads!"

The dragons roared in anger, and torrents of green fire issued out from their mouths, narrowly missing Cal and his friends. Uriel dove, dodging the blast with unexpected speed.

Fools!

Their heads whipped this way and that, trying to track the movement of the horse and its riders.

The Raven Queen has claimed this world for her own and has given us dominion over the air! Whatever rebellion you hope to stage will be swept up in the wake of our fire and her might!

Uriel came to a halt, his flanks heaving with outrage and exertion. Cal stood to his feet in the saddle, his hand upon the hilt of his ancient blade.

You dare to come at us with mortal metal and a winged pony, when all the might of Nogcwren and her Nocturnal army are upon your hovel of fools?

Cal drew his sword, and Gwarwyn exploded in a burst of silver and violet light. The dragons reared back, turning their heads and shutting their vile green eyes against the brilliance of this magical blade.

"This world and all that is in it belongs to the THREE who is SEVEN! And it is by His light you will know that truth. So by this blade, if I must, I will rid this world of your tyranny!"

The sword of Caedmon!

The sneering voices of the dragons transformed into a roar of protest.

"And the bow of Blodeuwedd!" Astyræ shouted, her violet eyes burning with hatred as she notched one of the silver fletched arrows and trained it upon the breast of Abaddon.

Deryn flew out from beyond the shelter of Cal and unsheathed his tiny azure blade. His wings, minuscule compared to the leathered monstrosities of the dragons, beat with the fury of vengeance for all of his kind who fell long ago to an evil such as this.

"And the children of the Jacaranda!" he exclaimed.

The luminous blast of the sword of the dragon slayer cast a brilliant light, a beacon to all who could see, both Raven and Ram below. Its presence was so unlooked for that the mighty dragons of the Sorceress had to retreat from it.

Astyræ let loose her arrow and it pierced the shoulder of the fleeing dragon. Though it did not slay him, its righteous wound burned deep in the wing of the serpent.

ROOAAR! The startled dragon shook the sky with his angry bellow.

"Cal, quickly!" she urged him. "We must pursue them, I wounded one! And they are afraid of us ... of your sword! Let's be after them and be done with them before this war has a chance to even begin!"

Cal looked down into the valley as Johanna and his woodcutter friends still marched towards the base of the mountain, and then looked again towards the retreating dragons. Deryn flew near, his tiny chest heaving beneath his silver armor. Cal had never seen his eyes so filled with fury. "Are you alright, my friend?"

Deryn sheathed his sword and exhaled his rageful breath. "I don't think they expected us," he said.

"All the more reason to be after them!" Astyræ insisted. "While we have the element of surprise, while there is fear planted in their minds!"

"I know," Cal said as he sheathed his own blade. "But that is not our quest. We may have bought our friends a safe passage for the moment, but I fear those dragons will return even more enraged at our opposition."

"And it will take more than speeches and swords to overthrow them," Deryn agreed.

"But Cal!" she pleaded. "I wounded one already. What if we—"

He cut her off with a hand on her shoulder. "I know," he said, kindness and understanding filling his eyes. "But we have been charged with the task of seeking the light, and if we ever had hope, true hope for

Aiénor ... it is in the new light, not these ancient weapons."

She stared out into the distance before them, considering his words. The sight of these vile servants of the Sorceress fueled her wounded heart, but she knew that Cal was right.

* * *

The dragons flew out past the river and just beyond the sight of their unexpected foes, hovering above the marching army of the Raven Queen. When a break between the ranks came into view, the twin serpents landed upon the rocky ground with a soul-chilling thud. The sound of their collision reverberated against the mountainside. They stood, talons upon the soil as they waited impatiently for the escort of their mistress to arrive.

Her driver stood at the helm of her winged chariot. From his pierced hands and forearms trailed thousands of thongs, each saddled to the body of a green-eyed raven as they pulled their queen onto the field of war. Durai, the lone commander, was mounted upon a massive, black horse whose eyes shone with the same sickly, green glow. He halted his approach and waited for his queen to address the dragons.

The driver let out a soul-chilling scream as the black cloud of birds came to rest at the feet of the dragons. The queen rose, her eyes yellow with bloodlust, her hands gripping the onyx scepter, whose rune-carved wand finished in a deadly point.

"My children," she said, her voice like satin against the harsh reality of war. "What have you to report? What have you—"

Her words stopped short of her unfinished question, for her eyes caught the silver glint of the arrow that protruded from the shoulder of her dragon.

We have encountered the rider in the sky. We have seen the blade and the bow and the bereft fruit of the broken trees.

She walked up to the wounded Abaddon as their voices reported to her in angered unison. He bowed before her, wincing at the pain of the barb in his shoulder. "And did you destroy them in the midst of such a ... *skirmish?*" Her voice seethed as she examined the ancient missile, her pale finger tracing its hallowed shaft.

The light that came forth overcame us, we were blinded in its presence. We flew hard and fast to report to you, our queen.

"Are you not the son of ruin and the daughter of power?" she fumed, her silken voice sharpening itself against her iron rage. "You have leveled cities, swallowed up entire armies in a blast of your fury! Kings have kneeled before you in homage to me … and yet you *flee* from a single rider?!"

The dragons bowed their heads, their wounded pride growled in their throats as they spoke.

This was no single rider, and not just any sword. The Tarrthála bore them, and the blade that he wielded was the blade of Caedmon, the one who slew our forebearers.

Her eyes went wide at the mention of that long-forgotten name, and she saw a vision from another life. Wounds long forsaken were made fresh at the mention of Caedmon. Sorrow, though briefly revived, gave birth to a bitter rage. A single tear fell from her eye as the runes that covered her milky flesh began to swirl about the skin of her body.

"*Them?*" she asked finally, tearing herself from her reverie.

The daughter of Aius rides with the sword bearer, and she carries the Moon to the sword's Dawn.

The Raven Queen stood in shock for a moment. "Are you sure?" she whispered.

Yes, my Queen. She is the violet-eyed daughter of your general.

"Do not forget, those eyes are also as yellow as my own," she cooed. "It is by my magic alone that she can even draw breath." Her tears dried as a ravenous smile crept back upon her face. "She is mine."

And the Spriteling?

"He will burn with the rest of them," she said dismissively. "Captain Durai, have you received word from General Aius? I would so like to reunite him with his daughter."

"My Queen," Durai said with a bow of his head, his raven-plumed helm held under his grey-mailed arm. "Dispatches were sent and received. The general has already ordered the removal of the army from the fallen city. He heads north back to the Wreath by the same route he used to take Haven."

"Very good news, Captain," she said, sensing her ultimate victory was close at hand.

"By now he should be just beyond the Halvard Pass, with a dozen battalions in tow," he reported to her.

Glints of firelight off in the distance, dancing against the base of the mountains, caught the attention of the Raven Queen. She smiled a reptilian smile and reached up, taking the protruding arrow in her fist. In one swift, unexpected motion, she ripped it free from the scale-covered flesh of the dragon.

Abaddon roared in protest and bore his yellowed fangs as a deep growl hung in the air between them.

"Do not let sword, or bow, or anything in this whole damned world stand between you and my victory!" she shouted at the top of her lungs as black blood dripped from the wound of the dragon, hissing as it splattered upon the grass below. She held the point of her scepter at the massive, green gaze of Angrah as she spoke.

"Now go!" she ordered. "And prepare these hidden rebels to meet their new queen!"

The dragons looked at each other and with a roar and a hurricane of wind, they climbed high into the darkened sky above them.

Nogcwren surveyed the silver arrow in her hand, her rage subsiding. In its place came the assuredness of victory that only a lopsided battle could produce. "It looks as if your woodcutter brothers have led us right to them," she cooed to the long-haired man that stepped out from the shadow of the queen's carriage.

"I have sought these traitors for over a hundred years, and now your foolish friends have led me right to their hiding place!" She laughed with delight. "If only I had captured your city sooner. Isn't that right, Yasen?"

The mighty woodcutter nodded his head in agreement.

She considered him for a moment. His left eye was not yet green, and a leather patch still covered his right eye. "Can you not see yet?" she said gloatingly. "It won't be long now until the un-light of the dragons takes its full hold on your vision." She told him as she walked closer to where he stood. "You do have a strength about you to so resist its full hold for this long."

"But I already can see in the dark, my Queen," he said flatly.

"Yes. But you will soon see this world as I see it, Yasen." Her armored bodice now pressed into his stout chest as she cooed in his ear.

"My Queen?" he asked.

"*As mine!*" Her voice screeched in his ear, but he did not recoil. She took a step back and gave him a look at her venomous smile as she snapped the arrow in two. "Please give my thanks to your friends."

Yasen remained unaffected, and she turned in satisfaction.

"Captain Durai," she called out without turning to meet his eyes.

"My Queen," came the voice of the mounted commander.

"Make for the base of the mountain," she ordered. "Our victory lies in its shadow."

"As you command," he agreed with a bow, spurring his green-eyed steed off towards the vanguard of his forces.

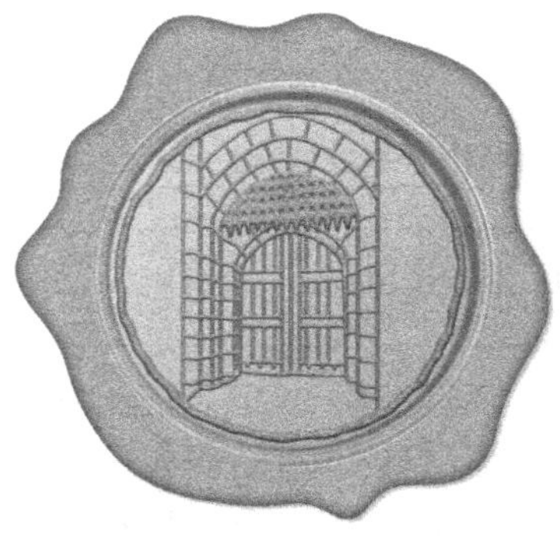

Chapter Thirty-Four

"ARGH!" came a roar from deep within the bowels of the giant. "Gather yer friends if ye can, and bar the doors! The Ravens have returned!" The giant seemed to leap his way down the stairs, growling with every infuriated step.

"Fryon, see about stringing those bows, and be quick about it!" Michael ordered his friend as he followed after the giant.

"Michael?" came the worried shout of Margarid as she ran through the great hall looking for him.

He nearly crashed right into her as he stumbled down the steps at the back of the great hall. "Michael, did you hear them?"

"Yes," he said, doing his best to catch his breath. "Where is everyone? Make sure they are all accounted for, Mar. I don't want anyone left outside these walls." He cinched his belt and scabbard about his waist as he spoke.

"And just where are you running off to?" she cried out worriedly.

"I've got to make sure that Vŏlker doesn't get himself killed!" he shouted back over his shoulder as he ran down the steps and out the large entryway into the courtyard beyond the walls of the keep.

"Portus!" Margarid called out. "Help me find something to bar those doors!"

Timorets entered in a hurry, his face washed with panic. "What is happening? Did anyone see anything? Are they close?"

Preparations in the great hall continued as Michael ran outside, chasing along after the giant. He stopped dead in his tracks as the sight of the Raven army came into focus, three, maybe four hundred paces away. "God help us," he prayed as he kissed the flint around his neck. He caught up to Volker, who was mumbling and growling in the courtyard. The giant had a large iron helm atop his head, and he was gathering up his discarded, massive hammer in his hands.

"Vŏlker, wait!" Michael shouted after him.

"Me has been waiting, Michael," he said coldly. "Ever since these *crows* stole me Hlíf from me."

"I know you have," Michael said, trying to reason with the enraged giant. "But don't just throw away your life! One giant, against the entire army!"

Vŏlker twirled his mighty war hammer in his massive hands as he considered Michael's words.

"You just showed us an entire armory! If you go at them alone, they eventually will overrun you. But if we defend the Halvard together … maybe this place could keep us all safe." He ran to his friend. "And maybe you can still have that vengeance of yours."

A black bolt shot through the air, narrowly missing the head of the giant. "Please!" Michael urged. "This is what they want! To cut you down and make their way back to whatever hell they came from on the other side of this gate. Do not give it to them, Vŏlker!"

"Have it yer way, Michael," Vŏlker said, resigning to reason. "But Vŏlker will have me vengeance."

Arrows flew at them again, and the horns of the enemy rang out their ominous tones. "Of course you will, now run!"

The two of them ran back towards the keep, raven-fletched arrows narrowly missing them as they darted back inside the ancient, stone walls. Vŏlker slammed the heavy, outer wood door shut and lifted a huge beam from against one of the stone walls, placing it in the cradle of the door brace.

"That is not going to hold off the entire army for long," Celrod said.

"He is right, Michael," Margarid agreed.

"Find what you can to block the door... anything at all to slow them down," Michael ordered. "Everyone else ... to the battlements!"

"The battlements?" Harmier asked. "To do what? We need to run! We need to hide and let the damn Ravens have this place if that's what they want."

"There isn't time for cowardice, Harmier," Margarid said. "Besides, if we don't make a stand against them here, in a place like this ... then who would dare to stand against them in the wild out there?"

BAROOM!

"How long, my friend?" Michael asked Harmier as he busied himself with the defense of the stronghold. "How long will we run ... and to what end? If we are to make a stand, this place and its ancient strength might very well be the best chance we have."

The group could feel the walls reverberate with the sound of the approaching army. "Whatever we do, it won't be long now before they are upon us for sure," the brewer said.

"He is right," Celrod offered. "Maybe we *should* run. But I, for one, was not built for all this running." He patted his significant midsection with a kind-hearted laugh. "And besides ... this is the first place that has felt like home enough for me to want to make a stand on its behalf."

"And maybe that is no accident," Margarid said sagely.

The sound of the marching army was closer now, and the noise of their approach sent a grave chill through the warm hall.

"Get to the wall, now!" Michael ordered. "Vŏlker, is the gate secured? Is the portcullis locked?"

"Aye, it is," the giant answered, never taking his eyes off of the large door below him at the bottom of the steps.

"Go now, Michael," Vŏlker said, calm and cold. "Arm yer people and do your worst. When the ravens get in here, Vŏlker will do mine."

Michael looked to the enormous giant, who had become such a friend in his time here. "Thank you, Vŏlker. Thank you for everything."

"Go now," the giant replied as the sounds of marching grew louder.

Michael complied as he quickly ran up the back spiral staircase to the armory where Fryon was busy passing out helms and armor, bows and arrows.

"Michael," Timorets said as he tossed him his own bow and a quiver of faded, yellow arrows.

"Why are they back?" Georgina asked worriedly. "I thought they wanted our city."

"I don't know, girl," Michael told her. "I thought they wanted it, too."

"I say, if they are going home, then we should let them be on their way already," Portus argued. "We want them to leave, don't we? Why should we stand in their way?"

"Because if we just let them leave, without so much as a stance or a fight," Margarid said fiercely, "then no place in this world will be safe enough to make a home in. They just walked into our city and broke our walls, broke our families, and burned our homes. They killed Vŏlker's wife, too. We can't just let them take everything and then leave as if none of it even mattered."

"She is right," Celrod said as he tested the string on his bow. "And think about it ... they *want* to leave, which means something on the other side of this fortress is more important to them than our whole city. I, for one, would like to make it rather difficult for them to return to it."

"They are here!" Fryon's brother reported as he ran into the armory from atop the battlements.

"No torches," Michael told his friends. "We want to make it hard for them to see us. But take as many arrows as you can manage ... and stay low!"

"But what if they get inside?" Georgina asked.

"Right," Michael agreed. "Vŏlker is waiting for them there at the entrance to the hall. Harmier – you, Georgina, and a few of the rest barricade those steps leading down and make a position here inside the armory." He pointed to the narrow stairwell. "At least from this position, you won't have to fend off more than two at a time."

Harmier put his arm around Georgina and nodded his understanding.

"Alright then, let's go," Michael said as he put one of the ancient, bronze-feathered helms atop his head.

They ran up the remaining flight of steps and out into the cold, north winds that blew hard atop the battlements of the Halvard. Spreading out among the merlons down the length of the barbican, they drew their arrows and held their bows at the ready.

"Steady!" Michael whispered.

The remnant took aim, sighting thousands of green-eyed warriors that were bottlenecked there at the entrance to the gate.

"Fire!" Michael ordered.

"Let them have it!" Timorets called out.

The arrows made contact, and they saw several of the Nocturnals begin to fall. But where they once stood, there were countless more to take their place. Raven arrows were fired in return, bouncing harmlessly off of the grey battlements of the barbican. "Careful now!" Celrod urged them. "This monster has teeth!"

Sounds of loud hammering could be heard below as the army beat against the great wooden door to the side of the main gate.

"Aim for the door," Michael ordered them. "We can't let them get inside!"

Bodies began to pile up, but the hammering did not cease.

"Keep up your fire!" Michael shouted as a raven-fletched arrow breezed just past his face, causing a chill to run down the center of his spine.

"Michael!" Margarid shouted with worry.

"I am alright!" he shouted in return, feeling a disrupted ribbon of metal there on the side of his helm where the bite of the arrow had just missed him.

BAROOM. BAROOM.

The long, soul-chilling blast of the sickly horns sounded again.

BAROOM.

"What does that mean?" Fryon asked his younger brother as he notched and let loose another of the Terrian arrows.

"I hope it's not those damned dragons again," his brother answered in return.

The long blast sounded yet again, followed by two more brief ones. Instantaneously, the Raven army ceased fire.

"What is going on now?" Margarid said to Michael as she, too, let loose another arrow, finding her mark and dropping another enemy.

The ranks of the surrounding soldiers began to part as a team of black beasts drove a sinister-looking chariot up through the sea of warriors and out into a clearing in the courtyard.

The green-lit torches that burned at the heads of their Raven-marked standards whipped and danced in the cold wind. The remnant of Haven saved their arrows and watched nervously as a large man, robed in black and wearing a helm adorned with raven feathers, stepped down from the seat of his chariot. He walked fearlessly out into the body-laden space before him.

"Keepers of this northern pass," the general said in a booming, emotionless voice. "Nogcwren, Queen of Aiénor, commands that you lay down your arms and raise the portcullis at once."

Margarid looked at Michael, searching his eyes for a sign of what to do next. He swallowed back his own fear, his mouth devoid of any moisture.

"Open these gates at once," General Aius continued coldly. "Our battle waits beyond these northern mountains, and I will not suffer delay. Your lives need not be lost in the waste of a puny resistance."

"We will not allow you passage!" Michael shouted boldly from the hidden safety of the battlement.

Aius turned his singular, glowing, green eye towards the direction of the defiant voice. "Your queen demands it."

"She is not my queen!" Michael shouted, more brashly this time, his courage fueled by his defiance. "She is queen to none of us!"

"Then die as an enemy of the realm," the general angrily said as he motioned with his hand to a sortie of the Raven soldiers.

"Michael?" Celrod said as he worriedly watched the soldiers part their ranks again and move a giant, black, iron scorpion into position. "They have a siege engine."

Michael peeked out over the stone merlon just as the mighty crossbow shot a massive, black arrow deep into the wall of the tower above them. The black barb bit and caught in the ancient stone, and trailing behind its iron shaft was a thick, knotted rope.

"They are going to climb the tower wall!" he whispered desperately.

"You have made your choice, foolish men of the dead tree," the general said in flat disgust. "Now you will die by it."

THWACK! The bite and crack sounded again as another of the enormous arrows were hurled against the other ancient stone tower wall.

"Fryon!" Michael ordered. "We have got to cut those ropes, or the whole damn raven army will soon be upon us!"

Fryon and his brother understood, nodding in agreement as they tightened their grips on the hilts of their blades.

"Quickly, now!" Margarid shouted after them as they retreated into the archways on either side of battlements. Below, the sounds of ramming and pounding resumed on the great wooden door.

"We cannot let them gain entry, we have to keep them outside this keep!" Michael urged his friends. The remnant concentrated their fire there at the entrance to the Halvard, and as dozens of their arrows rained down upon the besieging army, hundreds of the enemy replaced the fallen.

"Michael!" Celrod shouted as he fired his own arrows and then quickly shrunk back behind the stone merlon. "Look, over there! It's Fryon."

The dark-haired young man had signaled to his friends below from high in the parapet of the eastern tower. Raven soldiers had already begun to climb the rope, scaling the wall amidst a barrage of arrows.

Fryon looked out at the hopeless battle before him. His friends, not even a score in number, loosed what resistance they had upon an army a thousand strong.

One of the black barbs of the scorpion was just twelve hands below the arched window, but his blade was not long enough to reach the rope that was tied behind it. Fryon took a steadying breath and hoisted himself through the slim opening of the window at the top of the tower. His hands were sweaty, even in the biting, cold air. He gripped the brick-lined edge and slowly began to lower himself down, inch by nervous inch.

His boot searched and probed the old, stone walls, feeling desperately for the iron barb to make safe purchase. *THUANG!* An arrow clicked against the wall next to him.

"Come on, where the hell are you?" Fryon growled between gritted teeth. His foot bumped into a hard, resistant object and he knew at once he had found what he was looking for. "Steady now," he told himself as his second boot followed the first onto the shaft of the arrow. *THUANG!* Another arrow ricocheted off the wall. He let out an exhausted breath, turning his head to see the enemy below.

"They've spotted me, the bastards spotted me," he said to himself.

"Fryon!" he heard from the wall below. "Hurry!"

He could feel the vibrations in his feet as the Ravens climbed their way up along the rope, closer and closer to him.

"Hurry!" a voice yelled up to him.

"I can't bloody reach the rope," he growled as he bent his knees to lower himself closer, steadying himself against the wall with his hands. Suddenly he felt a great shift of force as some of the Nocturnals swung off of the knotted rope.

Screams and shouts came from below him, and he looked down to see Timorets and Celrod fending off attacks from the Raven soldiers who had just landed on the top of the barbican wall.

THUANG! Another arrow barely missed his head. Fryon steadied himself, grabbed the iron shaft with both his hands, and then let his feet drop out beneath him. He hung there, swinging in the wind as he inched closer and closer to the rope attached to the end of the barb. Once he grasped it with his hands, he securely wrapped his feet around it, working himself down the rope as fast as he could. Out of the corner of his eye, he saw his brother following suit on the opposite side as he climbed out the window of the western tower.

Fryon came down as close as possible to the top of the wall, watching as a whole contingent of Raven soldiers climbed up towards him. He reached for his blade and cut the rope beneath him, releasing those below into a heap of blood and brokenness upon the ground.

Fryon sheathed his sword and used his feet to run sideways across the side of the tower until he could swing his body out and over the top of the wall. He released the rope and rolled in the dust as he landed near his friends.

"Where is my brother?" he asked, breathless and quite amazed to still be in one piece.

"There!" Portus said as he helped him to his feet.

"Everyone take cover!" Michael shouted amidst the madness as a volley of arrows rained in upon them. Screams and shouts could be heard as every member of the remnant tried to make themselves smaller in the wake of the hells that were being unleashed upon them.

Fryon dove back to the ground, using the merlons of the wall to shield his body, when a loud *THUACK* cut through the clamor.

"They got me!" Celrod shouted through his pain. "The bastards shot me *again!*"

"Is everyone else alright?" Michael yelled again as he turned and loosed another arrow towards the invading army.

"Michael!" Timorets shouted.

Michael turned and looked, and what he beheld made the world around him go silent.

"No, no ... NO!!!" Fryon shouted as he ran desperately towards the bleeding, broken body of his brother. Arrows flew and the remnant cowered, but Fryon paid these dangers little mind.

"Get down, Fryon!" Michael shouted.

Ignoring him, Fryon ran across the battlements of the wall, raven-fletched arrows flying wildly about him, and at last reached the body of his brother. "Brother! Brother, no!" he cried out as he cradled the limp, lifeless head of his younger brother.

Margarid had crawled over towards Celrod to examine the wounded schoolmaster; the flesh of his left arm had been pierced clean through with one of the black arrows. She tore the hem of her dress and tied it tight, just below his shoulder. Through gritted teeth and a pained wince, Celrod nodded his permission. She reached up and snapped the head off of the arrow, then quickly pulled it free of his sizable arm.

Celrod growled in pain, but quickly silenced his protest when his eyes found the tear-filled face of Fryon. "God, no." He kissed his flint.

Tears began to stream down the faces of all who saw, for a friend and a brother had died trying to save them all. But their grief was short-lived, for a mighty pound and a splintering crack wrenched them all out of their momentary mourning. The Raven army flooded into the Halvard as the resolve of the mighty wooden door finally gave way to the assault from below.

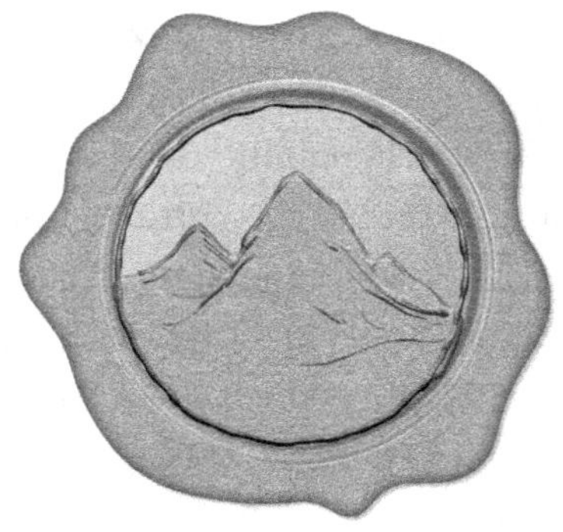

Chapter Thirty-Five

Keily, Marcum, and the other survivors had been ushered through the hallowed halls of the mountain palace, Petros. Although wonder flooded their thoughts, rest was the priority for this group of weary travelers. The Poets tended to their wounds, changing soiled bandages for fresh ones while seeing to the endless questions of the children. Though the circumstances were dark, and the danger all about them was severe, the company was a joyful and welcome change for everyone in the Poet home of Kalein.

As time passed and wounds healed, Keily began to feel better about their current situation. "This place," Keily said as she sipped her warm, spiced ale while her eyes scanned the massive, arched ceilings of the great hearth room. "This place feels like it is from another world."

"That is because it is ... well, sort of," Klieo said kindly as they sat and warmed themselves near the smoldering coals. "From an age long-past, really. This room here was a great ballroom once. Kings and queens, lords and ladies, gathered, danced, dined, celebrated, and mourned ... right here in this very space. Though that was an eternity ago, it would seem."

"What happened to it?" Keily asked, "How did it fall into such ruin?"

"A great evil, dear one," Klieo told her. "Evil will always destroy what it can't manage to control."

The old Poet stood to her feet, her aged joints cracking and popping as she rose. "We don't know the whole of the story, but we did find a library here in these ancient halls, and we have been able to piece together bits and pieces of what befell the kingdom of Terriah."

"I guess we are not much different, us and them?" Keily said. "I could never have thought that Haven itself would fall as it has. If you would have asked me, or any of my patrons, we would have called you mad. We would never have believed the great walls could be toppled, or the city burnt and ruined." She took another long draught of her warm ale. "And now, look at us. Homeless wanderers, taking refuge in the ruins of another dead kingdom."

"It was Šárka," Klieo said, her eyes fixed on the long, dark corridor just beyond the great hall, watching the comings and goings of the Poets and their guests.

"I'm sorry?" Keily said, feeling as if she must have missed something.

"The downfall of this place," Klieo continued. "The demise of it all, really. Terriah, Haven ... and many other kingdoms, I'll wager."

"I don't understand," Keily tried.

"She was a magician, a Sorceress of dark magic. But Queen Herrah took her as an advisor. The queen's husband, King Faramund, son of the High King Æðelric, convinced Šárka to return with him back across the Dark Sea as an honored guest, but secretly he wanted to collect her as a novelty for his court. Her hatred of Terriah grew as she was forced to be nothing more than entertainment for the lords of the East. Though her malice was concealed from them, she plotted, in the depths of her dark heart, to bring forth her wrath." Klieo shifted her eyes from the hallway to directly meet Keily's.

"She preyed on the kindness and superstitions of the queen, and her royal curiosities fueled deeds vile and dark."

"What kind of deeds?" Keily said, the hairs on the back of her neck prickling under the eerie chill of the story.

"While Faramund voyaged long and far, Herrah would safeguard his passage and assuage her worry by employing the charms and spells of the Sorceress. We don't rightly know all that bewitched her ... but we do know that all of Terriah feared the shadow that followed the queen."

"But I don't understand how Šárka destroyed Terriah? Did she have dragons like the ones that attacked Haven?" Keily asked.

"No. A beautiful maiden named Branwen was one of Queen Herrah's ladies in waiting. Some say she was the most beautiful woman in all of Aiénor," Klieo went on. "She attended to the queen, went where she went, gathered where she gathered ... and in turn participated in the very same dark enchantments that Šárka performed for the queen."

The old Poet leaned forward. "Her heart became poisoned by the Sorceress. When Reynard the Wise finally managed to entrap Šárka with his powerful magic, it was too late for Branwen's mind and heart to be rescued from the evil it had embraced. The young woman forsook king and kingdom, husband and home. With the imprisonment of Šárka, she took command of her evil serpent creations. She became the very embodiment of her mistress, and the hatred within her sought to destroy all that was bright and beautiful."

"Much blood has been shed because of the witch from the west, and many an innocent has been corrupted by the darkness she brought with her," Elder John, who had sauntered over to sit with them mid-telling, interjected. "The beauty of Terriah has become the beast that hunts us still."

"Do you mean to say ... is Branwen... the Raven Queen?" Keily asked them.

"The very same, dear," Klieo replied.

"Did she destroy this palace like she did our city?" Keily asked.

"No ... not in the way you might think," Klieo said. "She broke its heart rather than its walls. And once the heart is dead, there isn't much of real worth to keep fighting for."

Keily thought on the words of the old Poet for a moment before she spoke again. "Did you learn all of this from the books and the scrolls you found in the library?"

"Some of it, yes," Klieo said with a sad smile. "And the rest, the Sprite Queen Iolanthe told me, though I suppose there are parts that she witnessed that are still left unsaid."

"Witnessed? Queen Iolanthe? Were they both really here that long ago?" Keily asked, bewildered at the thought of someone so old. "That must have been—"

"Centuries ago," came the even, regal voice of the queen herself as she approached the group that was starting to gather in the great hall. "Yes, dear child, but the sad tale of Šárka and her progeny is of little help to us now." The queen turned to the elderly Poet beside her. "Klieo. Are they mending?"

"Meledae and Eógan have been hard at work tending to the wounded. Between their healing arts and the soups Clivesis has been conjuring up ... their strength is nearly fully recovered," she told her.

"Yes, we are all nearly recovered. Thank you, your majesty," Keily said humbly. An awkward silence hung in the room for a moment. "My Queen?" she asked finally. "Klieo said you knew her ... the Raven Queen, I mean?"

"No," Iolanthe replied. "I never knew this Sorceress who commands dragons and fells cities with a brutal fist of darkness."

"But I thought—" Keily tried to protest.

"I knew the wife of Caedmon the dragon slayer," the queen interrupted. "I knew the beautiful young woman who once dined in the flowing, white halls of Islwyn as my guest. I knew Branwen, friend of queens. But I have never known this ... this Sorceress that assails all of Aiénor."

"If even you do not know much about her," Keily said with a frustrated sigh, "then how will any one of us know how to defeat her?"

The queen flew over towards Keily and sat upon the long bench beside her. "My child ... do you not know?"

"I'm sorry?" Keily asked.

"There is not one of us who can defeat her," Iolanthe said gravely. "Her power has grown far too great, surpassing our own, fueled by the resignation of all who have lost sight of the coming dawn. Her dragons, the devils of Aerebus, haunt the skies and devour whole cities in their fury. Her Nocturnal armies far outnumber what little remnant of the faithful still remain in Aiénor."

A silver tear fell down the Sprite queen's face. "Neither the love of men nor the skills of my healers could stay the venom of Šárka poisoning Branwen, though we labored long and tirelessly. We shall not be able to stop this Raven Queen from exacting her vengeance."

"Then what hope have we?" she asked as exhausted tears formed upon her brave face.

"None, if your hope is in the strength of men or sword," the queen replied.

"What, then?" Keily said, her anger sparking. "Hide here? Wait here for her dragons to lay waste to this half-dead city all over again?"

"No." Iolanthe spoke without emotion. "Though, wait we must. Our hope lies only in the strength of the new light of our Great Father. If we are to see victory and beauty restored to this world, it will be by His light alone."

Keily turned her back to the Sprite Queen. The enormity of the moment unfolding in these ancient, ruined halls sent a flood of emotions and thoughts racing through the inner workings of her heart and mind.

"Keily?" came the familiar voice of a little boy. "Keily, what is the matter?"

"Roshan," she said as she wiped her tears on the sleeve of her tunic. "I am alright, my boy."

"Keily, where is everyone else?" he asked with childlike frankness.

"What do you mean?" she asked, as Iolanthe and the gathered Poets looked on.

"There were many more with us when we left Piney Creek. But they didn't come with you to find the mountain palace. Where are they now? Why haven't they come here?"

She knelt to meet his worried gaze. "You did a very brave thing, riding like you did to find us help. But the rest of them ... Roshan, I am afraid we are all that is left."

"That can't be!" he said, his brow furrowed and his voice adamant. "It just can't be."

"What do you mean?" she asked him patiently.

He scrunched up his little-boy face as he thought of the words he needed to convey his thoughts. "*We* made it out of the city, but we can't be the only ones that did so. There has got to be more of us out there ... somewhere, out there."

"I hope you are right, Roshan," she said truly.

"Well then, we have got to go and find them! We have to help them find this place too," he demanded.

The same fire that had driven her to fend off the boisterous patrons of the Gnarly Knob, the fire that drove her to muster her bow to the top of the wall, and to scrape and grapple for every inch past the fallen city, was now the same fire that caught wind in the words of this young boy.

"He is right," she said as she stood to her feet and addressed her rescuers. "We have got to search for others. How will they know of this place if there is no one to guide them here? And how, in the midst of all of this hell, will they know to hope if there is no one to tell them of a coming dawn?"

"Tell me, my dear," came the old voice of Tolk from out of the shadows of the hall. "What do you propose we do?"

The lot of them talked for what seemed like hours, putting together plans and gathering a heroic energy as they spoke of bringing other survivors to the safety of Petros. When at last they came to an agreeable conclusion, Tolk stood to his feet to address them all.

"The intention of this plan is true, and it is most certainly good, but let us not be *foolish* in our foolhardy endeavor ... for rescue alone is our great mission. The enemy of darkness is not might, nor power, nor strength of arms. No ... light is its only true opposition."

The gathered remnant of men and women from Haven, the Poets, and the Sprites all nodded their heads with grave understanding.

"Now, with that settled, who do you propose should lead this rescue mission?" Tolk asked expectantly.

"My men and I will," Marcum said, speaking through a pained expression as he stood at the entrance to the hall.

"Nonsense!" Clivesis said, with little regard for decorum. "You are clearly wounded! Though you may be noble and brave, this is no mission for a wounded man, whether he be guardsman or goldsmith."

"I will do it, the duty is mine," Keily said matter-of-factly. "I am a good rider, and whatever scrapes and bruises I may have had are well on the mend."

"But what about the children?" the Miller asked. "Who is going to see to them?"

"Oh, you old fool," Meledae said with a shake of her head.

"What?" the Miller said, oblivious to the insult. "She brought them here, I thought she might know best how to care for them."

"We have plenty of capable hands to mind the children," the Poet woman said with a scolding tone. "What we don't have is skilled riders who are fluent with a bow and arrow."

"Very well," Tolk said, his bushy eyebrows raised high in amusement.

"I will go with her," the white-bearded corporal said as he stepped forward. "We can move swiftly, and I know these outlands, at least the ones between the Kings' Road and the wall."

Keily smiled at him gratefully.

"I'll gather some provisions and fresh bandages and balms from my workshop," Marigeld said aloud. "If you find any poor souls out there, they will probably need a good mending."

Just then, in a flurry of violet light, the doors to the great hall burst open. Arthfael and his Sprite scouts flew into the council gathering.

"My Queen," the Sprite said, his breath labored and his brow beaded with sweat.

All eyes went to the center of the room as they waited anxiously on the report.

Iolanthe rose to her feet and calmly addressed him. "Go on, Arthfael, tell us what you and your brothers have seen."

"My Queen," he said with a bow. "We have spotted the army of the Sorceress, in full parade, making its way through the black mountains of Cair, heading east without delay."

"How many did you espy?" the queen questioned.

"Thousands, my Queen," Arthfael reported.

"And the dragons?" Faolan, his commander, asked.

"No, Captain." Arthfael said. "None that could be seen."

"They move without the cover of dragons?" Faolan said, perplexed at the imprudent strategy.

"East?" the miller blurted out. "Why in the damnable dark would they be heading that way? There is not much out there but rocks, shadow cats, and a few miserable sorts."

"He is right, though I hate to admit it," Clivesis chimed in. "The city ... I thought they wanted Haven ... and now they are headed into the middle of nowhere?"

"Leaving?" Keily said, hope now coloring her voice. "I don't understand. Why would they do that?"

"Perhaps it wasn't the city they were really after this whole time," Tolk pondered calmly through a puff of his pipe smoke.

"What else could there be?" Marcum said gravely. "And where the hell are those dragons?"

Iolanthe closed her eyes as an unlooked-for gust of wind blew up from the bowels of the hidden grove and into the great hall of the mountain palace. The fragrant smell of blossoms filled the air about them as the fire in the great hearth began to whip and dance in the wake of the gusts. Violet petals rode upon the current of cool, fresh wind. Voices in triad harmony, singing words unknown to all save the queen herself, were whispered amidst the breeze.

The Sprites knelt and bowed their heads while the queen stared into the swirling cyclone of petals and power. Almost as suddenly as the beautiful storm was upon them, it ceased. And in the receding of its might, the petals that had moments before swirled in delight upon the gust of wind, now fell limp and lifeless to the stone floor of the great hall.

In the silence, a small knocking could be heard from somewhere off in the distance, interrupting the awe that had enraptured them all in the holy moment.

"Let him in," Iolanthe spoke to the white-bearded corporal.

"But how do you—" Meledae tried to ask.

"Llinos has returned from the eyrie of the Watchers," she said with confidence.

Johnrey turned and left without so much as a questioning glance, seeing to the outer door at the queen's bidding.

"Is that what the wind told you, dear queen?" Tolk said humbly.

"No, that is what my heart told me," she said with a kind smile. "That, and the small sound of his young fist. I am quite sure he cannot manage to open so large a door by himself."

"But the wind?" Elder John pressed. "We all heard it speaking. What did it tell you?"

"The voice of our Great Father has spoken," she said as the room drew near to her radiant glory. "We shall gather the host of the Sprite army, and with the spirit of our Great Father, the fruit of the trees of beauty will fly east in pursuit of the army of darkness!"

"What? But you just said moments ago that they could not be defeated!" Klieo argued. "Why would you needlessly sacrifice yourselves for a lost cause?"

"The Great Father knows and sees more than any mortal eye could ever behold," she said definitively. "When He speaks, we must answer His call."

"My Queen!" came the small, frantic voice of the young Sprite.

"Llinos!" she said, worry coloring her face as she beheld the tattered and wounded Spriteling.

"Forgive me, I would have been here sooner, but I was waylaid by a hoard of ravens and barely escaped with my life," he said as he awkwardly landed before the gathered council.

"What say the Watchers, dear one?" Iolanthe asked.

"They fly west, my Queen," he said, as bravely and as resolutely as he could under the weight of his wounds. "They fly west, for war."

"For war?" Keily whispered aloud.

"War?" came the confused clamor of the gathered crowd. "What war?"

"I thought the war was here?" Marcum reasoned. "What could they possibly..." his voice trailed off as the thought of the colony of Haven came into the forefront of his mind.

"The colony!" Keily blurted out nervously.

"That is why the Raven army is headed east," Tolk said quite assuredly. "To return by the very same way they came to Haven ... to finish the war, once and for all."

"Then we will stop them before they reach the Western Wreath!" Faolan said as the fire of battle lit his violet eyes.

"But we are too late," Johnrey said. "The Ravens are already on the move, your scouts just told us!"

"Ah, my dear guardsman," the queen said, as her eyes, too, blazed with the fire of destiny. "You have not yet seen us fly!"

Ardghal, the herald, shot high into the rafters of the mountain hall. With his silver trumpet to his lips, he let loose a bright and terrible blast of proclamation.

"Éist leat go maith ó dhúchas an domhain agus tá súil agam. Eaglaim ort anois ar arm na dorchadais, mar a bheidh an óstach an Violet ag eitilt go cogaidh sa mhéid seo!"

"What is he saying?" Keily asked nervously.

"Hear thee well, oh darkened world, and take hope. Fear thee now, oh army of darkness, for in this very moment the violet host will fly to war!" Arthfael told her with a mischievous glint to his eye.

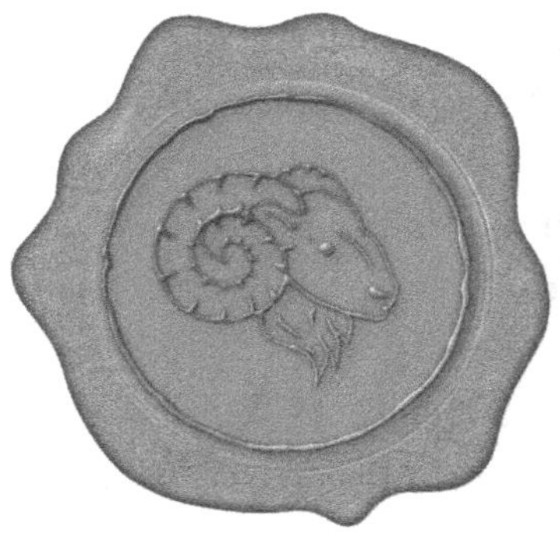

Chapter Thirty-Six

Uriel wheeled about, back towards the Itxaro, and Cal exhaled a sigh of relief as he watched the last of the woodcutters reach the fortifications at the base of the mountain.

"They made it!" Astyræ exclaimed. "They are safe ... at least for now."

"Safe?" Cal asked, the worry in his voice as thick as the cold fog that rolled upon the ground below them. "I would not name them safe, not with those winged devils still out there."

"Well," she said, undaunted by his worry, "then at least they are not exposed and defenseless like before." Her arms squeezed him with whatever reassurance she could manage.

"Perhaps the Itxaro might provide shelter enough to make a worthy stand against her and her army," Deryn agreed.

Cal's heart was indeed glad that his friends had made their way safe enough to meet Navid and his Ramsguard, but he knew that their only true safety would come not from barricade or battlement, but rather from the brilliance of a new light alone.

"Alright then ... safe enough." He managed to give a worried smile in return. "Uriel, can you take us to Johanna?" he asked the lord of horses.

Uriel agreed with a snort, and with great haste he made his descent towards the base of the mountain. As they landed, they were greeted by a sea of curious eyes.

"The queen!" Cal shouted as he leapt from the back of Uriel, and lent a hand to Astyræ to help her down and released the tether between them. "I must speak with the queen!"

"Son of Haven," came the voice of the queen, out from behind a cleft in the mountainside. "Tell me, what in the name of the Giver of Light did you see?"

"They are nearly upon us. There, just over the ridge, her army is coming," Cal told her as he turned around to look at the darkened horizon before them.

"How many did they number?" she asked, her voice grave and steeled for the truth.

"Seven, maybe ten thousand," he said, unsure of his answer. "I can't be certain ... but they number far more than we do."

"How many heavy horses?" the queen asked.

Cal thought on it for a minute, tilting his head as he did. "None. None that I could tell."

"Well, that is a good report at least." she said. "And the brilliance in the sky? All of us saw the blast of light you raised against the dragons. Is this the light that you have sought?"

Cal fingered the hilt of his ancient blade as he thought on her words. "No, it is not the same. Though I do guess that its origin is near enough." He sighed an exhausted breath as he continued. "If I am honest... I am not altogether sure where that light came from. I raised my blade in defiance of the winged serpents, and light issued forth."

"Then we have found a true weapon to ward those vile creatures off for good!" Navid exclaimed.

Cal shook his head. "We have startled them away, is all."

"But the light drove them back in retreat!" Sendoa argued.

"It was unexpected, by them ... it was unexpected by me, too," Cal replied.

"But they knew this ancient blade. Just as I knew its forebearer and the justice that came from its edge," Deryn interjected. "I can promise you this, Calarmindon Bright Fame: fear has indeed struck the hearts of those who previously prowled the dirt and sky so brazenly."

"But will it keep our friends safe?" he asked as he turned to look at the thousands of Shaimiran soldiers entrenched in the rocks before him.

"That, I cannot say," his Sprite friend told him. "But you two have dealt the first blow in this battle, and that might just be enough to turn the tide of this war."

"Perhaps the Giver of Light has not forsaken us just yet," Johanna mused aloud.

BAROOM! The sickly sound of the enemy's horns sounded off in the distance. The momentary elation of the gathered council seemed to vanish in the instant that the sound reached their ears.

"Commanders," Johanna ordered.

The two men bowed their heads, and in a flurry of deliberate action, orders were given and soldiers were made ready.

The forces of the Raven Queen marched quietly in unison along the cleft of the valley. The sight of their ranks began to flood the minds of the Shaimiran troops with cold waters of fear. Their banners were illuminated by the sickly-green fire of the torches held by their bearers; each banner and each torch representing a company of the Nocturnal warriors. The line of the enemy stretched out before them, moving in a fluid, almost hypnotic motion as the army began to span the borders of the valley floor.

"Dear God," Goran whispered as he and his woodcutter brothers kissed the flints that still hung around their necks.

"There are so many of them," Oren agreed as they watched from behind the dwindling safety of the large rocks of the foothills.

"Eh," Alon argued. "I've seen bigger."

"You have?" Oren said, raising a black, bushy eyebrow. "When was that, brother?"

"Well," Alon replied, his eyes scanning the ever-growing horizon before them, "no, I haven't. I just ... well, I was trying to make myself feel a bit better, I guess."

"Did it work?" Goran asked as he fingered the edge of his axe.

Silence hung there for a moment, interrupted only by the sounds of hard swallows and churning stomachs. "No. I don't suppose it did," Alon relented.

Goran shook his head, and a sad smile crept across his large, bearded face. "How many do you suppose are out there, old man?"

Gvidus held a spyglass up to his eye and squinted as he began to count the gathering enemy before him. "Six, no ... maybe seven thousand. It is hard to say."

"That's not so bad, then," Goran tried to reason. "By the time those bastards make their way across the field, I'm quite sure the arrows of the Ramsguard will cut their numbers down to something much more manageable."

Just then, the Raven army halted, with naught but a league of ground separating them from the entrenched men of Shaimira. The drums continued their pounding, the deafening rhythm moving faster and faster in a crescendo of power.

"What in the damnable dark?" Cal said as he fixed his ancient helm tightly upon his head.

"They are coming," Deryn said ominously. "The servants of Šárka are coming."

Astyræ whirled around, her violet eyes searching the sky for signs of the winged enemies again as she notched another of the silver arrows upon the string of her ancient bow.

Cal. The voice of the horse lord sounded in his mind. *It is time for us to leave.*

BOOM. BOOM. BOOM. The ever-growing tempo of the war drums seemed to signal the arrival of some great weapon.

"Go *now*?" Cal argued. "But the fight is upon us, and I hold the sword of the dragon slayer!" Cal hesitated, conflicted, for he knew that he should listen to the urging of Uriel, but an overwhelming concern for the safety of his friends stopped him from leaving.

This is not your destiny. You were not called to slay the dragons, light seeker. And I was summoned to bear the seeker in his quest."

"But what about the enemy? What about the dragons?" Cal continued. "Who will defend all of these people from them?"

Such wisdom and knowledge have not been given to me, Calarmindon.

"Cal!" Deryn shouted, as he recognized the distress upon the face of his charge.

Cal turned to look at the amassing forces. He caught the eye of Johanna as her dark hair blew in the winds, her face steeled and brazen. Then he glimpsed his woodcutter brothers, huddled behind the rocks, ready to engage the first enemies who would make it across the field.

"Cal!" Deryn said as he flitted up to grab his attention. "We have to leave now if we hope to escape the watch of the dragons."

Cal sighed a resigned breath and let loose his grip from the hilt of his blade. "Alright, then," he agreed. "This search for the light costs me much. I wonder if it will ultimately cost me everything." With those words he reached up and took a handful of Uriel's luminous, white mane and hoisted himself atop of the saddle. Astyræ reached out a hand, and he helped her join him atop the back of the horse lord. She held on to him tightly and, in a whirl of wind and wings, Uriel flew up and away.

"Where are they going?" Sendoa grumbled under his breath. "Do they not see the battle that is waiting here before us?

"Perhaps they have seen something that we have not," Johanna replied as she watched the *Anahiera* bear these two allies higher into the darkened sky above them.

"Forgive me, my Queen, but I thought the *Anahiera* were supposed to be the salvation of our people," Sendoa asked as he returned his gaze to the waiting army before him.

"Perhaps they will yet be," she said resolutely.

Without warning, the reverberations of the drums came to a halt. In their eerie absence, the *WHOOSH* and the weight of the predatory beasts filled the silence with their ominous presence.

The crashing sound of heavy talons upon the trembling ground startled the gathered army, though they had been poised and waiting for it. In a display of fury and strength, twin streams of green fire scorched the grasses of the field ahead of them.

Sheep of Shaimira. Men of the dead tree.

The voices of the dragons echoed in the minds of all who huddled and waited for war.

Your resistance is no longer tolerated, and your war-making is no longer necessary; for we bring you good tidings from the Queen.

"They are so loud!" Goran shouted in a whisper to his gathered brothers. "I can't make it stop!"

Salvation has come for you, and we bring it on the mercy of her wings. Receive her blessing, and all wars will forever cease, all darkness will forever be transformed into the brilliance of a glorious un-light, and all death will be forever stayed.

Johanna looked out as the sea of enemy soldiers began to turn and part, allowing the passage of someone of great importance to make their way to the forefront of the army.

Behold! Their voices rose in hungry anticipation. *Your queen has come for you!* Torrents of green fire lit up the darkened sky as the flood of fury spilled out between the fangs of the winged heralds.

A cloud of ravens flew ahead of her and squawked their homage as they pulled the carriage of their queen behind them. Their driver let out a blood-curdling scream. In response to his otherworldly order, the birds ceased their flight and landed upon the scorched ground before them.

The onyx carriage came to a halt and all eyes watched in frightful anticipation for what it was that might just happen next.

"For over a hundred years, you have hidden yourselves from me and struggled in the dark," Nogcwren said, her voice poised and as smooth as luxurious satin, yet somehow easily heard across the distance. "And yet, here I am. Ready to rescue you. Prepared as ever to offer my *gift* ... the same gift your foolish forefathers refused to embrace, choosing rather to scrape together a life in the shadows when they could have lived in the great expanse of my enlightened kingdom."

Her sultry voice echoed off of the rocks of the mountain face, and though ten thousand stood in attendance, no other sound could be heard beyond her words. She stepped deliberately down from her carriage, her boots claiming the ground beneath them with each footstep. "People of Asier, consider this your *last invitation* before my generosity runs dry." She stood, proud and greedy with lustful anticipation, her scepter gripped firmly in her right hand as she spoke. "Receive my gift and join the rest of Aiénor in the peace of my rule, or die with the fools who chose to cling to the failure of a God who does not care for his creation."

The wind whipped across the field, banners and braziers dancing in the cold breath of the chilled North; but no response was given. Neither boot upon stone nor throat being cleared, not even the bleat of the rams of Navid could be heard in reply.

She smiled a serpentine smile, the runes upon her skin forming ancient curses as they moved about her. "If you will not heed my offer, then perhaps," her voice lingered heavily. "Perhaps you will consider the plea of one who once thought of me as you do."

She turned and nodded to her newest pet, beckoning him with the lift of her brow.

The tall, bearded man whose fur-clad cloak could not be mistaken, strode out to meet her, accompanied by Captain Durai.

Goran watched in stunned disbelief as he pressed the eye piece of the spyglass firmly to his eye. "What in the damnable darkness?" he whispered to his brothers.

"What? What is it?" Gvidus demanded.

"I don't believe it ... not for one second!" Goran spat back in reply. "It's devilry, witchcraft I tell you!"

"What in the hell are you rambling on about?" Oren demanded. "I can't hardly see anything besides this blasted rock in front of me."

"It can't be," Goran whispered.

"I am no fool, people of Asier. I know you have welcomed help from the east, from the few surviving citizens of the once-mighty Haven. But what you do not know is that Haven is now mine, and so are its people, even those who have escaped its walls." Nogcwren continued. "Even this once proud and unenlightened wolf of Haven has forsaken lesser illuminations and has found both a new light and a place in my kingdom." She spoke proudly, knowing full well the devastation that was sure to come.

"Yasen?" Goran whispered.

"Liar!" came a shout from within the ranks of the woodcutters.

Her eyes smoldered with satisfaction. She raised her scepter, and with a single word she commanded the North Wolf to do her bidding. "Kneel."

Without hesitation, the tall, one-eyed chieftain of the woodcutters dropped to his knees before her.

"It is trickery!" Oren yelled into the silence.

"It must be! Yasen would never bend a knee to her!" Alon agreed.

"Shut up!" Gvidus ordered in an angry whisper. "This is exactly what she wants. To get us raging mad and foolish."

"The old boar is right," Goran said, his wits still stunned at the sight of his friend and brother kneeling before this witch of a woman. "Do not walk straight into her snare."

She looked at this long-haired woodcutter of hers, kneeling there before her like the good subject she expected, and a smile crawled across her dark lips as the yellow in her sickly, envious eyes smoldered with delighted anticipation.

The field of battle was silent. Not a stir or a protest could be heard over the tension of the land.

And then, into the hellish moment, the singsong voices of the dragons rose in the minds of all who were gathered.

Receive your queen and live. Deny her, and you will feel the scorch of the green flames upon your flesh.

Silence was the only response of these last free peoples of Aiénor.

Without so much as a raise of her gaze, the voice of the Raven Queen cooed her order to her winged twins. "Burn them. Burn them all."

ROOOAARR!!! The rush of green fire spewed from their mouths as their wings began to beat against the air, and the mighty serpents took flight towards the base of the mountain before them.

The dragons swooped low, their mighty, bat-like wings extended as they hovered just above the field before them. A flood of green fire poured out of their mouths, washing the grasslands in a baptism of unholy flame.

"Fire!" Sendoa shouted the order, and a volley of a thousand arrows flew high into the sky from the ground below.

"Release!" Navid ordered. The clank and crank of their iron machines on the mountain notched and racketed as one ballista after the other unleashed their mighty barbs.

The massive black arrows flew through the air like missiles, hurtling towards the approaching dragons. Abaddon and Angrah pulled up just in time for the ballistae barbs to scream past them and impale dozens of the Nocturnal soldiers who stood in formation, waiting for their queen to order their next move.

As the dragons climbed, the arrows bounced and skittered off their inky black scales, harmlessly falling to the burning fields below. "Damn it!" Sendoa cursed. "Save your arrows for the soldiers, men! They have no effect on the flying beasts."

The sounds of clanking metal as gears turned and pulled could be heard amongst the ranks of the entrenched Ramsguard, who were making the ballistae ready for their next assault. Navid caught the eye of each of his lieutenants, ordering without a word for them to wait for his signal.

The dragons circled back around, and the rush of air from their powerful wings caused the standards of the Raven army to whip violently below them.

"Steady lads!" Goran shouted to his brothers as they hid behind the massive boulders that littered the base of the mountain. "Make yourselves small now, they are coming 'round a second time!"

Navid raised his arm, and the silver of his gauntlet caught the firelight of the hidden braziers. He watched as the dragons came closer and closer, their green, glowing eyes alight with maniacal glee. Green fire came raging forth, washing the mountainside. Navid lowered his hand at the release of their flames, and a dozen of the black barbs launched straight at the dragons before them. Three or four of the massive arrows ripped through the wings of Abaddon, though the rest deflected off of his sister's scales.

The dragons roared and screamed in wounded protest. Abaddon tried to fly, but his wings could no longer enslave the wind. Angrah circled back, watching in furious horror as her brother glided clumsily to the ground below.

Navid's men cheered in victory as they hurried about the work of reloading the mighty weapons of war, but it was the screams of burning men below that spurred them to make ready with a greater haste.

Johanna smiled, grateful for the small turn in the tide, though she did not wholly trust it to hold. "He is wounded, but not mortally!" she called to her commanders. Ready yourselves, men of Shaimira!" She surveyed her defenses and her heart sickened as she watched men, her men, rolling and writhing in maddening pain. She saw the green fire devouring the scrub pine and mountain grasses, grateful to know that the rocks and the outcroppings still shielded most of her warriors.

Fools! The furious screams of the dragons invaded their thoughts. *None will be spared another day in this world! We will not rest 'til we have feasted on your burning flesh, and have become drunk on your red, boiling blood!*

BAROOM! The war horns sounded again. So deep and sonic was their tone, that at their very reverberation the dust between the stones and the courage in the hearts of those who opposed them began to rumble in disquieted tremors.

Company after company began to march towards the mountains before them, where the dragons still assaulted the hillside from the ground.

"They are coming!" Goran said as he crouched behind the rocks. "Make sure your axes are in hand!"

"Make ready!" Sendoa ordered his archers. "They will feel the point of our resolve, or may they burn in their own flames before they get to us!"

Though the fields were ablaze in green fire, the Raven army advanced unabated and undeterred. They marched through the flames that were roiling and licking at the sky above them, and all of the Shaimiran troops watched in horror as not a one of their assailants were hindered by the blaze.

"What in the damnable dark?" Gvidus shouted.

"How is that possible?" Alon asked, his eyes disbelieving what they saw.

Oren held his flint to his lips and kissed it with desperate worry.

Abaddon shook his head, clearing the pain from his mind, and began to claw at the rocky terrain with his razor sharp talons, climbing towards the clefts where the woodcutters laid in wait.

Angrah lifted off the ground again, unleashing green flames on anything that wasn't already burning. Men screamed and thrashed, trying desperately to extinguish the unholy fire.

"Now!" Sendoa called, and his archers let loose a thousand arrows into the ranks of the approaching army. The arrows found their mark, and a wide swath of Nocturnals fell without so much as a single protest.

"Again!" Sendoa ordered, and again a volley of arrows were loosed, piercing the muted armor of the invaders and cutting them down. But though they slew hundreds upon hundreds of the enemy, thousands more continued their march.

"There are just too many of them!" an archer called out.

"It does not matter how many they be," Sendoa said as he surveyed the blood and the burning and all the horrors of war. "What matters is our resolve." He handed the archer a fresh quiver of arrows. "And it matters that you loose these! We have got to take down as many of them as we can before they get to the base of the mountain."

The young archer wiped his sweat-sodden brow and notched one of the new arrows in his longbow. "Yessir," he said, falling into the rhythm of all those who defended this place.

"It matters!" Sendoa shouted against the sound of falling rock and screaming men. "Your arrow matters, guardian!"

"Yessir," the archer agreed as he fired another at the incoming horde.

"What is your name, archer?" Sendoa asked.

"Dorey, sir!" the archer answered.

"Keep them coming, Dorey... it matters!" Sendoa said as he walked the line of archers. "And you, son?" he asked the archer next to him.

"Graunt, sir," the young man said, never taking his eye off of the enemy before them.

"And you?" he asked the next in line.

"Khris, sir" the tall archer answered him.

"Jordain, sir!" came the excited reply of the next archer on the line, though he was not directly asked.

"All of you!" Sendoa shouted. "It matters! Your arrow matters! Your fight today means everything for our people! The enemy may be many ... but they have not taken these mountains yet, and by your arrows and the grace of the Giver of Light, they never will!"

"ROOAARR!!!" came the enraged screams of the flightless Abaddon as he spewed forth his fury upon the mountain base. Arrows whizzed past him, deflecting with a hopeless *plink* as they bounced off the hardened scales of the serpent's back.

Chapter Thirty-Seven

"Cal!" Astyræ pleaded. He could feel the pounding of her heart against his back as she pressed into him, desperately scanning the crags and clay at the base of the mountain. "We have to do something, we have to help them!"

Cal turned his head, peeling his eyes from the mountain heights where he had been doggedly searching for a sign of the Stag. What he beheld made his stomach drop in utter fear. From this vantage, he saw the endless army of the Sorceress marching relentlessly towards the fire-riddled defenses of the Shaimirans.

"God, please!" he half-prayed and half-lamented amidst the horrific symphony of this last and brutal battle.

"They need us," he said to the lord of horses.

This world needs you to seek and find the light, Calarmindon.

Cal's eyes reluctantly went back to the rock face. The sky was dark, save the violet glow that their flickering hope managed to illuminate for them. Uriel, with mighty, outstretched wings, glided as close as he could to the stone, while Astyræ held onto Cal with one arm so she could turn to see the war behind them.

Back and forth they swept the mountainside, and yet they saw no sign left by the White Stag. "What if we are looking in the wrong place, Deryn?" Cal said, hopelessness entering into his voice. "I've seen nothing, not a glimpse or a marking ... not since we passed through the Falls of Ammon. "

"I know," Deryn reluctantly agreed. "I have seen nothing either, my friend."

"What if we are supposed to be down there, with them?" Cal argued. "You saw what happened before ... the light ... the magic that stunned the dragons." His eyes went back to searching the face of the rocks, but his words continued. "What if we can help ... what if they need us?"

Just then, the sound of a familiar horn's blast carried on the wind and caught Cal's attention. "I know that sound ... that horn." He turned back to take in the battle below. "That is the horn of the woodcutters. Something is wrong. They need our help."

"Alright then, groomsman!" Astyræ told him. "Let's go!"

"Uriel!" Cal directed. "We are getting nowhere here. Take us to the woodcutters. It looks as if my quest will go through the heart of the battle, to save those whom I love." Cal said unwaveringly. "Now please! To the woodcutters!"

Very well, though, in my heart, a shadow lies over this decision. Uriel spoke as he banked hard to the right and began his dive towards the men of Haven. *I will bear you to your friends.*

As they started downward, they saw the mighty Abaddon crushing rocks and boulders as he climbed up the hillside towards the fortifications on the mountain. The ground around him was scorched and littered with hurled stones and spent arrows. The woodcutters of Haven were hidden, huddled behind a large outcropping not three hundred paces above the vile serpent of Nogcwren.

At the same time, Angrah flew back and forth across the face of the mountain, drenching the defenses in a tumult of fear and fire.

Uriel was like a meteor hurled from the heavens above, barreling ever closer to the fire-breathing dragon below. Cal took in all the carnage, watching wave after wave of Ramsguard arrows loosed upon the approaching army. He saw the sickly green dragons' fire consuming both men and mountain below him, when, all of a sudden, a glint of glowing, white light caught the corner of his clouded eyes.

"There!" he shouted to his friends. "I thought I saw something, a glow, maybe... over there!" His hand pointed to the cleft beside them.

"Where?" Astyræ asked as she followed his finger with her eyes.

"Right there! In the cleft of that rock, where it looks as if the mountain has been split in two!" he shouted against the rushing of wind. "Maybe we should turn around—"

ROOOAARR!!! The scream of Abaddon pulled their attention away from the rock as a flood of fire bathed the hiding place of the woodcutters.

Men of the dead tree. Why have you traveled half the world away only to die in the same manner as your brothers back home? But don't worry. The sinister glee dripped from each mocking word the dragons spoke. *Your bodies will burn just like theirs did.*

Just then, a silver shaft pierced the wounded, winged shoulder of the beast, Abaddon, who let forth an enraged growl.

"Be gone, spawn of Šárka!" Deryn shouted, his tiny, azure blade outstretched and ready to do his worst upon any who would oppose him.

Cal looked back over his shoulder, but the faint, glowing light was no longer visible. He took note of where he had seen it, knowing that if he lived long enough to return, he would not waste even one moment more searching for it.

The Raven army pushed in further, following Angrah's enraged blasts upon Sendoa's defenses that washed hundreds of archers in her unquenchable flame.

Cal drew his sword and pointed it at the beast below, the hilt of

Gwarwyn aglow in silver and violet. The sight of the lord of horses and the sword of Caedmon bolstered the resolve of the woodcutters, so they grabbed their axes and steeled their hearts, knowing that their time had come.

With a mighty horn blast, nearly forty bearded warriors with axes brandished came rushing out to meet their enemy as they had met so many of their foes before: head on.

The dragon fixed his stare on Cal's mount as he flew closer and closer towards him. *All hail lord of the horses, last of your kind.* His mouth curled in a snarl as he spoke, his fangs dripping with the blood of his vanquished enemies. *Today I rid this world of your lesser kind, vermin of the sky!*

Cal saw the eyes of the dragon grow wide with lust and hatred, and his own mouth went dry at the realization of what was about to happen. The sinister grin grew to a gaping, teeth-lined abyss, and green flame issued forth. Uriel collapsed his wings, then dove beneath the torrent of fire, hurtling even faster now towards the ground below them.

"Hold on!" Cal shouted to his friends.

Goran and his brothers charged the beast, and because his attention was fixed upon the flying warrior, he did not notice the company of axes that bit into his talons and legs. Abaddon shook his head in pain, and his fire quenched for a moment. He lunged for the woodcutters, sweeping his tail back and forth, trying to rid himself of these men with axes.

THUANG! Another silver arrow buried itself in the opposite shoulder. Twin screams of pain could be heard as Astyræ found her mark yet again.

Goran's axe bit hard and cleaved two toes from the rear foot of the dragon. Fire came flooding the ground, and the woodcutters that were not consumed in the fury scattered.

Angrah found a ballista and ripped it from its moorings, hurling it into the huddled defenses below to defend her brother.

Uriel was nearly upon the wounded dragon again, and Abaddon turned his head to meet his foe with fire. As he did, the lord of horses turned hard and to the left, and Cal leapt from the saddle with the blade of the dragon slayer brandished before him.

Goran saw what was about to happen and blew his horn, calling his brothers that were still left to turn and run towards the fight.

"Is that Cal?" Alon shouted with a shake of his head and proud smile upon his singed face.

The shouts of the woodcutters came as they rushed to the aid of their friend. The dragon roared and screamed his fury, and in trying to find the horse lord, he did not notice the man in forgotten, feathered armor with an ancient blade soaring through the air and crashing into his scaled side. Cal landed hard, the jolt nearly knocking the teeth out of his head, but the blade found its mark and plunged past the inky, impenetrable scales like a hot knife through butter.

He held on with two hands as the screams of the dying dragon shook the mountains themselves. The beast writhed in agony, sending his assailants scattering.

It burns! It burns sister!

The dragon's twin crashed into the side of the mountain, the pain of her pierced brother stalling her destruction with its horrific intensity. She slid down the side of the mountain and gained her footing on the ground beneath her. Shaking her head to clear it of her brother's pain, she narrowed her eyes at the fight that ensued about the wounded beast.

Deryn flew to Cal's side, sword out and worry etched on his face. "Are you alright?" he shouted.

"I don't think I can hold it much longer!" Cal shouted through gritted teeth and held tightly to the pommel of the sword that was buried to the hilt in the flank of this vile beast.

The blood that leaked from the wound was as black and as molten as the evil that lived within the dragon; as the beast rocked and writhed, the blade dug deeper in. A spray of the blood burned Cal's forearm and he partially lost his grip. Managing to hold tightly to the hilt with his remaining good hand, he fell and took the blade with him.

Cal landed on the ground in a heap, his sword falling from his hand and skittering on the rock below. His arm was burned badly, red and angry from the boiling, black blood of the dying dragon that had begun to spray like a geyser out from his wounded flank.

Abaddon reared up on his hind legs, blood gushing from his wounds, his face a mix of fear and fury. *If I am to die, at least it will be with the satisfaction of knowing I killed you first, relic of Terriah and bastard of Éimhear!*

Cal stood to his feet, his arm furious in agony. He grabbed the sword with his other hand, bracing himself for whatever might come next. Deryn remained at his side, continuing to protect his charge no matter the danger.

Deep from within the ranks of her Nocturnal army, Nogcwren screamed in furious protest, her yellow eyes burning with offended rage as she watched the attack on her dragon.

The dragon tried to breath its fire, but instead of a torrent of green flame, a choking cough erupted. His eyes narrowed with even more rage at his impotence.

"Cal!" came the far-off voice of Astyræ.

He turned, taking his gaze off of the hulking serpent that stood before him. As he looked up, he saw the most beautiful sight he had ever beheld. The blonde hair of his beloved billowed in the wind behind her as she loosed the last of her silver shards into the belly of the dying beast. The arrows found their mark and buried themselves effortlessly past the armored scales, piercing the bowels of Abaddon with their righteous intent. The dragons screamed again in horrifying unison, their pain shared through the spilling of the black blood.

Cal and Deryn jumped out of the way just as the felled beast collapsed in a heap. They rolled in the dust, and the debris of the deadly collision barely missed them. They could hear the cheers of the archers and the Ramsguard, but it was the sound of boots running towards them that woke them from their daze.

"Cal! Are you alright?" Goran asked, his mighty chest heaving with worried breath.

"I think so," he said as he rose to his feet, dusting off himself. He winced as his raw and wounded arm growled in protest. "Is he dead?" Cal tightened his grip on the hilt of his blade.

"I think so!" Goran said, beaming with pride. "That lass of yours found her mark alright!"

In the distance they heard Angrah's scream of outrage as she struggled to get up off the ground.

"Seems when you killed him, she fell as well," Goran explained. "Though it doesn't look like we were lucky enough to actually injure her, too."

The dragon climbed up from out of the rocky lands just below the Ramsguard and into the air. Hundreds of arrows deflected off her hardened scales as her wings beat against the sky.

"Come on, brother!" Goran urged. "The whole damned Raven army is nearly upon us; you don't want to be food for those carrion, do you?"

Cal grabbed his blade, and with strength from where he knew not surging through his veins, he walked closer to the fallen dragon. He surveyed the carnage all about him: the approaching army, the screaming men, the fire and blood and broken bodies. Then he looked at the sword of the dragon slayer, and thought about the man who had long ago guarded the realms of men and Sprites by the bite of its very edge. Suddenly, both the tarnish and the weight vanished as Cal approached the beast.

"Your reign of terror ends this day, spawn of Šárka," he said with an authority that was not his own as he raised Gwarwyn over his head. "Go back to the dark abyss with the rest of your vile breed!"

Abaddon's eyes shot open in a dying wash of sickly green.

Fool! You should have taken her gift. The end has come for you, Cal-ar-min-don.

Without a moment for another word, Cal swung the blade of Caedmon and freed the serpent's head from its hideous body. Black blood began to pour out like a river, catching rock, grass, and tree alike in unholy fire.

The beating of wings upon the air suddenly sounded a bellow of doom, and he looked up with horror to see Angrah hovering over the flames of her fallen brother.

"Cal!" Goran shouted. "Run!"

Cal stood there, frozen, his mouth dry with fear.

"Cal, come on, brother!" the other woodcutters called out to him.

Angrah narrowed her furious gaze, her teeth dripping with the spilled blood of the brave soldiers of Shaimira as she spoke, her voice oddly singular.

How dare you! I shall feast on your flesh, in retribution for your foolish insolence!

Cal tried to run towards the outcropping of stone where his woodcutter brothers took shelter, but the dragon cut off his escape with a stream of fire. He ran back the other way, and yet again more fire hemmed him in.

Angrah laughed.

I will have my revenge; and it will be the last thing you see and hear and feel before I devour you and all of this world with fire.

"Deryn!" Cal shouted against the roar of the blaze. "What do we do now?!" He whirled around, desperately looking for an escape from this fiery snare. "This is all my fault! We should have just kept searching for the mark!" he shouted again. "Now we will never find the light!"

"Cal!" his Sprite guardian called, flitting up to catch his gaze.

"I don't see a way out, Deryn!" he continued. "I failed them ... I failed Him."

"Cal!" Deryn said again as he fought for his charge's full attention. "This is not failure!"

Arrows rained in upon the approaching army, and the few remaining ballistae took their aim upon the hovering dragon, though her scales repelled the massive, black darts. Navid signaled to the Ramsguard to mount their beasts and secure their helms, preparing them to charge the Nocturnals.

Across the field of battle, Nogcwren smiled a serpentine smile as the pieces of destruction were nearly now all in place.

"Deryn!" Cal shouted, softer now, resigned to the fire that awaited them both. "Thank you, my friend … for everything."

Angrah opened her mouth, her eyes hungry, famished for revenge. Then, without warning, the sound of a screech pierced the air.

"What in the damnable dark?" Cal said aloud as he beheld a sight he never dreamed to hope for.

"The Oweles!" Deryn said excitedly. "The Oweles have come for us! Oh, thank our Great Father!"

Cal watched in awe as the mighty Oweles collided with the dragon. Talons ripped and tore into flesh. Feathers and fangs alike clashed and bit, ravaging with an intense ferocity.

"Cal!" called the voice of Astyræ from up above.

He looked up and saw her there atop Uriel, beckoning for him to move from the center of the ring of fire. As he did, the lord of horses landed on the ground below, and Cal held his majestic white head in his hands for the briefest of moments. "Thank you," he sighed in gratitude.

"Cal!" Astyræ shouted at him. "Hurry!"

Cal looked at the soldiers of the Raven Army that began to rush in, now not a dozen paces from them. He held tightly to the mane of the white horse and threw his leg up and over the saddle.

"Fly now!" Cal urged.

Uriel beat his wings, and as he did, the flames of the green fire began to dampen and extinguish in the wake of his righteous wind. The lord of horses took to the air as the Raven army overtook the hill of the dead dragon.

"Thank you!" he said, looking back over his shoulder. "That was … I mean, I thought we were—"

"We aren't," she interrupted him with a kiss upon his cheek.

He smiled. "Alright then. Thank you." Cal looked to the battle that raged in front of and below him. The blasts of green fire and the scourge of razored talons rending the sky with their bloodlust above and the collision of Ravens and Rams below.

Hail, Calarmindon Bright Fame.

A familiar screech sounded inside his head as a white-winged bird soared alongside the lord of horses.

And hail to you, Uriel, Lord of the Tarrthála and brother to our cause. I, Edur, bring you tidings from the Watchers.

"Master Owele," Cal said with head bowed. "You have saved us all."

I have watched over you upon each leg of your journey as the THREE who is SEVEN has commanded. I have seen, and will see, to the carrying out of His will alone.

"And what is the will of the THREE who is SEVEN, Edur?" Cal asked as he held tight to the mane of the white horse.

His will for me is to bring aid to the lost children of Ádhamh in their time of need.

Cal watched in amazement as another mighty bird flew before the entrenched forces of Shaimira and beat his wings against the violent, green fires of the dragon. So powerful were the winds issuing forth that the men had to cling to their gilded helms for fear of losing them amidst the gale. Within moments, the fires that had ravaged man and mountain had all been extinguished in the wake of the wings of the Owele Haizea, the *"Wind of God".*

"Uriel!" Cal spoke to the horse lord. "Quickly now, back to the cleft in the rock ... we have to help them all, we have to find the light."

Horns began to blow, and the mighty dragon Angrah retreated back into the ranks of the Raven army. The Oweles circled overhead, watching as Navid's men came barreling down the highlands and collided with the vanguard of the Sorceress' men.

Do not be afraid, children of Ádhamh! The screeching words of Ruarc *"Storm Words"* resounded. *For a new light is near, and by it all shall truly see!*

A horn blast from within the Nocturnal ranks rang out a second time, and a volley of black darts, thousands strong, was let loose upon the men of Shaimira. Crashes and screams and blood-soaked gasps could be heard as both man and ram alike fell under the assault.

Ram and Raven fought relentlessly, metal against metal, as desperate hope pounded against thoughtless destruction.

Johanna watched from the mountainside. She saw her commanders give their orders and fire their arrows. She saw them run through a sea of evil with their lances buried to the hilt in the black blood of the Raven army. She watched as dozens and then scores of men at a time were cut down in the field of battle against an army that far outnumbered them.

It was the sight of the Owele Zigor, *"Punishment"*, with a boulder clenched between his armored talons, that allowed the words of Ruarc to flicker in the darkness of her doubt. The mighty Owele swept fast and low, releasing the massive stone with such force and such speed that it plowed a cut right through the ranks of the enemy.

Owele after Owele began to follow suit, soaring in from the peaks of the Itxaro to drop a payload of retribution upon their foes. Arrows came faster and in greater number, and though rocks found their marks, so too did the black barbs of the Ravens cut down the assault from above.

Edur turned his violet gaze down upon the Nocturnals, his eyes ablaze in righteous fury, though no protest dared to pass the beak upon his holy face.

"Fire!" called the Queen of Shaimira. "We have got to drive them back from Navid's men! Cut them down!"

Goran looked to his brothers, some bleeding heavily, while Gvidus tended to his badly burned arm. He peeked his head out from behind the outcropping of rocks and looked to the sky for any sign of the dragon's return. "Well, brothers ... I can't see what sense running is going to do, and at least that damned dragon is not out there burning the hell out of us all."

"Aye," Oren agreed.

"And those birds?" Alon added. "What in the damnable dark are they?"

"I'm not rightly sure," Goran said in reply. "Though they appear to be rather friendly at the moment."

"Aye," Oren agreed.

"What about Yasen?" came the voice of another.

Goran thought on it before he spoke. "He is out there. Bewitched, if you ask me."

"Can't we go get him, then?" Alon asked, innocently enough.

"Aye," Oren answered.

"Well, let's be on with it then," Gvidus said, wincing and grunting in wounded exasperation as he stood to his feet.

"Aye," Goran answered.

"Aye," came the reply of the remaining woodcutters.

They grabbed their axes and cinched their belts, and at the nod from Goran's large head, the men of the North let out a blast from their horns and a terrible yell, and then ran into the fray.

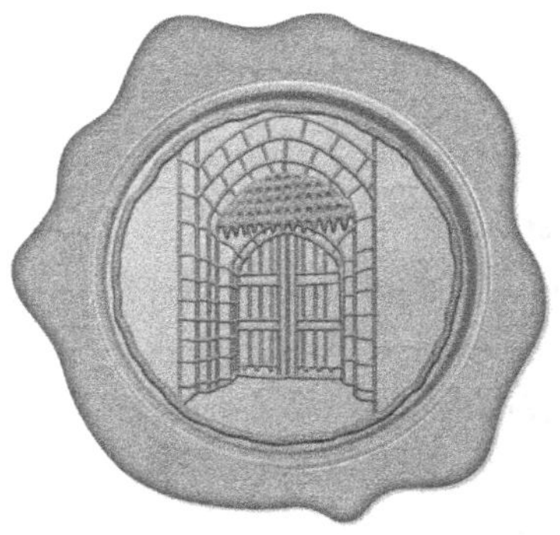

Chapter Thirty-Eight

The great courtyard door burst open in a storm of metal and splintered wood, and the cold, ominous winds of the North whipped up the stairs and into the great hall, blustering into the flaming hearth of the Halvard.

Vŏlker tightened his grip upon his mighty war hammer, and through gritted teeth he spat doom upon the horde of Ravens coming up to him through the breached door.

"Ye have come for your death, now, have ye?" the giant growled. "I'll have me vengeance for me Hlíf!" And with a soul chilling shout, the giant let loose a fury of swings, snapping necks and collapsing helms of the invading army.

"Vŏlker!?" came a shout from the stairs behind him. "Are you alright?"

But the giant paid little heed to the concern of his friends as he piled body after broken body upon the stone floor of the hall.

The clanking of the siege scorpions could be heard over Vŏlker's vengeance, as more spikes with more ropes were fired at the towers above.

Harmier risked a peek out from the protection of the rounded stairwell at the back of the great hall, and his heart nearly fell into despair at the sight of so great an army. The merchant fired a lone arrow that pierced the eye of a nearby attacker before he turned and ran back up the flight of stairs and into the armory above.

"What is it, Harmier?" Georgina asked as he rushed in, joining the few who had nervously entrenched themselves behind toppled tables and barrels of lamp oil, with their bows drawn and at the ready. "What is happening?" she begged in her bravest little girl voice.

"It is lost," he said as he looked at his worried friends. "The door is breached, the enemy will soon be upon us all."

"What?" came the shaking voice of an older woman.

"What do you mean, it is lost?" Georgina demanded. "I can still hear Völker!" she shouted in a frightened cry. "What do you mean, Harmier?!"

But the merchant dropped his bow and ran out past the door up to the battlements, fear overtaking his senses as he searched for a way of escape.

Arrows flew up from the ground below, and the remnant did their best to release what repellant they might down upon the army below. Harmier looked at the vast horde below and saw the doom that waited for them, hunger and bloodlust glowing in their sickly green eyes. He walked, stunned by the terror that he beheld, not heeding the danger around him, without so much as a crouch to hide himself from the angry bolts that buzzed furiously overhead.

It was Portus that spotted him first, as the large tanner had been desperately trying to burn the siege ropes that hung from the west tower near where Fryon was still grieving. "Harmier!" he shouted to his friend. "Harmier! You must get low! What are you doing?"

The rest of the remnant looked up from their targets below and saw the pale, panic-stricken merchant, walking obliviously through the storm.

"Harmier!" Margarid shouted out to him. "Harmier, get down!"

"It is lost," he began to shout back at them. "It is lost … it is all lost!"

"Harmier!" Michael shouted. "Get low, you fool!"

"It is lost … it is lost!" he continued as bolts zipped murderously past him.

"What are you talking about?" Michael shouted, furious at this display of recklessness in the midst of a battle.

"The enemy has breached the hall, and the army of darkness has come for us all!" he said as grief-filled tears ran down his cheeks.

Portus ducked low and ran towards his friend, tackling him to the stone floor as a score of raven-fletched arrows zoomed just overhead. "Are you mad?" the tanner shouted at his friend. "They are going to kill you!"

"They are going to kill us all!" Harmier screamed as spittle flew from his trembling lips, and tears fell from his bloodshot eyes.

"And you would just let them?" Portus said, his sizable brow furrowing in confusion at the posture of his merchant friend.

"Why resist, Portus? Why drag out the torture of life when death has so certainly marked us all with its doom," he said as he struggled against the large calloused hands of his friend.

"What are you saying?" Portus asked as he relaxed his hold a bit.

"Let me be, Portus!" the merchant screamed and spat. "The Ravens have come to pick my body clean, and I would rather not suffer the torture any longer than I must!"

"What?" Portus asked, all the more confused.

"Let me be!" he said with a violent shove of desperate strength, causing the tanner to raise up above the merlons that sheltered them. As he did, a half dozen bolts pierced the ancient bronze armor that Portus wore, biting deep into the flesh of his side.

"Portus!" Margarid shouted and screamed. "No!!!"

Michael ran towards them, arrows flying past as he tried to get to his friend.

"Why?" Portus asked in shock as he pulled his hand from his side and beheld the crimson stain of his leaking life.

"Let me be," Harmier said, rising to his feet and surveying the hopeless scene before him. "Just let me be." Before anyone could stop him, he took a step out from between the merlons and threw himself down into the throng of Raven soldiers that waited for him at the base of the Halvard wall.

"Harmier, no!" came the shouts of his friends.

Portus began to cough as blood spurted from his lips. Margarid leaned back against the safety of the wall as she held and stroked the head of her dying friend. "Portus, no! You are going to be alright! Right, Michael?" she begged, her beautifully sad eyes now wet with tears. "Right? He is going to be just fine... you'll see!"

Portus coughed again and blood leaked down his chin. He struggled to speak as the gurgles of death came for his body. "He said the hall was lost. We've got ... to ... we've got to help Vŏlker."

"Shhh. Rest now, Portus. Rest now, my sweet friend," Margarid cooed as she dabbed his bloody face with the hem of her dress.

"Portus, I am so sorry," Michael whispered.

"Ahhh!" The scream of a little girl sounded from the direction of the armory.

"Go," Portus replied.

Michael looked back at the entrance to the armory and then reached for the hand of his dying friend. "Seek the light, my friend," he said with a sad squeeze, and then ran, crouched, towards the sound of the scream.

As he came upon the barricade, he saw half a dozen Raven soldiers, felled and bleeding their blackened blood upon the ancient floor outside of the armory. He angled himself against the doorway, where he could see both the stairs going down to the great hall as well as the battlements atop the wall.

"Are you alright?" he asked the two ladies who were entrenched within, arrows drawn and aimed at the opening before him.

They were too stunned to answer him. The sounds of Vŏlker's mighty hammer and enraged curses could still be heard from the chamber below, but they could also hear the sounds of more boots upon the stairs.

"They are coming again," Michael said as he notched an arrow to his bow string and readied himself for whatever torment came next. The sight of the green glowing eyes and the muted iron of the Ravens' blades glinted out from the darkened bowels of the stairwell. Without so much as a single whisper, the weary remnant of Haven fired their arrows to defend their position.

"Michael!" came the tear sodden voice of Margarid. "They are on the wall!"

He turned his head to look out past the opening and saw that several of the damned devils had climbed a rope and scaled the Halvard wall, headed straight for the bleeding body of Portus and the lady Margarid. He notched his arrow and loosed it through the back of the helm of one of the invaders, just as three more came up the stairs into the armory. Two of them met their doom from the volley already fired, but the other leaped at Michael with a broad blade, narrowly missing his throat.

"Michael!" Georgina shouted at him as he drew his blade just in time to parry the thrust of the Raven soldier.

Screams came from atop the battlements, but he had neither the time nor the wherewithal to turn and see whose screams they were. More invaders came rushing up the stairs, and Georgina did her best to pierce their advance with her own arrows while Michael swung his blade and buried it into the belly of the beast that assaulted him.

A scream rose up again, and this time he was certain that it was the lady Margarid. He saw her fire upon one of her assailants, but another followed right behind the one she had just taken down. Margarid reached for another arrow, but her quiver was empty. The Nocturnal raised his blade, his sickly green eyes glowing with a hunger to devour the life from her. All that stood between his blade and her body was the pierced body of her friend the tanner.

"No!" she screamed. "Michael!"

Portus, using the very last of his strength, reached his massive hand up to catch the black blade before it buried itself in the amber-haired head of his screaming friend. His hand found iron, and just as the sharpened edge of the sword cut through flesh and bone, the point of an arrow shot through the mouth of the Nocturnal and sent him in a heap to the mob army below.

Michael ran, his bow still in his hand, and his heart pounding uncontrollably in his chest. "Margarid! Margarid, are you alright?" He tripped and stumbled to his knees, nearly crawling on all fours to get to her. "The blood!" he shouted. "There is so much blood! Are you...?" He tried to speak through worried labored breath. "Are you alright?"

She nodded and sobbed. The blood of her friend had soaked her body and covered her face. The black blade of the Nocturnal still protruded from the chest of the tanner as his fingers laid scattered upon the battlement floor.

"Oh, Portus," Michael said through his own tears. "Thank you." He looked at her and carefully helped her up and away from their large friend's dead body.

"Michael! There!" Celrod shouted and pointed toward the same siege rope that had given entrance to the enemy.

"Burn it!" Celrod shouted at him.

Michael looked about and saw a torch at the entry to the armory still burning in the grip of the iron sconce.

"Stay here!" He ordered. "Shoot everything you see!"

He ran towards the torch, and as he came close to the armory doorway his foot nearly slipped in a puddle of slick wetness. Worry was heavy upon his mind as he feared the worst for his friends who were so bravely defending them from inside. But the smell of leaking lamp oil calmed his worry and gave him cause to hope.

"Georgina ... are you hurt?" he shouted as he sniffed the wetness that soaked through his leather gloves.

"No, we are alright ... but we don't have many more arrows left, Michael," she said, as bravely as she could muster.

Just then, a loud, soul-chilling scream reverberated from below. Not a moment later, a great crash sounded upon the ground below them.

"Vŏlker?" Georgina cried. "Vŏlker, no! Not you, too!"

"What now?" the old woman asked, terrified. "We haven't the arrows to repel the whole bloody Raven army!"

The smell of lamp oil caught his nose again, and he knew in an instant what needed to be done. "The two of you, get out here, and stay low! Grab what you can to hide behind, and fire whatever you have at anything that comes at you."

"What are you going to do, sir?" the old woman asked.

Without so much as a word, Michael slammed his blade into the side of a barrel, spilling oil down the stairs as he did. He toppled the large barrel and sent it bouncing and crashing into the great hall below. The sounds of the enemy could be heard as they began to march up from below. Michael reached up and grabbed the torch from the sconce, and with a silent prayer on his lips, he threw the fire upon the lake of oil.

The stairwell erupted in a blast of flame, the fire racing like the white water of the Abonris, cascading down the spiraled steps and into the great hall. The sounds of screaming and grunting were followed by a sound of rushing wind cutting through the noise of the battle. The small, frightened remnant that huddled upon the battlement above watched as a burst of flames shot through the broken front door and lit the darkened courtyard below.

"What now?" Timorets said, his breathing labored and heavy as he saw their only means of escape engulfed in flames.

"Indeed!" Celrod said as he slid back down behind the cover of the merlon. "And what about the giant? Where is Vŏlker?"

Michael shook his head, the emotion of so much loss on this dark day beginning to well up in his eyes. He wiped at his face with the sleeve of his tunic and took a deep breath to steady his voice.

"We dig in. Here." He spoke as bravely as he could. "The west tower is lost, but we have the wall and the East tower. And at least we know from which direction these Ravens will be coming from."

"And how long will we be able stand here?" Timorets asked. "There are so few of us left, and I haven't many an arrow left."

"Aye ... he is right," the schoolmaster agreed. "I have about a half a quiver."

"And then what?" Fryon said flatly.

Michael let out an exhausted sigh. He knew horses, not battle strategy. His eyes caught the soft green of Margarid's, and though he knew not what the best laid plan would be or should be; he knew that he wanted to protect her in any way he could.

"I don't know," he said honestly and with great sincerity in his voice. "But I am not ready to give over to despair, and I am certainly not ready to give this dark army my life, or any of yours, without a fight."

"That fire won't hold them for long, you know," Celrod said matter-of-factly.

"That's okay, Celrod. The fire isn't the light we are hoping for, anyhow," Margarid said softly as she squeezed Michael's hand.

He looked at her, confused at her musing.

"Cal is still out there, and I believe he will yet find the light that Engelmann spoke of. We haven't come this far for it all to end in darkness. It can't."

Michael's eyes went wide with wonder at how he could have forgotten that Cal was still out there, seeking and searching.

"That may be," Celrod replied. "But he is just one man in this great wide world, and they," he motioned to the Raven army below, "they are still an army right here at our door."

"But it only takes one to seek and to find," Georgina spoke up. "At least, that's what Engelmann told us."

"One with hope enough for us all," Margarid agreed.

"Well if it's going to be anybody ... it's going to be my horsed-faced cousin," Michael said with a tired albeit hopeful smile.

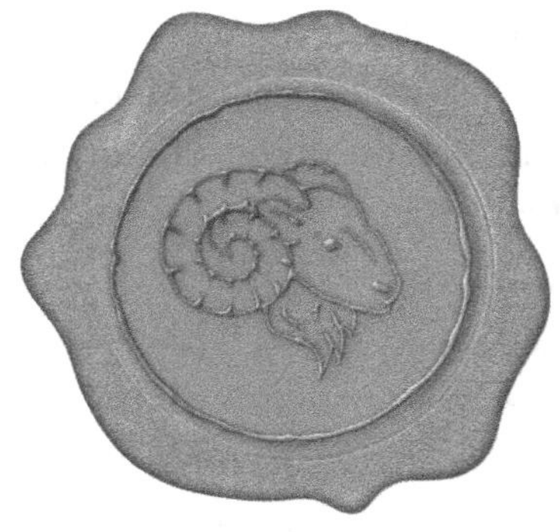

Chapter Thirty-Nine

The clash of metal upon metal rang loud and long in the dark sky. The Oweles continued their assault, first with stone and then with talons, as they unleashed their doom upon the advancing Nocturnal army.

The woodcutters worked their way along the ridgeline, the edge of the river giving them some semblance of protection as they relentlessly drove their axes, cutting deep wounds in the mighty forces of the Sorceress.

Angrah had retreated to the rear of the enemy army, seeking the aid of her Queen. The mighty dragon landed beside the black, winged carriage, her strength leaking out from the wounds upon her bloodied back.

My Queen. The Oweles have come to their aid, and their number is beyond my strength. If I but still had my brother-

"Enough!" Nogcwren shouted into the madness about her. "You are mine to rule, mine to order into battle, mine to command to ravage a thousand enemies if I wish it! You are not permitted to retreat or surrender, no matter what feathered pests litter the sky!" She pointed her scepter between the eyes of the dragon. "They are nothing but vermin." Her tone subsided into a more seductive timbre. "You are the offspring of Ahriman, the great serpent, the father of dragons. Never would he think to leave the fight, nor to disobey his mistress, Šárka."

Angrah growled in chastised protest.

"And yet, it would seem that I have been given his weakest of daughters," she said with hatred burning in her eyes. "A dragon afraid of a bird ... you honor your father well, Angrah."

My Queen. The dragon seethed with reproach.

"Captain Durai," the Raveness called. "General Aius has not yet joined us on the field of battle, has he?"

"No, my Queen," he answered, coming forth from the shadows. "Our scouts in the north have not brought word from the northern rim lands, but I am sure that he and the main host will join us soon."

She turned, her yellow eyes aglow with lust and menace as she watched her army marching ever closer to the last defenses of Shaimira. "These annoying pets of his, the foul of the sky," she turned to meet the gaze of her commander, "will the pointed barbs of our arrows not pierce their foolish feathers?"

"I would say so, my Queen," Durai agreed with a nod of his head.

"Then what are you waiting for?" Nogcwren ordered angrily. "Have the archers focus the whole of their assault on the sky, and perhaps we shall rid the air of their filth, once and for all!"

He bowed and left her presence, mounting his black horse, her orders fresh on his lips.

She looked to her driver who waited upon the front seat of her carriage with thousands of thongs pierced and threaded through his flesh. "If my dragon has neither the strength nor the stomach to fight the birds, maybe it's time we even out this fight." She nodded to him, and he raised a blood curdling, otherworldly scream. The flock of ravens rose from the ground in a murderous black cloud, snapping both thong and skin as they did so.

Angrah surveyed her scales and blew a blast of green fire over herself, cauterizing each bloodied wound by her own fire. She screamed in protest, but her pride was far greater than her pain.

I will avenge my brother and the honor of my kind ... and you will know gratitude for the AŽDAHĀ once again! She roared with such hatred and might that even the Sorceress herself was momentarily taken aback.

Nogcwren's composure quickly returned, and a satisfied smile crept across her pale face. "We shall see, won't we, Angrah?"

At that, Angrah burst forth in a rush of wind and rage, flying into the sky and bent on destruction.

"Tell me, what is it that you see?" she asked the tall figure behind her. The large dark-haired man walked up next to her carriage and raised a long, slender spy glass to his not-quite completely green eyes, surveying the battle before them.

"I see the birds, and the men. We outnumber them six to one, and yet their arrows rain down, and their knights still ride, and..."

"Yes?" she said, waiting for the large man to finish his thought. "Tell me!"

"The woodcutters." A growl of disgust colored his voice. "There, along the eastern flank and by the river. Looks like they are coming this way."

"Ah," she cooed with delight. "It looks as if your reward will be given as promised, Seig. Or should I say, *General.* Ready your men."

Seig turned to meet the face of Yasen, who stood a dozen paces behind him. "It seems you will finally get to prove your loyalty, North Wolf." Seig beamed with self-satisfaction. "Tell the men to ready themselves, for it is nearly our time for glory!"

Yasen looked at Seig, and not a trace of malice could be found upon his wounded face. His lone eye had not yet turned fully, but he stood at attention, as obedient as a dog to the heel of his master. "As you command," the once-mighty woodcutter replied as he bowed his head and turned to gather the remaining guardsmen of the first colony of

Haven.

They watched as Angrah unfurled her large, leathery wings as she approached the forefront of the battle, hovering not forty hands above the marching forces.

The Oweles were cutting swaths through the approaching enemy, while Navid and his Ramsguard barreled their way through the ranks on the backs of their mighty rams.

A company of Nocturnal archers halted their advancement and raised their black crossbows, aiming them high into the sky in the direction of the Oweles. With a wordless command, hundreds of the black barbs flew into the sky. Three of the ancient birds screeched in agony as their feathered bodies were pierced with the hatred of the Raven Army.

Ruarc screeched his indiscernible orders, and the company of Oweles spread themselves out along the line.

"There it is!" Johanna shouted as she spied the dragon hovering just above the field of battle. "The ballistae, now!"

THUNK. THUNK. THUNK. The sound of the great war machines reverberated across the clearing as they fired their terrible black arrows, one after the other.

"The dragon!" Cal shouted as he willed Uriel to turn and face the opposition once again. "Uriel, the serpent is back, we can't leave them!"

"Cal, no!" Astyræ reasoned with him. "We are nearly back to the cleft, I can see it!"

"I don't care!" Cal yelled. "We are going back to help them."

Angrah let out an assault of green fire as she approached the vanguard of the mounted, Shaimiran warriors. Ruarc called to his fellow Oweles, and within moments they had abandoned their lesser battles for this greater fight, turning their attention now back to the dragon.

Screeches filled the sky above, while Johanna looked on in horrified wonder as her men burned and battled in the shadows. She and her archers felt safe enough for the moment, while the winged monsters did their worst out in the not-so-far-off distance.

Another of the Oweles screeched and fell as the black barbs of the Nocturnals cut him down in a storm of biting metal.

"No!" Deryn blurted out as he saw the holy servant fall to the ground only to be trampled under brutish boots and hooves.

"We have got to concentrate our fire there, on their archers! Right there, do you see them?" Johanna said to Sendoa as he, too, looked through the spy glass to survey the field of battle.

"Yes, my Queen, I see them." With little regard for decorum, he ran from her side down the line of his archers, telling them where in the darkness to aim. As they began to fire, the Raven archers began to fall.

"My Queen?" came the voice of Mezulari. "What kind of devilry is that?" He drew his blade and pointed at the dark cloud of green eyes that was rushing ever swiftly towards their position.

"Have mercy!" she whispered to herself, then raised her voice to call to her warriors. "Swords, now! Draw your blades!"

Sendoa looked up at the sound of his queen's voice, unsure of the change of orders after they had just begun to concentrate their efforts, when what he saw made his blood run cold with terror. "Blades! Now!" he shouted as he, too, drew his own sword from the blue, leather scabbard that hung on his belt.

Just then, the storm of crows rained down upon them. Green eyes and sharp beaks crashed into bright armor and brighter blades, keeping the archers from firing a single arrow upon the advancing forces of the Sorceress.

The Oweles reached the enraged dragon, their armored talons gleaming in the firelight below.

Angrah. Ruarc screeched in authority. *Darkness is nearly over, for a new light is advancing upon Aiénor, swiftly on the wind of the coming dawn.*

The dragon roared in protest, torrents of green fire issuing forth in the direction of the holy birds. None, save one alone, altered their course to fly into the path of the rushing flames. Haizea began to beat his wings, and the rush of holy wind that followed collided with the vile fire.

The collision of forces thundered, the rolls of its magnitude breaking the noise of war with an unrelenting sound. The fire split and divided, never penetrating the wind.

Angrah's leathery wings caught the tempest, and the force sent her tumbling over herself. Unable to regain control, she crashed into the sea of Raven soldiers, crushing the warriors under the force of her fall.

The dragon waited only a moment before she stood up and shook the dirt and blood off of her hide, narrowing her gaze at the Oweles off in the distance. She gathered her strength and exploded from the ground, shooting high into the sky until the battle was nearly out of sight.

"Are you alright?" Cal shouted to the Oweles, as they approached him, diving in and out of the fray, dodging black arrows and sharp spears.

Calarmindon Bright Fame.

Edur's voice pierced through the battle, his violet eyes burning with a righteous fury.

Seek the light.

Without warning, a sound like a mighty rushing river came from overhead. Cal looked up to see what kind of devilry it was, and he saw the blazing green eyes of the dragon hurtling right towards them.

"Edur! Look out!" he shouted, but it was too late. The outstretched talons of the serpent cut through the feathered flesh of the great Owele, *"Snow"*, who had watched over him for his whole journey. The dragon screamed in pain as the silver blood of the Owele began to burn and torment the beast that had spilled it.

The Oweles, sensing the felling of their brother, turned their attention once again to this vile creation of Šárka.

Angrah roared, her voice pained and proud all at the same time. *I will rid this world of your miserable kind, if I have to do it one infuriating bird at a time!*

Cal urged Uriel closer, the light of the hilt of his sword glowing with duty.

"Cal, what are you doing?" Astyræ said. "We have already defeated one dragon, barely escaping with our lives! We have got to do as the Oweles said! We have got to seek the light!"

The Oweles swarmed and darted in and out of the fight. Angrah let forth blasts of green fire as she swiped hard with her razored talons. Blood was drawn by both bird and beast, cuts and tears bleeding both silver and black in this war in the heavens.

"She is right!" Deryn shouted. "Cal!"

But he would not hear their words, determined to rescue these warriors of the sky.

Angrah's yellowed fangs caught Basajuan as he was darting for the throat of the dragon. With a screech and a crunch, the *"Lord of the Woods"* was pierced and torn by a hundred vile teeth.

On the ground below, Sendoa's men swung their blades blindly into the cloud of ravens. They screamed and cried as the birds tore and pecked at their faces. The birds gave no heed to their own safety, for their only thought was to do the bidding of their queen. Blades cut through their tiny black bodies while Johanna and her guard tried to ward them off with fire. They waved blazing torches at the rushing cloud, but the birds did not relent, even as the flames consumed them.

Zigor flew up from underneath the dragon and let his talons rake their punishment from the tail to the belly of the beast. Angrah screamed and whipped her bleeding tail, crushing the bird and sending him careening into the face of the mountain wall.

Cal pointed his blade at the neck of the dragon and kicked Uriel in the flank with little reverence and pure determination. The lord of the horses folded his wings to speed his assault, but in that very moment, a dozen black arrows were loosed from the crossbows of the Nocturnal soldiers below.

Unlooked for and unaware, Remiel intercepted the assault of the enemy, as the mighty Owele was pierced so that Cal would be spared. The *"Mercy of God"* let out a screech, and the burning violet of his eyes faded to black as he, too, crashed onto the field of battle below.

Cal was within striking distance now, and the attention of Angrah was caught by the remaining Oweles. He raised Gwarwyn to strike the dragon, and the hilt of the sword erupted with light as the bite of the blade sunk deep into the shoulder of the serpent. So shocked and so pained was the dragon that she whirled about with her other arm and struck a deadly blow to the body of the flying horse.

Cal lost grip his on the sword as he and his friends were sent hurtling with impossible force into the rocks of the mountain's face.

Angrah screamed at the blade of the dragon slayer that was buried deep in her bleeding flesh. She reached around, trying to claw it out of her shoulder. Though she was desperate to rid her body of the sword of Caedmon, the blade that killed her kin, she could not get to it.

The Oweles flew higher out of the reach of the enemy arrows, surveying the suffering of the dragon. Black blood and green fire rained with fury upon the battle below, and Angrah twisted and turned, screaming and bellowing as she rent the darkened sky.

Azrael, the mightiest of the Owele warriors, closed his eyes as he listened obediently to a voice no one else could hear. When he opened them again, the violet had turned into a raging blue flame. The *"Angel of Death"* screeched his offense at all of this blood and beguilement. In a calm, deliberate move, he flew right up to the face of the beast and tore the horrified green eyes of the abomination clean from her head. He held them in his gilded talons and screeched in finality as he landed upon a small outcropping, high upon the mountain face, and began to devour them one at time.

Angrah seemed to float motionless in the sky for the briefest of moments, her inky body bleeding from head to tail. Ruarc screeched, though none could hear his words, and the dragon plummeted towards the ground below, crushing Ram and Raven alike as she crashed.

A shout went up from what was left of the Ramsguard, and their vigor was set ablaze at the sight of the two dead dragons. "Victory is nearly ours, men!" shouted Navid to his battle-weary guardsmen. "Gird yourselves now! Find the fight, find it quickly!"

As the ancient serpent exhaled her last, toxic breath, a cloud of green poison loomed over the battlefield. Navid's men and Nocturnals alike began to choke in the wake of its fumes. The few remaining Oweles circled high above, searching for their targets and then dive-bombing with ferocious intent, cutting through metal armor and greying flesh with their sharpened talons.

Haizea began to beat his wings in protest of the smog that stole the breath from both friend and foe. The gale blew back the noxious, green cloud, but as the fog began to lift, a volley of raven-fletched arrows pierced his feathered body, and the *"Wind of God"* fell lifeless, trampled underfoot by the once-again advancing enemy.

Across the battlefield, Nogcwren screamed frustrated fury. Thunder rolled off in the distance as a punctuation to the maniacal displeasure of the Raven Queen. "The Mal'akhim!" She spat in disgust. "How dare he send the Oweles!" Her yellow eyes burned like molten sulfur as she gathered herself and then spoke in a calm voice. "Captain Durai."

The commander of the advancing Nocturnal forces stood tall and unwavering, ready to receive his orders. "Has General Aius sent word from our army in the east?"

"No, Raveness," the commander said cautiously, not wanting to cause further displeasure to the volatile Sorceress. "Our scouts have reported no word as of yet, and we have seen no evidence of his movement."

"Evidence of his movement?" she turned on him. "*Evidence*, commander? It is an army nearly ten thousand strong! You will feel the very trees uproot themselves to get out of his way, the ground will shake at the sound of the boots of my forces coming down from the north!

"My Queen," Durai said apologetically.

"He is not slinking around, hiding behind the cover of the forests like some bumbling peasant, commander! He is a bloody *army*! My banners unfurled, my horns shaking the resolve of every ear who hears them! And no bird or beast, no hiding ram is safe from the guile of the hunter, commander!" she seethed in anger. "You need not *search* for evidence of his coming. Either he is here … or he is not." As she finished, the ink markings on her pale flesh were writhing like a nest of angry vipers.

"I will have my scouts send word as soon as we see him," Durai offered.

She looked at the commander with hatred in her eyes, then turned her gaze towards the tall, dark-haired hero of Haven. "Fools," she said as she looked him over from head to toe. "Do you want to see how to win a war, General?"

Seig's eyes had begun to turn green, and they glowed in their Nocturnal lust at the beckoning of this lethal beauty. "Of course, my Queen."

"Well then," she cooed. Her voice, not moments ago rough and biting, was now luxuriously velvet, like dark wine on a drunken tongue. "Follow me." She turned and strode off towards the field of battle.

Seig smiled like a man being led to a new and foreign bedchamber, licking his lips in anticipation of her appointment. "Men, gather your arms," he ordered the once-pious guardsmen of Haven. "We will be escorting the queen to her victory."

"Captain Durai?" she said, not looking over her shoulder as Seig and his men gathered about her in a shield-like formation.

"Yes, Raveness?" he answered compliantly.

"Kill the damned birds, will you?" She ordered. "The Mal'akhim. Shoot them all."

"Yes, Raveness," he said with a bow.

Chapter Forty

"Cal!" Astyræ shouted, wincing in pain as her bruised and battered ribs screamed in protest. "Cal, are you alright?" She gingerly crawled to her feet, searching for her friends who had been thrown violently into the mountain when Uriel was struck by the dragon.

"Deryn? Cal?" she shouted into the night, the heart-wrenching sounds of war echoing up from the battleground below. The wind caught her golden hair, and she labored to keep it out of her eyes so that she could search for her friends.

She took a deep breath, wincing again as she did so. "Argh," she groaned to herself as her hand went instinctively to her side. "Cal! Deryn! Where are you?"

"Astyræ!" she heard Cal's weak voice below. "Astyræ, are you alright?"

She cautiously walked to the edge of the rocky ledge. Steadying herself against the stone beside her, she peered out over the edge to see if she could spot him. "Cal?" she called again. "Are you alright? Hang on!"

Cal had been thrown from the back of Uriel, but he did not land upon the relative safety of the ledge. Rather he had crashed and tumbled further down the face until, by some grace, he was caught in the gnarled branches of a scrub tree that was growing in the cracks of the Itxaro.

"Aye!" He shouted up to her. "I'm pretty banged up ... but I'm alright."

"Can you climb up here?" she shouted back.

"I should be able to," he said as he found a bit of rock to place his boot upon and a secure handhold to begin the climb up thirty or forty hands to where she was perched. "Have you seen Deryn, or Uriel? The dragon, I didn't even..."

"No! Not yet," she told him as she looked hard into the darkness, scanning the face of the rock for any sign of their friends. She searched as Cal labored his way up the side of the mountain, and just when weariness was about to give way to despair, her eye caught a glimpse of an azure light just above and to the right of her.

"I see them!" she shouted down to him, but was startled when one hand and then another took hold of the ledge by her feet. "Cal!" she gasped, then winced at her own startled breath. "I think I see them there," she said, pointing in the direction of the glow.

Cal pulled himself up and onto the ledge, his face a smattering of blood and dirt. His tunic was ripped, and his feathered armor was dented, but he was alright. He grunted as he stood to his feet, his scraped and bloodied hands pushing the hair out of his face. "Where? Where did you see them?"

"There," she said, pointing with one arm, still holding her wounded side with the other.

"That's him, alright," he told her as his clouded gaze returned to her pained grimace. "What about you, my lady?" he said, taking her own bruised and bedraggled face in his hands. "Are you hurt badly?"

"My rib, it might very well be broken," she told him.

His eyes were locked on her own violet gaze; compassion, relief, and worry swirled about them. Just then, the sickening sound of the horns of the Raven army broke them out of their wounded reverie. Cal looked down and saw the horrors of war still raging like a violent storm; his friends were doing their best to weather the tempest, all the while knowing that the waves of darkness would soon crash their finality upon them all.

"Can you climb?" he asked her, taking her hand.

"I think so," she said, steeling herself for the pain that was sure to follow.

"Come on then, Astyræ, we have got to find them. And then, we have got to find the marking of the Stag."

The two of them clung to whatever their hands could grip. They shimmied and climbed, pulling their weary bodies and wounded spirits up the face of the mountain. It wasn't much more than twenty hands up and to the right from the ledge where they started that they came upon a cleft hewn out of the rocky face.

"Deryn!" Cal shouted. "Deryn, where are you?"

Cal pulled himself up and over, onto the rock. He quickly spun around and reached out his long arm, offering his hand to Astyræ below. "Take my hand, quickly now!" he told her.

She reached up and out for his hand with her own slender fingers, but her arm was not nearly long enough to meet his grasp. "I can't reach you!"

"You have to!" Cal shouted back down to her. He looked frantically, his eyes surveying the face of the rock below. "There! Just put your foot right there, and when you step, reach out and take my hand."

She held on tightly to the relative safety of where she was, and with a steadying breath she placed her foot upon the very place that Cal had showed her. "Alright!" she said as stones and pebbles skittered out from under her feet.

"Take my hand, Astyræ!" he said, his voice willing her to trust him.

She swallowed hard against her fear, then nodded her understanding to him. "Alright, Cal." She reached up, her fingertips grasping at the air between his hand and her own, her face wrinkled in pain at the fire that tore through her side.

"Come on! A little further now!" he said as he too strained against the rock ledge, willing his body to meet her own. "Further up!"

She let out an exhale as she shifted her weight from the safety of the ground and onto her other foot. In one motion, she leapt towards Cal's hand. Skin found skin, and Cal grasped her wrist as the rocks from where she propelled herself upward went skittering down the face of the mountain and into the battle below.

"I've got you!" he told her through gritted teeth. "I've got you, my lady!"

She turned her head to look at the battle below and swallowed her fear back down into her bile-churning stomach. Her eyes found his again, and she nodded her understanding. It wasn't but two more calculated steps and a generous tug of her arms until she and Cal both lay in a heap upon the mountain ledge above.

Her chest was heaving and her breath came raggedly, a cold sweat clinging to her face.

"You did it, my lady," he told her as he rose first to his knees and then to his feet. "You are alright now."

She stared into the black sky above her, the noises of war drowned out by the sound of rushing blood in her ears. "Thank you, groomsman."

Cal smiled, nearly forgetting why it was that they had labored so to reach this place. It was the sounds of wounded breath and agony, mingled with the soft silver song of the Sprite, that woke him from the glow of this small victory.

"Deryn," he whispered. "It's Deryn. Come on, we have got to find them."

The faint, azure glow of his winged companion illuminated the dark rocks ahead of them. "Deryn! Deryn, I am here! Are you hurt?" He heard his own words grow quiet as his clouded eyes took in the sight before him.

There, laying in a heap of blood and bowels, was the mangled body of the lord of horses, his brilliant white coat now stained a violet-crimson. "Uriel!" Cal blurted out, his voice breaking under the weight of the emotion.

The *Anahiera* wheezed and labored as the torn flaps of his flesh bubbled and bled with each excruciating breath. Cal ran towards him and fell to his knees, taking his fabled friend's head in his own stained hands.

"Uriel," he pleaded. "No! Not you, too!" His eyes filled with tears as he looked at his Sprite friend, who also had two silver tears streaming down his face. "I am so sorry!" he lamented.

"Oh no," Astyræ said, walking up to the carnage.

Cal's hands traced the angry, gaping wounds on the white flank of his friend. "It was the dragon," he said, choking back the anger and sadness. "Uriel took the brunt of his talons. He saved our lives, by giving up his own."

The sounds of the horse's painful breathing were nearly too much to bear, so Cal did the best thing he knew to do to bring peace to the equine friends he had known all his life; he began to sing. He reached out his hand to trace the ancient lines of Uriel's mighty face as his shaky voice managed to bring music into the moment.

Astyræ gratefully listened to him sing for a few minutes before she placed her slender hand upon Cal's shoulder. "He is suffering," she said. "It is not right for the lord of the horses to lay here like this."

He nodded slowly. "You are right, my lady." Cal reached for his sword, but did not find it in its scabbard. "Gwarwyn?" he said as he looked in vain for the sword that lay buried in the smoldering flesh of the fallen serpent. "Only ... only I have lost my blade." He looked at her helplessly as a tear ran down his dirt-stained face.

"It is only right that I bear the burden of his final wound," Deryn said as he reached for his tiny, azure blade. "For we are kin of a sort, given both wings and feet from our Great Father. I would rather him depart from the pains of this world by the hand of a friend."

Cal placed his hand on the throbbing neck of the dying beast. His heart was broken at the sight of such injustice for the kingly steed. "I am sorry, Uriel, I am so sorry," he whispered.

He heard the sound of Uriel's shaky, gasping voice in the recesses of his thoughts. *Seek the light, Calarmindon Bright Fame.*

The winged horse snorted a weary, exhausted pardon, and then he nodded his permission to end the suffering.

Deryn walked to the neck of the dying horse, barely able to see over its girth. He held his blade in front of him, the point of the sword hovering just above the throat. He bowed his head and prayed in words unknown to Cal and Astyræ, but with a meaning that needed no interpretation.

"Clota sneachta Uriel tigherna an Tarrthála, le do dhoimhneacht agus íobairt; ní mór fianaise mhór ár n-athair a fháil riamh.

(Hail Uriel, lord of the Tarrthála, may the great light of our Father be found by your doom and sacrifice.)

"May it be so," Cal said in agreement as Deryn plunged his blade deep into the throat of the lord of the horses, ending the life that had been given to spare their own.

Astyræ put her arm around Cal's shoulder as the violet-crimson blood leaked out upon the stony floor of this cleft in the Itxaro. They stood there for a moment and waited for the last movement of air to pass from the magical beast before them. Finally, Cal wiped his cloudy eyes on the sleeve of his sodden tunic, noticing the whirlwind of war still raging on the battlefield below them.

"Now what?" he said as he turned about to survey his surroundings. "We are trapped up here!" he said angrily. "Is this the end? I chose to help my friends for a few brief moments instead of finding the light, and now we've lost everything? I have failed. Again."

"All is not yet lost," Deryn said as he wiped his blade clean upon the hem of his own tunic. "Three times you have failed, as was foretold. And three times, you will choose ... even now ... to persevere, Bright Fame."

"But how?" Cal asked them. "Our friends are dying, and the Sorceress would murder the whole world before she would see a single soul left standing in defiance of her rule. We don't have a way down from these heights, and I don't have a sword to wield, even if we could find our way down." Cal sat down hard in a seat of his own self-pity, staring out over the fields below. "What kind of victory can we even hope for now? We are useless up here!"

Deryn looked directly at his charge. "What if the only victory we could have ever truly hoped for was to see our way clearly through this war?" Deryn asked him. "To escape the battle long enough that we might yet seek the light with the clarity of sight along the path that our Great Father intended?"

"My heart is breaking with so much death, Deryn, so much destruction and evil. Can't we do something about it?" he argued. "What good is seeking the light anymore if everyone who might see by it is already dead?"

Astyræ looked about the cleft of the rock as they talked. The small ledge curved inward towards the heart of the mountain, but then came to an abrupt halt, not ten paces past the bleeding body of the last of the *Anahiera.* She noticed that the blood that spilled from Uriel's body ran down, rather quickly, towards the wall of stone at the innermost part of the cleft. Something about this odd flow of blood caught her attention.

"So much blood from so great a beast, and yet..." she whispered to herself, paying no attention to the conversation of her companions.

"We have done *much* about it, my friend," Deryn said with great confidence. "We have rescued prisoners, we have defended our friends, new and old. We have fought bravely, albeit recklessly, against the serpents of the enemy; yet still one thing remains."

Cal nodded his head, and with a surrendering sigh, he understood. "It is much simpler, you know, to swing a blade and fell a foe, than it is to seek a power beyond all reaching, whose true might ... was never meant for keeping." He shook his head and smiled a sad smile, looking to the Sprite for approval of his rhyme.

"My warrior poet friend," Deryn said with a tired smile. "That clarity ... might yet still be our victory."

"Cal! Deryn!" Astyræ called out. "Come quickly!"

Cal stood to his feet and made his way through the passage of rock towards the sound of her voice. He saw Astyræ standing at the end of a stream of violet-crimson blood, her face alight with the most peculiar expression.

"I have found something," she said excitedly. "Look! Right there, do you see it?" She pointed to the stream of flowing blood.

"It is Uriel's blood, my lady," Cal replied, clearly not seeing what it was that excited her so.

"That is what I thought too ... at first, I mean," she told them. "But why is it not pooling, then? Uriel is a mighty beast, and with so much bleeding, this rock should be covered."

A wave of understanding washed over Cal's face as he connected her excited thoughts.

"Look there, at the end of the stream. It is flowing beneath all of that rubble and that bush of brambles right there! It is draining into the heart of the mountain, Cal!"

Cal looked at Deryn and then back again at the mess of stones and sand, branches and scrub brush, and hope entered into his heart all over again.

"If it is flowing... then perhaps—"

"There might be a way inside for us too!" Cal finished her thought. "Come on, then. Let's see what passage we might find."

The three of them went about the messy work of removing debris and rolling away the stones. Cal took hold of the base of the bramble bush, whose roots had spidered out all along the face of the rock, just above where the blood had been flowing. He put his boot firmly upon the rock, and with all of his might, he pulled. Finally, the vine relented its grip to the persistent tug of the groomsman's body, giving way with a rumble and the clatter of splitting stone.

With one final heave, the bush's roots released, and he yanked it free from the mountain face. As he did, the rocks, which had been held securely in place by the roots, began to crumble in a heap upon the stony floor. Cal fell back upon himself, landing in the stream of Uriel's blood.

When the dust had settled and the sounds of falling, skittering stones finally ceased, Cal saw with his clouded eyes the glowing marks of the White Stag there upon the inside wall of the newly formed cavity.

"What in the damnable dark?" he said in wonder.

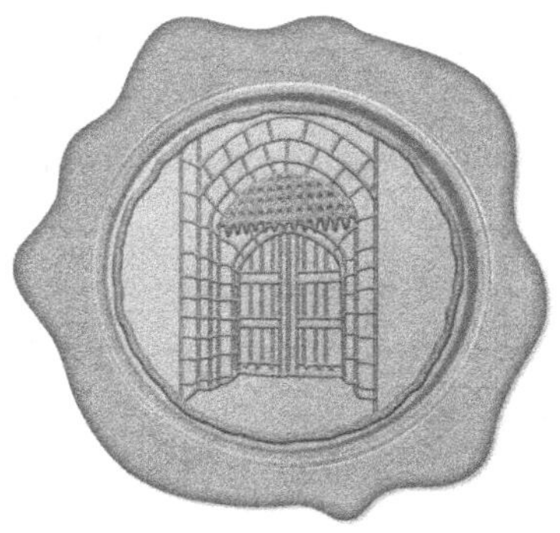

Chapter Forty-One

CRACK! The sound of the flame-ravaged rafters buckled and broke under the storm of fire.

"Come on," Michael said to his friends, feeling the tremble of the crumbling tower beneath his feet. "We have to move to the east tower. They are going to come for us, but we sure as hell are not going to make it easy for them."

"Stay low!" Fryon pleaded. "No more careless deaths today, alright?"

The small band of men and women nodded their agreement and crouched behind the protection of the wall, moving quickly across the expanse of the battlements and into the archway of the eastern tower.

A loud CRASH and BOOM startled them all as the floor above the great hall fell in on itself, burying a mass of Raven soldiers and the broken body of their friend and protector, Vŏlker the giant.

"Vŏlker," Margarid said, a sob catching in her throat.

"Quickly now!" Timorets ordered. The group began to roll leather trunks and crates filled with books and scrolls from the upper rooms out into the archway in front of them.

"How many arrows do we have?" Michael asked the group.

"Forty … maybe fifty at best," Celrod said with a forlorn face.

"And swords?" Michael continued to take inventory of their defenses.

"We have those, for what good we can do with less than a dozen," Timorets replied.

"Well, we will have to make the arrows count. Wait 'til they are on the battlements before we even take aim. We can't waste them firing into the horde," Michael told them.

"If nothing else, we will pile their cursed bodies high enough to slow them down," Fryon agreed.

"Right. Fryon, you and I will wait at the ready with blades in hand," Michael said as he placed his hand on Fryon's shoulder. "We will let the rest of them do the shooting while we defend the east tower."

Fryon nodded his understanding and secured the leather strap of his ancient, feathered helm tightly under his chin.

The fire slowed the Raven army down, as the rubble had buried the easiest point of entry to the tower. None of this would have mattered in the least to the Nocturnal army of several thousand soldiers, save the fact that the gatehouse held the only release to the lever holding the mighty portcullis in place, and the gatehouse was securely fortified at the base of the east tower.

The clank and the click of the siege scorpions cut through the noise from the army below them. With the stairwell of the west tower blocked by flame and rubble, the Ravens would have to climb their way atop the wall.

THWACK! CRACK! The sounds of the black scorpion arrows shook the remnant as the barbs bit and grappled into the ancient stone of the Halvard.

"They are coming," Michael whispered to his friends. "Wait 'til they are firmly upon the wall, and be true with your aim."

The invaders climbed the ropes and leapt atop the battlement. Half a dozen of them at first, but with a silent wave of Michael's hand they were cut down and dispatched from this world by the sure-fired arrows.

This happened over and over again, and with each little victory, their stock of defense dangerously diminished.

"Your supply is dwindling, and your champion has fallen!" came the booming, emotionless voice of General Aius from below. "Open the gate and let my army pass, and I will allow you to live in the ignorant darkness of your choosing!"

"Shhh!" Michael said as he raised a finger to his lips.

Timorets raised his head up to steal a glance down below, and he saw the general mounted upon his green-eyed steed, a raven perched upon his shoulder. He notched one of his last arrows and took aim at the leader of this evil horde.

"Timorets, no! What are you doing, man?" Celrod said in a worried whisper.

But the brewer paid him little mind and loosed an arrow at the general. The missile flew with great haste, but still narrowly missed the head of the general as it screamed by him in a defiant fury.

"Time is running short, and my Queen requires her army at once!" he roared, angered now. "And you play a fool's game? Open the gate and be done with it, or I will see to it that you and all your kind are fed to the twins of the air, one limb at a time!"

The remnant was silent as they took inventory of what little hope they had to survive this assault.

"Maybe we should just let them pass and be done with it," Celrod said, the defeat thick upon his voice. "We haven't the means, Michael."

"And let them march freely through the north, all the way to whatever hell is being inflicted upon someone else?" Margarid asked incredulously.

"What else can we do?" Celrod reasoned. "I doubt we can fend off much more than a few of their waves, and last time I peeked out over the wall, there were still thousands of those damned Ravens coming for us."

"Tell me this, schoolmaster," Margarid fired back. "Which is the greater woe? To stand and fight against these forces of darkness by what little means we may have left, or to let them pass, saving ourselves at the expense of God knows how many others?"

The remnant was quiet and ashamed, for somewhere in all of their hearts, even the bravest amongst them, it was all too easy to surrender to the temptation of self-preservation.

"Besides," Michael spoke up, "Cal is out there still."

"You don't know that, groomsman," Timorets replied.

"I believe it more than I know it," Michael told them. "And I, for one, can't send the whole bloody Raven army out after him ... not while there is still hope that he might find what we are all looking for."

Margarid reached over and took his hand, squeezing her affection with her own.

"We will not!" Michael shouted out over the wall. "We will not open the gate, we will not allow you passage."

"There is going to be too many of them!" Celrod said.

"Right," Michael agreed as a spray of violated stone crumbled down around them. "Fryon, you get down to the gatehouse below. I need you to break the lever, smite the chain ... do whatever it takes to make sure that this gate will not open easily, even if there are none of us left to defend it."

The brave man, who had just lost his brother to the bite of the Ravens, nodded his silent understanding and took off through the maze of barrels and trunks, down to the bottom of the east tower.

"Come on, Cal. We need you to find it for us, horseface," Michael whispered out his prayer. "I don't know how much longer this world has left."

He kissed the flint that still hung around his neck and steeled himself for what he knew he must do now. Suddenly, the hands and heads of the climbing Raven soldiers peeked out overtop the merlons of the wall.

"They are here!" Celrod shouted in a whisper.

"Wait 'til you have the clear shot!" Margarid said as she tried to steady her shaking breath.

THWACK! A violent crash came again as the scorpions unleashed yet another assault upon the wall.

"Fire!" Michael ordered as a dozen Nocturnals landed upon the battlements and squared off to fight them.

The arrows of the remnant tore through their muted, metal armor, and in a spray of blackened blood the assailants were cut down.

"Reload!" Timorets called.

"We only have a few more of these left," the schoolmaster reported. "At this rate, two … maybe three shots each."

Michael looked at the forlorn faces of his friends and at their dwindling supply of defenses. He swallowed his resolve and took off towards the bodies of the fallen enemy soldiers.

"Michael!" Margarid shouted out after him as he ran in a crouch down the barbican.

"What is he doing?" Georgina asked worriedly.

"Is he mad?" Celrod said.

Michael slid next to the lifeless Nocturnals and began to pluck the bolts from their broken bodies. He grabbed the ones closest to him and took a steadying breath as he turned and faced his worried, waiting friends.

More hands and more heads came over the wall just as he began his awkward retreat towards the relative safety of the east tower.

"Michael!" Margarid shouted, her eyes wide in terror as a second wave of assailants leapt from the wall and landed with violent intent, not ten paces from where Michael crouched. "Michael, get down! Now!"

Her words registered and he dropped flat upon his stomach as a blast of angry wind shot over his head and buried its pointed barbs in the chests of the Nocturnals that pursued him.

The bolts found their marks, though not all of them fell dead on the spot. For there were many more enemies than there were arrows, and one of them was nearly upon him. Michael rolled to his side, narrowly avoiding the bite and crack of the ugly blade of his green-eyed foe. The

Nocturnal raised his sword up and over his head, ready to unleash his fury once again.

WHOOSH! Another arrow flew overhead, and in an instant the Raven soldier dropped his blade and staggered back. Michael scrambled backwards on all fours as he tried to make his way to his friends; and as he did, he felt the hope-killing crack of the recently recovered arrows snap under the awkward weight of his escape.

"No!" he cursed under his breath.

"Michael, hurry!" his friends yelled out after him as the sight of more hands and more helmed heads cleared the top of the wall.

He got to his knees and drew his ancient blade from its ancient scabbard. His desperate eyes found the waiting, worried gaze of Margarid, and without a single word passing between them she knew he was not returning to the tower.

"No!" She screamed as she leapt out from behind the girth of the stacked trunks and loosed an arrow in the face of the first Raven soldier. Michael ducked, narrowly missing the sword of the Nocturnal, then swung his own blade, opening up its ashen neck.

Margarid notched one of her last remaining arrows and fired over Michael's right shoulder, ending the advancement of yet another assailant.

Blades crashed and sparked, and black arrows flew up from the frigid ground below. Timorets and Celrod were moved by such a display of bravery, and they, too, rose from their perch and ran out to meet their friends in the chaotic fray of battle. For every enemy that was cut down, another climbed up the wall and took its place. Exhaustion began to take its toll, and traces of warm red appeared on the wounded limbs of those who wielded their violent defense.

Then, an unlooked for sound, simultaneously sweet and angry, cut through the clamor of war with a bright-noted melody.

"What is that?" Margarid said as she slashed and parried with her own blade.

Again it rang out, clear and bright, from the west.

"I don't know!" Michael shouted back, his movements now labored and clumsy beneath the weight of his own sword. "I can't see anything!"

"What in the damnable dark?" Celrod said as he risked a glimpse up and over the line of merlons.

Another sound, this one dark and soul-chilling, rang up from the ranks of the Nocturnals below; its very tone stood in pure contrast to the brightness of the first sound.

"What is it?" Margarid begged, her heart afraid to hope.

"I don't know!" Celrod shouted as he sunk his blade in the gut of another enemy. "But it is beautiful!"

"What?" Timorets turned his head, confusion lining his bearded face.

The dark, sickly tone rang out again, but as it did, the darkness about them erupted in a burst of violet light.

"Michael, what is that?" Margarid shouted as she stopped swinging her sword and stood still, amazed and overcome by the unexpected onslaught of such beauty out here in the forsaken lands of the Halvard.

Michael's eyes went wide as a fragrant wind blew in from the west, and his mind registered the fantastical scene that unfolded before them. "Sprites!" he yelled, hardly believing the words that came from his own mouth. "The Sprites ... the Sprites have come ... they have come for us!"

Chapter Forty-Two

Enemy arrows flew in a violent storm of raven feathers, loosed from the crossbows of the Sorceress' archers. Her fury was so great at the murder of her dragons that she cared not whether her bolts cut down her own forces as they extinguished the lives of the traitors.

"Kill every one of them, every damned bird, every ram, and man who dares to defy my power!" Nogcwren screamed as she strode fearlessly into the line of battle.

Seig's green eyes glowed with fierce obedience as he and his men marched in formation about the Sorceress. He eyed Yasen at the opposite end of their column, wondering if by chance a blade might mistake him for one of his unenlightened brothers.

Nogcwren held her arm high above her head, and in her hand was her onyx scepter, whose deadly point thirsted ravenously for the blood of her enemy.

THUANG! Arrows loosed and riddled the sky in pursuit of the

Oweles that had assaulted her troops.

A contingent of Navid's Ramsguard barreled recklessly though the line of her spearmen, their white-horned helms now nearly black with the blood of slain soldiers. They screamed and shouted their defiance as their mounts hooked and bucked against the ranks of foot soldiers, and their mighty, curved blades slashed and bit into greying flesh.

The Sorceress held her scepter high, and with a flash of her rune-covered arm, whipped the head of the weapon towards the ram riders. A blast of green lightning, like the web of a hideous spider, shot forth to squeeze the life out of an Amaian warrior. He choked as a jolt of electricity coursed through his body.

"See your Queen!" Seig shouted in elation.

The men of the Ramsguard froze momentarily in terror, and then, resigned to the doom all about them, continued to fight as if their death had already befallen them. The sky above them hissed and popped as more arrows were fired, though not all of them were raven-fletched. Nogcwren raised her scepter again and shielded herself from the assault that rained down upon her.

The screams and grunts of her guard rang out as the shots of Johanna's archers found their mark. The ranks of Seig's guardsman began to diminish as it became evident that the protection of the queen did not extend far beyond her own flesh.

Metal upon metal, blade against bone; the battle in the shadow of the Itxaro Mountains waged heavily on. The Sorceress used dark magic as an extension of her own fury, while Seig and his guardsmen fought desperately to guard her flank.

Pyrrhus swung his sword, felling men with little joy, as he fought to protect a queen and a commander that no longer needed him.

"There she is!" came the shouts of the woodcutters. "The witch is right there!"

"To me!" Seig ordered his men as he saw the horde of bearded mad men charging at the queen.

"Argh!" came the shouts of the Northmen, their axes at the ready and their eyes burning with furious determination.

Arrows flew, and men fell, and still the woodcutters charged. Goran reached the line of guardsmen first, and with one mighty swing of his axe, he released the heads of two of his former countrymen from their now-lifeless bodies.

Seig gritted his teeth and swung his blade, burying it deep in the flesh of an assailant.

The Sorceress continued to wreak her havoc as her sinister magic pierced both the armor and the resolve of all who opposed her.

Goran made his way through the battle until he came in sight of Seig. The large woodcutter looked for Yasen, still unbelieving that his friend had fallen to the side of this mad man and that witch.

"Have you come all this way just to die, woodcutter?" Seig taunted as he came near.

"Where is he?" Goran shouted. "What have you done with him?"

"With who?" Seig said playfully as he narrowly avoided the flash of an axe blade that swung within a handbreadth of his face. He kicked, landing his boot upon the sizable stomach of the woodcutter and placing a breathable distance between the two of them.

"You know damn well who," Goran roared as he swung again, sparks erupting as the weight of his axe collided with the metal of Seig's sword. "Where is our brother?"

Seig's blade sparked and then snapped as a myriad of razor-sharp shards raked across his face. He looked at his broken blade and felt the now-black blood of his own Nocturnal flesh run down his cheek.

"Do you not know?" he chided. "He has taken the gift of the Raven Queen," he said with a sinister laugh. "He's now more *my* brother than he will ever be one of yours!"

Goran looked at the governor and saw his glowing, green eyes alive with the light of such hatred. "Yasen!" he shouted. "Yasen, where are you, brother?" Goran searched the fray of Rams and Ravens, his eyes desperate to find his chieftain and his friend.

"If you want to join him, all you have to do is bend the knee!" Seig shouted as he charged the large woodcutter and buried his broken blade in the belly of his enemy.

In the same moment that the sword bit flesh, Goran spotted his friend across the field of battle, and his heart sank in despair. Yasen stood, axe in hand, at the defense of the Sorceress herself.

"Yasen!" he shouted in surprised agony.

The North Wolf heard Goran's call and turned. As he spun around, their eyes met across the carnage. "No!" Yasen shouted, his eye wide in terror.

Pyrrhus heard the cry, too, and turned to see where it was coming from.

"You see, woodcutter," Seig gloated, whispering in Goran's ear as he twisted the iron deeper into the bowels of the woodcutter. "He has chosen the side of glory, and you ... fools, all of you, will water the grass of her kingdom with your insolent blood."

Confusion washed over Goran's dying face as he beheld the single eye of his friend. "Tell me this, Governor," Goran choked out amidst crimson coughs. "Why isn't his eye devil-green like yours, huh?"

The smug smile on Seig's face fell, turning into a confused scowl.

"Ha!" Goran grunted. "He has been playing you for the fool this whole damned time! He's only got one good eye, you know."

Pyrrhus watched as the North Wolf ran towards his dying friend and raised his axe as if he meant to throw it. "What in the damnable..." he whispered in confusion.

WHOOSH! The rushing sound of double-bladed vengeance echoed overhead as Yasen hurled his mighty axe across the field, burying it into the back of the once-proud Governor of Haven.

Seig let out a grunt of pain, and then slumped to the ground in a heap of wasted and ruined flesh.

"Goran!" Yasen shouted as he ran over to his wounded friend. "Goran, are you alright?" he asked as the battle raged all about them.

"I thought we had lost you to the devil herself," he whispered with blood-frothed words. "But then I saw your eye, and thanked the THREE who is SEVEN for that damned bear."

"And for the patch Keily sewed for me, old friend," he said as he held the head of his dying friend. "I switched it when they forced me before the dragons."

"I never doubted you," Goran said, laboring as he watched his brothers wield their axes all about them, cleaving helms and taking arrows. "Hollis would be proud."

A tear rolled down Yasen's scarred face. "He would be proud of you too, brother."

"Would you say the words for me?" Goran barely managed

"Aye." Yasen agreed, his voice proud and profoundly saddened. "By your body broke … come birch and elm, pine and oak."

Goran closed his eyes as the last of his life passed through his blood-stained lips.

Yasen rose to his feet and placed his boot upon the back of the fallen governor, gripping the handle of his axe and freeing it from his flesh.

Nogcwren whirled about, her rage and magic striking like an angered serpent at all who came within reach. The screams of the men and beasts pierced by her devilry cut through the clamor with a soul-chilling clarity. Yasen walked towards her, unopposed, through the diminishing line of guards. When her glowing, yellow eyes met his determined stare, she knew she had been deceived.

She pointed her scepter at the chest of the woodcutter, who was not more than forty paces from her. "Betrayer!" she shouted as a current of electricity shot forth and gripped him in a violent hold. "Fool! How can this be?!"

Yasen froze where he was, arrested by the force of her sorcery, writhing in tortured pain.

"*None* have kneeled before my children and looked into the fire of the un-light without being taken by its power!" Her very body seemed to be roiling and glowing with rage, as she used her magic to lift him up off the ground.

Yasen screamed in agony as her malice tightened its grip on his suffocating body. Oren and Alon and the host of the woodcutters ran to the rescue of their chieftain, felling guardsman and Raven alike as they did.

Pyrrhus watched in horror, and his face did not betray the storm of emotions inside his head and the confusion of it all. "How did ... he didn't take her light?" he mumbled to himself.

So terrible were the shouts of the woodcutters that even Durai fell victim to the fear they evoked in this last and final charge. The ground began to rumble and quake, and the woodcutters hurled their axes towards the sorceress as they ran.

She batted them away as if they were nothing more than a minor nuisance, but her gaze would not leave the face of the dog who betrayed her. "I offered you immortality! I gave you the gift of sight, and you spurned my affection? For what?" she screamed. "To join your dying brothers on this field of death?"

The ground began to shake even more violently now, and men and beasts everywhere began to lose their footing, stumbling amidst the scattering battle.

The screech of an Owele could be heard as Azrael descended from the sky above, his violet eyes blazing with righteous intent.

"This world is mine!" Nogcwren continued. "Look around you! This is the last of the resistance, and all you have left is but to stumble and fall at my feet!" She screamed and cursed, her yellow eyes burning with hatred. "Bring on the birds, bring them all, every last one of them!" She laughed and snarled as she looked up at the Oweles. "Blind servants of a dead God!"

Yasen's eyes caught a movement behind her, though he couldn't see just what it was. All of a sudden, the bright glint of iron shot through the rune-covered chest of the maddened witch. Blood, crimson and yet somehow fouled, began to pour down and pool in the swell of her breasts. The sorcery that burned in her eyes flickered and failed as she beheld the doom that had pierced her very heart.

The mighty bird tore through the air with such speed that the

Sorceress had barely the time to understand what fate had just befallen her. Her eyes went wide, and her slender, once-beautiful neck opened wide as Azrael slashed his talons to sever the head of the imposter Queen.

Yasen crashed to the ground in a world of pain, watching the body that was bereft of a head fall to its knees and then crumble in a tortured heap. He couldn't believe what he had just witnessed for standing where, not moments ago, the Sorceress had been inflicting her wrath upon him, Pyrrhus now stood with his crimson-stained sword still in his one remaining hand.

Chapter Forty-Three

The three light seekers peered into the man-sized opening in the side of the mountain, seeing only by the violet glow of their growing hope.

"Where does it lead, do you think?" Astyræ asked them.

"Further in, I guess. And further up," Cal said, still in wonder of it all. "Was the way like this the whole time?" he asked as he took his first, timid step into the passageway. "Hidden, I mean. I only say that because, well ... all the other markings were in plain sight."

"Plain sight?" Astyræ said with a playful smile as she followed him inside the cavernous hallway. "Neither Deryn nor I could see the way of the Stag, no matter how hard we looked."

"She is right, Cal," their Sprite companion said, the blue glow of his wings now reflecting off of the glittering walls inside this mountain of the Itxaro.

"Alright, alright," Cal said, his clouded eyes still searching for any markings that might be ahead of them. "What I meant was, why was this one hidden? Why the stones? Why the bramble bush? If it wasn't for the blood of Uriel, I don't know if I would have even guessed to look." He thought on it a moment more as the three of them continued their journey deeper into the heart of the mountain, twisting and turning each way the path led them.

"Maybe it wasn't always that way, groomsman," Astyræ said, interrupting his reverie. "Maybe the stones just fell, and maybe the bramble grew over time."

"The light of our Great Father has ever been in this world, but only a very few of His children have chosen to seek it." Deryn added. "Perhaps the ancient paths are subject to the complacency of those content not to tread upon them."

"It is sad to me that King Illium never found this part," Cal continued. "So close he was to it, and yet he died never reaching the promise he sought."

"I would not be sad for him, Cal," Deryn said, flitting up alongside him. "For your story is a part of his story, and you continuing to seek might very well ultimately reveal the shared hope of a shared promise."

Cal looked over his shoulder at his friend, a grateful smile breaking across his now-bearded face. "You are a wise little Sprite, aren't you?"

"Cal?" Astyræ said rather startled. "What is that?"

Cal looked as the path that had been winding back and forth for what seemed like hours now opened up into a magnificent chamber, higher than their violet sight could see, as rotund as the courtyard of the kings back in Westriver.

"What in the damnable dark?" Cal whispered in awe.

The three of them walked deeper into the chamber, spinning around as they did, straining to take in all that their eyes could see. The walls of the rounded chamber were adorned with intricate carvings, one flowing into the next, telling a story with detail that none of them had ever seen etched upon stone in such a way before.

"What does it mean?" Astyræ gasped.

Cal turned around in wonder; the measure of the beauty and detail was nearly overwhelming. "Look!" he exclaimed, his eye catching one the carved reliefs. "I know this place!" He ran over to the wall and traced his fingers upon a familiar sight, a palace carved out of a mountain, whose large doors he had passed through near the beginning of his journey. "Only ... it is not how I remember it. It is much more ... *brilliant* here, younger, not ruined as when I stumbled upon it. Petros is its name," he said in wonder. "Tolk ... I hope you and the others are alright, my friend."

The three of them found spaces upon the massive chamber's wall, each drawn to a particular scene. "I know this man!" Deryn said as he looked at the image of a mighty warrior standing upon the fallen flesh of an ancient serpent.

"Who is it, Deryn?" Astyræ asked.

Cal ran over to see who he could possibly be referring to, bewildered. As he approached the scene, he stopped dead in his tracks.

"Is that?" he whispered, for fear of scaring the revelation back off into the shadows.

"Caedmon, yes," Deryn said with silver tears in his eyes. "And that vile abomination is *Ahriman,* lord and sire of the AŽDAHĀ. I remember this day all too well my friend; the ruin of Terriah, the justice of Éimhear, and the treacheries of Šárka."

"Is that Gwarwyn in his hand?" Cal said, looking even closer. "It is, isn't it?!" he exclaimed as he reached for his blade to compare, then remembered it was now lost on the field of battle.

In that moment, surrounded by wonders and stories unknown and unimaginable, Cal remembered his friends who were still in the midst of battle: Johanna of Shaimira, Goran, Gvidus and all his woodcutter brothers. His mind reeled with a renewed sense of urgency.

"Cal look," Astyræ said nervously as she peered at a carving several scenes down along the great chamber's wall. "You have to..." she swallowed her fear back so as to finish her thought, "you have to see this."

"What is it, my lady?" he said as his eyes scoured scene after scene.

He beheld images of great towers erected, of the once-great burning tree of Haven, of beasts and creatures long forgotten, and of battles and beauty and the becoming of the world of Aiénor. He stopped just beside the golden-haired beauty, placing his hand upon her shoulder. When his clouded eyes gazed upon the carving, he too felt a sense of foreboding.

"That is the ship, *Wilderness*! Illium's ship, stranded! Just as we found it!" He wondered disbelievingly.

"It is, groomsman, just ... as ... we found it." Her voice was cold and ominous. "Do you see who is there ... in the stonework, I mean?"

His eyes searched the impossible lines, chiseled into the glittering stone walls with unmatched detail by some unknown artist. "Is that?" he paused, furrowing his brow and reaching up to touch the three small figures there at the bottom of the frame. "It can't be!" He turned and looked at her violet eyes, his own equally befuddled. "How can it be?"

"You?" came a voice from the center of the rotund hall.

The three light seekers wheeled around, all of them instinctively reaching for their blades and bows, only to find that Deryn alone still carried a weapon.

"Who are you?" Cal said as he scanned the stone floor of the hall, looking for something to defend himself with. "Who are you?" As he spoke, he noticed for the first time that the same sort of carved images stretched out underneath their feet, lining the entire floor of this great hall with more of the artist's handiwork.

"Who am I?" the voice replied in a deep and ancient tone. "Who am I?!"

An impossible wind began to blow inside the chamber from seemingly nowhere, breathing to life a long line of dormant torches that clung to the walls of the chamber with a familiar, silver fire.

The three of them whirled about, their eyes tracking the gust of wind as they watched the great hall explode with illumination. The dust from within the etched cracks of the chiseled history took flight and swirled about, creating a thick haze around them.

"Who am I?" the voice bellowed, the depth of its timbre thundering off the walls as the shape of a bearded man appeared in the cloud of dust. "I am who I have always been, and I will be who I always am."

Cal and Astyræ kneeled in respect and fear as the robed body of the man of dust began to take form. "We did not mean to offend you, sir. We were led here by the White Stag, and we have come seeking the light of the THREE who is SEVEN," Cal shouted into the wind.

The man raised his hand above them, and they saw that it held a hammer. In his other hand was a chisel that looked to be fashioned out of pure silver lightning.

"Please!" Cal begged, confusion and dread washing over him.

The man of dust narrowed his blazing blue gaze, his mouth moving with words unfamiliar to the ears of men and Sprites. As the storm about them continued to swirl and rage, Cal reached out to take hold of Astyræ's hand. She looked at him, her eyes grateful for the touch and grieving what might come next as they remained on their knees and looked up. A deep exhale came from the dust-formed mouth of the bearded man above them and at that ... all sound ceased.

In an instant, the chisel was planted onto the glittering, stone floor beneath them, and with a scream of horror and desperation they beheld the mighty hammer fall swiftly. Though they feared its strike was meant to smite them, its blow instead found only the head of the magnificent chisel.

BOOM! The crashing sound of the hammer reverberated off the carved walls of the chamber. Cal's eyes were wild with disbelief as he watched the floor beneath their knees writhe and crack, while blue tendrils of lightning bit into the stone, carving a new image before their eyes. He looked at the floor, and then at the man of dust, hovering over them.

"I never grow tired of watching," the man said, his eyes glowing with satisfaction as his handiwork began to take shape before their very eyes.

"Watching what?" Astyræ said, her voice quivering with relief.

"The story," he told them. "I never grow tired of watching so great a tale unfold before the theater of its maker."

"What do you mean, the story?" Cal asked again, his eyes drawn again to the scenes that decorated the stone around him. "Do you mean the carvings?"

Deryn did not tear his gaze from what was happening on the floor beneath his friends. "I think he is referring to us." Deryn told them, his words measured and ominous. "Look, Cal." His tiny hand pointed at the stone below them.

Cal and Astyræ turned their gaze to follow the Sprite's hand, and as their eyes beheld the image, their skin pimpled with goose flesh and the hairs on their necks stood tree tall.

"What in the name of the THREE who is SEVEN?!" Cal said disbelievingly.

"So you do see?" the man of dust replied.

"That is *us*!" Cal blurted out. "And there! Over here!" he said as he walked over to the image of the three of them just as they had found the wreck of the ship, *Wilderness*. "This is us too?"

"You are correct," the man of dust said with a bow of his large head. "All of this ... all of these," he waved with his massive, dust hand, "are but chapters in the greater story, the epic, the Requiem of Elior."

"Elior?" Cal said.

"The THREE who is SEVEN, as you know Him, or the Great Father, as the Spriteling may be more familiar with," the man of dust replied. "God who is light ... Elior."

"Then why are we here? Why are *our* images carved upon these stones?" Astyræ questioned.

"Daughter of Aius, have you not guessed?" he said as he turned his back and strode toward the center of the massive chamber.

"Guessed what?" she said, completely confused.

"That you three are part of the story," he told them.

Cal turned and saw the image that had been newly created in the floor below them: the three of them kneeling before a dust figure with a great hammer. He looked to his friends and then back to the floor, his brow furrowed in concentration as the gravity of understanding fell upon him with an all-consuming weight.

"Yes, Calarmindon Bright Fame," the man of dust said. "Even now, His story is still being told. The walls of the *Harel Lior* have told of deeds great and small, joyful and joyless, yet all have been a part of a grander tale, the tale of a light that will chase away the darkness forever and heal the hurts of Aiénor."

"All of it?" Cal asked. He thought back to the Oweles upon the walls in Westriver, and of his time with the woodcutters, and of how he found his Poet friends and his Sprite guardian. He thought of his appointment to the first colony, and then of finding Astyræ in the tower of Enguerrand. He thought of how one word, "Shaimira", had led them through so many more moments, right up until this one. And he thought of every failure, every flaw, and of how many times he nearly abandoned his quest for lesser paths.

"Yes, indeed. Especially our failures," the man of dust answered, almost as if he could read Cal's very thoughts.

The room sat silent for a moment as Cal took in what the man of dust was saying.

Finally, Astyræ spoke out with urgency. "Sir. We have been searching for a very long time, following the way of the White Stag. War is raging below us, at the base of these mountains, even now." She pointed back towards the entrance to this chamber of mysteries. Her voice was nervous, and her words came in a rush. "Can you tell us, please ... is this the place we have been looking for? Our friends are dying out there, and we have got to help them."

The man of dust peered at them, his glowing blue eyes plunging the depths of their intentions as he held his own council deep in thought. "Tell me, daughter of Aius, son of Poets, and offspring of the Jacarandas ... what is it that you truly seek?"

Cal took a step forward, speaking on behalf of his band of travelers. "We seek the light."

"And why is it, Calarmindon Bright Fame, that you seek such a thing?" the man of dust asked. "Why have you traveled through water and wilderness? Why have you both drawn and shed blood?" As he spoke, he began to grow in size, his swirling form hulking high above them now, his eyes blazing with question. "I am the Keeper of the Secret Flame!" he said, his voice growing louder. "I have tended the light of Elior since before Aiénor was breathed into existence!"

As he spoke, tablets made of swirling dust appeared in his hands, images flashing and forming in the air about them, each telling a tale of this ancient history.

"I have watched your kind ravage this creation over greed and power! I have witnessed the forsaking of the bright for the worship of the dark! Tell me, son of Ádhamh, why is it that you seek so holy, so great a treasure? What are you truly looking for?"

Cal's mind continued to race, and all the longings he had felt since he was a young boy flooded his senses as he stood before this monolithic guardian. Wind and flame danced about the chamber's walls while the man of dust heaved and pulsated with righteous indignation. Cal squeezed Astyræ's hand, then smiled a true, albeit exhausted, smile at Deryn. He exhaled and turned his gaze once again to meet the eyes of the mighty man of dust.

"Home," he said as a tear streaked his dirt-smudged face. "I have always been looking for a place in this world to call home." He swallowed back his emotions as he spoke. "And so are we all ... are we not? Searching for a place where the light shines free, where we will never again be lost in the dark? I have always hoped to find a Kingdom, a place where the hurts of this world have been truly mended, and where light has once and for all dispelled the darkness from its borders. I have been dreaming about and seeking that for all of my days ... I only thought that at the end of this path, I might find it here."

The man of dust reached into some unseen fold of his cloak to retrieve his hammer and chisel once again.

"Please!" Cal shouted into the storm. "Shine your light on me, on us."

The wind began to blow and swirl even faster. The torches of silver fire whipped and danced in a frantic motion, and the ground below their feet seemed as if it were humming. Words, in a language ancient and hidden from the ears of man and Sprite, began to grow louder and louder, crescendoing in an almost harmonious chorus of unknown speech.

"Cal?" Astyræ shouted against the tempest. "We should leave now! The whole place is going to fall in on us!"

"No!" Deryn replied. "I do not feel fear in my heart. While I do not understand what is happening, I sense that we are in no danger."

The storm grew louder and louder, and the winds and flames whipped the air about them. Just when they thought they might endure the whirlwind no longer, they heard a whisper buried in the heart of the uproar.

May it be so.

The man of dust raised his hammer high, and at the very center of the *Harel Lior,* he brought it down with ferocious obedience. At the point of impact, a light both silver and amber erupted from the bowels of the ancient Itxaro, and it shot forth up and through an oculus at the crest of the rotunda.

Cal and his friends shielded their eyes against the brilliance, only to find that its intensity only startled and did not harm them. The winds that had been moments before swirling and circling about them shot forth in all directions, and the walls around them began to rumble and quake. All around, they could hear the sounds of crumbling rock and falling debris, though, save for the floor below them at the center of the chamber, the ornately embellished room did not falter.

"Cal!" Astyræ shouted amidst the noises of chaos about them. "Look! The floor!"

Cal tore his gaze from the magnificent beam that was erupting out through the top of the room and followed it to the floor from where it was coming forth. At the center of the room stood the mighty beam, brilliant and beautiful, unwavering in its glory. As they stared in awe, the stones that had been laid in meticulous circles began to collapse, folding in and spiraling down into an ornate, stone staircase.

The man of dust watched as his handiwork shone in a new and radiant glory. His burning, blue eyes began to drip liquid sapphire-like tears upon the floor below.

"We have got to get out of here," Cal shouted to his friends.

"Agreed! But we cannot go back the way that we entered," Deryn replied. "How would you two ever descend the mountain?"

The floor beneath them continued to rumble, the quaking getting stronger and stronger with each passing moment. Cal looked about, but there seemed to be no other entry or exit along the curved cave walls.

"The steps going down at the center of the floor!" he shouted to them. "We will have to try it!"

"Is it safe?" Astyræ asked nervously.

"I hope so," he said, taking her hand. "Come on, my lady!"

They ran across the stone floor, their balance unsteady and their footing unsure, until they reached the outer rim of the spiral.

"What do you see, Deryn?" Cal said as the Sprite guardian hovered out over the precipice.

He looked down, and then looked up to where the shaft of light continued to shine.

"I sense no malice here ... I feel no warning in my heart, Cal," he told them bravely. "Come, let us continue."

And with that, the two of them put their feet on the sinking stones and made their unsteady descent, round and round, through the heart of the mountain. The light blazed in the center of the spiral stone stairwell, shining up through the center of the cavern. Although its brightness did not cast a shadow, there was no fear of burning, for its breath was cool and pleasant.

"Do you hear that?" Astyræ asked her friends as they descended with shaking steps.

Cal put his hand upon the wall to steady himself as the reverberations threatened to send him sprawling in a heap, all the way to the bottom. "What? What do you hear, my lady?"

"It's singing," Deryn answered.

"Yes! That's what I hear, too. Only, not words … just music; from a thousand quiet voices."

"What in the name of the THREE who is SEVEN?" Cal wondered, as he began to hear the unseen melodies. "Where are they coming from?"

"I believe … I believe they are coming from the *light*," Deryn said, his own voice awash in wonder.

Cal looked at the center of the brilliance. "Is this what we have been seeking all this time?" he asked reverently.

"I do believe so, Cal," Deryn replied.

"I hope that it is strong enough to chase away the Sorceress and her army," Cal said, unable to tear his eyes fully away from the sight.

"Beauty is always stronger than evil, and hope more powerful than hatred," Deryn said, with a great smile upon his small face.

The sounds of crashing stones and crumbling debris woke them from their silent contemplations.

"Well, I hope we make it out of here in one piece to see for ourselves!" Astyræ chided. "Come on now, boys … we are not safe just yet!"

The three of them made their way, warily and cautiously down the seemingly infinite spiral of stones steps. The walls about them shook and the dust of the trembling air glowed as it caught the brilliance of the beam of light.

They lost sense of both time and space as they made their journey through the heart of the mountain. When they finally reached an arched opening at the bottom of the stairs, their brows were slick with sweat and their chests heaved and gasped for air.

"Where are we?" Cal asked through labored breath.

"At the bottom? It seems that we have finally made it!" Astyræ replied as she doubled over, hands upon her hips.

"Yes, but made it … where?" Cal asked, scanning his surroundings.

"That is quite the question now, isn't it?" Deryn said as his own azure eyes went wide in wonder.

"What in the name of the THREE who is SEVEN?" Cal said, his voice barely audible to his friends.

They looked up, but what they all beheld seemed impossible to even imagine. They were standing inside a large hall, surrounded by white, alabaster walls that were ornately engraved with branches and vines. Upon the vines were flowers, alive in the most magnificent array of colors. The floor of the chamber was as translucent as ice, yet not the slightest bit cold to the touch.

"Is that?" Astyræ asked as she bent down to touch the shimmering floor.

"It's crystal!" Cal said, disbelievingly. "Or maybe even diamond!"

"But, I don't understand. Where are we?" Astyræ rose once again to her feet and whirled about, taking in the splendor of such a place.

BOOM! The sound of a terrible crash echoed from the other side of the spectacular walls that surrounded them. They looked at each other, the scent of jasmine and rose petals filling the uncertain air between them.

Cal spotted a columned doorway at the opposite end of the chamber, and though he was not ready to leave the sanctuary of this place, he knew that his quest was not yet finished. "There!" he said, pointing out the exit. "Come on, we have to get out of here, we have to see about our friends."

With that, they walked. Slowly at first, their senses still overwhelmed with all that they beheld, but soon enough they were running towards the doorway. As they reached its threshold, the enormity of what they had set into motion assaulted their already befuddled senses. Out beyond the tranquility of the great hall, they saw a vast city that expanded in white-stoned brilliance out into the farthest reaches of the Itxaro.

"What ... is ... this?" Cal barely managed to whisper.

"Cal?" Astyræ asked him as she took hold of his arm in her own. "How can this be?"

They looked around, and to their even greater amazement, they could see as far as their eyes could behold. Everything was no longer shrouded in shadow, but was illuminated in the same, soft, amber and silver brilliance as the light in the stairs.

"There!" Astyræ blurted in astonishment. "I know where we are! There's the river, and the highlands! And Shaimira ... it's there, right inside this great city! There's the falls, and the battlefield—" Her words caught in her throat as she viewed the remains of war.

"Cal!" Deryn called, breathless with excitement.

Cal turned, whirling about in incredulous disbelief. His eyes traced the skyline of this unexpected city; the white and jasper walls seemed to encircle all that had previously been the Itxaro Mountain range itself. At the center of the shining city, a pillar of light erupted its soft amber and silver brilliance from the top of the white tower that he and his friends had just descended.

The crashing sounds around them and below them continued to shake the ground and confuse their already overwhelmed senses.

"Cal!" Deryn shouted again for his friend, but Cal's eyes were transfixed on the scene unfolding before him.

The shell of mountains must have contained this hidden place, and now they seemed to have sloughed off, like a heavy coat from a road-weary traveler. The shale and dust, boulders and brambles, had fallen and crashed into heaps from the heights that they had once called home, covering the blood-stained battlefield below. Like parchment unwrapped to reveal the gift inside, the mountains were falling away. With each crash and world-shaking boom, the splendor of this new city was all the more revealed.

"Cal!" Deryn said as he flew to his friend and took his face in his tiny hands. "Cal, the darkness ... *it is gone!*"

"The light?" Cal asked, his clouded eyes welling with joyful tears.

"Yes!" Astyræ answered him, her own tears cutting clean lines down her dirt-stained face. "Yes!" She laughed as she wrapped her arms about him, embracing him as tightly as her tired arms could manage.

"We found it," he said in a whisper. "We found the light."

"Yes, we did, Calarmindon Bright Fame," Deryn said as the rumble and boom of the crumbling, mountainous exoskeleton punctuated his joyful proclamation.

Astyræ looked up at Cal, and her gaze was somehow different.

"My lady?" he whispered.

"Yes?" she answered him, her words breathless with glee.

"Your eyes!" He took her tear-streaked face in his hands. "The yellow ... it's gone!"

"Now is not the time for jest, groomsman," she told him. "Now is the time for celebration! You were right, Cal! You sought it out ... and you found it!"

"No ... I am not joking, Astyræ," His brow furrowed in wonder. "The yellow is gone from your eyes, not a single trace of it is left."

Deryn turned to meet her gaze, and his own azure eyes filled with silver tears at what he witnessed right in front of him. "Not a trace of yellow," he told her.

Her face wrinkled in confusion as her eyes sought the faces of her two companions. When not a trace of insincerity could be found, her jaw dropped, and her own hand reach up to cover Cal's.

"Only violet, my lady. Only beauty remains." He did not give her a chance to respond, for his lips tenderly and with great celebration found her own.

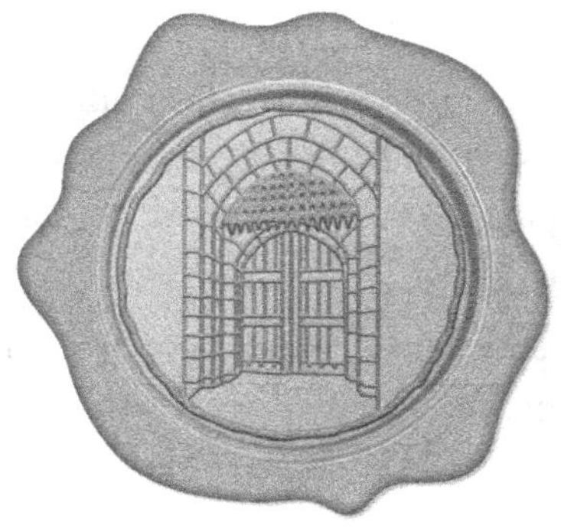

Chapter Forty-Four

Out from the ranks of the violet host, a silver star shot up into the sky. Ardghal, herald of the queen, raised his silver trumpet to his lips and blew the bright song of victory over the armies of darkness.

At that very signal, Faolan, captain of the Sprite host, drew his radiant blade. The host followed suit, and the sounds of their unsheathing rang out in harmony to the herald's song.

Aius barked his order, and the Raven army turned their attention from the remnant upon the wall, filing into rank to defend themselves from the surprise arrival of the Sprites.

"For our Great Father, for the Queen, and for Cal!" the silver-winged captain shouted to his warriors.

"For our Great Father, for the Queen, and for Cal!" they answered in melodious union.

Without so much as another word, the Sprite host exploded in a fury of weapons and wings as they began their assault upon the Ravens before them. The Sprite warriors darted in and out and in between, like famished hummingbirds upon a field of poppies; their blades buried themselves between armor and into flesh, drinking deep of the black blood of their enemies.

Arthfael, the largest of the Sprites, flew up and above the battle, wielding his mighty, brown blade, *Mathgham.* He severed the necks of each of the scorpions' ropes, sending them falling in heaps upon the heads of the Ravens below.

The Nocturnals loosed their arrows, but the Sprites flew swiftly out of reach, and even though the winged warriors made quick and deadly work of the Ravens, they were not impervious to the edge of their enemies' blades. Both Raven and Sprite fell upon that field of war, in the shadow of the great Halvard. As the battle raged, Michael and the remnant watched in bewildered wonder at the host that fought on their behalf.

"Have you ever in all your days seen such a thing?" Celrod wondered aloud.

"I have never, in all my days, even imagined that I would see the things my eyes have beheld," the brewer said as he wiped a tear from his eye with the sleeve of his tunic. "Dragons, and armies of green-eyed madness, and now this! I never even knew such beings existed to begin with!"

"I can't!" Fryon called out with labored breath as he emerged from the stairs of the east tower and came out onto the battlements. "I can't break it ... I haven't the means—" The oddness of the scene playing out before him stole the very words from his mouth.

"Looks like help has come for us, after all," the old woman said as she patted his back.

"I don't understand," he mumbled in confusion, his chest still laboring under his hurried breath.

"Neither do we," she told him. "But it don't rightly matter much, does it? Not now that it looks like we are safe."

"We are going to be alright, my lady," Michael said. He wrapped his arm around Margarid's waist and held her auburn head against his armored chest as they watched with cautious hope behind the merlons of the battlements. "I've met one, once before."

"What do you mean? Who have you met?" she said as her eyes took in the battle below.

"One of them ... a Sprite," he told her, his eyes never leaving the scene before them.

"You never told me that before," she said, disbelieving.

"Well, you would have never believed me," he said with a laugh.

"No, I guess I wouldn't have, would I?"

"They are rather violent if you cross them, I nearly learned that lesson the hard way," he told her.

"Oh?" she was curious now that the threat of death and destruction seemed abated.

"It was the last time I saw him, Mar," Michael told her, his eyes misting over. "Right before Cal left for the Wreath. I didn't believe his stories of Oweles, and dragons, and ... Sprites." He chuckled a bit, which was right for the story, but seemed so out of place amidst the carnage all about them.

"I said something stupid, and I offended him. The Sprite, not Cal. And before I knew what was happening, the little fellow had burst out from inside the cover of Cal's cloak and nearly opened me up from hind to head." He kindly kissed the top of her head. "That was the day I realized that there is much mystery in this damned darkened world of ours. All of it surprising, and some of it ... some of it even *good.*"

"Michael?" Georgina asked nervously.

"Yes?" he said as he knelt down to meet the brave little girl's face. "What is it? What is troubling you?"

"Don't you feel it?" she said as she reached up and took his hand.

"Feel what?" he asked. "Georgina ... you are trembling. What is the matter?"

"It is not me that is trembling ... it is the ground," she said worriedly.

"What?" he said, not quite understanding. He shot to his feet, convinced that as he peered out over the edge of the battlements, he would surely espy some witchcraft destroying the very foundation of this ancient fortress. The ground trembled beneath his feet, and quite quickly every one of them began to feel what the little girl had first perceived.

"Michael?" Margarid asked nervously. "What is it … what do you see?"

"I don't know! Nothing is happening to the tower that I can see. All the Ravens are still focused on the Sprites!"

The stones of the battlement began to crack, and dust scattered down. The Western tower, burned and crumbling from the inside, started to sway. Sand danced upon the top of the barbican, and soon the remnant was clinging to each other to steady their quaking resolve.

"What is happening?" Celrod shouted as he dodged the falling rocks that began to rain down upon them from the mountain face above.

The crashing sounds of the collapsing Western tower punctuated the intensity of the moment as the quake grew more and more violent all about them. Michael squatted down, his back to the wall. "Everyone, against the wall, and get close!"

As they huddled together, their fragile joy tossed all about by a hurricane of winds and tremors, a beam of light ripped through the west and shot high and violent into the heavens above.

"What in the damnable dark is that?" Timorets asked.

The pillar of light, a soft amber and silver beam, extended into the sky beyond the scope of their sight, shining a luminous glory that was not diminished even here in the east.

"Is it … is that fire?" Celrod asked.

"Some kind of devilry?" Timorets shouted against the crash and rumble of the quaking world about them.

They all looked on in amazed wonder as the height of the beam seemed to finger and fan out, spreading from its origin in a sea of brilliance.

"He did it," Michael whispered to himself, not sure he wanted to risk believing his own words.

"Michael, look!" Margarid exclaimed. "Look! It's happening! The shadows... the darkness..."

"They are fading!" Georgina finished her incredulous thought.

Timorets dared to rise up above the battlement and saw that the Sprites had turned their attention from the fight, pausing to kneel in what looked like reverence to the growing brightness.

"What in the damnable dark?" he exclaimed again.

The light grew and began to recolor the grey, shadowed world. Its amber and silver reach extended from the center of the pillar, returning colors vibrant and nearly forgotten, as they began to unfurl their splendor like great, masted sails of the mightiest of ships.

"Michael! You've got to see this!" the brewer shouted to his friends.

Michael rose shakily to his feet. The sight of what he beheld confirmed the hope in his heart. "He found it!" he said with tears in his eyes.

Without warning the quaking ceased, and at that moment a deep and nearly subsonic *BOOM* reverberated out from the center of the pillar, sending out a shockwave of wind to the four corners of Aiénor.

The Nocturnals wordlessly screamed as their sickly, green eyes beheld the new light of the THREE who is SEVEN. Those unbroken by the blade or the bow desperately covered their ashen faces, trying to shield their eyes from the assault of brilliance. The winds raced in a tidal wave of pronouncement, and as they reached the battle of the Halvard, the bodies of the slain Raven soldiers were reduced to dust and ash, carried away by the spirit of the light to the halls of Elior.

When the storm of wind had passed, and the new light of the THREE who is SEVEN had risen high and covered the whole of Aiénor in its golden illumination, the remnant beheld something truly unimaginable.

Thousands of Nocturnals, who had moments before screamed and shuttered against the onslaught of light, now blinked, peering about this newly illuminated world with the eyes they once had seen through, before the bewitching of the Sorceress.

Ardghal raised his silver trumpet to his silver lips and blew a note of victory that seemed to pierce the hearts of all who heard it, rendering the unanswered questions vying for attention of no great importance in this moment of redemption.

The herald rose upon his silver wings and sang the proclamation with joyous tears in his bright eyes.

"Feic, go bhfuil ár n-Athair Mór ag maireachtáil do chréachta an domhain seo. Ar mhaithe leis an olc agus a scáth, tá sé mar thoradh ar a ghrá."

(Behold, our Great Father is mending the wounds of this world. For evil and its shadow have been conquered by the light of His love.)

The Raven soldiers began to kneel as the words of the Sprite, though foreign to the ears of men, woke their slumbering hearts again.

Off in the distance, a sound could be heard: horns of some sort, though not nearly as magical as the Sprite herald's trumpet.

"Come on, everyone," Michael said, his own eyes wet with wonder. "Let us be done with this wall … I think it is safe for us to go down now."

"Are you sure?" Margarid said as she held his hand.

"What about those other sounds, the horns? It could be the enemy," Celrod tried to argue.

"No. It couldn't be," Michael said with complete confidence. "Not anymore, not since my cousin found the new light."

"But how do you know?" Celrod questioned.

Michael placed both hands upon the large shoulders of the schoolmaster. "I just know. Besides, I doubt there will be much to fear anymore; we can see, brighter and more clearly than ever before!"

They made their way across the battlements, the bodies of the fallen Nocturnals no longer littered on the barbican as they had been turned to dust and carried away by the winds. When they reached the entrance to the Western tower, they saw the wreckage of what was once the armory and the great hall, cascading out from the wall in a hill of rubble.

"Mind your step, now," Michael ordered them. "It looks manageable enough, and we have all traversed much worse than this already. But don't be foolish about it, either," he said with a playful wink to Margarid.

And so it was that the remnant began to make their way down, slowly but surely, until they reached the courtyard in front of the portcullis, where just moments before, the battle for their lives had raged on. Michael reached for his blade as he came closer to the mass of bewildered men whose eyes had not beheld anything but darkness and un-light for what must have seemed like an eternity.

"Careful, groomsman," Fryon said warily, his hand firmly gripping the hilt of his own blade. "Their eyes may have lost their rotten enchantment ... but we don't yet know if these men were spoiled all the way through."

Michael stared in wonder. The army of death and ravenous destruction looked less like the monsters they seemed to have been fighting, and more like his own bedraggled remnant of friends who were just opposing them.

"What is your name?" Georgina asked. She had broken away from the group and walked up to a bearded man. "Mine is Georgina," she said with kindness in her eyes.

"I never..." the older man tried to speak, but his voice was not used to the practice, and it cracked as he stumbled over long-lost words. "I never meant harm ... I did not know what I was doing."

The child reached out and took his filthy hand in her own without a hint of fear. "I know. And it's all over now. Can't you see it? It's beautiful!"

Tears began to roll down his war-stained cheeks. "Yes, girl ... it is beautiful."

"You may call me Georgina, sir," she said with a smile that would melt even the coldest of hearts.

"I am Diggory," he said with a sheepish smile. "Have you seen my son and my wife? I followed *her* in order to save them ... do you know where they are?"

"No, I am sorry," she said, her eyes saddened at her own report. "There is no one else out here but us ... and, well ... the Sprites."

"Hail, friends of Aiénor," came the melodic voice of the great herald as he flitted down from on high and greeted the remnant. "I am Ardghal, herald of the High Queen, and these are my brother and sister Sprites."

Michael reached out and took Margarid's hand in his own as he and the rest of his friends beheld the violet host that descended and landed about them. "Can you believe this?" He shook his head and squeezed her hand in wonderment. "If only Cal could see me now."

"Pardon me, son of Ádhamh," the captain of the host, Faolan, said as he landed last in a display of his command. "What did you say?"

"I am sorry, Lord Sprite. I meant ... I mean..." Michael stammered over his words, partly in awe, and partly out of fear of offending these regal rescuers. "I only said, I wish that my cousin, Cal, could have been here to see all of this, and all of you."

A murmur could be heard, rumbling through the winged host, and it was the captain who turned back to address the remnant again. "Are you saying that you are kin to Cal—"

"Calarmindon Bright Fame," finished the unlooked-for voice of a woman, high born and of great nobility.

"My Queen," Faolan said with a bow as Iolanthe, High Queen of Islwyn, descended from the bright sky in all of her violet splendor to meet the object of her rescue.

Michael instinctively went to one knee and bowed his head as the violet eyes of the silver-haired queen met his own. "Your Majesty," he said.

His friends all followed suit, their eyes wide and their mouths agape in stunned disbelief.

Her laughter was like music, and her voice like calm water as she spoke. "Yes ... I can see the resemblance in your manner, Michael."

"How do you know my name?" he asked nervously.

"Our Great Father reveals much to me," she said, her eyes aglow with kindness as she reached out for his bearded chin and raised his head to meet her own eyes. "Though I feared we would be too late for this moment," she smiled, then turned to address all who remained, man and Sprite alike. "But it would seem that the Light Seeker has found the gift our Great Father had hidden away, the gift created for the mending of the world." She turned back to address the remnant. "And in doing so has given flesh and blood to the hope we had all held in our hearts."

The affection and wonder felt as thick as a fog on the morning pasture; it clung heavy and hopeful, binding all present as witnesses to something truly amazing. It was the silver voice of Ardghal that broke the silent reverie as a song poured out from his silver lips.

"Ritheadh an oíche, agus tá an solas nua tar éis an saol seo a ghlanadh i rith an lae inniu. D'aimsigh an t-iarrthóir, agus is féidir go mbeadh gach croí áthas anois. Ardaigh do chuid guthanna do na cinn go léir a chruthaigh tú agus lig do mholtaí do dhaoine a bhfuil meas orthu i bhfianaise nua na beatha!"

(Night has passed, and the new light has bathed this world in the coming dawn of creation, for the seeker has found, and all hearts might now rejoice. Lift high your voices all ye created ones and let the praise of your admiration usher in the new light of life!)

Tears began to well in the eyes all who heard the song, and Michael whispered in Margarid's ear as they watched the herald fill this valley of war with the balm of sweet song. "What does it mean?" he said, emotion thick in his voice.

"It doesn't really matter, does it?" she said as she smiled at him.

"No ... I suppose it doesn't," he said as he squeezed her hand.

When the song had finished, the Queen addressed the remnant once more. "Rise, sons and daughters of Ádhamh. Aiénor will require all of us, irrespective of our deeds prior, to aid in its mending."

"What about them?" Celrod said, still unsure how to treat those who, not moments before, would have run him though with a blade.

"Aiénor is wide and it is wounded. Many hands, all of our hands, will be necessary, dear one."

He nodded his obedience. Though he was unsure how to reconcile it in his mind at the moment, he was also confident after looking into her eyes that he need not understand all the intricacies at this particular time.

"Turn your vision to the sky! Look up and see the light of our Great Father, shining for all to behold." The Queen rose upon her wings to address the gathered people. "And then let your vision turn inward, towards your own hearts, and witness how the light of the Father chases away the shadows of fear and doubt. Then, my friends ... may your vision focus out upon this world before us, as we build, together, HIS new kingdom."

All stood silent for a moment and considered her words, letting the spoken wisdom do its good work in all their hearts. In the quiet, they could hear the sound of horses and wagons from the road west of the Halvard. The remnant looked to each other, wondering just who might be approaching now.

"Excuse me ... Queen?" the small voice of a little girl spoke over the noises from the road.

"Yes, my child?" Iolanthe answered graciously.

"What about our friends? Can we say the words over them?" Georgina asked, thinking of Portus, Vŏlker, Harmier, and all the rest who had been slain.

"We will honor them, my child, together." The smile of the beautiful Queen touched the wounded part of the child's heart with a salve of compassion. "But first, let my Sprites see to your wounds and your hunger, for we have much work to be about, and you all will require your strength."

The snort of horses sounded again as a wagon rounded the turn in the road.

"Woah ... easy there, Ransom," a voice called out. "Well, I never!" said the same old man. "I think we've found it!"

"I had no idea that it would happen like this!" came the voice of another. "Did you?"

"Of course I did," said a third.

"Like *this*?" said the second voice.

"Well ... maybe not just like this," the third old man said.

Michael tried to see who it was that had arrived, bringing with them the commotion of such banter.

"Who is that?" the brewer asked.

"I don't know … I can't see over everyone's head," Celrod reasoned.

"What is that smell?" Timorets asked, the scent of something savory caught in his nose.

"I hope you are hungry!" called the voice of a wizened old woman from one of the carts.

"And thirsty … don't forget that!" said a white-bearded man. "My ale is prize worthy, and just the thing for a day like this!"

"It's good ale, we all give you that, Miller," the beardless old man agreed. "Not that we will ever catch you drinking a drop of it."

"Yes," the woman said again. "Plenty to eat and plenty to drink."

"It would seem that our friends have arrived!" Queen Iolanthe said with laughter in her royal eyes. "Come, all of you … fill yourselves until you are content."

The remnant wasted no time, for the fighting had sapped them of their strength, and it was not until the savory aromas had wafted over the field that their bellies remembered they were indeed famished.

The Sprites looked on as the Poets greeted the remnant with great joy and hospitality in their eyes. Faolan and the host began to collect their injured, whilst Eógan tended to the wounds.

"Why do you not go and eat, children of Ádhamh?" the queen said to the former Nocturnals as they stood in the shadow of the Halvard, outside of the celebration.

"This was our cause, our doing," said a tall, broad-shouldered man, whose silver beard was braided. "How could we dare presume to partake of your provisions when it was by our blades that your own blood was shed upon this ground? We do not deserve your hospitality, Sprite Queen."

She observed him, and in her heart, she knew him. There was nobility in his tired, sad eyes, and though neither of them had ever encountered the other before, there was a chord woven between them.

"Our Great Father's hospitality is not contingent upon the deeds of men, no matter how noble - or otherwise - they may be," the queen told him. "A table has been set, a humble banquet to usher in the mending of all things. You and your newly-liberated brothers are to be included and invited to participate in that very same mending, right alongside the rest of us."

"I don't understand," he said, raising his once-proud face to meet the eyes of the Queen of the children of the Jacarandas. His own eyes met her blazing, violet ones, and at the very sight of them, a tear of longing and sorrow rolled down his face.

"His will is not contingent upon our understanding, either, son of Ádhamh," she said with a sincere smile. "Now come, our Poet friends have plenty of beer and bread for all of us to eat and drink together."

Aius exhaled a tired laugh, and then looked around at the thousands of men who were once under his command. He undid the buckles that held his armor to his body and, in moments, the muted mail that had been forged in the depths of Aerebus lay discarded as rubble upon the field of battle.

The rest of the men looked to their general and followed suit, glad to be rid of the mark of the Raven Queen.

"Looks like you have your work cut out for you," Elder John said to Eógan, the Sprite healer.

"There are many of our kind wounded, but I am confident in both my skill and in the heart of our Great Father," Eógan said with a smile.

"Oh, I don't just mean our Sprite friends, Eógan," Elder John said as he watched the throng of men make their way towards the wagons.

"Oh?" Eógan said in reply. "I am sure their cuts and bruises will heal well enough when I apply my arts to them."

"Aye, their bodies will heal, master Sprite," Elder John said as he handed out loaf after loaf of sweetened bread. "But their hearts have been half-dead for who knows how long, used to living in the dark. I would say that it will take some adjusting to learn how to live in the light again."

"That might just be the greatest of all glories, my dear Poet friend,"

Eógan said as he wrapped a bandage made of white linen and leaves from the trees of beauty. "To see their hearts fully alive again. Though I would say that it will require all of us for that kind of healing, I think."

"I suppose you are right," Elder John said as he handed out bread and nodded his permission to the men who bade him thanks. "I suppose you are right, indeed."

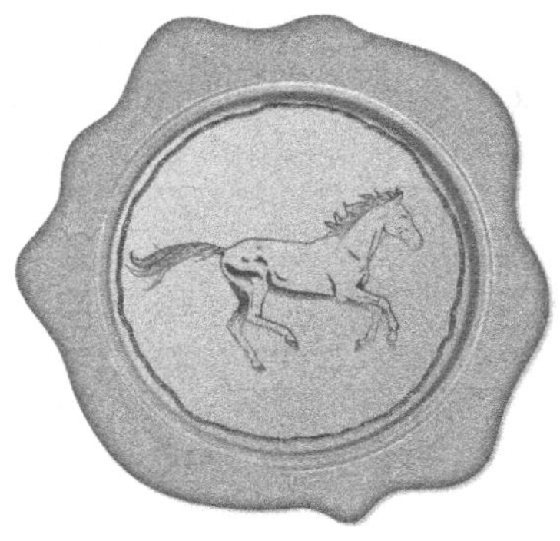

Chapter Forty-Five

Cal and his companions walked out from the center of this new city, from where the light rose high above the clouds and reached deep into the heavens above. A stream of water, which began as a gurgling spring in the fount of the sanctuary, flowed into a river that flowed out beyond the reaches of the white-stoned wall of the city. As they walked, they passed mansion after mansion, and saw gardens with flowers and hedges in full bloom, the likes of which they had never witnessed before upon this once-dark world.

As they passed the ornately carved archways and jeweled streets, they did not see another living soul.

It took them a long time of walking before they reached the white wall, and when they came upon one of its many entryways, a strange thought occurred to Cal.

"That is quite odd now, isn't it?" he said to his friends.

"What specifically do you mean, groomsman? This whole place is quite peculiar and odd, if you ask me," Astyræ told him with laughter in her eyes.

"My whole life, I lived behind the walls of a city," he told them as his hand reached out to touch the massive, carved stonework before him. "And never have I seen a walled city whose gates had no doors, not even a portcullis? This makes no sense. Why a walled city with no way to secure its walls?"

"I can see the sense in it, groomsman," Deryn said as he flitted up to examine the empty archway.

"I don't understand," Cal asked his friend.

"Perhaps these openings in the wall were not designed to keep people out, but rather, to welcome them inside," the Sprite said.

Cal shook his head, still confused. He took Astyræ's hand in his own and they walked through the shadow of the great entrance together. "Come on, then. I am sure this place will still be here when we are ready to come back. Our friends are still out there somewhere, and—"

"Halt!" interrupted the voice of one who did not sound like he would suffer foolishness long. His call was followed by the sound of fifty bows being drawn, and the clang of blades being unsheathed.

"Careful, now!" the man barked. "Show yourselves, or we will have no choice but to fell you where you stand."

Cal swallowed back his uncertainty. He raised his hands, and Astyræ followed suit.

"We are unarmed ... and we are looking for our friends," he told the man on the other side of the wall as he stepped through the great archway.

A gasp sounded from the waiting guards, and quickly the creaks and yawns of the slackening bowstrings stole the silence away from the shock.

"Cal?" came a familiar voice. "Is that you? I don't ... how could it be?"

"Sendoa?" Cal said. At first there was caution in his words, and then with great celebration he cried out to his friend. "Sendoa! Sendoa, it is you!" He took the warrior by the arm and then grabbed him in a delighted embrace. "Are you alright? What about the battle?" He looked up and over his shoulder, peering out onto the field of war. His voice was awash in confused curiosity. "What happened? Is it over?"

"We are alright, Cal," he answered, surprised at such an unlooked for embrace, here at the entrance of this unlooked for city.

"And yes," came a voice from behind the archers. "The battle is over."

The warriors parted, and a clearing opened up before the Lady Johanna, Queen of the Amaian people. Bandaged and rather war-torn, she strode out to meet them.

"Johanna!" Cal said. "What happened?"

She looked up, her eyes drinking in the bright and beautiful city that rose up before her. "What happened, you ask, Son of Haven?" she said with an incredulous shake of her bandaged head. "We all should be the ones asking you the very same question. When the dragon sent you reeling towards the face of the mountain in a heap of blood and fury..." Her eyes teared up at both the former fear and the newly found relief of the moment. "I had thought the tide of battle had surely turned against us. And yet, here we stand, dear groomsman of Haven."

Cal smiled, and an exhausted laugh escaped him. But as he surveyed the remnant of the Shaimiran army, his brow furrowed at how few remained. "Is this everyone? Are there any more survivors?"

"The Ramsguard is still searching for wounded, though there are not many of them left to do the searching," Sendoa said, with saddened words.

Cal looked to Johanna, his face still searching her own for the answer he truly sought.

"It is true. Navid and his guard rode and fought bravely," she recounted for him. "And though they cut down many of our foes, the barbs of the Raven army were too numerous to overcome."

Sendoa's men bowed their heads in reverence at the mention of the fallen captain.

"I am sorry; truly," Cal said. "And the others? Did they...?"

"Did they what?" came a loud and brashly familiar voice.

Cal's whole countenance raised at the sound of this friendly voice.

"Did we get cut down, too?" the large woodcutter bellowed as he made his way to the front of the line. "No brother ... we did not." A wide grin grew across his large, bearded face.

"Besides," Oren said. "We woodcutters are much better at the felling of things!"

"Aye!" Alon agreed, then glanced at the queen. "Not that you are not, too! I mean ... I didn't ... I wasn't saying that you weren't a fine army, a fine army indeed," he stammered apologetically.

"Lady Johanna," another voice from within the throng spoke up, his words noble and kind. "Please forgive my brothers. They have spent too much time alone among the forests, and have forgotten that they are not the only ones who live and die in these lands."

"Right ... I meant no harm by my words," Oren said, stumbling over his apology.

Cal looked about, trying to see who it was that spoke with such eloquence and authority, but he couldn't quite find the man among so many gathered.

"I am sure that no ill will was indeed intended," Johanna said, "though I would have you remember, woodcutter, that the blood of our warriors and your brothers has become indistinguishable out there on the *Tristura Eremua.*"

Cal looked to Deryn for the translation of the ancient words.

"*Tristura Eremua.* It means, the 'Fields of Sorrow,'" the Sprite whispered reverently.

The woodcutters raised and kissed their flints as the Amaians bowed their heads in remembrance.

The voice Cal had been searching for spoke again. "Never will we forget, though our joy momentarily robs us of our senses," he continued as he walked closer to the front of the crowd. "We are now kindred, a family born of blood and brilliance." As he said these last words, he bowed his own head in full view of the queen, and when he raised it to meet her eyes, Cal could not help but to blurt out the man's name with true elation in his voice.

"Yasen!" he said as he ran towards his friend. "Yasen, it is you! What in the name of the THREE who is SEVEN? I don't … I mean, I thought you were gone!" he said, stumbling over his joy as he took his friend by the shoulders and embraced him with great force.

Yasen's face went momentarily grave as he remembered the horrendous events of these last days, but that storm soon passed as the light of this victory shone once again in his unpatched eye. "Aye brother, but that is a story for stronger ale, on a less momentous day. Besides," he said as he looked around, taking in this unexpected miracle, "it would seem that you have indeed found what it was that you went searching for so long ago. And that, Cal, will require celebration, and not sorrowful tales." Yasen stretched his arms out to clasp Cal's shoulders.

Cal smiled, his own clouded eyes misting over with emotion. "Indeed, Yasen. Indeed," he agreed, his hands gripping the back of Yasen's neck.

"What is this?" Yasen said as his gaze caught the violet glow in the familiar face of the beautiful, blonde, Wreather woman. "It would seem to me that you bested the bravery of the governor's men after all, lady Astyræ." He looked to Cal with growing approval as he spoke. "And you are not the least bit worse for wear, it would seem."

She walked up to this tree man from across the Dark Sea, the man who had hidden her safely from the mob of guardsmen. She smiled a most grateful smile, and rose to the tips of her toes to plant a kiss upon his bearded cheek. "Thank you, woodcutter. I owe my safety to you, as well as to Cal."

"Think nothing of it," he said as he remembered his barmaid half a world away.

Queen Johanna walked into the middle of their joyful reunion. Her heart was cautiously hopeful that her people were free of danger, but her mind would not wholly let her guard down until she knew for certain. "Cal?" she asked, interrupting the moment. "You must tell me now … what is this place?"

He smiled at her and looked back up at the pillar of light that erupted from the high tower at the center of the city. "I do not know, Queen Johanna, but that light right there ... that is what we have been looking for all our lives, even when we did not know it. It is the light of the THREE who is SEVEN, the one He promised us."

"It would seem so, Cal," she said still taking in the mystery of this hidden city. "But this *place*, these walls and these roads ... the tower; whose kingdom is this?"

"That, I cannot say for certain," he said, reaching out to take her armored hand. "Though it does not trouble me as it does you, it would seem."

"No," she said, her eyes glancing through the entryway to the many mansions and glittering gardens all about her. "You are right, Cal, but my responsibility is to guard and protect my people. So before I lead them into an unknown danger, I would like to know for certain."

"Know what, for certain?" he asked her.

"That this place can indeed be trusted," she said, signaling Sendoa and his men to spread out and begin to secure the perimeter.

Sendoa ordered his men into formation, surrounding the queen and Cal alike, as a column of soldiers began to march their way into this white city of light. Cal and his friends followed along with the Shaimiran army. The air about them was fragrant with the scent of flowering jasmine and lavender. The gardens teemed with fruit trees and vegetables and row after row of berries. The silent air seemed to somehow buzz with electricity, but not another sound penetrated the weight of the quiet.

Along the borders of the walls were scores of homes, mansions built in a vibrant array of color, and next to them were storerooms teeming with linens and leathers, sugars and spices, and of every desirable good one could think of. A few of the scouts reported libraries, and great kitchens with majestic hearths. They found innumerable barrels of wine and ale, and great concert halls with unknown instruments of music.

"Something is odd to me, Cal," Yasen said as he listened to the reports of the scouts, detailing all of the richness and the beauty of this city.

"What is it?" he replied.

"Not one single scout has reported finding an armory, or a barracks. Not a prison hold, not even a locked door … let alone a sentry to guard all of this abundance." He furrowed his brow in concentration. "Why do you think that is?"

"Perhaps, dear woodcutter," Deryn said, his response nearly bursting from his smiling lips, "there is no need for guards or weapons in this new kingdom of light."

The column halted as they came upon the grotto of the great tower of light. The space was massive, and at its center stood the spiraling tower, high and bright. At its base, the silver waters of the river found its origin.

"What say you, Sendoa?" Johanna asked her commander.

"We have found no hint of an enemy, nor of any danger. No sign of anyone at all," the commander said with puzzlement to his words. "Though, my Queen, nothing seems spoiled or time worn. It is as if everything were bottled and barreled and bloomed this very day."

"Alright, then," she replied. "See to it that the gates are secured. With so many riches here, we are sure to have another war on our hands over the possession of this place."

Sendoa bowed his head and turned to gather his men.

"No!" Deryn said to Cal, worry now replacing his previous joy. "This is wrong … we can't—"

But his protest was interrupted with the sound of mighty hooves upon the glittering, stone street. Everyone turned in a hurry, while bows were drawn and blades unsheathed. Though the land around them was bright and unshadowed, they had to cover their eyes at the sight of the rider before them.

"Do not dismay, children of Ádhamh. Lay down your instruments of death, for the days of war are over and done with." The voice in the brightness implored them with great authority. It sounded as trustworthy as an aged grandfather and as virile as the roar of a great lion; its tone demanded both trust and awe with each faintly familiar word spoken.

Sendoa looked to his queen, but did not hesitate to lower his own sword, and so his men followed suit. They looked in awe at the sight before them, struggling to see with their eyes what their hearts already trusted. Finally, they began to see Him. The brilliance of the rider before them did not fade, so much as the eyes of all who gathered began to accommodate to so great a presence.

"Who are you?" Johanna asked with a trembling voice as her own eyes beheld a rider robed in white, mounted upon one of the *Anahiera,* crowned in the majestic, triune horns of the White Stag.

"I am known by many names, and I have taken many forms throughout the ages," the white rider proclaimed. "But do not fear, Johanna, Queen of the Amaian people, you may trust that I am indeed good."

As He spoke her name, her heart softened in an instant. She looked at Him carefully, searching the bright face of this white rider once more for any sign of malice or un-truth, but her heart had already been satisfied. And so, the knees of the great queen bent in reverence to His brilliance.

The gathered remnant followed the example of the queen, kneeling before this rider in white.

"The days of darkness are over, for hope has led you to the halls of *Ziohnia,* the Kingdom of Light! As foretold, the wounds of this world will be mended." He turned and found the face of Deryn as He continued. "For in our Great Father's kingdom, there are many mansions, and room enough for all."

Cal ignored the tears that fell joyfully down his war-stained face as he listened, his heart drinking in the words that he had always longed to hear.

"Yours is now the task of ordering the broken things of this world, joining in the mending of its wounds by the grace of the THREE who is

SEVEN." The rider turned to meet the gaze of the kneeling queen. "But temper not the welcome of this city, nor spare the larder of its storehouses. For all are welcome here, though they may have once been seduced or enslaved by the now-defeated darkness. All may call My kingdom ... *home.*"

The gathered children of light looked upon the rider with the deepest gratitude they had ever experienced, trusting in both His words and His generosity.

"The old order of this world has passed, for My light is alive, and the dawn has indeed come for us all." And with those last words, the *Anahiera* reared up on his hind legs, and the rider in white held high a familiar blade, whose flowering hilt shone and sparkled in the reflection of this new light. "May it be so!"

The mighty winged horse shot high into the bright, blue sky, leaving the whole of Aiénor with the charge and the adventure of the great restoration of all things.

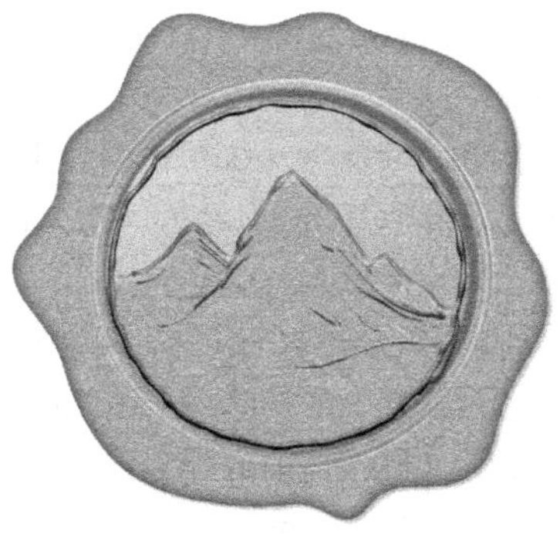

Epilogue

Many bright days had passed since the rider in white had left them there in the brilliant streets of this new kingdom. True to her word, Johanna did not bar the entrances nor turn any away from its shelter.

Astyræ had first joined with Aysa and the healers of Shaimira to bring aid to all who were wounded and battle-weary. But as they all soon discovered, in the light of this new world, there was no place for infection or festering, and the wounds of war were mended with great haste.

There was no throne, nor any seat of power in the city of *Ziohnia*, for it was quite understood that this kingdom was a gift that did not belong to any one person or peoples. The citizens did, however, look to Johanna for guidance and leadership, though she no longer saw herself as a queen. Rather, now, more than any title she had ever held before, *steward* suited her best.

Cal walked into the covering of a great tent out in the field of battle where so many men had died. He found the former queen working quite intently over a desk full of maps.

"Queen—" he caught himself as he spoke. "I mean, Lady Steward," His cheeks flushed. "It is sometimes hard to unlearn the old ways, even in the light of the new ones."

She laughed and smiled, her face beautiful and alight with purpose. "Calarmindon!" she exclaimed. "Oh my dear friend, for what reason does the light seeker come to my tent today?"

"Well," he said, almost reluctantly, "it is time, Johanna."

"Oh?" she asked, puzzled. "Come and sit, Cal, and tell me about what time you speak of." She motioned for him to sit and as she did she turned to address Sendoa. "When will you be ready to march? I would like to make our way as soon as we are able; there might yet be those imprisoned in the depths of Aerebus that need our help."

"Yes, Lady Steward," the commander said with a salute. "By tomorrow morning, our provisions and our men will be ready for the journey southward."

"Very good!" she said, quite pleased. "Will you excuse us, Sendoa?"

He nodded and smiled as he met Cal's eyes with his own, then quickly turned and ducked out from the cover of the tent.

"There is still so much to do, Cal," she said as she poured a delicious smelling wine into two metal chalices. "And undo, for that matter." She offered him a glass and then drank deeply of her own. "Even the wine tastes better in the light of this new world!"

Cal sipped and smiled. "Aye, it does."

"Tell me again, what is it that you were saying?" she asked him.

"I believe that it is time, Johanna," he told her as he rested his drink upon the table. "Time for me to return home."

"But this is your home now, Calarmindon," she said in confusion. "You spent your life dreaming and hoping for this place, and then ... then you found it." She placed her hand on his. "Why would you ever want to leave this place?"

"Because," he said sweetly as he clasped her hand. "Because, it may be that there are survivors, from Haven and the outlying lands, that do not even know this place exists. And there is plenty of room here for them, too."

"And your friends?" she asked as she espied the violet-eyed Astyræ, the azure winged Sprite, and the bearded band of woodcutters waiting just beyond the flowing walls of her tent. "Will they be going with you?"

"Yes," he told her. "Though I do not suppose this will be the last you will see of any of us. I've got to find them, if they are lost out there somewhere. I have to at least try to seek them out, to see if there is mending and restoration that can still be done for Haven."

"That is certainly as noble a cause as any we have been pursuing here," she said supportively. "What do you need of me? I haven't any ships to carry you across the Itsaso, but if anything you wish is in my power to grant ... it will gladly and freely be yours."

"No, thank you," Cal said easily. "We are not looking for a ship; I have had enough of the Dark Sea to last a hundred lifetimes," he laughed. "If only you had some horses, I would most certainly be grateful for an equine companion again."

Her kind and noble eyes fell in disappointment at this request. "If I had them to give, they would already be yours. But please, accept our finest rams, and the carts to carry your friends who are too, well ... too *mighty* to ride upon their backs."

"Thank you," Cal replied. "We would be honored to receive such a gift."

"Consider it done," she said with great generosity. "I will have the herd master ready them for you." She squeezed his hand and raised her brow as she searched his eyes. "When will you be leaving us?"

"As soon as it is possible ... tomorrow, if the herd master can manage," he told her.

"Very well, then," she said. "Mezulari, will you please see that Gelinda prepares provisions for our friends' great journey eastward."

The captain of her guard bowed his head, his stern face now remade in the kindness of peace. "Of course, Lady Steward," he said as he left to see about her request.

The amber-hued day carried on much like the last many days here in this bright kingdom of the new light. The smithies were particularly busy as they melted and reshaped the ugly, metal blades and armor of the once-vast Raven army into plowshares and tools for the replanting and the rebuilding of Aiénor.

Shaimira was not abandoned, though many of its former residents found new homes in the mansions of *Ziohnia*. Daily, it seemed, wanderers from all about the Greywood were drawn to the tower of light. As they came forth, they were welcomed with a great feast each silvery evening.

The Oweles did not tarry long in these western lands after the war had been won. Only of few of them had survived after the fighting was finished, and they soon bore their slain brothers back, with great lament and honor, to the eyrie of their birth.

When the great light had burst forth from of the bowels of the Itxaro, the bewitching of the Sorceress, and all the ancient seeds of Šárka, perished under the glorious illumination. Men and women everywhere no longer needed to see in darkness, and so they left behind the former to join the new kingdom of light.

The following morning, the small band of friends awoke with great intention and anticipation for the journey that they would soon embark upon. While the woodcutters and Cal busied themselves with securing their provisions and packing their belongings, Deryn whisked away his violet-eyed friend to show her the makings of his own plan.

In the great courtyard of the shining city, an arbor of Jacaranda trees had sprung out of the new earth, ancient plantings hidden before the beginning of time, resplendent in their violet beauty. Deryn marveled often at them, for the thought of new Sprites being born again into this world filled him with great joy.

"Oh Deryn!" she said as she beheld the sight. "When will these trees bring about your kind?" Astyræ asked as her own, violet eyes marveled at the white trees.

"I am not wholly sure," he said as he perched upon her slender shoulder. "But I suspect they are waiting to meet their Queen before these flowers will produce any fruit. I do hope to tell Iolanthe all about them soon." He shook his tiny, azure head as he thought on it. "Can you imagine? *Éimhear* herself couldn't contain my excitement if she had ordered it so."

"Will there be more, do you think?" she asked him.

"Oh yes," he smiled. "At least ... if I have anything to say about it."

"What do you mean, Deryn?" she asked, her smile inquisitive as she watched his excited face.

Deryn beckoned her to come and see, taking her to a small, carved chest that was sitting at the heart of the arbor. "What is this, dear Sprite? A fairy box?" she laughed playfully.

He shook his head, not offended by much at all these bright days. "Look for yourself!" he told her with great delight.

She kneeled down and lifted the metal clasp on the small chest, opening its cover to reveal seven, small, purse-shaped pods, brightly glowing in a violet aura. She picked one up in her hand and recognized the treasure she held.

"Where did you come by these?" she said in awed wonder as she stared at the Jacaranda seeds.

"I picked them myself," he said proudly.

"But Deryn?" she protested.

"They are but seeds until a Queen has come for them, never you worry," he told her with great confidence. "I mean to plant them on our journey back, in hopes of binding the grove of Islwyn to this very arbor here!"

"Those are great plans, my friend," Cal said as he walked in on their conversation. "Great plans, indeed."

"Is it time?" Astyræ asked. "I have never been to the east, tree man, and I cannot wait to see where it is that you come from."

Cal walked over to her and took her by the waist, pulling her close for a sweet kiss. "Aye, and if there is any of it left, I will be glad to show you, indeed. Now, come on already, Johanna is ready for us and it would seem that all of *Ziohnia* is waiting to see us off."

She bent down and picked up Deryn's chest, taking one last look at these trees that had sewn their violet thread through the center of her life.

The three of them walked to the easternmost entry, followed by the small band of woodcutters. What they saw gathered before them made their hearts nearly burst with affection and their eyes fill with joyful tears. Great banners and streamers of fine linen danced in the breeze of the morning, and as they made their way down the brilliant streets, a great cheer went up from the thousands who gathered before them. Bright horns rang out their jubilant notes as they approached the Lady Johanna.

"Seems a bit much doesn't it?" Oren asked playfully.

"Ah, not at all!" argued Alon. "I was expecting fireworks and maybe even dancing! But this will do, I suppose."

"Shut up, brother," Oren said with a playful punch to his shoulder.

The procession of travelers included Yasen, Oren and Alon, Gvidus, and the remnant of the woodcutters. Pyrrhus, the one-armed fire knight of Haven, also travelled with them, along with Astyræ, Deryn, and Cal. The Lady Steward stood before them all, a smile upon her face and tears streaming from her eyes.

"I know you must leave, for there may still be those in need of rescue; but I charge you all with this: return to us soon, and return to us often," she said.

A collective agreement sounded from the gathered friends as they laughed and made their promised intentions known.

"I have carts for you, woodcutters, and strong teams of rams to pull you by," she told them. "There is plenty of food and wine to drink."

"And ale?" Oren asked childishly as Alon elbowed him in his side.

"Yes," she laughed. "Plenty of ale, too. For the stores of Ziohnia are more than abundant! The herd master has given his best rams for your journey, and they are saddled for you, Pyrrhus and Astyræ. May they bear you well along your journey."

A commotion could be heard as the crowd about her began to part. An older man, whose long, white, hair had been braided and hung in the center of his back, held the leather reins of a silver-white horse.

"Who is this?" Cal exclaimed as he gazed at the horse, whose majestic head sat high upon his muscular neck. Finally, he turned and met the eyes of Johanna. "How did you come about him?"

"Well … he is no *Anahiera*, but he is beautiful; a descendant of his Amaian forebearers," she said as she reached up to stroke his braided, silvery mane.

"But how did you come by him?" Cal asked as he moved closer to the tall, sculpted horse, hands outstretched and a smile on his lips. "You said that your people had abandoned horses?"

"I did not tell you false, Calarmindon. This horse came to us," she replied in wonder.

"A prince this one is, surely a descendant of Sigrid herself," he mused as the grey muzzle of this silver-white horse greeted his hand with a warm, soft welcome. "Yes, indeed," he whispered in a sing-song voice.

"Perhaps the rider in white sent him to aid you on your journey home," she told him.

"Does he have a name?" Cal asked.

"That is for you to decide, I think," the Lady Steward replied.

"A prince among horses, indeed," Cal cooed.

"May I suggest Tersk?" she replied. "It means 'the prince of horses'; a noble name for a noble purpose!"

"Tersk, huh?" Cal said as he placed his hand on the horse's high-set neck, just below the jaw line. The groomsman could feel their two hearts pulsing as one, and when the horse let out a long exhale of a breath, it seemed as if the two had melded together.

"Yes," he said, turning to thank Johanna. "That is a fitting name for such a horse, and for such a gift." He embraced her, and she him, and the whole of the gathered people let out a cheer of great delight.

"Alright, alright," Gvidus said as he labored to climb atop the cart.

"We have a long journey, groomsman, and I hope that there are some friendly faces waiting for us at the end of it."

"Very well, then," Cal said with a beaming smile on his face. And with that, he placed his foot in the leather stirrup and hoisted himself upon the back of Tersk. The horse whinnied and let out an agreeable snort.

"Good boy," Cal said, stroking his neck.

"One more thing," came the voice of Sendoa as he moved towards the mounted hero of Aiénor. "The journey may be long, and there still may be dangers unknown along the way." The captain unwrapped a blue scabbard that held a broad sword within its protection, whose hilt was formed of the wings of the *Anahiera,* and whose pommel resembled the mighty face of Uriel.

"I know your sword was lost in the battle," Sendoa offered. "And well ... we thought we might honor both you and Uriel in this way."

Cal picked up the blade, incredulously. It was much lighter than Gwarwyn had been, though no less beautiful.

"Its name is Ikehr, the *Visitation,*" Sendoa told him. "Euria the smithy crafted this in homage of the visitation of the *Anahiera,* the second salvation of our people."

"I will wear it with great honor, and each time I draw it forth ... it will be done in remembrance of Uriel, and of all of you," he said as he cinched the scabbard belt and sheathed the blade. "Though if I am honest, my heart tells me it will be for remembrance sake alone that I will hold it aloft. This light," he said as he looked high into the brilliant pillar overhead, "has chased away the brooding shadows of the most dangerous places."

"Return to us soon, return to us often," Johanna said with great affection. "All of you."

With that farewell, the departing host rode eastward along the foothills of the Itxaro and into the wilderness north of the Dark Sea.

Every three days as they journeyed along the way, Deryn and Astyræ would plant one of the seven Jacaranda seeds. The Sprite would sing a song of unknown consecration and smile with great anticipation, hoping his Queen would soon return along the same road to give her blessing upon the young saplings.

"You can plainly see the route by which the Raven army took through these lands," Yasen said to the group. "The ground was abused under the weight of so many men and their machines of war."

"Good God. How many were there, I wonder?" Pyrrhus said as he beheld the aftermath of their movement. "There must have been nearly ten thousand in the Wreath. Could there have been that many over here as well?"

"It's hard to tell," Yasen replied. "But for our city's sake … I hope we are just misreading the tracks."

"Who knew the world was so big?" Astyræ said as she rode beside Cal, taking in all of the grandeur of these lands. They had begun to turn southward days ago, and as they did, the mountains crept in all about them, on both sides of the trail. They rose high, with grey rocks and black granite and not much green, save the brambles and scrub pines that protruded from the rock face.

"And it is so much bigger now … now that we can see it all," he said with a smile.

"Yasen!" came the voice of Gvidus from atop one of the ram carts. "There is something up ahead you should see."

"What is it, brother?" Yasen replied warily.

"I don't rightly know," he told him. "But whatever it is … it's big."

"Careful now, lads," Oren cautioned. "We don't know what kind of Ravens could yet be hiding in the crook of these rocks."

"I thought all the Ravens were gone," Alon argued. "You know, now that the Sorceress is dead and all."

"I mean … I don't really mean *Ravens* now, do I?" Oren retorted. "I mean some kind of scoundrel, or highwayman … or Yasen's damned demon bear, for all we know."

"He is right," Yasen agreed. "Keep a sharp eye about you. Cal, Astyræ, Pyrrhus … ride with me. We need to get a closer look."

They all nodded their understanding and spurred their mounts as they rounded the outcropping of rock and came face to face with a giant, iron gate, set within the smooth, stone walls of some ancient outpost.

"What is that?" Yasen said aloud as his eye scanned the battlements above. "A fortress? Out here?"

"It's not one of ours," Pyrrhus offered. "I don't think our maps even go this far east, and if they did, we had no reason to use them."

"No, it is much older than Haven," Cal said as he cautiously rode Tersk closer to the massive wall. "It reminds me of something, someplace I have been before."

Cal dismounted Tersk and bade him to stay put as he got a closer look. He ran his hand upon the seamless stone, finding no imperfection in its craftsmanship. He looked high above his head at the ruined and crumpled mess that must have once been a tower. "Do you see that?" he said as he pointed to the heap of rubble.

"Aye," Yasen agreed. "It doesn't look as if that mess is as old as this place is."

"Agreed. I'd wager some great battle happened here, not too long ago," Cal said.

"Do you smell that?" Astyræ said as she sniffed at the air.

"Like an old fire," Pyrrhus replied. "But not too old ... the smoke is still present in the morning air."

"Look at this!" Cal exclaimed curiously as he ran his hand over the ancient, iron portcullis. "It is badly damaged ... but from the inside."

"Whatever it was that ruined this place wanted out ... not in," Yasen surmised. "Does it move, groomsman? Will it lift?"

"Certainly not by my strength alone," he said as he tried to manipulate the heavy gate. "Deryn," Cal called out, "can you fly through and tell us what you see?"

Deryn, in a whir of blue light, flew through an opening in the portcullis and onward to see what was on the other side of this ancient gate. "There was a battle alright," the Sprite shouted back to his friends. "The ground is littered with the arms and armor of the Raven army!"

"Is there any sign of life?" Cal asked his friend.

"Not that I can see," Deryn admitted.

"Then who opposed them, huh?" Pyrrhus muttered. "The Ravens didn't just break themselves against the wall. Somebody held this place and defended it against them."

"You are right," Yasen said. "But why would they defend it, and then abandon it? That just … doesn't make much sense."

"It would if they found someplace better," came an unfamiliar voice from inside the gatehouse.

Instantly the company drew their blades, fixing them in the direction of the voice.

"Who goes there?" Cal asked bravely as the light of the morning glinted off the blade of Ikehr.

"As one who is trying to gain passage, I think it should be you who first answers that question," the voice said.

Cal looked to Astyræ, asking without words if she could see who it was behind the gate. She shook her head no to answer him, and then the blue glint of their Sprite friend gave them cause for hope.

"To gain passage, you say?" Cal said playfully. "We have already made it through."

"What do you mean—" the voice began to say, but was quite suddenly interrupted by the point of a tiny, azure blade.

"Please, sir," Deryn said as he held the point of his sword in the flesh of the man's neck. "We have journeyed far, and still have much to do before our quest is over."

"A Sprite?" the man said warily. "I don't understand … is this a jest?"

"I assure you, sir, that my Sprite friend does not jest with his blade," Cal pressed. "Why would you say that?"

"Cal!" Astyræ whispered as she espied some movement.

Yasen and Pyrrhus flattened their backs to the ancient wall, weapons at the ready.

"Because the Sprites are our friends, that's why," the man said, all suspicion now gone from his voice.

"I don't understand," Cal said aloud.

"Tell me your name, friend of Sprites," Deryn said, not relinquishing the advantage for a single moment.

"My name is Johnrey," the white-bearded man said. "I was once a corporal in the army of Haven. I served under Captain Armas, and I serve now alongside Lieutenant Marcum."

"Johnrey?" Pyrrhus said as he came away from the wall to have a closer look.

"And what Sprite do you claim friendship of, Johnrey?" Deryn persisted.

"All of them ... I mean, I thought it was all of them," he said, dumbfounded at the question. "Though I would say the Queen has the affection of all who have made their home within the mountain."

Deryn released his blade from Johnrey's neck and flitted over to meet his gaze. "My name is Deryn, a sentinel of the house of the Queen herself," the Sprite said as he sheathed his blade. "I was sent to aid and to guide Calarmindon of Haven on his quest to seek the light of our Great Father."

"And now that we have found it," Cal added, "we come in search of our friends."

Johnrey moved out from behind his concealment and into the open light on the other side of the iron gate, and what he saw filled his face with utter joy. "Raise the portcullis!" he shouted to someone out of view.

"I can't believe it!" he said as he walked through the now open gate and over to Cal. He nearly put his hands on Cal's shoulders, pausing only at the blade that was still brandished before him. "Are you the one everyone has been talking about?"

"I ... I don't know—" Cal tried to say before being interrupted.

"The one that found the Poets, and the Sprites? The one who left with the colony in search of Illium's light?" Johnrey was bumbling with excitement. "They are never going to believe me!"

The sound of footsteps upon the stone stairs cut through the moment.

"Lower your weapons," Cal said, still unsure of what had just happened, but trusting in the goodness of it. He sheathed his own blade and reach to shake the arm of this guardsman, Johnrey. "We are going to be just fine."

Bows were lowered and blades were sheathed as the company came forward to be greeted by a small contingent of guardsmen, dressed in a mix of the green and silver, but adorned with armor that reminded him of his own.

"Where are we?" Yasen said as he, too, greeted Johnrey.

"The Halvard," Johnrey said as he watched a woodcutter, a captain of Haven, and a violet-eyed beauty walk through the gate before him. "This was once called the *Guardian of the Rock* by the people of Terriah, or so I'm told."

"Of course!" Cal said. "It reminds me of Petros."

"And how did you come to be in command of it?" Pyrrhus asked.

Johnrey just shook his head in amazement as he and his men beheld the sight before them. "That is quite a long story, and I will save it for after we get you all settled and fed. For there are going to be many who will delight to hear of your return." The corporal turned to one of his guardsmen. "Lower the portcullis!"

"Not so fast, Corporal," Pyrrhus said, holding out his one remaining arm. "The rest of our friends have still to join us."

Yasen smiled at this kindness, and then raised his horn to his lips and let out a single blast to signal the woodcutters. Whips were cracked, and the rams' carts woke to life, making their way round the rocky road and through the Halvard Pass. The company rested in the shadow of the ancient stronghold. Unbelievable stories were shared by the silver light of evening time. When morning came and their fast was broken with cheese and honey and toasted pieces of rough-cut bread, Cal and his company bade the guardsmen farewell.

"Thank the THREE who is SEVEN, my new friends," Johnrey said as he embraced these unexpected guests of his. "I never, in all my days, believed we would witness such histories as we have."

"And just think, Johnrey," Cal said as he slapped his back in warm affection. "This is just the beginning of a new age, and we are invited to be a part of it."

"May it be so," the old guardsman said with a salute across his chest.

"I am not so sure that you need to worry about the portcullis anymore, Corporal," Pyrrhus said. "On the other side of the world is a bright kingdom, a good kingdom … and I doubt there are any left who would want to oppose it."

"I have my orders, Captain," Johnrey respectfully disagreed.

"I know you do," he said with a smile as he placed his hand upon the corporal's shoulder. "And they will soon seem foolish enough."

They set out westward, ranging from long bouts of silence to hours of wonder-filled conversations. They followed the instructions of the men at the Halvard, but as they stepped onto the soil of the retreating forest, both Cal and the woodcutters knew exactly where they were.

"Home," Yasen whispered reverently.

"It looks a lot different in the light of day, doesn't it?" Gvidus mused.

"Less dangerous, for one," Oren said.

"Aye … and a lot sadder," Alon added.

"Makes a grown man – a woodcutter, at that – do a lot of thinking about all we have done … and what good it did us, or anybody, for that matter," Gvidus continued.

"We did what we had to," Yasen replied. "For what we thought was best, even if we were wrong in the end … we did not labor wrongly."

"Aye," Gvidus said between puffs of his pipe. "I suppose you might be right."

Days passed and the journey was slow, for the ground had been ravaged in the march of the Nocturnals. It wasn't until they came upon the old timber roads that they felt as if they could move with any real haste.

"How much farther?" Yasen asked.

"About a day, maybe less, once we reach the Altar," Cal said with anticipation as he scanned the horizon.

"And we shouldn't be too far away from there now, if I remember correctly," Yasen continued. "To think this was all forest, once, and rich hunting grounds."

"And it will be again," Cal said, hope ever in his eyes. "That's what I believe, anyway. Look!" he said as a tall shape came into view, not half a league before them. "The Altar! We are nearly there, my friends ... nearly there."

"Well, that is not how I remember it looking," Gvidus mused as the company beheld the ruined and desecrated altar.

"Aye," Oren said, matter-of-factly. "As I remember it, the thing was in one piece."

"Well ... I am sure there is going to be quite a lot of this same conversation as we continue to explore our homeland," Yasen said. "I'll wager our city didn't fair nearly as well as this did."

They didn't stop as they came upon the Altar; they continued onward, each taking in the foreshadowing moment of all that would be required of them as the ruined places were built anew. Westward they continued, the ground about them unchanging for the most part, until the sounds of the river Abonris began to reach their ears.

"Well, that is a welcomed sound," Cal said as he spoke to Astyræ.

"Oh?" she said playfully, and with a smile in her eyes. "Why is that, groomsman?"

"It was the river, Abonris, that led me to where we are going. If I hadn't tried to run away..." His eyes went wide in horror as the sudden realization of something very important crashed in from the recesses of his memory.

"Cal?" she said, puzzled at his expression. "Cal, what is the matter?"

"The reason why I ended up in the river to begin with was because I was trying to escape ... *her*."

"Who is *her*?" Yasen asked.

"I don't really know," Cal said as they continued on. "She had eyes like Morana, and like Nogcwren; a sickly yellow."

"A witch, then?" Yasen offered.

"Maybe a demon, or some foul, evil spirit," Cal said. "She wore the body of a sad, beautiful maiden. And then as she spoke, a wretched old witch would just … I don't know … take over. Frightened me to my very bones."

"I don't understand," Astyræ said. "Did she throw you into the river, or trick you somehow?"

"She guarded some ancient bridge, probably Terrian. I had never seen it before, or heard of it, for that matter," Cal told them as they drew closer to the place he remembered. "She meant to entrap me … to keep me from, well … seeking the light. I suppose I see that now. And when we ran, Moa and I … we ended up in the river. We almost drowned."

"Is that the bridge?" Astyræ said as she pointed out into the distance.

"I believe so," Cal said, shaking his head at the full circle of his journey.

"That doesn't look very scary to me, brother," Yasen said playfully.

"Nor does it to me, anymore," Cal said thoughtfully. "Perhaps the horrors we have seen and fought makes this place seem… well, less horrific. I mean, the bridge was never evil itself… though somehow she was bound to it."

"Well, you are not alone this time, groomsman," Astyræ told him with a sweet smile. "And just because you might not need to travel half-a-world away anymore to seek the light, it does not mean your quest now is any less important. So, we will all be on our guard with you."

Cal laughed, but he knew her words were not making light of his story. "Thank you, my lady," he said, with a dramatic nod of his head.

"I don't see anyone," Pyrrhus said skeptically. "I think it is safe to cross it."

"No," Cal replied, examining the small, stone bridge. "I don't see anyone either."

"Do you think?" Gvidus offered. "That when the light came … maybe it destroyed her?"

"Maybe so, brother," Cal replied.

"I guess the rider in white meant what he said, then," Alon said with laughter in his voice.

"Of course he meant what he said," Oren countered, with an exasperated shake of the head.

"But look!" Yasen told them as he pointed to something metal that bisected their passage.

"What is that?" Gvidus looked harder.

"It looks like some kind of manacle, chained from one side to the next," Cal offered. "Though I have never seen one like that before."

"And it's broken, at that," Astyræ said with a smile.

"What is she saying?" Oren asked in confusion. "Is she saying that there is some damned witch running around here now? She wasn't destroyed ... she was ... released?"

"I thought you just said that the rider in white killed all the witches," Alon argued.

"No!" Astyræ said sharply. "What I am saying is ... maybe the weeping maiden is now ... free."

"Ah!" the woodcutters said in union.

"Still," Oren interjected one last time. "I am not touching those cursed things if it is all the same to you."

The company laughed as they crossed the bridge, unopposed and undeterred, towards their final destination. It wasn't much more than a half a day's ride from there, and soon Cal and his company found the ancient, paved roads of the mountain palace. Their eyes began to mist over with emotion as the stone reliefs told the tales of a place they had never before known existed.

A blast of a horn, and then another to answer, woke the sky of the dwindling day, and voices, dozens and dozens of voices, could be heard, going about some excited business. When at last the company came to the great grotto in the shadow of the Hilgari, they looked upon the ripe and teeming fields of the gardens of Kalein and onto the deep, blue water of the Dark Sea.

As the group of travelers was spotted, people ran towards them, curious, then excited, then overflowing with joy. They laughed and cried and embraced wholeheartedly, reveling in the glory of a reunion they had not dared to hope for. Yasen scanned the heads of the gathering crowd for the curly-haired barmaid that had won his heart and saved his life with her affections.

"Keily!" he shouted out, as he climbed atop the ram's cart to get a better look. "Cal, I don't see her," he shouted worriedly over to his friend. "Can you tell if she is here?"

Cal just smiled, his own eyes misting over as he watched the brave and beautiful barmaid climb undetected into the back of the very cart where Yasen stood. "Do you see her, brother?" his face betraying the longing in his heart.

Cal laughed and nodded his head as spoke. "I do … I do, brother."

"What?" Yasen replied, unsure and frustrated. "What is that supposed to mean?"

"It means that I don't know how you made it all the way back to me alive, if you couldn't even spot a lady climbing up into your own cart," Keily told him playfully. "Maybe if you had two eyes…" she tried to finish her teasing thought, but the strong arms of the woodcutter grabbed her roughly and picked her up off of her feet, bringing her in tightly and fiercely into his own arms.

"I don't know either, girl," Yasen said, his smile unguarded and beaming with joy. "But I am sure glad I did." He kissed her deeply and she returned the passion, while all of the woodcutters let out a riotous roar.

"I have missed you … so much," Yasen told her amidst the celebration.

"And I you, North Wolf," she whispered, her cheeks stained with the tears of utter relief.

"Is your uncle here?" he asked. "I would like to hug that old woodcutter's neck." He scanned the crowd of people for his chieftain and friends. "Where are they all? Where are my brothers?"

She shook her head. It seemed a lifetime ago that Hollis and nearly the whole camp of woodcutters were brutally and savagely slaughtered at the hands of the Raven army. "Brádách is here, and the cook ... oh, and that Priest, what a fighter he turned out to be," she said kindly, trying not to smother such celebration in the quicksand of lament.

"The others?" he pressed, needing to know the truth.

"No," she said, with a sad shake of her head. She reached her hands up to take his face, drawing his saddened gaze back down to meet her own. "But *you* are here. We are here ... and we will live to honor their sacrifice and build a brighter world."

Yasen took a deep, steadying breath and nodded his understanding, his hand sliding up her strong arm to find her beautiful face. "Aye ... we will."

"Well, you sure didn't get any uglier over there in the wilderness of the Wreath," Cal heard a familiar voice shouting through the noise of it all. "I thought for sure you would come back looking like him," Michael said as he pointed to Yasen from across the way.

Cal laughed, his eyes overflowing with tears of joy. "Oh, thank the THREE who is SEVEN! My horse-faced cousin is here!" he said with irreverent sincerity. "Come on, then!"

The two cousins, brothers really, ran and embraced each other. "You look good ... and in one piece, too!" Cal said as he held Michael by the shoulders.

"Barely! I nearly lost my head a dozen times!" Michael said as he kept shaking his head in disbelief at it all. "You wouldn't believe the things I have seen!"

"Oh, I promise I would, Michael, and I can't wait to hear all about it!" Cal said.

"Cal?" Michael said as he brought his cousin closer in a hard embrace. "You did it ... you really did it. You were right this whole damned time. I should have never doubted your Poet heart, brother."

"I found him, you know," Cal said with a smile.

"Who?" Michael asked. "Who did you ... wait, you don't mean?"

"Aye ... I found him," Cal said with a nod of the head. "I found his ship. I fought alongside the grandchildren of some of his men. I said my prayers at his grave." Cal looked up and shook his head at the sight all about him. Poets and woodcutters, guardsman and outliers, Sprites and even a Priest; every heart filled with joy at so great a reunion.

"He never stopped seeking it, you know," Cal continued. "Never once, the people told me. He never stopped seeking the light."

"And neither did you, Cal," Michael said proudly.

A golden-haired woman with violet eyes walked from the outskirts of the celebration to take Cal's arm.

"And who is this?" Michael said playfully. "My horseface of a cousin isn't much for manners, you'll have to forgive him, my lady."

"Michael, this is Astyræ," Cal said as the grin grew ever wider across his face. "My lady ... this is my cousin, Michael."

She reached out and shook his hand, nervous and elated to be here amongst his family. "I've heard so much about you Michael, and I am honored to finally meet you. Though," a mischievous grin crept across her face, "I am glad I got the handsome one."

The three of them erupted with laughter as Margarid found them and shared in the joy and release of those who loved and overcame insurmountable odds.

"Welcome, brothers and sisters of the new light!" came a booming voice, whose youthfulness was only betrayed by his aged body. "This is our home, Kalein ... welcome to Petros, and to Islwyn, and to the new world!" Tolk said as raised his arms high and wide. "You are now home!"

A cheer went up from all who were gathered.

"Daily, it seems now, new friends are finding their way along the ancient paths to the heart of the Hilgari," Tolk continued as his face beamed with the joy of hospitality. "And daily our scouts are finding those still lost amidst the aftermath. Our ranks are swelling ... and that, dear friends, is worth celebrating!"

"Now, let's be about a feast, shall we? For friends new and old have sought and found ... and I am sure they are rather thirsty by now!" Elder John chimed in.

"I think the guest of honor, Cal, should be the first one to drink the first draught of victory!" Meledae decreed.

"Agreed!" Clivesis said as he raised his pipe high in smoky punctuation. "Besides ... the Miller has been hard at work, and he will tell you all about it himself." He gave them a wink and a smile. "Don't tell him I said so ... but it may be his best fermentation yet!"

"Well, come on then, Cal!" the Poets jovially demanded.

"Alright, alright!" the groomsman of Haven said as he took Astyræ by the hand and led her to the center of the celebration. "It is good to see you all, but I must admit I am no singular guest of honor. Deryn, come on, my friend!" he said as he beckoned his noble companion over to join him. "I will not drink a drop of this legendary ale unless you drink with me!"

Cheers again erupted, and the people clapped and laughed.

Bright notes rang out as the trumpets of the Sprite Queen announced her arrival. In a royal parade, the host of Islwyn flew out to greet the victors and welcome them back home. Iolanthe laughed, and her laughter was like the music of the Sarangrael. The banners of her sentinels danced in the fragrant breeze as she approached the three of them at the center.

"Well done, Calarmindon Bright Fame," she said through broken tears. "Well done, Deryn of my house. And well done," her face changed as she beheld the violet eyes of Astyræ, and wonder washed over her expression. "Forgive me, my daughter ... but I do not know your name. Yet, in my heart, I feel I know you."

She looked nervous and felt out of place, but so great was her awe as she beheld the Queen of the Sprites that she stood there speechless for a moment.

"My child, what is your name?" Iolanthe asked again.

"My name is—"

"Astyræ?" came the deep-voiced question of a tall man, who was desperately making his way to the center. "Astyræ, is it you? Is it really you?" he begged with tired eyes.

"Pappa?" she answered in disbelief. "But ... how is it possible?"

"Oh, dear girl," Aius said as he dropped to his knees and hung his head. "I don't deserve so great a gift! Please, forgive me, I am so sorry for all I have done, for all the mess I've made, for all the loss."

The crowd went silent as the scene unfolded. And she thought long on his words, for it had been many years since she had seen his face or heard his voice, many years that she had wished for a chance to make things whole with him again. Cal squeezed her hand, nodding with encouragement. "Go on," he whispered to her.

She squeezed his hand back, and then let go of it. One step, and then another; she walked up to the father she never really knew and kneeled before him, wrapping this mighty warrior in her brave, slender arms. "It has been a lifetime since I have dared to hope for a moment such as this. Yes, of course, Pappa ... I'm sorry too."

She threw her arms around her father, and he held her in his own, and they wept and they laughed. All who witnessed felt the unmistakable calling of beauty and redemption in this moment.

The Miller came to the center with flagons of his finest, amber ale, and a small chalice for Deryn. "Alright then ... let the singers sing, and the troubadours play, for victory deserves a great feast ... and a great feast deserves a great ale!"

"Hurray!" came the shouts and the cheers. Cal took his flagon and walked over to Astyræ to give her one too. "Come on, my lady, the party is waiting for us." Together, they raised their drinks high, and Cal shouted his words for all to hear. "In the name of the THREE who is SEVEN!"

"May it be so!"

THE END

<h1 style="text-align: center;">Afterword</h1>

Dear Reader,

It is a surreal experience to pen this letter to you, to think of what comes *after* the telling of this tale. When I happened upon this story – or rather, as Elder John would say, when I found myself answering the call of beauty – this moment seemed a true impossibility.

Much has happened in my life since that fateful day at the intersection of Bell Shoals and Bloomingdale when I first heard the whispers of Haven. And for all of those happenings, I am most truly grateful. I am grateful that this story indeed had to be told, and that it chose me to do its telling.

I'll never forget finishing Calvin Miller's *The Singer Trilogy*. I had just preached a sermon the Sunday before, and suddenly – or rather, seismically, the seeds of this story crested the dirt and began to reveal themselves to me.

Haven started right there, inspired by the prose of Miller's books and by the same message that I had spoken the week before:

"I wonder, as I am sure you might have before, why doesn't God reappear in the burning bush? Why doesn't he make an appointment with Moses and all of his followers on a regular basis, at a regular time? Tuesday at 3pm sounds good for me. I am sure that we would be quick to remember to remove our shoes before we approached the emblazoned shrub.

I think He knows us a little better than our good intentions. He knows our obsessive natures and our tendencies to ritualize impactful moments … and He has rightfully surmised that we might be less concerned with hearing and meeting the voice of God than we are with seeing the fire and walking barefoot.

I bet He understands that we would be content to wander the mountain where God once spoke, and to invite others to follow likewise, rather than to worshipfully obey the assignment given. I think God is quite familiar with His creation, and so He has in turn provided us not with our predictable longings to revisit the glory days when bushes were ablaze, but has set with in us an intense need to seek and to find the smoky scent of a fiery God.

I am learning that worship is not held in the enshrinement of once-hallowed ground, but rather is found in the preparing of fresh soil to be made holy."

This Epic is an allegory of sorts, though perhaps not in the on-the-nose kind of way that some allegories have a way of displaying themselves. This is the story of hope. It is also a story of the seeker, the church, the self-righteous, and the prodigal. This is the story of my dearest friends, my cruelest teachers, tragic enemies and ... well, redemption.

This is not meant to be a theological treatise, nor a triumph of word designed to produce uniformed disciples; rather, I present to you an epic of ethos; a lens, as C.S. Lewis (Clivesis) might say, whereby we might glimpse a deeper understanding of the heart of God.

Now, don't get me wrong; there is quite a bit of action, romance, war, and wizardry that makes for a damn good story if you ask me. But if you want to look just below the surface, there is another story altogether, right in the midst of this one.

In case you haven't gathered or haven't noticed, let me be the first to point out that nearly every single name in the Epic of Haven, whether person, place, or object, has been chosen with deliberate intention. The Poets are indeed real people, and many of my friends are present throughout these pages, too.

This might not matter to most of you, or change the way you love or hate the story. For me ... there was instant depth. The history and mythos of knowing that a name is not just a random assignment of letters, but rather a foreshadowing, brought a gravity of responsibility to tell those parts with a deeper meaning in mind.

Though this trilogy is now completed, there are still many stories to be told in the wonderful world of Aiénor. I long to learn the tragedy of

Caedmon and the fall of Terriah, and I still want to experience the Great Darkening of the world through the eyes of Illium. You never know, my friends, when the great stories might start whispering to me all over again.

I pray that you have enjoyed this final chapter in Haven, and that the journey of Cal and Michael and the rest has filled your own heart with a dream of a new and epic way of living.

Seek the light,

R.G.

INDEX

Caution: This Index contains spoilers for Book Three.

CHARACTERS:

Abaddon: dragon of the **Nocturnal** Raven Army with byzantium colored scales, vile green eyes, and a serpentine body; moves and talks in symmetric synchronicity with his sister dragon, **Angrah**

Ádhamh: the first man of **Aiénor** sent by **The THREE who is SEVEN** to sire the people of **Terriah**

Æðelric: the first High King of **Terriah**, father of **Faramund** and **Ermendrud**

Æsc: mighty leader and Lord of the **Walha**, father of **Hildræd**

Ahriman: great serpent lord and sire of the dragons (**AŽDAHĀ**)

Aius: General of the **Nocturnal** Raven Army; previously was the last steward of **Dardanos**, father of **Astyræ**

Alexio: young male attendant of Lord **Johanna**

Alon: woodcutter of the **Western Wreath** colony; yellow-bearded jovial brother of **Oren**

Amaians: self-named group of people who refused the un-light of the **Raven Queen**; founded the protected city of **Shaimira**, *"New Beginning"*

Anahiera: name used in **Shaimira** for the legendary winged flying horses; revered as the salvation of the people

Angrah: dragon of the **Nocturnal** Raven Army with byzantium colored scales, vile green eyes, and a serpentine body; moves and talks in symmetric synchronicity with her brother dragon, **Abaddon**

Annsley: child and remnant companion of **Marcum**

Arborists: tree-like stewards of the hallowed, great burning tree; keepers of ancient magic and prophecies

Ardghal: Sprite, silver-winged arch-herald messenger of the Queen, *"Herald of High Valor"*

Arianrhod: ancient magical bow given to **Astyræ**, *"Silver Moon"*

Armas: leader of **Haven's** Northern forces against the **Nocturnal** Raven Army; died on the **Melania** battlefield

Arthfael: Sprite, large silver-winged scout leader, *"Bear Prince"*

Asier: Johanna's great-grandfather's grandfather who founded the city of **Asier** after escaping the cruel desert slavers of the south

Asierians: people from the abandoned city of **Asier** on the **Western Wreath**; led by Lord **Julen** to the new city of **Shaimira**

Astyræ: beautiful, mysterious woman from the **Western Wreath** with violet eyes and yellow pupils who accompanies **Cal** on his quest, daughter of **Aius**

Aysa: preeminent healer of **Shaimira**

AŽDAHĀ: name used in **Aerebus** for the dragons or serpents

Azrael: Owele, mightiest of the warriors, *"Angel of Death"*

Bakaren: old woman of **Asier**; member of the council of elders

Barkas: Captain of the Capital Guard for King **Illium**; crew member aboard the ship *Wilderness*

Basajuan: Owele, *"Lord of the Woods"*

Blodeuwedd: Sprite, armorist who made both the sword, **Gwarwyn**, and bow, **Arianihod**

Brádách: woodcutter of **Haven** who walks with a limp after burying an axe in his own foot

Branwen: raven-haired, beautiful wife of **Caedmon**, before the evil of **Šárka** corrupted her and turned her into **Nogcwren** (the **Raven Queen**)

Caedmon: hero dragon slayer of the ancient Kingdom of **Terriah** who wielded the magical sword, **Gwarwyn**; his wife was **Branwen** before she became the **Raven Queen**

Calarmindon (Cal): groomsman who is called by **The THREE who is SEVEN** to seek a new light for the Kingdom of **Haven**; he rescued the sword **Gwarwyn**, *"Bright Fame"*

Cascarie: past King of **Haven**, father of King **Illium**

Celrod: round-bellied schoolmaster of **Westriver**; member of remnant group led by **Michael** that defended the **Halvard**

Clivesis: Poet of **Kalein**; keeper of wisdom and of stories

Črotmir: Commander of the **Nocturnal** Raven Army; ordered to **Haven** so that **Aius** could return to the **Western Wreath**

Dacain: guardsman for King **Illium**; crew member aboard the ship *Wilderness*

Dani: member of **Wreather** family hiding from the **Raven Queen**, mother of **Delilah**

Delilah (Dilly): member of **Wreather** family hiding from the **Raven Queen**, sister of **Mahlah**

Deryn: Sprite, blue-winged warrior who is **Cal's** companion and guardian on his journey to find a new light

Determination: three-masted, silver-sailed ship that brought the first colony to the **Western Wreath**

Diggory: soldier of the **Nocturnal** Raven Army; befriended by **Georgina** after the battle of the **Halvard**

Dorey: archer of **Shaimira** under **Sendoa's** command

Dreamer: Cal's first horse; ran away into the wilds of the North, but was found by **Keily** and carried **Roshan** to the **Poets**

Durai: Captain of the **Nocturnal** Raven Army; ashen-skinned hulking commander of **Nogcwren's** forces on the **Western Wreath**

Ealhstan: past lord of the **Walha**, father of **Æsc**

Edur: Owele, white feathered guide and protector of **Cal**, "*Snow*"

Éimhear: High Queen of the **Sprites**, mother of Queen **Iolanthe**, **Niniané**, and **Gormlaith**; now entombed at the site of the royal tree, **Fionnuala**

Elder John: Poet of **Kalein**; humble fisherman helped by his mule **Ransom**

Elior: God who is Light; also known as **The THREE who is SEVEN** and the Great Father

Elmer: Arborist, green-haired and leafy-bearded brother of **Engelmann**; died helping **Margarid's** remnant group escape **Haven**

Engelmann: Arborist, green-haired and mossy-bearded brother of **Elmer**; died helping **Michael's** remnant group escape **Haven**, "*The Hopeful*"

Eógan: Sprite, golden-winged healer, "*Shepherd of the Weary*"

Ermendrud: second son of High King **Æðelric**

Euria: smithy of **Shaimira**; forged the sword **Ikehr** for **Cal**

Evande: Queen of **Haven** at the time the first branch fell, wife of King **Illium**

Everard: guardsman for King **Illium**; crew member aboard the ship *Wilderness*

Faolan: Sprite, silver-winged Captain of the Host, *"Little Wolf"*

Faramund: first son of High King **Æðelric**; brought **Šárka** to **Terriah** from the **Western Wreath**, husband of Queen **Herrah**

Farran: Cal's third horse, a dapple-grey courser horse that he rode while on the **Western Wreath**, *"Iron"*

Fionnuala: the royal **Jacaranda** tree that birthed the High Queen **Éimhear**; she is entombed beneath the glass of its crystalized remains

Fryon: older of two **Westriver** brothers; member of remnant group led by **Michael** that defended the **Halvard**

Gabriel: child and remnant companion of **Marcum**

Garaile: second-in-command of **Shaimira's** regular guards under **Sendoa**

Gelinda: citizen of **Shaimira**; hosted **Cal's** group in her house; descendant of **Barkas**

Georgina: young farm girl of **Haven**; member of remnant group led by **Michael** that defended the **Halvard**

Goran: woodcutter of the **Western Wreath** colony; mountain of a man with a big heart and a big appetite

Gormlaith: Sprite, daughter of the High Queen **Éimhear**

Graunt: archer of **Shaimira** under **Sendoa's** command

Gvidus: woodcutter of the **Western Wreath** colony; large-bellied and eldest member

Gwarwyn: magical, leaf-shaped sword rescued by **Cal** from the depths of the **Falls of Sarangrael**; the hilt blooms as he performs valiant deeds, *"Beautiful Dawn"*

Haizea: Owele, powerful white winged protector, *"Wind of God"*

Harmier: merchant of **Haven**; member of remnant group led by **Michael** that defended the **Halvard**

Herrah: past Queen of **Terriah**, wife of King **Faramund**

Hildræd: scout leader and sentry of the **Walha**, son of Lord **Æsc**

Hlíf: giant killed by the **Nocturnal** Raven Army while protecting the **Halvard**, wife of **Völker**

Hollis: Chieftain of the Northern woodcutters; died fighting **Nocturnals** north of **Haven** before the war began; fiery-haired uncle of **Keily**

Huckston: child and remnant companion of **Marcum**

Ikehr: sword crafted by **Euria**; in honor of **Cal** and **Uriel** saving the people of **Shaimira**, *"Visitation"*

Iker: Elder councilman of **Shaimira**, didn't believe **Cal's** warning of imminent war

Illium: King of **Haven** at the time the first branch fell; sailed to the **Western Wreath**, found **Shaimira**, and died there, *"Light Seeker"*, *"The Lost King"*

Iolanthe: Sprite, violet-winged Queen of the **Sprites** who resides in

Islwyn; daughter of the High Queen **Éimhear**, "*Violet Flower*"

Isme: herald of the **Raven Queen**; ashen-faced former nobleman who threatened the people of **Asier**

Jacaranda: trees that birth **Sprites** from their fruits

Jhames: Priest King and de facto ruler of **Haven** who took the **Raven Queen's** un-light in order to retain his power and position as ruler, "*His Brightness*"

Johanna: lord and leader of the hidden realm of **Shaimira** and Queen of the **Amaians**; later becomes the steward of **Ziohnia**, granddaughter of **Julen**

Johnrey: Corporal of the Northern cavalry, second-in-command of the **Haven** remnant under **Marcum**

Jordain: archer of **Shaimira** under **Sendoa's** command

Julen: Lord of the **Asierians**; lead his people away from **Asier** and founded the protected city of **Shaimira**

Kader: horse of **Rolf** the woodcutter

Kaestor: past King of **Haven**, father of King **Cascarie**, and grandsire of King **Illium**, "*The Mad King*"

Keily: former barmaid of the **Gnarly Knob**; courageous archer and leader of a remnant of citizens of **Haven** who escape to **Petros**; love interest of **Yasen**

Kemen: young hunter and messenger of **Asier** who finds and names **Shaimira**, nephew of **Zuriñe**

Khris: archer of **Shaimira** under **Sendoa's** command

Klieo: Poet of **Kalein**; historian and keeper of the library

Llinos: Sprite, green-winged young messenger of the Queen, *"Of Bird"*

Luken: young guardian of the pass of **Shaimira** under **Sendoa**

Mågąn: name used in ancient **Terriah** for the giants who lived in the lands northeast of the **Halvard**

Mahlah: member of **Wreather** family hiding from the **Raven Queen**, brother of **Delilah**

Mal'akhim: name used in **Aerebus** for the **Oweles**

Marcum: tall and long-haired lieutenant; commander of the **Haven** remnant who escape to **Petros**

Margarid (Mar): auburn-haired citizen of **Haven**; member of remnant group led by **Michael** that defended the **Halvard**; love interest of **Michael**

Marigeld: Poet of **Kalein**; painter and master gardener, *"Of Gardens"*

Meledae: Poet of **Kalein**; healer and horse caretaker, *"Of Songs"*

Mezulari: captain of the **Queensguard** of **Shaimira**

Mathgham: mighty, brown blade of **Arthfael**, the **Sprite**

Michael: cousin and closest friend of **Cal**; leader of remnant group that defended the **Halvard**; love interest of **Margarid**

Miller, the: Poet of **Kalein**; master ale brewer

Morana: evil sorceress of the **Isle Dušana** who lures men in to take control of their bodies and then devour their souls; was once the **Sprite** princess **Niniané**

Navid: captain of the **Ramsguard** of **Shaimira**; commander of the mountain defenses

Niniané: daughter of the **Sprite** High Queen **Éimhear**, she was betrayed and became **Morana**, the evil sorceress of the **Isle Dušana**

Nocturnal: green-eyed servant in the Raven Army

Nogcwren: the **Raven Queen**, evil sorceress who desires to enslave all of **Aiénor** to her un-light; controls the Raven Army of **Nocturnals**; was once known as **Branwen**, before being corrupted by the evil sorceress **Šárka**, *"Raveness"*

Oier: old man of **Asier**; member of the council of elders

Oren: woodcutter of the **Western Wreath** colony; yellow-bearded jovial brother of **Alon**

Osane: flatleaf herb with tiny white and violet flowers that helps to reduce fever

Oweles: large owl-like watchers and servants of **The THREE who is SEVEN**; protect and guide **Cal** on his quest

Payam: mariner for King **Illium**; crew member aboard the ship *Wilderness*

Poets: rival religious sect of the **Priests**, they believe in the powers of beauty and hope; live in the colony of **Kalein** hidden in the **Hilgari Mountains**

Portus: tanner of **Haven**, member of remnant group led by **Michael** that defended the **Halvard**

Priests: ruling religious sect of **Haven**, they believe in the powers of resolve and piety; live in fear of the great tree dying and the loss of light

Pyrrhus: one-armed knight of the **Western Wreath** colony; arrogant and cruel, but is redeemed during the battle with the **Raven Queen**, *"Fire Knight"*

Queensguard: infantry soldiers charged with directly guarding Queen **Johanna**

Ragnarr: wizard and chief advisor to Lord **Æsc** of the **Walha**

Ramsguard: cavalry soldiers charged with guarding the mountain barrier around Shaimira

Ransom: Elder John's trusty mule

Raven Queen: evil sorceress **Nogcwren**, formerly **Branwen**

Remiel: Owele, brown, red-tipped winged guide, *"Mercy of God"*

Reynard the Wise: trusted wizard of Queen **Herrah**; helped to defeat and entrap the evil sorceress **Šárka**

Rolf: woodcutter of the **Western Wreath** colony; older man with a strong work-ethic

Roshan: young lad and remnant companion of **Marcum**, rode **Dreamer** to the **Poets** to seek help

Ruarc: Owele, brown, white-tipped winged leader; started **Cal** on quest to seek the light, *"Storm Words"*

Ryder: child and remnant companion of **Marcum**

Šárka: evil sorceress of the ancient Kingdom of **Terriah**; destroyed the **Jacaranda** trees and corrupted **Branwen**, turning her into **Nogcwren** (the **Raven Queen**)

Seig: Governor of the **Western Wreath** colony; exhibits bravado and seeks glory; overall commander of the colony's guardsmen and woodcutters

Sendoa: captain of the guardians of the pass of **Shaimira**; commander of the ground defenses

Sigrid: fabled Queen Mother of all horses, *"Fair Victory"*

Soma: woodcutter of the **Western Wreath** colony; concerned for the safety of **Yasen** and his brothers

Soren: Chief of the guard-watchers of **Asier**; member of the council of elders

Sprites: magical, fairy-like race born from the last remaining **Jacaranda** trees of **Aiénor**

Tahd: guardsman captain of the **Western Wreath** colony; died after delivering first shipment of wood to **Haven**

Tarrthála: named used in ancient **Terriah** for the legendary winged flying horses

Tersk: Cal's fifth horse, a silver-white majestic horse that he rode back to **Haven**, *"Prince of Horses"*

The THREE who is SEVEN: God of the world of **Aiénor** who gave the world the tree of light; sent the **Oweles** and **Uriel** to help **Cal** seek a new light, *"Great Father"*, *"Giver of Light"*

Timorets: long-bearded brewer of **Haven**, member of remnant group led by **Michael** that defended the **Halvard**

Tolk: Poet of **Kalein**; leader and eldest member; present at **Cal's** baby dedication

Uriel: Cal's fourth horse, a white winged *Tarrthála* sent by **The THREE who is SEVEN** to help **Cal** on his quest, *"Lord of the Anahiera"*

Völker: giant inhabiting the **Halvard**; welcomed **Michael's** remnant and together fought the **Nocturnal** Raven Army, husband of **Hlíf**

Walha: exiled outlander group living in the harsh **Cair Mountains**; led by Lord **Æsc**

Watchers: another name for the **Oweles**

Wielund: blacksmith of the **Western Wreath** colony; friend of **Cal**

Wilderness: ship that carried King **Illium** and his crew to the **Western Wreath** to seek a new light

Yasen: Chieftain of the woodcutters of the **Western Wreath** colony; lost one eye and wears an eyepatch that his love interest **Keily** made for him, *"North Wolf"*

Zigor: Owele, *"Punishment"*

Zivor: guardian of the pass of **Shaimira** under **Sendoa**

Zuriñe: old man of **Asier**; member of the council of elders, uncle of **Kemen**

Zviad: soldier of the **Nocturnal** Raven Army; arrived with the **Raven Queen** on the *Determination*

PLACES:

Abondale: southern borough of the city of **Haven** devoted to farming and shipping

Abonris: mighty river that runs through the city of **Haven** northward to the **Hilgari Mountains**

Aerebus: dark castle on **Western Wreath**; birth place of the dragons and seat of **Nogcwren's** power

Ágoni gi: areas within the **Greywood** where the **Jacaranda** trees died, leaving teardrop-shaped shards of glass in the barren ground, *"the beautiful barren"*

Aiénor: the known world in which the Kingdom of **Haven** resides

Argiñe: wide river that runs from its hidden source in the **Itxaro Mountains** to both the **Dark Sea** and the **Falls of Ammon**

Asier: once great, redstone city on the **Western Wreath**; known for their horses; abandoned by its people for the safety of the hidden land of **Shaimira**

Aureole: mountain on the eastern edge of the city of **Haven** that contained the hallowed, great burning tree in a garden at its top

Bay of Eurwen: bay south of the city of **Haven** where the men of the first colony set sail

Cair Mountains: craggy, black granite mountain range northeast of **Haven**; home to the **Walha**

Clarus: once great, sea-foam colored city on the **Western Wreath**; known for their ships; abandoned by its people for lands across the **Dark Sea**

Dardanos: once great city on the **Western Wreath**; located at the southernmost point of the **Greywood**; childhood home of the lady **Astyræ**

Dark Sea: cold, deep sea surrounding the Kingdom of **Haven** and separating it from the **Western Wreath**

Enguerrand: long abandoned prison tower in the **Greywood** where **Cal** rescues **Astyræ**

Falls of Ammon: the western branch of the **Argiñe** hiding the entrance to the pass to **Shaimira**

Falls of Sarangrael: the ending of the **Abonris** River that nourishes the

Jacaranda trees within the hidden **Sprite** home of **Islwyn**

Gnarly Knob: tavern in the northern borough of **Piney Creek**; operated by **Keily** and her father

Greywood: wilderness forest in the central part of the **Western Wreath**; landing site of the men of the first colony

Halvard: mountain castle fortification guarding the only land entrance to **Haven**; sight of the last battle against the dark in the east, *"Guardian of the Rock"*

Harel Lior: round, cavern-like chamber where the guardian of the light records the events of **Elior's** story of **Aiénor**

Haven: great, walled city and seat of the eastern Kingdom; home of the once-burning, dead tree

Hekate': mountain range in the southern part of the **Western Wreath**; home to **Nogcwren's** garrison

Hilgari Mountains: beautiful mountain range north of **Haven**; home to the **Poets**

Isle Dušana: island in the **Dark Sea**; home of the evil sorceress **Morana**

Islwyn: hidden **Sprite** home in the heart of the **Hilgari Mountains** containing the last remaining **Jacaranda** trees, *"Secret Grove"*

Ithelum: extremely wide river that cuts off **Haven** from the east; the **Meinir** crosses it just under the surface of the river

Itsaso: ancient name for the **Dark Sea**

Itxaro Mountains: protective mountain range north of the **Greywood**; surrounding **Shaimira** and hiding a secret; sight of the last battle against the dark in the west

Kalein: Poet colony hidden in the **Hilgari Mountains**; part of the palace of **Petros** in the forgotten kingdom of **Terriah**, *"Beauty is Calling"*

Kelila: spiraled tower looming over **Shaimira** at the heart of the city

King's Bridge: bridge leading to the main entrance of the Capital in **Haven** and spanning the widest portion of the **Abonris**

Maris Tower: ancient lighthouse situated at the southernmost point of the Kingdom of **Haven**; guards the mouth of the **Bay of Eurwen**, *"Star of the Sea"*

Meinir: granite slab land bridge just under the surface of the **Ithelum** connecting both shores

Melania: field of battle outside of the northern wall of **Haven**; renamed for the defilement of battle and dragons' fire, *"Black Fields"*

***Oroitz Guardia*:** pair of massive, sculpted chariots flanking either side of the roadway to **Shaimira**

Palladium: house of wisdom and law in **Shaimira**; based on the one that was burned down in **Asier**

Pass of Kemen: underground passageway from behind the **Falls of Ammon** to the secret city of **Shaimira**

Petros: stone palace and royal residence of **Terriah's** past kings; now inhabited by the **Poet** colony of **Kalein**

Piney Creek: northern borough of the city of **Haven**

Shaimira: hidden city founded by the exiled **Asierians** and home to the **Amaian** people, *"Guardian"*

Terriah: ancient ruined city north of **Haven** in the **Hilgari Mountains**

where the **Oweles** live

Tristura Eremua: ancient **Terrian** for the battleground outside of **Ziohnia** meaning "*Fields of Sorrow*"

Western Wreath: forgotten wilderland across the **Dark Sea**; encircles the Kingdom of **Haven**

Westriver: western borough of the city of **Haven**; home to **Cal** and **Michael**

Ziohnia: city housing the new light of **Elior**; kingdom that **The THREE who is SEVEN** prepared for the people of **Aiénor**

Zuhaitz Dolu: graveyard on the east side of **Shaimira** for **Illium** and all the sons of **Haven**, "*Mourning Trees*"

ACKNOWLEDGEMENTS

When I set out to write this story seven years ago, I never would have dreamed just how many Poets it would take to bring it to life. I must first give my heartfelt thanks to all of those who stood by the story, supported us in its telling, and journeyed with us through page after page of this allegory. To my **fellow Lost Poets** … I am truly grateful for you.

To my editor, partner, and wielder of the mighty, fabled "Red Pen of Doom": **Melody Farrell**, I will forever be in your debt. My gratitude for you is boundless, and I hope to make up for it with many a feast.

Rich Kesky might be one of the most unsung heroes of this trilogy. Thank you, my friend, for taking the time to ensure that the details are exact and that the timelines are indeed true (or as true as we can make them). Your love of fantasy and adventure has helped to sharpen the telling of this story.

Rob Stainback, Chris Farrell, and **Amanda Farrell**, your design work is truly outstanding. Thank you for your care, your creativity, and your willingness to stick it out along the better part of the last decade!

To the proofreaders, **Jennifer Harris** and **Christy Freeman**, thank you for wading through my run-on sentences and grammatical travesties! I hope you were able to enjoy the forest amidst all the incorrect trees.

To **Grant Radebaugh** and **Jordan Thurmond**, your willingness and excitement to read from the unedited onset has been a gift to the way we hone the storytelling. Thank you for reading past all the errors and giving us your true enthusiasm for the story itself.

To **Brandon Hyde**, who would have thought that a few good

conversations between us nearly a decade ago would lead us on this kind of adventure? Thank you for believing in this story.

To **Mark Topping**, the way you have brought these people and places, these songs and stories to life has been a treasure I will cherish forever, my friend.

To my beautiful wife, **Katie**: thank you for making space and energy for me to finish this story, and thank you for being a champion of my heart throughout all of it. I will forever be grateful for you.

To my kiddos, **Annsley, Gabriel, Huckston,** and **Ryder**: one day, may you find your name in the midst of the remnant and know that I have always believed that you will be a part of making this world a brighter place.

To the readers and the fans, the obliging family members and even the critics who have waited these last long four years: I am proud to share this conclusion of the story with you. Thank you for sticking with us. I pray for great adventures for you ... and that in all things, you will seek the light.

Gratefully,
R.G.

MORE FROM R.G. TRIPLETT

Begin the adventure with

The Great Darkening

Book One in the Epic of Haven Trilogy

Available on Amazon:

https://www.amazon.com/Great-Darkening-Epic-Haven-Trilogy-ebook/dp/B00I8DVQUO

Continue the journey with

The Ravenous Siege

Book Two in the Epic of Haven Trilogy

Available on Amazon:

https://www.amazon.com/Ravenous-Siege-Epic-Haven-Trilogy-ebook/dp/B01JFF0GTA

Go deeper into the allegory with

Seeking The Light

Editorial companion guide for *The Great Darkening*

Available on Amazon:

https://www.amazon.com/Study-Guide-GREAT-DARKENING-Triplett-ebook/dp/B01F7E7K9C

www.ingramcontent.com/pod-product-compliance
Lightning Source LLC
Chambersburg PA
CBHW050958180726
48291CB00006B/1880